TURN THE OTHER
Chick

TURN THE OTHER
Chick

Edited by Esther M. Friesner

A Baen Books Original

Baen Publishing Enterprises
P.O. Box 1403
Riverdale, NY 10471
www.baen.com

ISBN: 0-7434-8857-1

Cover art by Mitch Faust

Distributed by Simon & Schuster
1230 Avenue of the Americas
New York, NY 10020

Production by Windhaven Press, Auburn, NH
Printed in the United States of America

Dedication

This book is respectfully dedicated to
Tanya and Grant Van Der Ploeg

Artists and Artisans

Contents

Introduction

Welcome to the fifth *Chicks in Chainmail* anthology. Allow me to offer you a comfortable chair, a bowl of popcorn, some corn chips and salsa, perhaps a few carrot sticks, and the healthful beverage of your choice before placing this book in your lap. No, it's not *Turn the Other Chick;* not yet. It's a family album.

"Whose family?" you ask. (Or perhaps you ask "What's this bushwah about a 'healthful beverage'? Gimme a chocolate ice cream soda, straight up, before I get *nasty.*" In which case, shame on you.) Maybe it's yours. It's definitely mine. The members thereof are a small selection of fictitious heroines who aren't represented in this book but who have had a whole lot of impact on changing how people think about women. They've put down the order pad, the bake sale brownies, and the *Why His Problems Are Always Your Fault* book and picked up the sword instead. I'd say they deserve at least a passing nod, a smile, and even a few words of thanks for all that they've done for us. (I wouldn't suggest a pat on the back, though. These chicks have got rather *enthusiastic* reflexes, they don't like surprises, and they're probably toting something sharp.)

There's the woman herself, Xena, Warrior Princess. She's gone now, as is her faithful sidekick Gabrielle who became a woman warrior in her own right before their story ended.

1

Ah, and Eowyn and Arwen from the movie versions of *The Lord of the Rings*! Not 100% true to the book, but that's the nature of the cinematic critter. The purist in me might sulk, but my Inner Child is brandishing an elven blade and whooping "Arwen finally gets to do something besides wait around for Aragorn to show up! *Yes!*"

Check out Princes Leia, who proved to a doubting world that just because you send out a wideband Damsel in Distress call you can still kick plenty of Dark Side butt when the opportunity presents itself.

And can this be little Buffy Summers? My, how she's grown. Yes, you *can* fight evil and still hold down a job in the exciting and high-paying fast food industry!

I apologize to those of my fellow J.K. Rowling fans who are asking why Hermione Granger isn't here. She's certainly a fighter, just not the kind that uses a sword.

Oh, very well, let's include her. I suppose you could argue that not every woman warrior fights her battles with a sword, and that a wand is close kin to Buffy's favorite vampire-slaying stake, Mr. Pointy. I can't say no to Hermione. Really. I *can't*. She slapped this *Let Me In Or Else* spell on me and I had no choice.

Ironic, that. Freedom is all about having options and until fairly recently, being a woman was not. We were forever hearing "But you're a *girl*, so you can't:

"1. vote.

"2. live on your own.

"3. manage money.

"4. be paid the same as a man who's doing the same job.

"5. defend your country or even yourself.

"6. compete in professional sports.

"7. save France."

Women warriors—all of us, not just the ones who look slick in video—stand ready to defend our hard-won freedoms, our options, and to strive for further triumphs on the battlefield, big or small. Our battle cry, a thunderous "Sez you!" is often underscored by a resounding Bronx cheer in the direction of anyone who tells us "You *can't* 'cause you're a *girl*."

Among these freedoms is the choice of keeping a sense of humor on your person at all times. On occasion we don't hear "You can't do that 'cause you're a *girl!*" but the equally snarky "You can't do that 'cause you're a *Feminist!*"

Oh yes I can. (See above: *Freedom.* Also: *Sez you.*)

You'll notice that the women I've mentioned all hail from movies and television, though some originally saw the light of day in books and some have come to have spin-off books written about them. Their sisters who exist in print alone are even more numerous, but the Received Wisdom of the modern world is that eye candy reaches more people (and thus has more societal impact) than brain food. I'm not going to debate the truth or error of that, though I'd be the Amazing Ostrichwoman if I denied the wide-reaching influence of TV and movies.

As long as the aforementioned influence continues to present us with powerful, independent women who know how to fight in defense of themselves and others, I'm not about to complain. The more people who get *that* message, the merrier.

"That is all very well and good," I hear you say, "but that is also the past. Xena and Buffy have gone to Syndication Heaven. Who's going to replace them? Or are we going to go back to the days when the most important battle ever fought by women in fiction was Betty versus Veronica to settle that burning, earth-shattering question, *Who will Archie take to the prom?*"

I wish I had an answer handy. There are plenty of people who would be all too happy to return women to being objects of Rescue, Ornament, and Enforced Cheerful Domesticity. This would be bad enough, if they limited these desires to women's roles in books, movies, and TV. It's a sad truth that many of our fellow human beings can't feel tall unless they're standing on someone else's face. For some folks a mad dash back into the Dark Ages ("When Underlings Knew Their Proper Place!") looks like progress simply because it's motion at high speed.

Are we going to see more strong heroines appear on the big and little screens, or are we going to get a pat on the head and the jovial reassurance that everything will be taken care of for us, go have a manicure and let the nice media moguls handle it?

Um, how many female media moguls are there, by the

way? And how many of them think of the rest of us as more than just a Marketing Demographic?

It's tiring, swinging a sword all day, and it's hell on that darling manicure, but it beats having to fight the same battles all over again because you assumed someone else would guard your freedom for you. If you haven't got a sword handy, you can always wield your wallet.

You can also choose not to worry your pretty little head about it. (Note: This is still your choice, not a constraint. For now.)

And while we're talking about choices, here's hoping all of us will forever be free to choose laughter.

Buffy would have wanted it that way.

You'll notice that the dedication of the book is for Tanya and Grant Van Der Ploeg. "Why?" you may ask. (Unless you are still demanding to know when the heck you're going to get your chocolate ice cream soda. Stop that.)

Go to *http://www.dolls-n-daggers.com* and you'll understand. Heh.

Mightier Than the Sword

John G. Hemry

Suzanne entered the temple hesitantly, her footsteps sounding small in the great structure whose marble pillars reached toward a ceiling emblazoned with pictures dark and bright. Before her, torches flared around the great statue of Inspiration, Goddess of Writers. To either side of the goddess, lesser idols in Inspiration's pantheon were ranked behind their altars. There stood proud Contract next to faceless Writer's Block, while Slush was almost invisible behind the pile of offerings on his altar. Not far away, several petitioners were down on their knees before the grim visage of Deadline, praying for the extra time only she could grant.

Suzanne rendered honors to Inspiration, then turned toward the cubicles lining the sides of the temple and approached the tiny cells where the Editors worked. One glanced up as Suzanne reached her desk. "Do you have an offering?"

"Yes." Suzanne knelt and proffered her manuscript, carefully settling it into the Editor's offering tray. "May I beg an audience?"

"An audience?" The Editor frowned, then shrugged. "You may speak."

"Oh, Editor, why have my previous offerings been rejected?"

"I'm afraid the Mysteries of Editing are not for the uninitiated."

"But, please, grant me at least a hint!"

The Editor sighed heavily. "Very well. You can scarcely go wrong if you follow your Muse."

"My Muse?"

"Yes. You do have a Muse, don't you?"

"Ummm." Suzanne looked around. "Would I know if I did?"

"Most assuredly. I'm afraid if you lack a Muse—"

The Editor was interrupted by a sweet voice coming from above and just to the right of Suzanne. "She lacks one no longer."

"You?" The Editor held up her hands, palms out. "Oh, no. Not Calliope."

"What?" Suzanne looked toward the voice and saw floating there the almost transparent figure of a woman perhaps two feet high. "A Muse? I have a Muse?"

"Wait!" the Editor cautioned. "That's Calliope!"

"Is that bad?"

Calliope answered. "The Editor cannot say, can you? For Editors cannot reject a writer's Muse. You see, dear writer, I have already revealed one of the Mysteries of Editing to you."

The Editor glared at Calliope. "You might mention to her that Editors can't reject the Muse but we can always reject the manuscripts that Muse helps create!"

"Oh, posh." The dimunitive figure began drifting toward the exit from the temple. "Come along, my writer."

Suzanne followed hastily, catching up just as the Muse floated out of the temple. In daylight, her figure remained faint but clearly visible. "I didn't know Muses could be seen."

"Only by our writers, and Editors of course. Now, let's have a look at your latest offering." Somehow, Calliope had retrieved Suzanne's manuscript from the offering tray. She quickly flipped through it, then frowned down at Suzanne. "Oh, dear."

"I was trying to—"

"My dear . . . what's your name?"

"Suzanne. Suzanne of—"

"Suzanne's fine." Calliope drifted down to eye level with

Suzanne. "If you have to explain to the reader what you're trying to do, you haven't done it. That's lesson one. Lesson two is that it really helps to write something interesting."

Suzanne rubbed her forehead. "Well, I try to write about what I know, you see."

"Haven't you ever done anything interesting?" Calliope paused in anticipation of Suzanne's answer, then hung her head theatrically. "You have to seek Inspiration in your experiences."

"But, if I imagine—"

"Who's the Muse here?"

"You are." Suzanne bit her lip and looked around. "I don't see anything interesting."

"You have to seek it! Come along." Calliope floated off down the street, passing through obstacles without hindrance, while Suzanne struggled through the crowd to catch up. When she finally did, Suzanne saw Calliope admiring an armorer's shop display. "This is just the place."

Suzanne peered at the armor and weapons. "For what?"

"If you're going to go adventuring, you need to be outfitted properly." Calliope's shape drifted inside the shop.

"Adventuring? What? Wait!" Suzanne rushed through the door, finding herself the object of the attention of several rough-looking men. "Excuse me." She slid sideways until she reached some shelves near Calliope. "What are you looking at?"

"Armor. Look at this one!" Calliope pointed to a gleaming mail shirt with mesh so fine it flowed like water.

Suzanne checked the price and yelped, drawing more glances from the men in the store. "I can't afford that."

"What *can* you afford?"

Suzanne scanned the shelves. "That." She lifted a stout leather shirt, stained and scored with damage, a sheet of scarred metal tacked to the upper chest. "I wonder why it's so cheap." In the center of the largest stain, her fingers found a thin hole about two inches in height in the armor. "Oh."

"It'll do," Calliope announced. "A writer's real armor is her imagination."

"Does that stop swords?"

"Now that you mention it, you also need a sword."

"Wait!" Suzanne once more followed Calliope, to where

the Muse hovered near a barrel of rusty weapons. "These don't look all that good."

"The price is right. Try that one with the nicks in the guard."

Suzanne hefted the blade doubtfully, then smiled as it seemed to fit herself to her hand. "It is nice! I think its name is Guardian."

"Guardian? Good. You'll need one of those."

"I thought you—"

"I'm a Muse, not a Guardian." Calliope waited with every sign of impatience while Suzanne paid for her purchases, then drifted back out onto the street as Suzanne awkwardly carried her new armament in the Muse's wake. "Now, you've a pen?"

"I always—"

"Good. Write something on your armor."

Suzanne frowned down at the battered leather and metal. "It's not the best writing surface."

"You must armor yourself with your imagination! Write something upon your armor that will strike fear into the heart of evil!"

Suzanne paused, her pen poised above the leather. "Isn't my Muse supposed to help me write?"

"I'm an agent of Inspiration, not a secretary."

"But what should I write?"

"Try a spell to protect you and smite your foes."

"I don't know any spells."

"Make. One. Up!"

"All right." Suzanne's pen paused again. "Should it be in a foreign language?"

"That's usually a good idea. Do you know any foreign languages?"

"No. Can I make up a foreign language?"

Calliope applauded. "Wonderful. Of course you can. That's thinking like a writer."

Suzanne patiently inscribed a series of nonsensical but impressive looking words upon her armor just beneath the metal plate. "Now what?"

"Put it *on*."

"In public?" Calliope's glare answered Suzanne's question, so she hastily struggled into the stiff leather. "Oh, it smells."

"That's called atmosphere. Comfortable?"

"No."

"Good. Let's go."

"Go where?"

Calliope glanced back as she began floating away again. "In search of Inspiration and adventure! You won't find that in a safe little town. To the countryside!"

"But there's bandits out there."

"Excellent! Follow me."

Suzanne tried to stand her ground, but found her feet moving briskly of their own accord. By the time they reached the gate to the city, she was sweating in the heavy leather and wondering if she should've listened to the Editor.

The guards at the gate frowned as Suzanne approached. "We're gettin' ready to shut the gate for the night. Come back in the mornin'," their leader announced.

Suzanne, momentarily managing to stop her feet with the greatest of effort, watched Calliope drift unheeding through the gate. "I have to leave now."

"Why? Got a fella out there?" The guards broke into laughter.

"No! I'm a writer and I have to follow my Muse!"

A guard with a brass ornament on his shoulder which apparently identified him as the leader gave Suzanne a skeptical look. "A writer? You look more like one of them barbarian sword maidens. Ain't that right, guys?" His fellow guards chorused in agreement. "How come a writer's wearing armor?"

"I . . . I'm going to a writer's workshop. They're going to criticize my writing."

The head guard eyed Suzanne suspiciously. "Not a barbarian? What's that on your armor, then? It looks like barbarian writin'."

Suzanne looked down at her armor. "It's a, uh, spell. I wrote it."

The guards exchanged glances. One of them came close, leaning to peer into Suzanne's face. "She ain't got on much makeup." He looked downward. "And she's wearing sensible shoes. Maybe she *is* a writer."

"I dunno." The head guard scratched his scalp with a spade-like fingernail. "Barbarian sword maidens wear sensible shoes, don't they?"

"Sometimes. But they always fight half-nekked. This one's got too much clothes on."

"That's true. There's not even a hint of cleavage visible on her. Hey, I know. Check 'er hands."

"Okay." The closest guard grabbed Suzanne's hands and turned them palms up. "She's got ink on 'em."

"Hmmm. Now ask her to spell somethin' hard. Like, uh, arachnid."

The guards looked from their leader to Suzanne. "Go ahead," one urged. "If you're a writer, spell that."

"Uh . . . a, r, a, c, uh, h, i, no!, n, i, d."

The guards looked to their leader. "Is that right?"

"I dunno. Sounds right. Okay, you can pass. Hey, can I be in your next book? Somethin', you know, heroic? No comic relief, mind you!"

The closest guard leaned even closer. "I got this great idea for a story. I can tell it to you, and you could write it up and split the money with me. Whattaya say?"

Suzanne smiled with what she hoped appeared to be sincerity. "What a wonderful deal. Let's talk about it later." Her feet were already moving again, pulling her along the path Calliope had taken.

Calliope slowed enough for Suzanne to catch up. Her form had taken on a golden glow as the sun began to set. "You've passed your first obstacle. Isn't it glorious?"

Suzanne glared at Calliope from under lowered brows. "I don't feel glorious. I certainly don't smell glorious in this armor. Did you hear those offers I got from those guards?"

"You have to expect to be propositioned when you're a writer."

"I'm not *that* kind of writer!"

Calliope sighed. "Ah, you're the artistic type. There's nothing wrong with selling your talents occasionally, you know."

"I really don't like the way you're describing this. Where are we going?" The sun kept sinking toward the horizon, and Calliope kept drifting down the road.

"To an adventure."

"It's getting dark."

"Mysterious night! What wonders and terrors does it hide?"

"My feet hurt."

Calliope gave Suzanne a disappointed look. "I thought you were an artist."

"I work best after a good night's sleep. And something to eat."

"You didn't bring anything?"

Suzanne opened her mouth but nothing came out.

Calliope peered ahead and smiled. "Here comes a rider! What adventurous prospects!"

"A rider?" Suzanne glanced around frantically. "I have to hide."

"Nonsense. You have a sword."

"A sword?" Suzanne glanced down at Guardian, swinging forgotten at her side.

"And your armor," Calliope added. "I'd try to avoid getting hit, nonetheless."

"Thank you." Suzanne drew Guardian and stood in what she hoped was a confident posture as the rider drew closer. It soon became apparent that the rider was male and, from his expression, in a foul mood.

Instead of veering his horse slightly to the side to avoid Suzanne, he aimed a kick at her. "Get out of the way!" As she dodged the kick, he took another look. "Hey. A babe. Out here all alone?"

Suzanne gritted her teeth. "And planning to stay that way."

The man grinned unpleasantly. "What's with the armor, babe? It just gets in the way."

Suzanne's eyes narrowed. "It helps protect me from jerks."

"Ah, that's no way to be. I bet you're hungry, huh?"

"Not that hungry." Suzanne tried to ignore the growling in her stomach, but it was obvious the rider heard it.

He rummaged in his pack and surfaced with an oblong object. "What say we make a trade? I give you this, and you give me something in return."

"Is that chocolate?" Suzanne stared at the bar. "Trade? What do you want?"

The grin grew into a leer. "Like I said, that armor gets in the way. Take it off."

"That's all? Take off my armor?"

"Then take off everything else. You'll get the chocolate when I'm done."

Suzanne's temper boiled over. "I'm tired and hungry and out in the middle of nowhere and you dare treat me like some kind of slut who'd sell herself for a single bar of chocolate?"

The rider frowned. "I've got two bars if that's—"

"Ahhhh!" Losing all control, Suzanne leaped at the rider, her sword swinging. The flat of the blade caught the surprised man on the side of his head, tumbling him from the saddle. "Not for two bars! Not even for three! I'm not a slut!" She stood over him where he lay in the road, her sword poised, her face glowing with rage.

The man stared up at her, fear filling his face. "What . . . what are you?"

"I'm a writer!"

The man scuttled away, still on the ground. "Take the chocolate. Take the horse." He scrambled to his feet and fled, vanishing into the growing darkness.

Suzanne blinked, looking around in surprise. "Well . . . that was nice of him. Why do you suppose he gave me the horse? He didn't seem all that nice a person."

Calliope had reappeared by her side. "He's not. I believe you frightened him."

"It serves him right for using chocolate to taunt an armed woman." Suzanne ate slowly, savoring the bar, then dug in the abandoned horse's saddle bags and found another. "Now what, Calliope?"

"You have a horse. Ride it."

Suzanne mounted the horse, who seemed unimpressed by his change in owners. "I'm sure that man didn't treat you very well, either, did he?" The second chocolate bar and the last traces of daylight vanished at about the same time. Suzanne shivered in the cool night breeze. Her sword scabbard kept slapping her leg in an annoying way, so she removed the scabbard from her belt and fastened it to her saddle, rather enjoying the sensation of being armed and mounted. She even rubbed her armor with some feeling of satisfaction.

It took her a while to realize Calliope had disappeared. With no Muse to follow down the empty road on a cold night, and with the last of the chocolate gone, Suzanne's brief pleasure in her adventure rapidly faded. Spotting a somewhat sheltered area among some rocks not far from the road, she guided the horse that way, dismounted a bit stiffly, then sat heavily onto the ground, thrown off balance by the weight of her armor. Muttering curses at Fate and Muses, Suzanne struggled briefly with getting out of the armor, then gave it up as too much trouble and simply leaned back against the nearest rock.

A sound woke her to bright day. Suzanne stared around, blinking against the light. "Calliope?"

"Right here," the Muse answered cheerily. "You really should wake up now. Your adventure is getting better by the moment!"

Beyond Calliope's shape, Suzanne saw a group of men approaching. Their generally scruffy appearance and ragtag assortment of arms and armor didn't inspire confidence in her. She struggled back to her feet, aware her hair probably looked frightful, and adjusted the leather armor, rapping the metal reinforcement on her chest for reassurance.

The group of men stopped when they saw her moving, then came on again, smiling with varying degrees of menace and anticipation. Suzanne counted their numbers and the scars on their faces with a sinking feeling. "Oh, Calliope."

"Yes?"

"I'd appreciate a little help."

"This isn't the best time to write."

"I don't mean with writing! How am I going to handle these men? They look like bandits."

"They are bandits."

The advancing bandit gang had halted as Suzanne talked with Calliope, looking around with puzzled expressions in search of the companion she was speaking with.

"Calliope! What do I do?"

"You're wearing your armor."

"Which didn't do its last owner much good."

"Then draw your sword, for Inspiration's sake."

Suzanne made a desperate grasping motion toward her side, finding nothing there. She glanced around quickly, finally seeing her sword about twelve feet from her. In its scabbard. Tied to her new saddle. Cinched onto her new horse, who was looking back at Suzanne with an expression which clearly communicated "if you take one step toward me I'll run away as fast as possible." "I don't have my sword."

"Well, then, draw your knife!" Calliope advised with a trace of aspersion.

"I don't have a knife."

"You must have something."

Suzanne felt frantically around her waist. "I've got my pen."

"Draw it!"

Gripping the pen firmly, Suzanne raised it in what she hoped was a menacing fashion. "Come no further!" The bandits halted their progress again. "Calliope! Now what?"

The Muse's voice had grown fainter, as if she were moving away. "You're the writer. Find a solution to your plot dilemma."

"What? Plot dilemma? This isn't a plot dilemma! I'm in serious danger!"

Calliope's voice could barely be heard now. "Surely you didn't write your primary character into a dead end? Didn't you plot this out beforehand?"

"No!"

The bandits, staring around again, jerked in surprise at Suzanne's howl of anger.

"Then use your imagination and your tools, writer. Create a way out for your character." Calliope's voice faded out completely on the last word.

Suzanne stared at the bandits, who stared back, then began slowly advancing again. "Stand back!" Suzanne cried. "I'm wearing armor!"

The bandits exchanged glances, then one near the head of the gang addressed Suzanne. "So are we. And we've got weapons."

"So do I!" Suzanne waved her pen at them. "Besides, this armor is . . . is . . . magical. See? There's a spell written on it."

The bandits paused yet again, their eyes locked onto the area just beneath Suzanne's chest. "What kind of spell?" the bandit chief asked warily.

"Uh, a powerful spell. Yes. Very powerful. Anyone who attacks me will be stricken . . . uh . . . stricken. Yes. Like . . ." Suzanne waved her pen again. "That."

One of the bandits spat and shook his head. "She ain't providing much detail, is she?"

"No," the chief agreed. "I think you're lying, woman."

Suzanne glared at the bandits. "I can be very detailed. I may be weak on imagery, but I can detail every detail in detail. I'm very good at that."

"Pah! Let's get her."

Suzanne lowered her pen's tip toward the bandits, extending her arm and settling her body into a fighting stance. "Don't make me use this!"

The bandits halted so fast some of them stumbled, then stood looking from Suzanne to the pen. "It don't look too dangerous," one whispered.

"It *is* dangerous," Suzanne insisted. "With this I can . . . I can create monsters! And terrible armies! I can create entire worlds!"

The bandit chief's smile held menace. "Then how come you ain't created any decent armor for yerself? All you got is that there battered leather. With what you say is a spell on it."

Suzanne drew herself up to her full height, adopting a haughty expression. "It does have a spell on it! A spell I created out of nothing! This armor is reinforced by Imagination and . . . and Desperation. It is the Armor With No Name! It is Ineffable! Ineluctable! Undistinguished! Inexplicable! Inadequate!"

The bandits gaped at her, their mouths open with awe. "She's casting a spell," one cried.

The bandit chief lowered his sword, his expression now guarded. "That stick can make anything, huh?"

"Well, so far I haven't made any money with it. I'm still working on that." The bandits looked angry and puzzled again. "But it wrote this spell on my armor! Believe me, one of us will regret it if you attack me!"

"She's a sorceress," one of the bandits warned. "She could be real dangerous."

"Or maybe she's crazy," another one added.

"Crazy women're dangerous, too."

The bandits shifted back and forth where they stood, holding their weapons between themselves and Suzanne's threatening pen. The chief tried to focus on the pen's tip, squinting as his entire head followed the wavering instrument. "Here, now. I've had enough. Are you a sorceress or are you just crazy?"

Suzanne's anger at the bandits, at Calliope, and at the entire situation finally flared. She raised the pen over her head, her eyes wild, her unkempt hair flaring around her face. "I'm *not* crazy. I'm a *writer!*"

The bandits stared wide-eyed at her for a moment. "Run!" several shouted at once, and the entire pack took to its heels.

Perplexed, Suzanne watched them go, holding her fighting stance. As the figures of the bandits dwindled into the distance, she finally lowered the pen, then ran her free hand through her hair. "I don't look *that* bad in the morning," she muttered.

Calliope reappeared directly in front of her, smiling with approval. "Excellent! You've had experiences worthy of interest. I'm sure you're just filled with the spirit of Inspiration."

Suzanne glowered at her Muse. "Yes. As a matter of fact, I feel inspired to do something right now." Her hand balled into a fist as she swung right at Calliope, but the Muse vanished like a burst soap bubble and Suzanne's attack swished through empty air.

Grumbling and feeling muscles knot up from sleeping all night on rocks, Suzanne limped toward her horse, now standing with no sign of skittishness. Suzanne eyed the beast sourly. "I'm going to call you Inconstant. You really don't seem to care what happens to your owners, do you?" It was impossible to tell for sure on a horse's face, but Suzanne thought Inconstant smirked at her words.

Riding in full daylight, the journey back to the city was an easy one. Suzanne found a writing pad in one of the saddlebags and worked on a story as she rode. A new set of guards were at the city gate when Suzanne arrived. They waved her through, though not without some worried comments that her attire might represent the first indication of a trend toward modest dressing by barbarian sword maidens.

This time, Suzanne strode firmly into the Temple of Inspiration, ignoring the flinches of those she passed close enough to that they caught a whiff of her odorous armor. She came up to the same Editor she'd spoken with before, kneeling briefly as she presented her offering.

"Another manuscript already?" The Editor took it, glanced at the first page, kept reading, and twenty minutes later looked back up at Suzanne. "Your offering is accepted." Suzanne smiled as the Editor painstakingly counted out a small pile of coins. "That's the standard payment rate. It's set by the goddess, so don't complain to me."

"It's fine." Suzanne swept up the coins.

"Can I expect more offerings from you?"

Suzanne smiled again. "Perhaps. First, though, I have to kill my Muse."

The Editor shook her head sadly. "Writers can't kill their Muses. A Muse can leave of its own accord, but it can't be killed."

"I can try." Suzanne paused before the idol of Inspiration to toss some of her new coins onto the goddess' altar, then headed out of the temple.

Calliope appeared, floating about ten feet away from her. "Your first accepted offering! How wonderful. Are you ready for more experiences?"

Suzanne smiled merrily as she drew Guardian from its sheath. "Sure. Let's talk about it. Could you come a little closer, please?"

"I'd rather not."

Suzanne drew forth her pen with her other hand. "Have I shown this to you? It's really a nice pen. Come look."

"No, thank you." Calliope began floating backwards as Suzanne took a step toward her.

Suzanne took another step and Calliope flew away at a faster rate. Still grasping her sword Guardian in one hand and her pen in the other, Suzanne jumped onto the back of her horse Inconstant and urged him after the fleeing Muse.

It wasn't until they reached the gate that Suzanne realized Calliope was leading her out of the city again.

A Late Symmer Night's Battle

Laura Frankos

Mustardseed grunted as she tightened the leather straps holding her armor in place. She twisted about, testing for mobility. Finding one couldn't move in combat could prove deadly . . . that is, assuming one ever got into combat again. She sighed, and flopped down on the grassy hillock.

"Is it all right?" a tiny anxious voice asked. "Shall I put in a few more stitches, just to make certain they hold well?"

Mustardseed peered into a mound of dandelions. There, among the gray fluff, she barely made out a chubby face surrounded by wispy silvery curls. A faint flutter of translucent wings sent dandelion seeds aloft. Who else but Moth, as pale and flitty as her namesake? If Mustardseed didn't reassure her, she was apt to tremble so much the nearest fairy ring would be awash in weeds.

"The straps are fine, Moth. Thanks for doing them; I can handle my sword, but not a needle."

"But you were *frowning*," Moth said, emerging from the weeds with a shake of her wings.

"Not over your work. I was just thinking how dull it was. It's so confounded peaceful. And now that Oberon and Titania have kissed and made up, we don't even have the chance to face off against the king's fairies."

"There's facing off and facing off, dearie," came a voice from behind her. "And some of Oberon's fellas have *nice* faces. Among other things."

Mustardseed didn't really want to hear it. She'd recently broken up with Robin Goodfellow. True, it was all for the best. They weren't suited for each other in the slightest: Robin was an incurable playboy with an infantile sense of humor, however much fun he was in the flowerbeds. Mustardseed's heart had mostly healed, but didn't take kindly to public references to "Oberon's fellas." She decided to put a brave face on it, and resorted to teasing back.

"You'd know best, Peaseblossom," she said. "People say you're responsible for half the fairy rings in the forest, you and your ever-changing partners."

Peaseblossom stepped into the clearing, her every move revealing why she was one of Titania's favorite dancers. And, Mustardseed reflected bitterly, one of the queen's best fighters as well. Peaseblossom proudly wore the black and yellow ribbon signifying she'd successfully dueled a humblebee. Mustardseed, while stronger by far, had no hopes of attaining such an honor.

"I can't help it. A cute guy, an empty patch of grass, and I just have to dance. And my latest beau is positively scrumptious." She twirled gracefully to Mustardseed's side, brushed some dust off a toadstool, and, after arranging her skirts just so, sat down.

"You could say hello to your cousin," Mustardseed said.

Peaseblossom blinked. "Sorry, Moth. Didn't notice you."

"Of course not. She's not a cute guy or a bare patch of grass. Never mind, Moth, some of us appreciate you."

Peaseblossom shook her curly pink locks. "I love Moth, and she knows it. Not that any of us have seen her lately. How, by the Queen's grace, did you manage to get away from the little monster, coz?"

"Ghosh is not a monster," Moth said. Her nearly-invisible antennae extended for a brief moment, then drooped again out of sight.

Mushrooms for all! Mustardseed thought. *Little Flutter showing signs of temper?*

"He's just active. Really, Peaseblossom, he's the sweetest baby and he'll make a wonderful page someday. No wonder their Majesties were ready to go to war over him."

Moth covered a yawn. "But I admit he's wearing. His latest trick is digging holes. I've had to put up signs warning people, or they'll fall in his excavations. The filthy places I've found that imp!"

"I saw him the other day," Mustardseed laughed. "I know he's naturally dark-skinned, being a little Indian changeling, but I couldn't tell where the mud left off and where he began."

"So where is the tiny, but grubby, paragon?" Peaseblossom asked.

"He's napping, so Philomel agreed to watch over him," said Moth. "I've been using the spare time to catch up on my leather-working. I fixed Mustardseed's armor straps, made a belt for dear Throstle, and started some pants for Ghosh. Of course, given what he does to clothes I'd be better off making them out of granite slabs, not reremice's wings."

Mustardseed and Peaseblossom both grimaced. Reremice were some of the nastiest creatures on earth: utterly vicious, completely destructive, and lacking in any intelligence beyond what was needed to attack their enemies. Both fairies had fought in the last great conflict with the winged devils; Mustardseed's left arm bore a scar from long, yellow fangs, and Peaseblossom's entire family had died when the beasts swooped out of the night sky, wrecking a fairy enclave. *Perhaps that's why Blossom's so carefree, choosing a different partner every week,* thought Mustardseed. *She lost nearly everything that mattered to her five years ago.*

Moth suddenly realized she had erred in mentioning the dread enemy before seasoned veterans. "Oh, I mean—I didn't mean—that is . . ." she stammered.

"Don't fret, old flitwings," Peaseblossom said with false heartiness. She clapped Moth on the shoulder, nearly staggering the smaller fairy. "At least we got a hefty supply of leather from fighting the big bug scourge of the night."

"Reremice aren't bugs," Mustardseed said mildly. "But do let's talk of something else."

"Delighted. I've been looking for you two. What else could get me to climb this hill in this heat?" Peaseblossom fanned herself with a burdock leaf. "Webby's home on leave! To celebrate her return, I'm throwing a grand bash tonight at the clearing by the musk-rose bush. I've spent the morning killing all the cankers in the buds, so the place looked splendiferous, and smells even yummier."

"Dear Cobweb!" said Moth. "We were so proud when she was accepted into the Queen's Archers. It will seem like we're all schoolgirls again. Of course I'll come, though I may have to bring Ghosh."

Peaseblossom's beautiful features scrunched in dismay. "Oh, if you must. I'd rather have you there with the Brat from Bombay, than not have you at all. But mind you keep him out of the shrubbery. Mustardseed?"

"I'll be there. For Webby." She hadn't felt like attending revels since the bust-up with Robin, but she couldn't miss the chance to spend time with an old pal like Cobweb.

It was a typical Peaseblossom affair, with more extravagance than style. And it was jam-packed with fairies, so crowded there was barely enough room in the circles to turn about. But Mustardseed, an indifferent dancer, was content to stay under a honeysuckle bower, chatting with Cobweb and watching Moth chase Ghosh.

Cobweb looked well, and the golden trim on her purple archer's uniform picked up the highlights in her braided hair. Like Mustardseed, she was one of those fairies with vestigial wings. Neither of them could fly more than a few paces, but they made up for it with greater strength. Webby's right arm positively rippled with muscles.

"So there we were, the new recruits, and what does the Master have us do? Hang pearls in every bloody cowslip's ear within sight. I tell you, we were ready to pack up. We'd come for training, not gardening! It wasn't until we returned to camp, bitching all the while, that we learned our next task: *shooting* the pearls out of the cowslips. Now that was a challenge worthy of us!"

"Amazing!" Moth breathed before distraction set in. "Ghosh! Don't eat that!"

"Dig, dig, dig," Ghosh said, brandishing his shovel and spraying dirt in every direction before dashing away. Moth hurried after him, sighing.

Cobweb and Mustardseed watched them go. "Moth hasn't changed," Cobweb said. "As domestic as ever, yet no kids of her own. Think she'll ever settle down?"

"If Throstle gets the gumption to pop the question. He's off with their Majesties on the Second Honeymoon Tour, though."

Cobweb pointed to a hillock, where Peaseblossom was regaling a mob of fairies. "She hasn't changed either. And to think she's currently got the infamous one on her string. Wonder how long that will last?"

"Oh, her new lovelight? I actually haven't heard much about him."

"Dewdrops! She's nabbed Randy Robin himself! She said he brazenly approached her at the last full moon ceremony and whispered in her ear, 'Wanna Puck around?'"

Mustardseed suppressed the urge to flinch. *I will not overreact; Webby has no idea Robin and I were an item. It's over and done with, and Blossom's welcome to him. But it hurts to think of him with one of my best buds.* "He probably used the 'let me put a girdle round you, baby' line, too. You'd think he could come up with a new routine." She pulled up some grass blades and methodically shredded them.

"Uh, right," said Webby, giving Mustardseed a curious look. "Hey, here comes an owl-rider. Wonder what's up?"

The ghostly white bird silently landed down by the brook, where its uniformed rider dismounted and ran to the side of Lady Quill, the ranking official in the royals' absence. Clearly, something was amiss. Fairies scattered like ants whose mound is disturbed, some flying, some running. Lady Quill herself zipped to the center of the clearing and called for attention.

"Ladies and gentlemen, I have grave news. The kobolds have attacked our border guards on the northern edge of the forest. They've beaten back our first line of defenders and are coming this way. They're expected by tomorrow night. I've sent messengers for additional support, but they might not arrive in time. For now, all military personnel are to report to General Pard. Civilians, take cover in Oberon's Glade."

"Rain and storms," said Mustardseed, "to think I was complaining it was too peaceful. My big mouth!"

The fairy forces seemed meager to Mustardseed's trained eye. A bare handful of archers, led by Cobweb; a division of hedgehog armor, thirty owl-riders, and the resident fox cavalry, to which she and Blossom belonged. *We'd gotten complacent. We haven't been challenged since the reremice war. Half the army's traveling with the royals or hunting that troll in the southlands. These blue-skinned Germanic devils could be grimm. Er, grim.*

As she mused over the coming battle, Mustardseed groomed her fox, Mr. Tod. Nearby, Peaseblossom was doing the same. Her beast, a skittish vixen, suddenly snarled as someone approached. "Easy, there," said the newcomer. "Just came to say my farewells to two very foxy ladies. I'm off to bring word of the invasion to their majesties."

"You!" Peaseblossom hurled her brush at Robin Good-fellow's head. It connected with a resounding *thunk*. "You skip my big party because you're off taking a trip to the moon with Miss Gossamer Wings herself, slutty Cinnabar. Get out before I throw something heavier at you."

Robin, rubbing the bump on his head, flashed that devastating smile on Mustardseed. "Mussy, honey, it's a long trip I'm making . . ."

"How nice. We can rejoice in your lengthy absence. Now why don't you show off that vaunted speed of yours and exit, preferably pursued by a bear?"

"Be that way, then." He buzzed off around a hedgerow, but the pair could hear him faintly. "Aurora, darling of the day! Had to make my farewells . . ."

Mustardseed and Peaseblossom looked at each other over their foxes' backs and burst out laughing. "He must be collecting good-bye smooches," Peaseblossom said.

"Probably timed his departure to the split second." Mustardseed scratched Mr. Tod's elegant nose. He whined in sympathy.

"Trouble is, Robin can kiss better than damn near anyone. The rat."

"More to life than kissing. Let's report to General Pard."

At the next sundown meeting, the officers gave a briefing on the enemy's movements. A captured kobold had explained the reason behind their invasion: they had been peacefully working in the silver mines in northern Greece when a bunch of humans evicted them. He said their families were homeless and the men couldn't find suitable jobs anywhere—but the officials warned this might be a play for sympathy.

"Whatever troubles they might have had, they can't barge

in here and steal our homes," thundered General Pard from atop his panther. "Cheeky Hun devils! Their General Hinzelmann is a nasty piece of work, too. Rides on a snake, if you can imagine it! Beats his own soldiers with a stick; heard he's dared to use it on humans, too! Scandalous! A hefty reward to any fairy that disposes of this vermin! Now take your positions. They're expected by midnight."

The battle proved to be more of a skirmish. Clearly, General Hinzelmann was feeling out the fairies' strength. He had superior numbers, more infantry than cavalry and few archers, but they were scrawny bastards. A stick-thin kobold on a weasel, who barely looked able to hold his own shield, managed to break Mustardseed's spear in a brief but fierce tussle. The others she fought with showed the same intense determination: physically weak, but fueled by obvious desperation.

The hedgehog armor did considerable damage to their line, until Hinzelmann himself rattled the nerve of the prickly creatures as he slithered by on a huge snake and laid about him with a great, walloping stick. Mustardseed tried getting near the enemy leader, but soon had to abandon her plans. One of the kobold colonels—a tall fellow, very dark blue and wearing a weird black felt cap—led his division in a clever feint on the right side, cutting off a dozen fox-riders from the main force, Peaseblossom among them.

Fortunately, the commander of the owl-riders immediately sent air support. Mustardseed spurred Mr. Tod into the fray, followed by other cavalry. She managed a swing at the clever colonel, but his beast, a pine marten with a striking orange patch on its breast, turned aside just in time. He had the effrontery to tip his cap and grin at her, his teeth white under a neatly trimmed black mustache. The tide of battle soon separated them, and the surrounded fox-riders broke out of the trap with minimal losses.

Fortunately for the fairy army, Hinzelmann pulled his troops back to regroup for another assault. Mustardseed, Peaseblossom, and Cobweb downed mugs of nectar and assessed the damages. "Not good," Cobweb said. "Some of their officers have little blue stones embedded in their leather coats. I saw two perfectly good shots glance off the cursed things. I was hoping to take out the maniac on the snake."

"The guy in the cap's a bigger danger," Mustardseed said.

"I saw him bring down an owl with a dagger in the eye, and he nearly destroyed Blossom's platoon. He's fast enough . . . What's that?"

But she knew too well what it was. Shrill piping filled the sky and dark shadows played across the moon. Cobweb, without hesitating, loosed two shots in succession. A reremouse fell to the ground, twitching until Mustardseed slit its throat. Its fellows shrieked in protest, and the fairies' camp was instantly filled with combat.

Reremice, however vicious, aren't good at coordinating attacks, and soon flew off. But, to the fairies' horror, they were heading for Oberon's Glade where the civilians were hiding.

"There's no help for it," Lady Quill shouted from the back of her massive owl. "What use fighting the kobolds if all our loved ones perish under vile fangs? Onward!"

The owls took flight and the foxes, many double-burdened with archers, leaped over the fields. "Bad, very bad," Mustardseed said over her shoulder to Webby. "Even if we beat the bats, the kobolds will pour down from the hills onto us."

"First things first," said Cobweb. "Hey, Lady Quill's owl just nailed two of the buggers! But what's that in the glade? That can't be Moth!"

The diminutive grey fairy was smacking a downed reremouse with a broom. She looked furious, her antennae sticking straight up. Other reremice were flapping in the sky above the glade, engaging the owl-riders in combat. Cobweb and her fellow archers immediately started shooting, bringing more leathery-winged demons down.

Mustardseed looked about in amazement. Save Moth, the glade was empty. "Where is everybody?"

"In the caves." Moth gave the corpse one more whack. "Ghosh found a tunnel last week while digging, leading to enormous caves. Room for all, and we can block the entrance until these creatures leave. I stayed to show you the way."

General Pard's panther pulled up just in time to hear Moth's news. "Wonderful! And even more wonderful: look, we've beaten them back, and they're heading for the kobolds! They'll get what's coming to them!"

Something twisted in Mustardseed's stomach. "Begging your pardon, sir, but I disagree. No intelligent beings deserve

to die under the reremice's fangs and claws. The kobolds,
for all that they attacked our lands, are a cultured people
with a sense of honor." The image of the kobold colonel
tipping his absurd cap came unbidden to her mind. "Do you
think *the Queen* would leave any thinking race to such a
fate?"

The general, who revered Titania, had the decency to
blush. "What would you have us do, then? Invite the devils to share our sanctuary?"

"Yes," Mustardseed said bluntly. "I am willing to ride to
their camp under a flag of truce and direct them to the caves.
Er, where are they, Moth?"

She pointed. "Near the tallest birch in that grove, just
under the outcrop of rocks that resembles a red crab. I left
Ghosh's bucket near the entrance as a sign."

"I must confer with Quill," mumbled Pard, gesturing
towards the air patrol, which was coming in for its landing.

"Do it quickly. Sir." Mustardseed's sharp ears caught hoarse
cries from the kobolds' camp.

Moments later, Mr. Tod and every other available fox were
bounding through the forest again. The beasts were tired,
but somehow picked up energy as they neared the fray. Foxes
loathed reremice.

There wasn't any time to present the flag of truce in any
formal way. The kobolds were backed up in a solid mass,
defending a cluster of wagons. Mustardseed heard tiny
kobolds wailing over the din of battle. The fairies charged.

Mustardseed glimpsed the face of Colonel Cap, who was
directing the defense: he clearly thought the fairies had come
to polish his men off, and registered complete crogglement
when he saw Titania's Finest whaling into the bats. Then
she had to concentrate on impaling reremice, having picked
up a new spear in camp. She turned three into shishkabobs
before getting close to the kobold defenders again.

The reremice had figured out that the most defenseless
morsels were in the wagons, and were dive-bombing them
in their haphazard fashion. Mustardseed watched in aston-
ishment as the colonel's pine marten hurled itself into the
air and snapped a reremouse in half while its rider cleaved
another. But then the colonel's luck failed; a brown streak
whizzed at his head and long claws raked through the black
hair. The felt cap flew off, and the kobold nearly lost his

seat. The reremouse pivoted in air, readying another attack. Mustardseed heaved her spear . . . and connected.

Two more of the monsters tried getting into the wagon, its canvas cover torn to shreds. Mustardseed glimpsed small, frightened blue faces within, and maneuvered Mr. Tod in between the wagon and the reremice. She fended off one with her sword, but when she turned to challenge the second, she saw the injured kobold had already dispatched it. Blood dripping down his face, he looked around wildly for more enemies. But the fairy reinforcements had driven them off, at least for the moment.

"Where's Hinzelmann?" Mustardseed asked him. *Where had that darn white flag gone? Oh, well.* "We've come to lead your people to safety. We have a refuge in the ridge, down by that glade."

The kobold shook his head, hoping to clear it and not succeeding. "Herr General Hinzelmann is wounded. I command." He looked about, dismayed. "*Die Fledermäuse . . .*"

"Yes, they'll be back soon. So let's get underground and worry about the details later, Colonel . . ."

He drew himself up, patted the neck of his exhausted marten. "Hödeken. So-called for my little hat, wherever it is." He bowed.

There's something incredibly appealing about such dignity in the face of disaster. And that mustache! "You'll need a new cap. That one's been haberdashed to pieces. Let's go."

"Who would have thought it would have worked out so well?" said Webby. Peaseblossom was again throwing another bash, this time for Webby's imminent return to archery training. She was in rose silks, which matched her flawless complexion, while Mustardseed was not only clad in silver but had the jewelry to complement it.

"What, the kobolds discovering that those caves go on for miles and contain more silver than their old ones did?" asked Peaseblossom, her hand smoothing the yards of lace in her skirt. "And Oberon and Titania working out a deal with their leader? Good thing that crazy snakey general of theirs died of his wounds. From everything I've heard, he was the one behind the invasion. The other fellows in charge seem much more reasonable. Here's Moth and the man of the hour! Little Ghosh! Aunty Blossom has a present for you! A new shovel! Such a good boy deserves anything he wants!" From a diamond-trimmed satchel, Peaseblossom withdrew a gold-handled shovel and gave it to the chubby toddler.

Who promptly tossed it aside. "Don' wanna dig. Wanna *fish*. Go fishing? Now?"

Moth picked up Ghosh and handed him to Blossom. "Good boy deserves anything he wants! Aunty will take you fishing, for a while, anyway. His gear is by the docks, Peaseblossom."

Peaseblossom gulped. Then she hugged Ghosh. "All right, let's fish, if that's the latest passion. After all, Moth has a Significant Meeting tonight with a certain Captain Throstle."

"And if he doesn't propose, we'll *all* thump him," said Mustardseed. "You know, I've never looked forward to a dance so much." She surveyed the crowd of fairies and kobolds, looking for a certain figure in black with a cap worn low on his face.

"I'm surprised," said Webby. "You're a lousy dancer."

There he was! He'd bear the mark of those claws forever, but at least they were healing without infection. She rose, and he saw her, his smile visible despite the distance between them. She turned to her pals. "I was a lousy dancer. But that was before Hödeken taught me to waltz. Later, girls."

Psyched Up

Michael D. Turner

My mom swore I'd outgrow my tomboy phase. And she would teach me to be a lady or die trying. May she rest in peace. It's not that I didn't try, I just didn't have it in me. I admit Momma made some inroads before she died, but the compromises were all going my way.

Being a service brat has a few advantages, and my family was determined to get all of them for me. In fifth grade, Mom got me ice skates. We were in Connecticut, and she was thinking figure skating. We compromised on Pee Wee Hockey. The next year in Hawaii, I got hula lessons. And started karate.

Then Mom died, and while I was shook up, I got through it, and my education and deportment fell to my dad. And Daddy had some different ideas. Dad is in the Navy, and does something that involves a lot of swimming and jumping out of airplanes and other stuff I don't talk about. And he thinks everyone ought to be able to "take care of themselves."

He's a great dad. He's taken me skydiving and scuba diving. He taught me to shoot and swim and run. He did not teach me to drive but had a friend in the secret service do it. He encouraged me to keep at martial arts, and when he's around we lift weights together.

He finally remarried when I was a junior in high school. To a nice Filipino-Hawaiian girl about eight years older than me and she is like my big sister. And her dad is my main martial arts instructor, which is how they met anyway.

All this is kind of a long road to tell you how I ended up being the Mistress of Mayhem. That's my professional name and it's the name of my website. I got out of high school and was not ready for college and needed to make a living. I tried exotic dancing and that paid the rent but it was a real drag dealing with the a--holes, especially the ones who ran the clubs. So I met this guy who designed websites, and it was a lot easier and paid better and so I launched my career. I came up with the theme myself, so I guess I have no one else to blame.

I knew my dad really didn't want me being a porno queen on the web. Mostly 'cause of all the flak he'd get from guys on base. So what I came up with was "Mistress of Mayhem," which was this thing where I did a lot of photo shoots with me wearing these costumes of armor or leather and things, usually holding weapons, in settings all over California and also down in Baja. It didn't start off all that well money-wise until Freddy, that's my web guy, talked me into getting a boob job. So a nice pair of B's got turned into a couple of rather full D's and the money just poured in. Best ten grand I ever spent.

Anyway a couple of months ago we got into streaming video. You know, a bunch of pictures taken in sequence automatically. And I started staging these fairly elaborate "battles," usually with one of the guys I know who's into the local reenactment scene. The battles are fun to do, and the suckers, ah subscribers, really dig them. I usually pre-record them and play them with my color commentary like a sports event on my live shows once a week. And I have this whole persona thing going with it. It works really well, which is how I'm buying a house in southern California as a twenty-year-old self-employed dilettante.

So last night I'm doing my show, and it's going over really good. I have about forty subscribers on, and at least three new ones. I'm spinning the story with clips off my CD, and the new battle is just kicking. It's easily the best thing I've ever gotten on disc. Eric, that's the guy I'm fighting, is huge, hairy and really muscular, and he's also a theater major at

UCSD who's into movie choreography and we worked this thing out really well. He's all in leather and I've got my chain mail nothing on, which is really just a couple of dance belts over my shoulders and crossing between my boobs, with a mail and elastic thong. It's my subscribers' favorite and more comfortable than most of my outfits.

And this battle looks really good, I mean real. Eric tosses me around the sand (we were at a beach near the Little Sur river) and I'm whaling on him. He used a couple of blood caps just like in wrestling, and, man, when we got there the viewers just went wild. I'm doing real well on the commentating and the show is just going great.

One of the newbies is really going on about this, like she (only about ten percent of my customers are female, but they are a very loyal ten percent) thinks this is real. Well, that's what live shows are suppose to be like, so I'm leading on like, "Well, yes, this is what I do." And she's asking like what do I charge for rescues? And I'm thinking she's giving me a come-on and that's cool. It's part of the business and besides, it's a good lead, 'cause in the next clip I finish trouncing Eric. Then my friend Morgen, who's spent the whole clip reclined on the dune behind us crying and cheering while wearing an anklet and a head band, gets to "reward" me with a little soft core girl-girl action. Nothing too hard, and I never minded doing the girl stuff. Morgen used to dance with me at the strip clubs.

So I made some fluff comment about working it out with the rescuee—I swear to Gods I don't remember exactly what I said, though I could play it back. Then this newbie types in, "It's a bargain!" There's this shimmering light, and all of a sudden—

I'm here. Looking at this chick in a see-through silk bathrobe who's looking at me like I'm the president or something. She's maybe eighteen, petite but filled out, and she is standing over what looks like a marble altar covered with wizard's gear and a magic mirror. It takes me a minute but finally I realize it *is* a marble altar covered in wizard's gear. With a magic mirror.

Before I can ask the seven hundred stupid questions guaranteed to make me look like a moron, she springs forward and drops to her knees, clasping my sword hand in both of hers and kissing it. "Oh thank you, mighty warrior, for championing my cause, for surely I need a champion in this dark hour."

If she'd said this with anything less than total sincerity with more than a touch of desperation, I'd have laughed in her face and blown the whole gig. But I managed to set my face into what my dad called a "mission face" and my drama teacher called a "stern countenance" and said in a level voice, "Just what is your current ah . . . problem?"

"The wicked lord of Wierdmark, John the Bastard's get, has challenged my right to rule from the throne of Ghemlan. And tomorrow I must send forth a champion to meet his and contest his claim. And I have none so mighty as to be able to best his champion, who is bespelled to be invincible to all in single combat!" she replied.

That didn't sound too good. And it did not explain how I'd become involved. Okay, so I had some strong suspicions. I wanted to hear it out loud and from someone who believed it. That way maybe I could too. So I figured to brazen it out until I got my feet under me.

"And how," I asked in what I hoped was a calm and steely voice, "did you come to choose me as your . . . champion?"

"When no one of my loyal subjects came forth who I thought could best John's champion, I assembled my late mother's magical apparatus to see if it would offer some hope. I used her magic mirror to scry the nearer dimensions. There I spied your combat with the hairy brute, and perceived your spells sent out to promote yourself as a sort of mystical champion. I followed the mystic threads from your image to the far place wherein you dwell, and using nearly all my mother's stores of magic power did summon you to me once you had agreed to my bargain," the princess fairly blurted.

Great, I thought to myself, she thinks I've already agreed. Terrific. Better not get in too deep.

"You're mistaken, I'm afraid. What you saw was mere entertainment. It's how I make my living. I record mock battles and play them out with a little sex on the side so my subscribers can get their, er . . . So they can enjoy the spectacle. I am a performer, not some sort of cosmic duelist. My reply was part of my act. I thought you were one of my subscribers." There, put it all out front. Now that she understood her mistake she could send me home and go back to looking for a real champion.

The princess looked like she was going to cry. I tried to head that off.

"Sorry about the confusion but I really can't help you. So just send me back and you can get on with your scrying out a real champion." I was going for nonchalant and missed it pretty wide, I'd guess.

Tears were streaming down the young woman's cheeks. I could tell she was really upset. And totally at a loss.

"B-but I can't send you back, it took all my mother's magic to get you here. It will take days to replace all that and send you back. And the challenge is tomorrow! And then I'll be destitute and won't be able to afford to send you back and, and, and you agreed! We have a mystical contract. You can't back out!" She was wailing now, tears in gushes and eyes getting all puffy.

Now I've never been much of a crier. I don't remember using tears on my folks but they would have been unimpressed with them. But I've never had to deal with them either. I felt so bad! I mean really. And I had agreed, I guess. And she looked so helpless and upset and all.

So I said, "What exactly does this challenge entail? I mean what do I have to do and who do I have to do it to? And when?"

"The challenge is tomorrow noon. A single combat, traditionally with swords though you may use any hand weapon. To death or surrender, with mercy dependant on the opponent's whim. You will fight Ursus Redbeard, Lord John's champion." The princess was drying up some.

"And just how good is this Ursus? How much experience does he have?"

"He has fought a half dozen duels as a judicial champion, and with high fee, till word of his bespellment spread. Since that time all who were faced with a challenge from his clients have capitulated their cases, rather than face a certain loss."

"Can you show me his last fight?" Looking around the stone walls and embroidered tapestries filling the chamber I started thinking MGM's *Robin Hood*. Probably not.

But the princess surprised me. "My mother's mirror can display all his bouts. But to what purpose? You have said you are no champion!"

I sensed another bout of tears coming on. I moved to head them off.

"Now look here. Look at me. Do I look like some soft actress fop? These muscles," I flexed my biceps. Not unimpressive, especially to a sheltered princess. "You don't think they just grew this way, do you? I won't back out of this deal unless I'm sure I don't have a chance. So turn on your magic mirror, princess, and let's look at the bad news."

And so she does. And the news wasn't all that bad. This Ursus guy was big and ugly, no doubts. His face looked stepped on and his arms had more hair than my . . . um, anyway, his gut hung way past his belt and while he struck with real power he was fairly slow on his feet. And he used a wide, slow broadsword, doubling up his hands for extra power or leaving his off hand to punch or grapple. He liked to move in on his guy but none of his opponents really tried to work around him and they were mostly armed like he was.

After watching all six of his duels about three times each, I had no doubts. I could take him. Except for the little matter of the spell.

"Just how do these spell thingies work? I mean what does the spell do to make this Ursus so invincible?"

The princess looked pensive and bit her lip at me. After a second or so she gave out a hesitant explanation. "It's not really a spell of protection. That could be countered. He paid a fen witch to cast a spell of prophecy. She pronounced that no single opponent would ever defeat him in battle."

"It must give him a real edge in a duel, knowing that. I mean confidence is important in these things." I ventured.

"Yes, indeed. And his opponents have also been confident of his victory. That has doubtless been a great boon to his career," the princess allowed.

"So if he thought we had his magic beat, he'd be behind a step, right?"

"If we had his magic beat? Perhaps but we . . ." She was backing off.

"I can take him!" I pronounced. "Provided you and I can agree to a fee." I gave my most evil grin. I had her squirming.

"I have seen your fees. If you win, I will pay it!" She looked quite nervous about this. I had forgotten about

Morgen's part in my show. That wasn't going to be near enough anyway. I decided to twist the knife a little.

"That was a performance, not a fee. For a real bout at which I'll be risking my actual life and limbs, I require far more."

"What more?" The tears were welling again, but now I was armored. This much she had coming.

"I'll be saving not just your life but your throne! As such, additional payment is appropriate. Gold! Jewels! As much as I can carry. And I want some assurances. Medical coverage for any wounds I receive!" If she thought she could work this off in bed, she had another think coming.

"Done!" She cried out with such enthusiasm I wondered what perverse pleasures she thought I would demand. Another thing came to my mind.

Glancing down at my barely clad body with its chain mail cutaway bustier and chain and elastic thong, I grimaced. The only gear I had worth a hoot was my sword, a beautiful Persian-style scimitar I got for modeling for a knifemaker's catalog. The rest of my gear was costume junk. "I'll need some real armor. With padding. And some boots. Nothing too heavy, but I'll be damned if I am going to fight in this ridiculous bedroom gear!"

"My guards have a complete armory, and the royal cobbler can do wonders! Is that all?" The princess was looking quite relieved.

"Just one more thing. Does your highness have a name?"

"Serenity." She quivered as she gave it. But she looked me straight in the eye while she did.

So I said, "Princess Serenity, if you agree to these conditions, I'll be your champion."

And so I was.

It was not all peaches and schnapps from there on in, but it went pretty well. She pulled a silk rope which rang a bell and summoned a goggle-eyed servant, which reminded me of my state of dress. For about a second, after which I figured he'd survive it and forgot about it while Serenity summoned the royal cobbler. He measured me for footwear while I explained to him what I wanted. I don't know if his sweating was at my urgent requirements or my nubile proximity but he got his business over with in a hurry and that was done.

The armory was harder as there were about a half dozen guys there, healthy young guys, and they made sure to take a good look while I went about my business, but as none openly leered, I took it in good spirits. Dad always says a warrior gets what he can when he can, 'cause who knows? At least they didn't ignore me. That would have been unnerving.

It was getting late. I bundled up my new gear and Serenity showed me to a chamber not far from her apartments where I had come in. I laid my new gear down on a table, bundled my old gear up on the nightstand, set my sword atop it unsheathed. I then lay down on the bed, found it had a feather mattress and promptly fell asleep.

I woke up that morning only slightly disoriented and, unlike every story I have ever read, I knew right where I was and what had happened and I knew it was real. So much for reading preparing one for life. I judged from the sun hitting the wall through the window that it was about eight o'clock. I did my morning stretches and my daily dozens and glanced around for something to wear while I searched out breakfast. Not so much as a stitch apart from my armor and my work mail. I judged both too uncomfortable for day wear. So I sheathed my sword and swathed a sheet around me sari style and was just preparing to venture out when my hostess arrived, with breakfast in tow.

I could tell Serenity was nervous. Heck, she was having kittens. But I didn't want to talk battle strategy over breakfast. So we tried for girl talk. It didn't take well and we mostly ended up eating in silence.

She had figs and dates and eggs and porridge. Mindful of the upcoming fight I had one egg, hard-boiled, a small bunlike loaf of dark bread, some yellow cheese, and cider. After being shown to the privy I came back to don my armor, very glad I was not going to stay here.

As I suited up, Serenity had a chest brought in. It was about half the size of an army foot locker with a sturdy handle on each end. In it she had set some small gold bars so that they covered the bottom in a layer about two deep. She had me lift it. Not much of a challenge but she didn't look surprised. Her men added some more gold and I lifted again. Then we went back and forth this way for some time until the chest became quite burdensome. I finally said that was enough gold.

Serenity then laid a tray of thin wood over the gold and onto this she poured jewels from a doeskin pouch. There were a couple of dozen, green and red and purple and yellow and shiny white, which I took to be diamonds. They ranged in size from about the size of the stone in my mother's wedding ring (a third of a karat) to about the size of the end of my little finger (which Gods only know is how much).

"That's fine, thank you." I mean what else was I going to say? I replaced the gems in their pouch. Then I tossed my bundled bikini mail into the chest, hefted it once to show I could carry it (which was not that easy anymore) and indicated for it to be closed up. Then I strapped on my sword.

"How much time?" I asked.

"Time enough for me, I trust?" It was the royal cobbler, my boots in hand. I glanced down at my still-bare feet and grimaced.

"Indeed."

The boots fit tolerably well, which was good 'cause if they hadn't, I would have been obliged to duel barefoot. Still the time was getting on and the princess was getting nervous.

"Serenity, what's wrong?"

"Are you sure you can beat both Ursus and his magic? You haven't told me how you mean to do it." She pouted prettily when worried. She probably practiced her look in the mirror. Why not? I did.

"Trust me, your highness, I've got his number." She looked quizzically at that but we moved along to a large hallway that led out of the castle and to the upcoming duel.

I really don't know what I expected for a field of honor. I suppose I had envisioned a greensward surrounded by gaily bedecked stands. Like in the movie *Ivanhoe*. We didn't even leave the castle. Well, not entirely. The main gate of the castle (which was huge, I never did get a feel for the entire size of it) was at a right angle to the main wall as the circle of the main walls did not meet square on. Surrounding this area was another wall, nearly as high but not quite as thick, with two stout towers forming a sort of barbican with another gate between them at a right angle to the first. All the walls and gates formed a space which I remember my dad, during a trip to Spain on which we toured several castles, telling me was called a killing field. Well, hopefully not this day.

The walls were lined with people in gaily-colored clothing, but I could not really see them as they were all on the tops of the walls, while I was down on the ground level. I was escorted out on the ground by the princess and about thirty of her guards, including a few of the fellows from the armory last night.

I winked at one. Hey, a warrior gets what she can.

Lord John the Bastard's Get was oily and sly-looking, overdressed in velvets and heavy embroidery. Then again he wasn't fighting. I looked around for his champion. Finally I noticed him in Lord John's shadow. Not nearly as tall as I'd thought. Maybe six-two. Maybe. Still a good two-sixty, maybe two-seventy. Also greasy-looking.

While the official people talked official talk in loud voices I took a deep, cleansing breath. I tune out the words and just follow the rhythms. I'm centered. I'm focused. Another breath. I run through an old joke in my mind. Just as I am grinning at the punch line the talk stops. Good timing. I'm loose and relaxed and focused.

Greaseball steps up. The sound comes back on as I glide out to meet him. He grins at me and draws his sword out and he says, "I cannot be defeated in single combat. It is foretold."

And I smile sweetly at him as I slide my scimitar out of its scabbard and look him straight in the eye and I say, "I'm not exactly alone, you know. I'm pregnant."

The look on the greaseball's face would have made this whole thing worth it. Even if he killed me. Which he tried to do with unseemly haste, coming in with a fast thrust up the midline. Oh yeah, I'd got to him. But now I had to make it work.

It was really the wrong way for him to come at me. I mean he was a head taller than me and twice as heavy. My blade barely brushed along his as I stepped offline. His off hand reached out for me and I cut below it, toward his leg. He skipped away and I followed my blade in and around at another angle, high and hard. The scimitar's well-tempered tip sliced through his heavy leather gauntlet and a few of the links of his mail sleeve, drawing blood. He came back with a heavy overhand slash which passed right through where he thought I was going. But of course that's not where I went.

Now I was not going to kid myself. I'm in terrific shape and I've been doing martial arts training for half my life. I was much faster than this guy, I had a weapon he wasn't used to, and I had seen him fight. But he was a pro with battles under his belt and I wasn't going to give him time to figure out my style. If I did he'd gut me.

My dad always said if you sweat more in training you'll bleed less in combat. And I had really tried to live that in my training. Thank Gods. Ursus Redbeard was slow and fat and totally lacking in finesse, and if I ever had to go one minute with him a second time he'd eat my liver. But this one time I got him. And I got him just about how I planned.

Twice more he came in and I moved offline, cutting in on an angle and out on a second. And each time I cut him, but not badly. The next time he made to come straight at me again and then cut off at an angle. I was waiting for it. I had set it up for him to do. He still nearly had me.

I feinted an angled cut and then charged in. His blade whistled at my head and somehow I moved it out of the way. I locked up his arm, brought my pommel down hard right on the juncture of blade and hilt. Then I dropped my hips down and over he went, landing hard on his tailbone with his sword arm, sans sword, twisted behind his back and my blade at his throat.

I hissed between clenched teeth into his dirty ear, "Do you yield? Do you want my mercy?"

It might have taken him half a second to reach his decision. "Aye," he hoarsely croaked.

"Then swear you will champion no one but the princess Serenity forevermore as long as you live."

"I swear it." Still a dry croak.

"Then yield."

"I yield! The princess wins!" This much clearer and louder.

A great cheer went up. I released my hold and removed my blade, stuck out my hand and hauled him to his feet. "And since you're going to champion the princess you might want to start bathing regularly." Serenity got that one free.

The rest of the trip was very smooth. I came out of the

fight without a single cut and only some strained muscles in my lower back. Not too bad, as I was still able to hoist my treasure chest. Which I did, right up the stairs and back to the princess' chamber. And I got the rest of my payment. Every penny's worth.

It took a couple of hours for her minions to gather the necessary wizard's stuff. I gave her the benefit of the doubt and assumed they had been working on it all day. I stood in a circle of silvery chalk and she did her thing (I didn't really see what) and I'm back in my bedroom in front of my computer holding a chest full of gold.

I was exhausted, so I took a quick shower and crawled into my bed. Sleep had never been so good.

This morning I woke up with the sun just peeking through my shades as usual. What was different was the nausea that sent me sprinting to the porcelain throne to loudly worship Ralph. And then leaning over the bowl after my second heave, it strikes me. I'm never sick.

And I thought I had pulled a smooth one over on old Ursus. Guess not.

Branded

Jan Stirling

Around the fire the women's faces were grim, though in the best of times there was little that even firelight could do to soften these faces. These were the noncoms and lower ranked officers of King Saldeg's mercenary legions and their experience lent a hardness to their features that even near darkness couldn't alter.

The scars, eye patches and missing teeth didn't help either.

Feric the magician sat silently among them, gauging their mood and worrying about Terion, his lover and friend. He glanced across the fire at her. Alone in this company, her face was untouched by war and very little by harsh weather. Her friends envied her for it, teasing that she kept Feric around to slide her best scars below her collarbone, for her body bore some spectacular ones.

Feric didn't mind the teasing; he was happy that they'd finally accepted his presence. And relieved—the incessant beatings were getting hard to take. Once Terion had to trounce ten different women in a week. That was in the beginning though; now they were accepted as partners. Of course, it didn't hurt that he was a good camp cook and knew an excellent anti-rust spell, as well as how to revoke it at any distance.

As if she sensed his gaze, Terion looked up at him, and though she couldn't bring herself to smile, her expression softened, then she looked back into the fire. She could at best be called striking, but to him her face was fairer than dawn in the vale of Darden. It grieved him to see her so sad.

The women shifted and someone spoke in tones of awe and horror.

"Branded."

"Marked with a coward's shame," another growled.

They shifted again and their eyes met and dropped around the circle. The silence became more charged still. Feric waited, but at last could stand the silence no more.

"What do you do when you're branded?" he asked.

Beside him Lieutenant Belta threw her grog into the fire, causing the flames to dip and hiss before flaring as the alcohol burned. She turned to him and her blond head seemed as big as a lion's.

"Do you fight for your name?" she asked him. "Is that what you mean?" She turned away and spat in disgust.

"Would that the Captain could," Terion said quietly. "But she ran. We all saw it."

"And we all saw *you* save the day."

The women looked round at the speaker. Prince Ennit strolled toward the fire, his richly embroidered velvet cloak held close around him, though the night was mild. Behind him, Peria, his sorceress and some said his lover, lingered in the shadows. She was a slender woman dressed in black, with almond-shaped dark eyes and hip-length black hair worn free.

Feric caught Peria's eye and nodded. She returned his nod—professional courtesy.

Terion stood and the others rose in belated courtesy.

"I only did my duty, highness," she said grudgingly. Ennit was a peacock and every soldier in the army looked down on him, for all his royal blood and fighting ability.

"What a pity that Captain Avia did not," the prince sneered.

The very air grew stiff and Peria moved forward a step. Ennit raised his hand and she stopped, then he made a throwaway gesture.

"But it is enough for my royal father and myself that

you"—he gestured at the warrior women around the fire—
"and your troops performed as they should. In fact he
proposes to give you a small bonus, Lieutenant, for your
efforts today." He paused, smiling.

"Thank you, highness," Terion said, her voice choked.

Never doubting that her voice was choked with gratitude,
rather than fury and shame, the prince smiled. Again he
made that throwaway gesture.

"But be seated, ladies," he said smoothly. "I did not mean
to interrupt your rest." Then he became solemn. "Unfortunately I have come with bad news as well." The prince
looked down and bit his lip as he paused, then looked up,
but met no one's eyes. "Though I have tried to intercede
with my royal father he will not rescind his judgement."
He blinked rapidly, as though fighting a tear. "Avia is to
be branded."

No one spoke, but shoulders dropped and heads were hung
around the fire.

"The one concession I could wring from him was that
the brand will be in a hidden place. Most likely one of her
buttocks."

Terion looked up at him, her face shocked. Then she
looked away. It *was* better than being branded on the face.
But the humiliation!

That this should happen to Avia Iron Breast, so named
because she actually had one (an exquisitely modeled pros-
thesis that covered an early wound).

The reason she'd had it made, she'd told Terion, was
because she'd gotten tired of being accused of being "some
war-god's Amazon doxy." Even though it was the wrong
breast. Steel would have worked as well, and might have
been lighter but didn't sound as good as Iron Breast. Gold
or silver would have made her too much of a target, and
"Avia Tin Tit" was right out.

Terion almost smiled to remember the Captain's amusement when Feric shyly offered his anti-rust spell while trying
to avoid the word "breast" and her honest pleasure at not
having rust stains streaking her muscled torso after every
battle.

Terion sighed.

This was the end of the Captain's military career. You
couldn't go back from something like this. They'd all seen

her running, white-faced and screaming, from the foe. Terion had managed to keep the company from breaking in confusion. But this was the end of the company as she'd known it.

As though hearing her thought Prince Ennit said off-handedly, "As Avia is to be banished, my father has given me command of your company, ladies." He smiled, and the smile mocked them. "Lieutenant Terion will be my second."

"Sir," Terion said, rising, "I'm not senior enough."

"You're too modest, Lieutenant. My decision is made." Ennit cast a glance over the company, nodded once and with a swirl of his elegant cloak, swaggered off.

Peria turned to follow the prince, then paused. Her dark eyes looked at this woman and that, lingering longest on Terion. Then her glance flicked to Feric. He nodded to her, his expression cool, she lowered her eyes and nodded back, then melted into the darkness.

Belta spat into the fire and cursed. "I hate that snake," she growled.

"Peria? Why?" Terion asked.

"She's dangerous!" the blond woman said.

"Not really," Feric said, tossing another stick onto the fire. "She's not even close to being as powerful as I am, and I wouldn't describe myself as dangerous."

Surprised, Terion tipped her head. "She acts like she's dangerous."

"Well, of course," Feric said. "If his nibs didn't think she was a powerful magicker he wouldn't keep her around."

"So she's a *liar*!" Belta snarled, glaring.

Feric blinked at her ferocity.

"If she's not powerful how does she do her spells?" Terion asked. "And how do you know she's not as strong as you are?" Her tone of voice accused him of engaging in some sort of magical pissing match.

"Her mother told me about her. You remember Sita Goldenhair?"

"*That's* her *mother*?" Terion couldn't believe it, Sita Goldenhair looked like a dewy twenty-year-old.

Feric smiled and nodded. "But then, she *is* a powerful sorceress. She sends a mix of pre-packaged spells to Peria several times a year that only need a little push to activate. Peria is well up to that."

"She's a cheat!" Belta shouted.

"Maybe," Terion said mildly. "But do you really want Ennit to have a powerful sorceress at his side?"

Belta grunted, looking unhappy, but undecided.

Terion shook her head. "It must be a great disappointment to Sita for her daughter to be so much less powerful than she is."

"It's more of a disappointment to her that her daughter is in love with the prince," Feric said, stirring the fire.

"Just when did you and the lovely Goldenhair have time to do all this gossiping?" Teri asked, eyes narrowed.

Feric smiled and blew her a kiss. "After she'd finished testing me and before you returned from getting your shield fixed."

Terion's answering grunt was lost in Belta's increasingly angry rumblings. "She can't do what she makes out she can do. She's taking the prince's coin under false pretenses! She's a *thief*!" This last was shouted directly into Feric's astonished face.

He wiped off the spittle and somewhat testily asked, "Why are you being like this?"

Looking shamefaced, Belta looked away. "I was born in this land," she muttered. "So I guess you could say Ennit is my prince."

"So how do you feel about your prince taking over the Captain's company?" Terion asked.

"Frankly, not good," Belta admitted. "Especially now his sorceress turns out not to be worth spit."

As they walked back to their tent Terion suddenly grabbed Feric's shoulder, pulling him to a stop.

"Feric, I need to talk to the Captain," she whispered.

"I don't think that's possible," he said, looking puzzled. "But I suppose you could try."

She grinned and leaned closer. "*We* could."

Feric pulled back, looking alarmed. He studied her face. "What are you asking me to do, Teri? Put them to sleep? With my lack of control and unpredictable power surges it could be for the rest of their lives!"

"Keep your voice down," she said patiently. "I was thinking more along the lines of a bribe."

"Oh," he said, somewhat abashed. Feric kept charge of

their funds for the most part. He clutched the communal purse thoughtfully. "I could put a spell on the money to make them think it's more than enough," he suggested.

"Whatever," Teri said. "C'mon." She tugged him towards the Captain's tent, where Avia was being held prisoner.

As Terion lifted the flap of the tent she regretted the bribe. From the looks on their faces, she suspected the guards would have let them in gratis. But there wasn't a guard in existence who would say "no" to free money. At least not in this world.

The Captain stood as Terion bowed her head and tapped her left shoulder with her fist in salute. As she raised her head, Teri saw that the Captain wore manacles, and gasped.

Avia smiled ruefully. "After my trial, his majesty said that a coward in the habit of running might attempt to escape justice. And so he added these to complicate things."

Terion took a deep breath and let it out in a rush. "Captain, you are not a coward. You've been my hero since before I took up the sword. In fact it was your example that inspired me to do so." She shook her head. "Something is wrong here."

The Captain sat and gestured to a stool. When Terion was seated she looked her lieutenant in the eye. "I've never had cause to think myself a coward," she said. "There have been times when I was afraid, but I've always managed to fight in spite of it." She shook her head, and her eyes were troubled. "Not this time, though. I controlled it for a time, but it grew and grew until it overwhelmed me." Avia spread her calloused hands. "But why? We weren't facing anything I hadn't met a hundred times before. Why should ordinary soldiers so terrify me?"

"That bothers me, too, Captain," Teri said, her eyes hard. "Did you feel anything strange just before it happened? Did you hear, or see, or smell anything out of the ordinary? Did you eat or drink anything unusual before the battle?"

"Like the other captains under the prince's command, I breakfasted with his highness. I ate and drank what everyone else did." Avia brushed her hair back and hit herself in the nose with the chain attached to her manacle. "*Ow.* At first I thought I must have been hit in the head because suddenly everything was so different. And it was painful in a

way. But afterwards there wasn't any sign of a wound." She
hung her head, spread her hands. "Now I feel strange, like
recovering strength after being wounded. But I'm not
wounded, merely ashamed."

Reaching out, Terion clapped the Captain on the shoulder, startling her out of her mood.

"There's something strange going on here, Captain. And
I mean to get to the bottom of it. Hopefully before they
mark you and Ennit takes over our unit."

"*What?*" The Captain leapt to her feet. "That popinjay . . . !"
She stopped herself before she could say anything else that
might be indiscreet and stood panting with outrage.

"He told us tonight," Terion said. "But surely if you're
no longer our commander, our contract is void and must
be renegotiated. Right?"

Avia pointed to a richly carved chest on her camp desk.
"The contracts are in there. Bring it to me, Lieutenant."

Teri did so and the Captain rifled through the box until
she found what she wanted. After reading for a while she
shook her head in disbelief, pointing at the paper in her
hand.

"I would never have signed this," she said. Avia flung
the contract aside and let rip a stream of impressive oaths.

Catching the paper as it flew, Teri paused to be impressed
by what she was hearing. The Captain had a way with
words. Then she started to read the offending passage.

*In the event of Captain Avia Iron Breast's death or
desertion, Prince Ennit will assume direct command of her
company.*

"We're a free company," she said to the Captain. "Even
if you did sign it, this article is surely illegal."

Avia gave her a pitying look. "Try explaining *that* to the
king. Especially since he dotes on Ennit."

Frowning, Teri considered the problem. "He's ordered me
to be his second."

The Captain raised a brow at that. "Don't get me wrong,
Lieutenant, you're good, and you have considerable potential,
but you're not ready for that post yet."

"I know it, ma'am," Terion assured her. "But he wouldn't
listen."

"And that, too, strikes you as strange." An odd expression came over the Captain's face and she touched her chest

just over her heart. She shook her head. "Fear again, but for you this time. Beware of him, Lieutenant, he's a twisty one."

"Then I have your permission to look into the matter?" Terion asked.

"And my blessing. But be careful, be very careful."

Terion crept closer to the prince's tent, senses stretched to their considerable limits, intent on discovering something that might aid her in helping the Captain. If caught she intended to claim that she was checking security. The words "standard procedure" were balanced on her lips.

She moved toward the sound of murmuring voices.

"My lord, it is too soon!" Peria's voice said. She sounded distressed.

"But I can feel it going, draining out of me. Can't you stop it? Can't you do *anything*?" Ennit sounded on the verge of panic.

Teri cut a tiny slit in the tent's fabric and peeked in. The prince strode back and forth, his face peevish and filmed with sweat. Peria watched him with her heart in her eyes and her hands outstretched.

"Please, my lord, calm yourself. This worry weakens you and dissipates the effects of the spell."

Ennit spun on his heel and glared murderously. "Are you saying that this is *my* fault?"

Peria bowed her head. "No, my prince, not at all. I merely meant that it is an effect of the spell."

"Then fix the spell!" Ennit screeched.

The young sorceress flinched but stood her ground. "Once the spell is cast, my lord, it cannot be altered."

He stalked toward her like a cat about to ruin some mouse's day. "Then fix the spell so that when it is cast the effect is permanent. Don't you understand that I can't bear feeling this way?" His hands reached out to her, pleading.

Peria went to him and laid her head on his shoulder, while his arms enfolded her. Her expression spoke of love, his of impatience.

"Why won't you help me?" he asked, looking bored, sounding desperate.

With a gasp Peria pulled back and looked up into his handsome face, now appropriately displaying sorrow and yearning. "I am trying, my lord. But to change a spell takes time and experimentation." She bit her lip. "It may also harm the donor."

He pushed her away. "I don't care about the donor! My concern is *my* future! What my royal father would say if he knew! These are the things that concern me."

"That is why we must select the donors more carefully," the sorceress insisted.

"I think that I am selecting the perfect donors," Ennit said haughtily.

Taking a deep breath Peria tried again. "But someone as prominent as the lady . . ."

"*Lady!* Call that horse a lady!" He laughed harshly. Ennit loomed over his sorceress. "She's a mercenary captain and hardly worthy of being called a woman, let alone a lady. She deserves everything she's going to get, and more besides." He clenched and unclenched his fists. "I shouldn't be second to that . . . female in any way. Nor to the next one I've selected!"

"As to that one," Peria said, looking nervous but determined, "she's a friend of my mother's."

"What do I care?" Ennit said with a laugh.

"My point," the sorceress said carefully, "is that I don't wish to offend my mother. And I assure you, my lord, neither do you."

He glared at her and his breathing deepened. Outside the tent Terion expected him to hit her and wondered if she dare interfere.

"I beg you to choose someone else," Peria said, clasping her hands before her.

Slowly Prince Ennit smiled. "No," he said and turned away. Then he glanced over his shoulder. "You may go. But send in Lita, you know, the little blonde." He turned away again, with a smirk on his face.

The look on Peria's face was downright scary.

I don't think I'd want to be little Lita at this point, Terion thought. *The poor kid's gonna come down with munga-twat at the very least.* She rose and moved carefully away from the tent, filled with misgivings.

Even though he matched her brisk walking pace, it was taking Feric awhile to catch up to her mentally. He looked at her, his mouth slightly open, with all the intelligence of a stunned cow. Terion sighed. You could get Feric on his feet and moving, but actually waking him up was a lot more difficult. Maybe she was being too indirect.

"I think they intend to do something to me tomorrow during the battle," she said, breaking the problem down to its simplest elements.

"Wha?" he mumbled.

His eyes seemed to be moving randomly and Teri considered slapping him but just couldn't bring herself to do it. It wasn't his fault he was a sound sleeper.

"I want you beside me during the battle tomorrow."

That got his attention. In fact he immediately seemed taller because his hair stood on end. Then he chuckled.

"You're joking," he said, waving a hand dismissively. "For a moment there I thought you were serious." He put his arm around her brawny shoulders.

"I am," she said.

"Heh heh," he replied. They walked on in silence for a moment, then his steps slowed. He turned to smile at her, the smile somewhat desperate.

"I am," she repeated. His hand squeezed her shoulder almost painfully tight. "Ric, you're supposed to pinch *yourself* to see if you're dreaming," she said somewhat testily. "And you're not."

He spread both hands on his chest, his eyes huge. "But . . . I'm . . . You're . . . I . . . You know . . ." After a moment he gave in to his shock and waved his hands, shaking his head, mouth open, not even attempting to speak.

"I need you beside me to protect me from Peria's spell."

"Couldn't I stand beside Peria?" he asked. He nodded quickly as though that would make her agree.

"Since she's usually beside the king's magician, who stands beside the king himself, I'd have to say, um, no." Terion put her hand on his shoulder. "I *will* protect you, even as you protect me." She leaned in to give him a kiss.

"I don't have armor!" he said, pointing a finger gleefully.

"We're with an army, sweetheart. Armor won't be a problem, believe me." Teri put her arm around his shoulder and walked him back to bed.

"We're a female company," Terion explained, amused at Feric's protesting the breast cups on his breast plate. "I would never have a male squire. And flat-chested you look like what you are—a man."

"I should hope so," he muttered.

"No one will know but you and me," she assured him. "If nothing happens then you just slip away, and if anything *does* happen," Teri shrugged, "same thing, I guess."

"I must warn you," Feric said, nervously plucking at his mail, "the iron in this may inhibit my abilities."

Terion jammed his helmet on his head, then lifted the visor and smiled. "When you're focused, my dear, *nothing* inhibits you." She kissed him lightly and slammed the visor shut, grinning at the sound of protest he made. Then she turned to her duties, trusting Feric to stay by her shoulder.

She'd gotten out of eating with the prince by saying she'd been up for hours and had already breakfasted. But there'd been no way to avoid the toast Ennit had offered.

"To the king, and victory!" he shouted. She'd even had to drink the whole draught as his eyes were on her the whole time. Sure as the goddess made little green men, Ennit was planning to attack her somehow.

She mounted Captain Avia's restive bay and Feric got on Terion's grey, "mounted" being far too elegant a description for what he managed. The grey snorted in disgust. Ennit pranced up to them on a huge black stallion that made the two smaller horses wicker nervously.

Nice to know we're all in agreement about this pair, Teri thought. Which was that they were better looking than behaved and dangerous in an attack-you-from-ambush-for-no-reason sort of way.

"Who is this?" Ennit demanded, indicating the well-disguised Feric.

"My squire, your highness," she said.

I need you beside me, she'd insisted last night and he'd finally stopped his protests. Now, in the face of the prince's suspicious looks, surely he could see that she was right. Terion hoped it would make up for the bronzed bumps on his chest.

Feric kept his horse just behind Terion's and between her and the prince.

Ennit glanced over his shoulder at him and there was no mistaking the irritation that shone in his eyes.

"Have your squire move back," the prince snapped. "Has she no sense? My stallion dislikes being followed so closely."

Terion waved a hand and Feric fell back slightly, while she widened the space between herself and the prince. When they reached their positions at the head of the mercenary companies, Ennit turned to Feric again.

"Get back!" he snapped. "I won't have you crowding me!"

Feric glanced at Terion, even as he obeyed, certain that whatever Ennit planned was going to happen soon.

I should be watching Peria, he thought anxiously. *Not cluttering up the battlefield like this.* He suspected that everything was in place, or almost so, requiring only that slight nudge of power from the sorceress.

Feric looked around and spotted the royal party on a slight rise in the ground behind them. The young sorceress was easily distinguished by her black clothing amid the brilliant colors of the courtiers. A glance at the prince showed that he was looking in the same direction. Peria raised her hand and Ennit reached out to touch Terion's shoulder.

Feric spun his arm in a great circle as though winding up and throwing a ball. There was a flash of light and the scent of ozone and a very soft, grinding sound—as of something very heavy slicing into the ground.

The prince's gloved hand bounced against something invisible and he pulled back his hand. Terion reached out cautiously and tapped her gauntleted finger against the barrier. Then she looked into Ennit's astonished eyes.

Before either of them could speak the enemy came rushing towards them, banners flying, men and women screaming their war cries and waving their weapons with feral abandon in a way that loosened Feric's bowels quite dangerously. Ennit turned toward the foe and his body bowed as though he'd been hit hard in the stomach. He backed his stallion, looking desperately around him.

"My lord?" Terion said. "What are your orders?" Her voice was cool and calm, and behind them the mercenaries held their lines, all of them looking toward the prince. "Shall I order the attack, or do we await them here?"

Ennit backed his horse still further making a sound like a very furtive steam kettle. Without saying anything he turned and fled through the ranks.

Terion splayed her hand on the invisible, but very solid,

barrier that had formed between her and the prince and turned to smile at Feric. "Perhaps you should follow his highness and make sure he comes to no harm," she suggested, with a little swing of her head that told him to slip out of his well-endowed breast plate before he did so.

Feric managed a realistic salute before he turned and rode off even more swiftly than the prince had. Behind him the armies clashed together with the sound of a massive hammer hitting metal. *Oh, goddess,* he prayed, *spare me and I'll do something wonderful for you. I'm too scared right now to know what, but it'll be good, I promise.*

He looked behind and pulled his horse to a halt as he was far enough from the fighting to be out of danger. Slipping out of his gauntlets he quickly removed and flung away the objectionable armor. Then he rode after the prince, visible now only as a cloud of dust. He saw a troop of the king's guard enter that cloud and, by the time he rode up, the prince's stallion had been halted and surrounded.

"What are you doing here?" the sergeant of the guard demanded of Feric, his hand on his sword.

"Lieutenant Terion told me to make sure the prince came to no harm," Feric answered.

"The prince himself has seen to that," the sergeant growled.

"She also suggests taking the sorceress Peria into custody. She suspects there was something going on between them that warrants investigation." Feric was proud of that statement, it sounded downright official.

King Saldeg sat his throne in a posture of dejection as his herald explained to Captain Avia how the prince had coerced his sorceress into casting a spell that transferred all of her courage, temporarily, to Ennit.

Ennit, standing to one side with his hands tied behind his back, had tears running down his cheeks by the time the story was finished.

"Please believe me, Captain," he cried, "I never meant you any harm."

Avia raised an eyebrow. "No? You raged about my cowardice and demanded that I be severely punished—branded and banished. You have humiliated me before my own company and nearly ruined my reputation. If that's your idea of doing me no harm, sir, I shudder to think what would have happened if you *did* mean to injure me."

Saldeg raised his hand wearily. "Because you have been so insulted by my son," he said, "and reminding you that even as he is punished he *is* my son and heir, I ask what you would have us do with him?"

Conscious of the honor the king was offering her, Avia bowed. "Your majesty, I shall paraphrase the prince. I do not demand that he be punished in public, but I do insist that I be the one to wield the brand."

"NO!" Ennit screamed. "Father, no!"

The king winced at his son's outburst. "Take him away," he said in disgust, refusing to look at the prince, his cheeks red with shame.

"Further," Avia said over Ennit's receding screams and pleas, "Peria the sorceress should be banished from your kingdom and delivered into her mother's care."

With a whimper the sorceress took a step back, only to bump into the guard behind her.

"Done," growled Saldeg. He didn't speak again until the sorceress had been whisked away. "I find there is no joy in empire building if my heir cannot hold what I've won," he grumbled. "I should like to appoint you my envoy, Captain Avia, and sue my neighbors for peace."

Terion tapped the invisible barrier, then *tsked!* in wonder. "What's it made of?" she asked Feric.

"Air," he said.

Her brows shot up. "Air! Well, there's a wonder. Solid air. Can you get rid of it?"

He blushed and shook his head. "I've a feeling it will dissipate over time, though."

She stretched her hand over her head as far as she could and still found the barrier.

"I believe it's circular in shape," Feric said. "I visualized a round shield when I made it."

Terion chuckled. "Good thing we had you in that power-inhibiting armor," she said. "Otherwise this shield might be dividing the world."

"Brrr!" Feric said and shuddered dramatically.

Terion grinned and put her arm around his shoulder. "Well, my contract's up, sweetheart. We're plump in the pocket.

Time we paid some attention to your needs. What say we try to find you a mentor, eh?"

With a sigh Feric shrugged. "I don't know, Teri. Everyone we've asked had either got an apprentice or says I'm too old to teach."

"Don't be discouraged, love. Someone, somewhere, has to realize we can't just leave you to your own devices. We'll be a package deal. You as apprentice and cook, me as a guard; surely someone will take us on. Didn't Goldenhair give you some names?"

"Yes, but you won't like them. Sylvia the Sybarite, Loreli the Lovely, Amber the Amorous."

"You're making those up."

"I'm not, I swear!" He held up his hand and crossed his heart.

"Sylvia the Sybarite? I don't think so."

"Goldenhair apprenticed with her. She's real."

"Hunh," Teri said. "Loreli the Lovely doesn't sound so bad. We'll try her."

He smiled fondly at her. "That's what I thought."

"Besides," Terion said, giving him a squeeze, "there's not a sorcerer born who can't be handled with a sword through their guts."

"Teri!" He pulled away from her. "I swear that's why some sorcerers have refused me."

"What?"

"You! You kind of glower and project I'm-going-to-kill-you vibrations at them. Magicians are very sensitive to vibrations."

"You're making that up."

"I'm not! You do! it's real."

They'd had this argument before, and they kept it up in an amiable way as they packed and as they rode away into the summer afternoon. Until Terion capped it with, "If she makes a move on you, I'm going to knock her teeth out."

Which so endeared her to Feric that he let her win.

The Girl's Guide To Defeating the Dark Lord

Cassandra Claire

Deep, deep within the earth are sunk the dungeons of Castle Bonespire. Bleak is my prison cell. The walls drip with moss and the howls and screams of the other prisoners are my only companionship throughout the endless nights. The hideous form of the Dark Wizard who rules this place is branded in my memory. Taller than a man, with a face like iron and a cruel smile, he snatched me from my chambers at my father's castle and brought me, flung senseless across his saddlebow, to this place. Surely he means to torment me, or even worse, to marry me and make me his dark bride! I pray each day that my father will send a champion to rescue me. But the days grow long . . .

I have never been so bored in my entire *life*. Thank goodness at least I had my diary in the pocket of my nightgown when I was kidnapped or I really would just expire right here on the floor. If only I hadn't gotten up in the middle of the night last week with a truly remorseless craving for butter tarts. If only I hadn't decided to sneak downstairs to the kitchen. If only I'd guessed that the night guard in the kitchens was in the pay of the Dark Lord Vexor. Ah, well, as my father always says, it's no use wailing over things you can't change.

All right, so my previous entry wasn't entirely accurate. My prison cell isn't damp, it's quite dry, with clean straw on the floor. There's a window, although it's covered over, so I might not actually be in a dungeon. I have no idea how I got here but I think it was probably by magic and not on a horse. As far as I can tell, there are no other prisoners, and if there are, they certainly aren't doing any screaming. Vexor is actually quite short, and if he has a cruel smile I haven't seen it. He comes by sometimes just to stare and look grim, but I can hardly see his face at all because he keeps his hood pulled down over it. For all I know he might be quite handsome, although I doubt it. If he was handsome he'd probably have a more cheerful disposition and then he wouldn't have any need to go around kidnapping people now would he?

Today counted all individual bits of straw in pile on floor. Counted up to 4,325 when Vexor came in and made me lose count. He still had his hood pulled down but I could see a little of his face. He has quite an ordinary chin for a dark wizard.

He was frowning. "Princess," he said, "another week has passed, and still no word from your father. Your doom draws nigh."

"I told you already he isn't going to send word," I said crossly. "It's not the done thing. They send their champions instead. He's probably holding tournaments right now to find the boldest and bravest knight for the task."

"And when his knight fails?"

"You are conceited, aren't you? He might not fail, you know."

"He will fail," said Vexor. "First he must pass the impassable mountains. Then he must defeat my troops, who are massed on the plain below." His tone was condescending. "As you can see, they are fearsome in number, and mighty in—"

"Actually, I can't see anything of the sort. I only have one window, and you bricked it up."

He looked sort of surprised. "I did?"

I pointed at it in an accusing manner.

"Oh," he said.

He shuffled around for a bit, and then he left.

When I woke up this morning, the bricks were gone out of the window. I have a view! I can see the front of the castle, some mountains. A little bit of drawbridge over a gorge and a sort of courtyard thing with a well in it. Am obviously miles from anywhere; no surprise there.

I can see troops practicing down on the plain in front of the castle—my sisters would call it a greensward, but it really is just a plain. They're all carrying Vexor's banner, which is a sort of snake with ropey things poking out the eyesockets. Quite nasty. And doing little marches in tandem.

Bread and jam again for lunch today. Every day, a little slot opens up in the door, and an Unseen Hand puts food through it. At least I expect I'm supposed to assume it's an Unseen Hand, and be properly terrified because after all, magic and all that. I'm just glad it's bread and jam. The first few days it was gruel.

Vexor came by again today and interrupted me while I was watching the soldiers practice. He just waltzed in and stood there sneering until I noticed he was there.

"Gazing out the window," he said darkly. "But of course. Waiting for your bold rescuer to appear?"

"I'm sure he's coming," I said airily. "He's probably been delayed by the rain."

The sky had been cloudless for days. Vexor gave me an odd look.

"I don't see why you care what I do anyway," I said. "All you want is my father's money."

"All I want," Vexor corrected me, "is the overthrow of the High King."

This was news to me. "You do?"

"Yes. And if I need more money to raise a proper army, than I'll just have to get it however I can."

"Including kidnapping helpless girls?"

Vexor made an indignant noise. "Spoiled princesses whose families grow fat off the backbreaking toil of their peasants—"

"I AM NOT FAT."

"Not yet," he said, eyeing me coldly.

"No wonder everyone hates you," I muttered. "I've heard peasant mothers keep their children in line by threatening them that if they misbehave, Vexor will get them."

This appeared, inexplicably, to enrage him. "What?" he sputtered. "Why, that's—that's outrageous!"

I blinked at him. "It is?"

With a grunt, he stalked away from me, over to the door. Which by the way, is double-planked oak with iron fittings. I kicked it a whole bunch of times the first day I was here and I didn't even make a dent. "I bid you good day, Princess."

"Well, all right, but I don't see what you're upset about, I really don't."

He paused for a moment, staring at the door. "No," he said finally. "You wouldn't."

Have discovered that if I wedge myself right into the window frame I can see down into the courtyard where the minions are having their practice maneuvers. Is just like watching the soldiers practice at home, except that here they keep their helmets on all the time, probably because of being so evil and unsightly and all that. I do enjoy watching the practice though. I used to watch the soldiers all the time at home until Father said it wasn't proper for a princess to hang about where men were getting all sweaty, especially not when they should be attending to their *own* training.

I have started to be able to tell the minions apart by number of stripes on their helmets. There's a little one I'm quite fond of; the other ones are always beating him in single combat during the practice sessions but he always gets up gamely and carries on. I've started calling him Tiny, because he's the smallest and hasn't got any stripes at all. Today he had to fight an absolutely monstrous brute in a helmet with horns on it.

I got so carried away watching that I started shouting encouragement down to him: "Right, parry *right*! Can't you see he knows you always attack from the left?" They all jumped about six feet in the air and stared up, trying to figure out where the noise was coming from. A couple of them pushed their helmets back. Very disappointing, really, everyone always said that Vexor's army was made up of red-eyed demon fiends, but they looked ordinary enough to me. I ducked right down out of the window before they saw me.

Damn and blast. Vexor came stomping by in a complete strop. "I'll thank you not to shout at my soldiers!" he ranted, clomping up and down in my cell in his great big iron-studded boots. "Boris almost got his ear taken off thanks to you!"

I wondered if Boris was Tiny, or the one in the spiky headgear. "They were doing it all wrong," I said sulkily.

Today his hood had slipped back. I could see his eyes. They were dark and flashing with rage. "And how would you know?" he demanded. "What training have *you* got? Attack needlepoint? Assault with a deadly spool? Killer embroidery?"

"It is apparent to me," I said coolly, "that you have some very outmoded views of what it means to be a princess!"

Vexor cut me off with a wave of his hand. "And I suppose that's why you're still here, waiting to be rescued?" he sneered.

"Well, it would be rude to Father if I just left," I said reasonably, "after all that trouble finding a champion."

"You are deluded," he said, quite peevishly.

"At least I know what proper weapons training looks like," I said. "If you don't arrange your troops with some gaps in the front lines, there's no way the secondary forces can move up while the first line of defense retreats."

Vexor stared at me and for a brief moment I thought he was going to ask me something else. But instead he just grunted. "Don't talk of matters of which you know nothing," he snarled, and clanked away.

Rained all the past three days and so there was no practice. Finally the sun came out a bit this afternoon, and when I climbed up on the windowsill I nearly got the shock of my life. Vexor was out there on the greensward, looking all dark and spindly in the sunlight, and there were the troops marching with *gaps in their formations*. I couldn't believe it! He'd completely nicked my idea, *after* telling me I didn't know what I was talking about!

I almost yelled "Oi!" down at him when I realized, with a sobering sort of heavy feeling in my stomach, that I'd just given perfectly good battle advice to the sworn enemy of the High King, the most evil wizard in the entire kingdom. Father was right, I need to think before I talk. I crawled down from the windowsill feeling chastened indeed.

Am refusing to watch the practices. Too hard not to shout advice down. I tried ducking out of sight when they all looked up, but this morning Vexor caught me and gave me a cheeky little wave. I hope Boris accidentally hits him with that pikestaff.

For the first time today Vexor actually knocked before he came barging into the tower. It was a bit pointless since it's not as if I can open the door but I suppose it's the thought that counts.

He came in, fidgeting slightly. "Princess," he said.

"Yes?"

"I just wanted you to know that I don't mind you watching the practices," he said abruptly. "Your advice—it was very good advice."

I continued to stare at him haughtily.

"I'm sorry I said you didn't know what you were talking about," he said, all in a rush.

I felt somewhat mollified. "All right."

"So." He had begun to play with a loose thread on his cuff. "Which one do you think is the best?"

"Which one of what? The minions?"

"They're *soldiers.*"

"Whatever." I screwed my face up thoughtfully. "Well, Tiny could be good except for always feinting from the left, and there's the two that always fight together, they'd be hard to beat. Really all of them need—" I broke off. "Wait. You're choosing a champion, aren't you?"

"Yes," he said.

"I can't help you," I said, shaking my head. "I can't help you pick which one of them is going to go out and kill innocent people—"

"Do you know what the first day of every month is in

the Four Kingdoms?" Vexor interrupted me, sounding strained.

"No."

"Tax day," he said. "And you know what the High King does to anyone who can't pay their taxes? He has them whipped, unless they can find a champion to fight for them. Of course if they could afford a champion, they could afford the taxes. You see how it is."

I started shivering. "I don't believe you," I said angrily. "The High King wouldn't do that and anyway, what do you care? It's not like you're above terrorizing the peasantry—"

"I've never terrorized anyone!" he yelled suddenly. "Those are just stories I spread so that the High King would be afraid of me!"

"You're trying to trick me." I put my hands over my ears. "Just go away and leave me alone! Go and—and be evil, or whatever it is you do!"

He stood very still for a second. "As you like," he said finally, and swept me an awfully formal bow—a real prince would have been impressed. Then he stalked out of the room leaving me feeling very out of sorts indeed.

Tonight I was woken up out of a pleasant dream about running Vexor over with a bricklayer's wagon by an enormous crash. I leapt to my feet brandishing a handful of straw only to see a young man in bright white and gold mail lying sprawled on the stone floor under the window, completely tangled up in rope.

I ran over and dropped down next to him. I had a horrible feeling he was dead, but as it turned out, he wasn't. He groaned as I rolled him over and looked up at me entreatingly. The first thing I noticed was that he was very handsome, with springy gold curls and eyes the color of violets. The second thing I noticed was that there was a sizeable arrow sticking out of the upper part of his leg. All around it the white mail was edged in red.

I knew I was supposed to address him as "Brave and valorous knight" but I was too startled and the sight of the wound was giving me a terrible fizzing sensation in my ears. I panicked. "Are you all right?"

"Fair maiden," he gasped, looking pained, "I lie wounded."

I rather thought this was obvious, but it would have been rude to point it out. "How did it happen? What can I do? Does it hurt? Who are you, anyway?"

"I am Prince Rupert, sixteenth son of the High King Edmund, and I have been sent by your father to rescue—"

He broke off with a gurgle. He was turning a luminous shade of green. I didn't think it was likely he would be rescuing anyone soon. "Of course you have," I said soothingly. "What happened?"

"Minions of the Dark Lord," Prince Rupert wheezed. "Shot me as I was climbing up the wall."

"You poor brave thing," I said comfortingly. "Just hold on a tick and I'll get that arrow out of your leg."

He looked alarmed. "Are you sure you know what you're doing?"

I nodded. "I've read plenty of manuals on field medicine," I assured him. "I know you're supposed to pull the arrow out right away. Or push it through the other side," I added, more thoughtfully. "I'm not sure exactly. I suspect it rather depends how the arrow's fletched and all that. Still, no time to waste."

He protested weakly. "I'd really rather you didn't."

"It'll go septic if I don't."

"I'll take that chance."

"Oh, don't be such a baby," I said, and yanked the arrow out.

"Auugh," said the Prince, and fainted dead away. There was a quite a lot of blood, too. I tossed the arrow aside and started ripping strips off the hem of my skirts for bandages. I'd made a tourniquet and was just tying the last bandage extra tight when the door opened and about twenty minions came pouring into the room, the Dark Lord on their heels.

The oddest thing about it was that I couldn't help feeling as if Vexor was somehow disappointed in me. He kept looking at the window and then at me and then at Rupert, and glaring. I don't know what he was astonished about; I *told* him my father's champion was on his way.

"You did say your father's wrath would be swift," he said, eyeing poor Rupert, who was still bleeding profusely onto the straw. "I suppose I had not expected it to be quite so inept."

I stuck my chin in the air and didn't say anything. A princess knows when certain things are below her dignity.

Vexor snapped his fingers and his minions snapped to attention. "Chain him up," he ordered, indicating Rupert. "Strip him of his weapons and armor."

"But he's bleeding!" I protested. "He might *die*."

"It appears to me," said Vexor, "to be a flesh wound merely," and with a curt nod, he swept out of the room.

Once Vexor had gone, the minions stripped poor Rupert of his armor and took his sword, his shortsword, his daggers, and even his nail-studded *boots*. Then they manacled his ankle to the floor and clanked off sniggering, the brutes.

I sat down next to him on the straw and pondered our tragic fate. Perhaps Rupert and I were doomed to die together at the hands of the Dark Lord, our relationship unconsummated and, I had to admit, largely nonexistent. He seemed a nice enough bloke and he did have cheekbones like knife blades, but I had to admit that, strictly speaking, we had not yet become close. Still, I had pulled an arrow out of his leg and in all the ballads that always signals True Love. Tired of watching him sleep, I reached out and shook him by the shoulder.

He came awake with a groan. "Roderick, I told you I wanted to sleep in—" His eyes focused on me and he let out another groan. "It's true then, isn't it? I've been captured by the Dark Lord?"

"Yes, unfortunately," I said. "But take heart, brave knight. We may yet escape."

"I hardly see how," he said peevishly. "You pulled that arrow out of my leg, didn't you?"

"Yes." I beamed and waited for thanks.

His sculpted lip twisted into a frown. "If your hamfisted attempts at medical treatment leave me with an unsightly scar, your father had better be prepared to handsomely recompense me for my mental anguish." His blue eyes scanned the room. "Where are my belongings?"

"The Dark Lord took them," I told him.

He collapsed back on the straw. "Then we are doomed," he moaned. "My enchanted armor! My inlaid daggers! My sword Durendal, that can cut through anything! I am helpless without them!"

"You named your sword?" My father always said that only prats named their swords.

He gave me a very unpleasant look. "Yes, and what of it?"

"Nothing," I said.

"I didn't actually think I'd be chosen as champion," Rupert confided suddenly. "I thought, why not try out? Seemed like a lark and there's not much to do if you're a sixteenth son, even if your father is the High King. And then I was picked and the money was pretty good. I couldn't say no. I suppose I wasn't thinking realistically. I never do. And now look. Cut off in my prime, not even twenty yet, ignominiously laid low by the blade of the sneaking enemy . . ."

I wanted to point out to him that it was his own fault for trying to crawl in the tower window in broad daylight and that the enemy hadn't been so much sneaking as simply doing their jobs. But I couldn't get a word in edgewise. He was already complaining about how if he ever recovered he'd probably limp forever and Vexor was probably off somewhere trying on his mail and stretching it all out of shape. For someone so handsome, he has an awfully squeaky voice.

Rupert continues to be useless. I thought he might get a bit better once his leg healed up, but he hasn't. He just lies on the straw and rattles his chains and sometimes he turns his face to the wall and murmurs that death befits a prince better than vile imprisonment.

"You know," I said to him today, "we should really work on escaping."

He gave me a hateful look. "If you hadn't noticed, Princess, I'm chained to the floor, and helpless without my weapons and armor."

Because you were so much use *with* them, I thought darkly. "Well, I'm not chained to the floor. The least you could do is help me think of a way for us both to escape. You're a prince and a hero, you must have escaped from dungeons before."

"This isn't a dungeon."

"You know what I mean."

He turned his face to the wall. "Leave me alone. I am disgraced, ruined. You're just a girl, you couldn't possibly understand."

I ignored this. "There's no way out through the window, since I can't possibly climb down and anyway, I'd be seen. It has to be the door. There must be some way to pick those locks. . . ."

"There isn't," muttered Rupert, who had been pretending to not listen.

I ignored him. I already knew that the door was three feet thick at least and made of oak. I supposed I could try to take Rupert's belt buckle away from him and tunnel through it, but it would take at least ten years to make it through to the other side. Maybe I could tunnel under it . . . ?

Then again, Father always said that the best way to deal with a seemingly insoluble problem was to try to look at it from the opposite side. An idea popped into my head.

I snapped my fingers. "Give me your belt buckle."

"What? No. You're mad. What could you possibly want with my—get off me! Thief! Madwoman! Leave me alone!"

It wasn't nearly as hard to take the hinges off the door with Rupert's belt buckle as I'd thought it would be. They popped off so quickly that for a moment I was worried that the door would swing out and hit me in the head, but it didn't.

"You can't just leave me here!" Rupert wailed as I levered the door open and slipped through the gap. "I'll scream until the guards come! You'll get caught!"

I popped my head back into the room. "Be quiet. I'm just getting the keys to unlock your manacles. I'll come *back*."

Rupert looked unconvinced. "You'll probably get caught and killed anyway."

"Then you won't be any worse off than before."

The hallway outside was bare with a vaulted ceiling and torches spaced at intervals. It was quite clean and neat; Vexor had good housekeeping. I took a torch down off the wall and crept down the corridor.

All the halls seemed to be deserted. I was just congratulating myself on my stealth when I turned the end of the corridor and smacked directly into a guard. I nearly knocked him over; he gave a bellow of surprise, righted himself, and came at me yelling and waving his sword.

I was hastily backing up when I realized from the striped helmet and the dimunitive size that this was Tiny. He swung the sword up and came at me from the left, but I was prepared—I ducked out of the way and hit him over the head with the torch. He went down with a grunt and strong smell of singed ear hair.

"I told you not to always feint from the left," I said severely, and bent down to grab him by the feet.

He was very heavy to drag and I'm afraid I hit his head against several uneven steps before I found a door, pushed it open, and hauled him inside. It was only after I'd dropped his feet and straightened up and looked around that I realized I'd wandered straight into Vexor's private chambers.

They were really quite plain. There was a long table covered with maps of the Four Kingdoms, some couches, and a high black bed hung all around with long glimmering curtains. They had the constellations picked out across them in slivers of what looked like either diamonds or glass. The bed was empty. I wonder where he is, I thought, turning around nervously.

It was then that I caught sight of him, wrapped in his black robes, lying prone across one of the couches against the wall. I was too shocked to scream, which turned out to be a good thing for two reasons. The first was that he was fast asleep. The second was that lying on the floor by the couch was Prince Rupert's sword and his mail armor, quite neatly folded.

I set the torch into a bracket on the wall and crept over to Vexor. I suppose I ought really to have been more frightened but he did seem so very asleep. Up close, without the mask on, he looked much younger and his hair was ordinary brown and in need of brushing. He had long eyelashes. If it hadn't been for the familiar boots and the black robes, I wouldn't have even guessed it was him.

I snatched up the mail and the sword and retreated to the other side of the room. Much as I would have liked a change of clothes, it didn't seem the time or place. I shrugged the mail on over what I was wearing—Prince Rupert wasn't that much taller than I was, so it only bunched a bit— buckled on the weapons belt, sheathed the sword, and, as an afterthought, pinched Tiny's helmet. I apologized to him when I did it; I had a feeling the other minions wouldn't be too pleased with him when he woke up.

The mail clanked so much that I was worried it would wake

up Vexor, but he didn't stir. Which was a good thing because as soon as I slipped out the door, I discovered that the hallway was full of guards. Why, oh why, did they have to go everywhere together? Before I had a chance to go for my sword, the one in front spoke, "Oi! Boris! What's going on?"

He thought I was Tiny! I pitched my voice low. "Nothing," I grunted.

"Thorvald thought he heard a noise," the guard went on, eyeing me.

Thorvald was the huge one. I looked at him with loathing. "I was just . . ."

"Where's Vexor?"

"Not around," I said quickly. "Gone to visit relatives."

"I didn't know he had any," said Thorvald.

They really were useless, I thought furiously. "He left explicit orders," I said. "We're to practice our underwater fencing all afternoon until he returns."

"But none of us can swim!"

"Time to learn, then!" I cried. "To the lake!"

Thorvald took up the cry. "To the lake! Everyone!"

The tromp of their boots hid the noise as I quietly slipped away and back down the corridor. When I got back to the tower, Rupert was sitting up against the wall moodily chewing on a piece of straw. It fell out of his mouth when he saw me. "How . . . ?"

I swung the sword at his chains and it cut right through them as if they were butter. "We'd better go," I said. "All the minions are down at the lake practicing their underwater fencing, but I doubt they'll stay down there forever."

Rupert goggled at me. "I can't believe it!"

I allowed myself a smirk. "I know, I can't believe it either. I've rescued us!"

"No, I meant I can't believe you're wearing my mail! You'll stretch it all out of shape!" He rubbed his chafed wrists and eyed me resentfully. "Give it back!"

Seems like I haven't written in this diary forever but actually we've only been on the road a few days. Thank heaven we finally found a wayside inn. If I'd had to hear Rupert complain one more time that the dry mountain air makes his hair frizz, I would have chopped it all off in his sleep.

I'd say I've never had such a hard time traveling before, but the truth is I've never traveled anywhere much. I guess that's why all the villages looked so small and poor to me and the people so dispirited. Somehow I was expecting the peasantry to be a bit more hearty and cheerful. I said as much to Rupert but he just told me not to get too close to them because they probably have fleas.

On the third day I saw six or seven men and women being whipped in the central square of one of the villages. Over Rupert's objections I rode closer to ask the magistrate what they had done. He said they hadn't been able to pay their taxes that month. I couldn't help remembering what Vexor had said about the taxes being too high for people to pay them.

As we rode away I asked Rupert what the High King spends the tax money on. He scrunched up his face in thought. "Just the usual things," he said. "Concubines cost a lot more than you'd think. Peacocks. My mother's collection of gold swan boats." He reached out and petted me on the head. "Don't worry," he said, "younger sons aren't allowed to have concubines. When we get married, you'll have me all to yourself."

Rupert's finally gone downstairs for a drink; I think I'll have a bath while he's gone. I washed already, but I still feel dirty.

Fell asleep after my bath but was woken up shortly by the sound of drunken carousing. I could hear glass smashing, chairs being thrown, and loud yelling. I slid my feet into my boots and clomped furiously downstairs. The first sleep I've had in weeks that wasn't on dirty straw or hard ground and Rupert has to ruin it!

I thought maybe he'd gotten into a bar brawl—I could imagine any number of reasons someone would want to punch his smirking face—but it wasn't a brawl. It was just a bunch of drunken locals crowded around Rupert. He was sitting atop a table like the royalty I suppose he is, a tankard in each hand. "Of course the silly girl was no use at all," he was saying. "She was so grateful to be rescued she just wept and clutched onto my leg. It made it very difficult to fight my way through the crowds of the Dark Lord's soldiers, but I managed it. We did get into a spot of trouble

when he imprisoned us, but luckily I had the bright idea
of taking the hinges off the door . . ."

I though about stalking over there and upending a tankard in his lap, but it didn't seem worth it. There were tears
in my eyes as I stumbled upstairs, not because I'd expected
any better from Rupert, but because I hadn't. By the time
I got back to my room my vision was swimming and I
almost crashed into a small figure who'd been lurking outside
the door, trying to look inconspicuous.

Even without the helmet I recognized him right away.
"Oh," I sniffled. "Tiny! I'd better warn you," I added sternly.
"I beat you once in combat, I can beat you again. You'd
better leave me alone."

He paled. "I have no idea what you're talking about."

"Did Vexor send you to bring me back?"

"I don't know anyone named Vexor."

I poked him in the chest, where the snake insignia was
embroidered over his pocket. "Don't be ridiculous."

"Oh, *Vexor.* All right, I do work for him. But I'm on
vacation. Just passing through. Nice to have bumped into
you again. It's a warm night, isn't it? I think I'll go for a
walk."

"Tiny," I began sternly. "I know perfectly well you've been
following me. Why? Because if Vexor's trying to kidnap me
back—"

Tiny sighed. "He's not," he said. "He just told me to follow
you to the border and look out for you. Report back if
anything . . . happened to you."

"An unlikely story."

"Vexor's not such a bad sort," Tiny said, rubbing his bald
spot thoughtfully. "I know he seems stern and forbidding
and all that, but he means well, and he was kind of fond
of you. He's just been moping out by the fountain every
day since you've gone."

"You have to say he's not so bad. You're a minion."

"I'm not a minion," Tiny protested, with some spirit. "I'm
a soldier. I applied for the job and everything. Vexor pays
us all regularly and he never beats us if we don't pay our
taxes. You can't say that for the High King."

I shuffled my feet around in my boots. "I suppose not."

He eyed me thoughtfully. "Vexor thinks the Prince isn't
very likely to actually marry you," he confided. "He seems

to think he's a bad lot, although possibly he just doesn't trust royalty."

"We're not all bad," I said. "Look, Boris—could you wait here for a moment? There's something I have to do." I smiled at his startled expression. "I'll be right back."

It only took us half as long to get back to Castle Bonespire as it had to leave it—apparently Rupert got us lost more than once. Tiny took the direct route, although he didn't mind me stopping in all the villages to distribute the contents of Rupert's purse to the peasantry.

Tiny said it was likely that the innkeeper back in town would be very displeased with Rupert when he found out that Rupert had no money to pay for his rooms, his food, or all the ale he'd drunk. At least he didn't have to worry about the cost of keeping his horse, since I stole it, along with Rupert's mail coat, his sword, and his boots, to which I had become oddly attached.

From a distance, Castle Bonespire actually looks quite pretty. Its towers stand out against the sky like lacework and the lake sparkles. I put on the mail shirt, buckled the sword on, took Tiny's helmet, and told him to wait for me on the far side of the crevasse. He waved at me as I galloped over the drawbridge.

A few of the soldiers tried to stop me as I rode in through the gate, but I batted them aside with the flat of my blade. I was very mindful not to hurt them and I think even the one that I knocked into the manure pile won't hold any hard feelings for very long.

There were a whole group of them chasing me by the time I got to the central courtyard. Vexor was there, sitting on the edge of the fountain with his chin on his knees, his black cloak blowing around him. He wasn't wearing his mask. He looked up as I rode in and his eyes widened. "You," he said, beginning to rise to his feet.

I pushed the visor on my helmet back. "Me," I said.

He looked astonished. "*You,*" he said again, but in a very different tone. "What are you doing here?"

I slid off the horse and knelt down at his feet. "I have come to present myself as your champion," I said.

"What?" For a moment I thought he was going to topple into the fountain. He ran a hand through his untidy hair in a distracted manner, and stared at me. "No. You can't possibly."

"I don't see why not," I said. "I've escaped Castle Bonespire, defeated your minions in single combat—"

"They're not minions, they're soldiers."

"Whatever. How many people have ever broken out of your fortress? Not many, I bet."

"Certainly you are the first one who has ever come back afterwards," Vexor said dryly.

"That's because I want to be your champion," I said. "Fight for your cause. At least mostly. There are some details we need to work out, but they're minor."

Vexor sat down heavily on the side of the fountain. "What kind of details?"

"Well, I won't fight with you against my father," I said. "But I don't think that'll be a problem, because it seems to me your real fight is with the High King, and none of the other kings like him anyway. If you could get them on your side, you'd be in a much stronger position."

"But they hate me," Vexor said. "You said so. Everyone hates me. Even the peasants are afraid of me."

"Well, of course they are. Look at you, hiding up here in the mountains, wearing all black, dressing your minions—"

"Soldiers."

"Whatever. Dressing them up in snake helmets, calling yourself Vexor the Dark Lord. Would *you* trust a man called Vexor the Dark Lord?"

"If his cause was just, I would—"

I shot him a look.

"Probably not," he admitted. "I just thought it would all be easier if everyone was afraid of me."

"Not at all," I said. "You'll see when I take you to meet my father. I'm sure he'll like you much better than he would have liked Prince Rupert."

"Rupert is a smug weasel," Vexor said. "He's my cousin, you know."

"Is he?" I got up from where I had been kneeling and went to sit next to Vexor on the edge of the fountain. "What's your real name, anyway?"

He smiled. He had quite a nice smile. "Simon," he said.

"That's a lovely name." I scooted closer to him on the

side of the fountain. "I was thinking," I said. "Maybe it would help if your men had more cheerful uniforms. Like, if they were blue. Or even pink."

Simon looked at me thoughtfully. "Pink minions?" he said. "You mean soldiers."

He grinned. "Whatever," he said.

She Stuffs to Conquer

or
An Army Marches on Its Stomach

Yvonne Coats

Crowded in here, isn't it? Hang on a minute while I shift my gear, and you can sit at the counter. All the sweets are great here . . . Oh, you know the menu already.

You say I look familiar, huh?

Yes, I'm Gloria Mondee, but I'm not working right now.

Yeah, I used to be called Little Glo, and a bunch of other names I never bothered to remember. And you can knock off that "Glorious Gloria" crap right now, or this conversation is over before it starts.

That pile of metal next to the wall is the "famous" armor. You didn't think it would be so pink? That's not pink. It's heart's blood red! Hmm, maybe it *has* faded a little. It's pretty old gear, I guess. It belonged to my mother and who knows how many women before her.

Listen, we'll get along better if you don't call me "ma'am," even if I am a person of substance these days.

You want to know how I went from being Little Glo to what I am today? My parents had a lot to do with it. Mom was a pretty gifted heavy cavalry officer in her day, and Dad—well, Dad was, and is, one of the best pastry chefs back home.

Are you really curious about this stuff? Well, okay, buy me lunch (I warn you that I'm a hearty eater), and I'll tell you the whole story, or as much of it as you'd want to know.

About ten years ago I broke both legs below the knees when my horse and I parted company on rocky ground. So there I was, flat on my back in bed, with big thick boards strapped to both legs, unable to get up, or even pee, without help. Let me tell you, it's deadly dull, especially if you can't read, and what first-ranked cavalry officer *can*?

Anyway, the duchess's troops—what duchess? It doesn't matter, they're all pretty much alike, just pay-masters, or -mistresses, who hire troops for dirty, dangerous jobs. These particular troops were moving out, my legs weren't anywhere near healed, and my mood was pretty foul. Long story short: They sent me back to my dad's to recover. Or not.

I arrived at Dad's tavern in style, on the back of a haywain. It's a comfortable enough ride, but dirty. I had hay and dust in places a lady doesn't mention. I'll show you where, later.

So there I am, wobbly on my crutches, glad to be off the wagon but not too happy about reaching my destination. I expected to die from boredom before my legs healed.

"If you keep eating like that, Glo, you're never going to fit into your mother's armor," Dad said.

"Golly, that would be bad, right?" the sixteen-year-old me retorted. I took another bite of plain, grilled trout and washed it down with chamomile tea. I hadn't had any of Dad's home brew since I started arms training. Lean and mean, that was me.

"I'm starting to think you'll never be woman enough to fill it." Dad's face turned as red as Mom's armor, but that didn't stop me.

"I'd never want to be as much woman as 'Sherma the Trough.'"

"That's Sherma the Tank!"

"Trough, tank—who'd want to be called after that big, huge, enormous round thing that horses drink out of?"

As if I'd reminded him, Dad walked over to the tavern's trough and ducked his head and shoulders in, almost up to his waist. His way of cooling his temper. After he shook off he came up close to me, slicking his thin hair back with both hands.

"Look, girl, I don't want to argue with you. I just want to do what your mother asked and make sure you take her armor when you join up with the mercenaries."

I couldn't imagine lugging all that heavy pink junk around, even if it had been Mom's dying wish, which it might have been. "Dad—"

"I'll give you an extra horse, for your gear." It was a bribe, and a good one.

I thought briefly about selling both the extra horse and the useless armor at the first opportunity, but one look at my dad's open, homely face told me that I never would.

He said something funny before I left, though. "Don't ever put it on unless you're sure you're big enough. Promise me, Glo." Since I couldn't imagine willingly ever strapping on anything so bright, bulbous and ugly, I promised.

So I still had the extra suit of armor with me when I wound up back at the tavern. I'd gained a bit of weight since breaking my legs, but I wasn't in Mom's class. Dad fixed that, though. He refused to listen to my requests for simple, small meals and instead plied me with all his specialities: butter-drenched croissants, butter-drenched spice bread, butter-drenched potatoes, butter-drenched . . . well, you get the idea. And the desserts must have been made of nothing *but* butter and sugar and air—and in Dad's kitchen, even the air was fattening.

Cooped up in the tavern, or out on a bench in the courtyard, food became my entertainment. I tried taking lessons on the mandolin and the lute, but music bores me unless there's a good-looking musician attached to the instrument. By the way, do you play anything? What? I'm just asking. Keep your shirt on. For now, anyway.

Since I couldn't get into leggings or trews while my legs were broken, I'd taken to wearing some silk robes that had been my mother's. They were soft and bright and roomy, and so comfortable after leather and armor that I didn't really mind wearing them. When they unwrapped my legs, I still had to use the crutches because my legs had gotten so weak. It seemed like I weighed double what

I had before, but I told myself that's because I'd been off my feet for so long.

When I finally tried to strap on my leggings, they didn't fit. And the jerkins and doublets? Forget about it! I tottered downstairs and out to the kitchen and started yelling.

"It will take me months to get back in shape! How could you do this to me?"

"You're still strong, Glo," Dad soothed. "You train for a couple of months, and you'll be as good as new."

"And about as light-footed as a plough horse."

Dad's face grew very still, and he looked me over from head to foot. "Try on the armor, now."

"Mom's armor? You're kidding."

"No, now you're ready for it."

"Well, it will certainly fit, but I don't see what good it will do. I'll still be wheezing after the first fancy footwork I try."

When Dad finally shooed me out of the kitchen, I pulled myself upstairs and stood in my room, looking at the trunk where the armor was stowed.

Eventually I pulled it out and put it on. By the time I picked up the helmet my body tingled all over. I thought I'd have to fumigate the old stuff, that cooties had gotten into it.

The armor was infested all right, and with a rare sort of pest, but I didn't know that right away.

When I put the helmet on, I heard a voice. *Sherma?*

I whirled around faster than I'd thought I could on my formerly busted legs. Nobody else was in the room.

Sherma? I heard it again, all around me.

"No, it's her daughter, Gloria Mondee." Silence. Just when I was sure I'd imagined the voice, it came again.

Baby Glo?

I snorted. "Not for a long time now."

Then Sherma is—

"Dead, when I was ten. Crushed while moving beer barrels into the cellar—one got loose. Who are you?" But I thought I already knew.

If I ever had a name, it's gone now. You can call me "Amory."

" 'Amory' the armor, who gets stored in the armory? You're kidding, right?"

I used to be an armorer, I remember that. At my death-bed there was a man, my patron perhaps, who swore that my spirit would live on in the glorious armor I'd made for his lady. This (I swear I could hear Amory shrug) *seems to be what he meant.*

"So, Amory, can you do anything besides talk?"

And, of course, he could, and the price for using the armor was a pleasure to pay, except maybe for getting called Big Pink for the first couple of years.

Why do I call him "he"? I never thought about it, but I guess it's 'cause he nags like a man. What? Sorry, I meant he nags like my dad—is that more "acceptable" language?

As for the price, you can probably guess. The armor helps me fight, makes me damn near invulnerable—maybe not to one of those exploding projectiles they have up north, but we haven't put it to the test yet. In return, I feed it.

Remember that tingling sensation I mentioned? That was the armor, feeding. Off *me*. I'm lucky that he only needs to feed when someone wears it. I guess he's not really "awake" unless someone's inside. Anyway, he never remembers anything when I'm not using him. Even so, the cost of my combat rations alone has caused some employers to reconsider the length of their campaigns.

After a week-long engagement I've lost as much as fifty pounds. Just wearing the armor around for a week uses about five. You'd think the armor would get big and clumsy when I lose a lot of weight, but it always feels just right when I have it on. That's magic for you.

So that's why you found me in a bakery rather than a tavern. None of the taverns around here know how to make a decent dessert, and I need about ten a day on top of my regular food, to maintain my fighting weight. Beer's good, too, but I get hung over if I drink enough to do the armor any good.

This might be my last fighting season, though I'm still pretty young. I'd like to settle down, maybe have some kids. It's nice being famous and practically invulnerable, but that suit is a real chatterbox. Vain, too.

You say you'd like to talk to Amory? No, you wouldn't. Besides, the only way to hear him would be to put on the armor, and I don't like to think what it would do to a skinny fellow like you. For that matter, it's not really . . . configured . . . for a man. It might be dangerous. You'll just have to take my word.

Anyway, you asked, and that's my story.

Now, what's yours?

You're no soldier, that's obvious. You don't look rich enough to be a prospective employer—also, you're too polite. And you already told me that you don't play an instrument, so I guess you're not a bard or a skald or whatever they're called in these parts. So, who are you, and what's your calling?

"Louie Baker"—that's a good name. Easy to remember. And you work here? As a *pastry chef*? Why, Louie, this could be the beginning of a beautiful friendship . . .

The Gypsy Queen

Catherine H. Shaffer

"It's a shame," Lorayne said as she nudged the gold-lamé-draped corpse of the evil sorceress Amygdala. "That *fabulous* outfit is ruined."

Coedric knelt down and pulled the amulet from around Amygdala's neck. Coedric (sedrick) of the Coelacanth (seelacanth) Clan was a powerful young man, a hand shorter than Lorayne, but mighty-thewed—a grimly efficient fighter from the wild and frigid north. His helm bore the likeness of his clan's totem fish, and he wore the coelacanth tattooed on his smooth bicep as well. He made a neat complement to Lorayne's lean, aristocratic figure, with her dusky skin, black eyes, and killer fashion sense.

"I'll take that, if you don't mind," said a smooth voice behind them.

Ordinarily, this was Lorayne's favorite part of the fight—the witty repartee. Lord Guano was a flamboyant ham of an evil overlord, and never missed an opportunity to say campy things like *Seize them!* and *Foiled again!* It was actually more fun than working for the law-and-order side, which tended to be priggish paper pushers. Of course, at least working for the good guys, she could count on a paycheck. Guano's credit with the mercenary guild was terrible. And this time, there was more at stake than a paycheck.

Lorayne turned to find Lord Guano framed by the tacky gold-gilt carvings. "You'll have it when you deliver my sister to me outside the city walls, with horses, rations, and water—as you promised."

Guano made a moue at them. "Oh, dear," he said. "I completely forgot about that." He put a hand to his cheek, then said, "No, I don't think so. Guards." With a gesture of his hand, a phalanx (Guano had a huge phalanx) of guards appeared and took hold of Lorayne and Coedric. Guano grabbed the amulet out of Coedric's hand.

"You filthy bastard," Coedric growled.

"Language, Coedric," muttered Lorayne. Louder, she said, "Really, Guano, darling, double-crossing is a nice touch, but we're playing it straight today. Give me my sister or die."

Guano frowned, and turned to Coedric. "What's she talking about?"

Coedric translated. "You filthy bastard!"

"Ah, yes, thank you," Guano answered. And to Lorayne, he said, "I'm sorry, my dear, but Esmerelda is too great a prize. I find I cannot part with her. I have no more use for you now. Take them to the dungeon."

The guards moved in on Lorayne and Coedric. "Wait!" Lorayne cried out. She thrust forward one long, lean, smooth leg, bare under a mail skirt, as per union bellatrix contract clause 739. "Take me instead," she invited, giving Guano her most seductive smile. Lorayne had always been the pretty sister. She was taller, thinner, with more dramatic coloring and tighter buns. Esmerelda tended to bookishness and heavy thighs.

Lord Guano laughed. "Not this time, my dear." He paused, looking confused. "No, somehow you're just not my type."

As the guards dragged them out of the room, Lorayne unwillingly delivered the standard tag line: "You won't get away with this."

Lorayne had lived within Amygdala's citadel for three months, disguised as a traveling dancer—aptly suited to her Romany background. Her time had been well spent, mapping every nook and cranny of the fortress. "Coedric," said Lorayne under her breath. "Ten, fourteen, twenty-nine, five, on three."

Coedric glanced sidelong at her and nodded. They walked along a curving hallway, and just ahead, it opened into a rotunda.

"One," said Lorayne.

"Shut up," said one of her guards.

"Two," said Lorayne.

"I said, 'Shut up,'" said the guard.

Lorayne turned and smiled at him, without breaking her graceful stride, which, she noticed with some satisfaction, the guard had trouble keeping up with. "Three," she said to him softly, then shoved him against the wall and brought her knee up hard between his legs. Anticipating an attack from the left side, Lorayne raised a fist, back-punching her other guard. She heard a scream that she knew was one of Coedric's guards falling over the rotunda railing, and landing with a thud two stories below. Coedric and Lorayne looked at each other, as the last guard stood between them, his weapon raised.

"Mine," said Coedric.

"Okay." Lorayne rolled her eyes. "Be that way."

Even at two in the afternoon, the Mincing Pony was dim and crowded. A shirtless serving boy moved between tables, weighed down by half a dozen tankards of ale. A hand snaked out from one of the long wooden tables to pinch his buttocks. The boy's eyes widened, but he didn't spill a drop.

"Lorayne!" squealed the Pony's owner, Barbara Faw. Mistress Faw was Romany herself, and she greeted Lorayne like a sister. An imposing woman, Barbara dispersed a group of teenaged footpads from a table and cleared it off for Lorayne and Coedric. Exhausted from the flight from Amygdala's citadel, Lorayne accepted gratefully. Of all the places in the world, the Mincing Pony was the closest thing to a home that she had.

All of her life, Lorayne had dreamed of being a sword-maiden. From earliest childhood, she had fenced with her shadow, with her cousins, with anyone who would hold a stick. She grew tall, strong, graceful, and yet her dream seemed only to slip further and further out of her grasp, for, lo, Lorayne was a boy, and her mother insisted on calling her Loris.

Here's a perfectly fine shirt of mail, Loris, her mother would say. And, *Try this nice leather jerkin*. But nothing would avail. It was Esmerelda's silks and dancing skirts she craved. And for fighting, she favored a stiff leather bodice that laced up in back, stuffed in front with stout woolen socks, and a pair of skin-tight pants, capris in the summer, with tiny slits just below the knee. When she came of age, she took up the profession of mercenary, and it wasn't long before she became known as the Gypsy Queen.

Coedric had already been drawn into a rowdy conversation with a group of barbarian body builders. "You see," Coedric said, rolling up his sleeve to display the totem fish tattooed on his arm, "the Coelacanth is wily, but he's not weak. Back in fifty-two, our clan had a dispute with Muskellunge clan that broke out into fighting. The Muskellunge bastards outnumbered us Coelacanths two to one—"

"Shhh! Coedric!" Lorayne gestured toward the other end of the tavern where a pair of Muskellunge clansmen sat glowering at them. Coedric ignored her.

Lorayne pouted. Her feelings about her longtime fighting partner were, to say the least, conflicted. She would almost have thought she was in love with him. And, on occasion, she thought he returned those feelings. Certainly he saved her life often enough. But that wasn't the confusing part. The heart that beat inside Lorayne was all woman, but she found that in matters of love, her inclinations leaned toward women also. Crossing swords was very well by day, but under the covers this was a prospect that made her squeamish. She cursed the fate that had made her such a freak. Life would be so much easier if she were a *normal* transgendered barbarian swordswoman, but, no, she had to be a *lesbian*, as well. And *that* was what she couldn't understand about her feelings for Coedric.

As for Coedric, he refused to speak of his past. Lorayne had always felt that he had secrets from her, that he had a lover back home. At least if he would admit it, she would know whom to be jealous of.

She pouted some more while he tried to impress the barbarian body builders. Then the minstrel walked by, all dressed in green silk with her Adam's apple sticking out, and she hadn't even bothered to shave her arms. Coedric pinched her behind, and Lorayne couldn't watch anymore. Barbara Faw plopped a pitcher of ale on the table along with a plate of roast duck and some hard rolls. Lorayne wrenched her thoughts to the problem at hand—how to save Esmerelda from Lord Guano.

The minstrel took up position in a corner of the room and began to sing, accompanying herself on the lute. Her voice was a dusky tenor, as she breathed out the first lines of her ballad, "I made it through the wilderness, you know I made it through-ooh-ooh."

Suddenly, Mistress Faw was at her elbow, whispering urgently. "The back door, Lorayne, hurry!" Lorayne looked up to see a half dozen guards in Lord Guano's colors, scarlet and gold, pouring through the Pony's front door. Mistress Faw intercepted them with an enthusiastic greeting, and two half-naked serving boys sidled up, smiling. The Pony's patronage was nothing if not loyal. Even the displaced footpads closed ranks around them, blocking the guards' view.

Lorayne grabbed Coedric's arm and made for the back entrance. But chaos broke out in front of them. One of the guards shoved a barbarian body builder, and the minstrel dropped her lute and smashed a clay pitcher over the guard's head. Another guard yanked her by the arm, and then all of the barbarian body builders jumped into the fight. In the midst of the melee, two of Guano's guards spotted Lorayne and Coedric making for the back door and ran to intercept them. Lorayne and Coedric elbowed through the crowd and turned to face the guards, their swords hissing out of their scabbards.

Two guards would have been no match for Coedric the Coelacanth and the legendary Gypsy Queen, but as fate would have it the two Muskellunge clansmen sulking at the far end of the tavern jumped up at that moment.

"Die, Coelacanth!" they shouted with rage, when they spotted Coedric, and then their clan battle cry, "Magnificent Mauling Muskellunge!" It took the drunken clansmen several tries to utter it.

Lorayne found herself facing two soldiers as the clansmen focused their attack on Coedric. She was a highly accomplished swordswoman, and was able to parry their first attacks with disdainful finesse, but she knew that before long one of them would slip under her guard.

Out of the chaos, Barbara Faw appeared. She threw a blanket over the guards' heads. Momentarily free, Lorayne turned on the Muskellunge men and forced them back. "Coedric, come!" she yelled, making for the back door. Reluctantly, Coedric followed.

As they ran down the alley behind the Mincing Pony, Barbara Faw followed. "Take a right!" she hissed. Lorayne and Coedric dodged into an even smaller alley that was not more than a crevice between two buildings, too narrow even for a horse. They heard cries behind them, booted feet pelting down the alleyway, scattering gravel. Barbara opened a door cleverly hidden in the stone wall and shoved them in.

The door closed on perfect darkness just as the pursuing guards ran by. Lorayne heard one call out, only inches away, then the voices faded.

The room was tiny, and crowded with three people in it. Something was stacked along the back wall and from the smell Lorayne surmised it was dried fish. "Oh, goddess," she said. "I am *never* going to get this smell out of my leathers."

Coedric inhaled deeply, and as Lorayne's eyes adjusted she could see dimly that he had a fierce grin on his face, only inches from her own. "The smell o' the northlands, love. That's the smell of home."

"Gross," said Lorayne, without much feeling, since she was distracted by being pressed up against Coedric. *Maybe it would work*, she thought, *if I just pretended . . .*

"What do we do now?" said Coedric. "Go back to Amygdala's coetidel?"

"Stop that!" said Lorayne.

"What?" said Coedric.

"You know very well, what," said Lorayne.

"I coertainly do not," said Coedric.

"You did it again!"

"Hush!" said Barbara Faw, as more voices passed by in the alley. When all was quiet again, she spoke. "This Lord

Guano has your sister, Lorayne, right? And he intends to marry her?"

"Yes," Lorayne answered.

"The Serpent God he worships requires forty days of fasting and a sacrificial goat for a wedding. Guano will be unwilling to wait. And he will be too cheap to pay for the goat. Not to mention the portrait-maker, the flowers, and the cake. And his family would never get along with yours."

Lorayne nodded. "I hadn't thought of that. Seating arrangements would be impossible."

"There's only one place Guano can take her where the rituals will be sufficiently . . . expedited . . . for his tastes," said Barbara.

Lorayne and Coedric exchanged glances in the dark, then said, in unison, "G'morra."

"Now," said Barbara, "We'll need disguises. Lorayne, we'll dress you as a boy—"

"Forget it," said Coedric. "She could never pass as a boy."

"Here's what we're going to do . . ." said Barbara.

The lights of G'morra were visible miles away as Lorayne, Coedric, and Barbara made their way across the Zyndian wastes. Barbara rode in a carriage borrowed from a certain young noble who owed Mistress Faw a debt of gratitude for her discretion. The nature of the Mincing Pony disposed a lot of wealthy people to be helpful to its proprietress. Coedric sat up front, driving the horses, while Lorayne rode a horse, quietly pouting in her plain soldier's garb: leather jerkin (*flat*), shirt of mail, bracers, gauntlets, leggings (not capris), rough leather boots, and man's surcoat. The unfamiliar clothing chafed her. Barbara Faw had even denied her the comfort of foundation garments. She cast a jealous glance at Barbara, draped in scarlet silks inside the carriage.

Barbara caught her look, "For goodness sake, Lorayne. *You* can be the Queen of Sheba on the way home!"

Lorayne sniffed. "That's what you said last time!"

Coedric snorted, giving the reins a jiggle. "Stay in character, *Loris*." Coedric was disgruntled as well, having been forced to put aside his coelacanth helm, and don the lavender livery of the imaginary nation of Sheba.

Lorayne straightened her shoulders, cleared her throat, and attempted a masculine grunt. Her one comfort was that she had some emergency supplies in one of her saddlebags: a compact, face powder, hoop earrings, a very sharp razor, and some moist towelettes.

Their small delegation was welcomed through the gates, into the city of G'morra, where a festival was held every day of the year. They drove up the main thoroughfare, towards the center of the city. G'morra, known as Vaygas among the Southerners, was laid out in concentric circles, penetrated by spokes. Around the inner circle were arrayed villas owned by all of the wealthy nobles of the realm. Since G'morra was liberal in its allowance of entertainments, many of the grandest balls, tournaments, and feasts were held here. The second circle hosted G'morra's permanent courtesans, courtiers, minstrels, elvish impersonators, and others who provided services to the nobility. In their leisure time, the courtesans, courtiers and their ilk visited the third circle, which was occupied by the bakers, butchers, armorers, grocers, common prostitutes, and inns with a triple-A diamond rating of three or less. The butchers, bakers, and common prostitutes could often be found in the fourth ring of the city, associating with the loan sharks, pickpockets, con artists, street musicians and lowly whores, purchasing tobacco and lottery tickets at the hop-in. And so the cycle was perpetuated, unto the eighth ring, where, it was said, there was no finer place on earth to go to drink yourself to death—if, that is, you could evade the cutthroats long enough to do it.

The main road into the center, though, was the most magnificent, and most decadent part of G'morra. Here dozens of taverns had sprung up, devoted to gambling and gaming in all its variations. Each one was more spectacular than the last, brightly lit all night and day, loud and boisterous, with prettily dressed young men and women standing in front, inviting visitors inside with the promise of wealth. Lorayne, Coedric and Barbara made their way up the strip, with travelers pressing in close on either side, coming and going.

Mistress Faw led them toward a certain second-circle inn where she had a connection. Their path took them through the heart of the city, a grand open courtyard wherein peasants dressed in gypsy costumes danced around a maypole. Lorayne suppressed a grimace at the quality of the dancing.

Liveried guardsmen in colors even more garish than the lavender of Sheba (*If there's no such place as Sheba,* Coedric had growled, *why can't we wear a sensible tartan?*) lounged about in front of their lords' villas. One of them whistled at Lorayne, who nodded back politely.

As they rode, Coedric tipped his head toward Lorayne and said, "In the northlands, this city is called Coencoenatti."

Lorayne answered back, "There's so much wrong with that, I don't even know where to start."

They emerged into the second circle on the far side of the city, and parked the carriage in front of The Headless Horse. A flurry of servants greeted them, taking charge of the horses and disappearing with their baggage. It seemed only minutes before they were seated comfortably at a table in the inn's common room with a pitcher of ale and a bowl of rabbit stew.

The innkeeper appeared, a wiry man of indeterminate age. "Babsie!" he squeaked, sliding into a chair at the table.

"Shhh!" said Barbara Faw. "It's 'Your Highness' if you please."

"Right!" said the innkeeper, putting a hand over his mouth. "So sorry! What brings you to G'morra, Highness?"

"I come bearing a wedding gift for the Lord Guano," Barbara said.

"Lord Guano!" the innkeeper's voice dropped to a whisper. "Why just yesterday a rider came with a reservation for Lord Guano for the bridal suite at Sir Gallahad's Folly!"

"I knew it!" said Lorayne.

The innkeeper glanced up at Lorayne, and looked back and forth in confusion.

"Charles, these are my bodyguards, young Loris and Coedric."

"The pleasure is mine," said Charles. Lorayne nodded and Coedric grunted.

A serving girl arrived with more ale, and stopped to give Lorayne a lingering smile. Lorayne smiled back. Coedric scowled. "No one deserves to be that pretty," he complained.

"Everywhere we go she has men and women falling all over her."

Lorayne blushed. Did this mean that Coedric found her pretty, or just that he was jealous?

"Charles, my wedding gift must be delivered at the occasion of the wedding, not later. Have you heard where that might be held? Lord Guano worships the snake god Lothar."

"Lothar!" said Charles. "Why then it would have to be the Little White Wedding Temple. Unless he went to the fourth circle. Guano's not cheap, is he?"

"Just try cashing one of his checks," said Lorayne, under her breath.

"Thank you so much, Charles," said Barbara. "We must away, then. No time to lose. We can't be late delivering Lord Guano's wedding gift, can we now?"

Coedric grinned and ran a thumb down the edge of the knife he was using to trim his nails.

The Little White Wedding Temple shared space in a cozy-looking ziggurat with several other wedding temples. Lorayne, Coedric, and Barbara entered through the mouth of a giant skull and found themselves in a small, but well-appointed Lothar worship space. A giant, stone carving of the seven-headed snake god himself loomed over the room. There was a blood-stained altar at the front, and a low rail surrounded the requisite pit of live poisonous snakes. There were only three rows of pews to accommodate witnesses. Two hulking men wearing nothing but skirts and black body paint lurked in a corner.

A hooded, black-robed priest swept out from behind the snake god. His eyes and lips were lined with black. He greeted the visitors with a smile. "Welcome! Welcome to the Little White Wedding Temple. And who is getting married today? The young man and the shieldmaiden?"

"Ha!" said Coedric as Lorayne glowered.

Barbara Faw cleared her throat. "Actually, we're here for the wedding of a . . . friend. I've come to surprise him with a gift."

"Hmmm . . ." said the priest. "We've had no advance reservations, but we get walk-ins all the time. Would you like a tour while you wait? Perhaps you'll choose us for *your* special day?"

Lorayne, Coedric, and Barbara looked at each other, then shrugged. "Sure," said Barbara.

"Right," said the priest. "We marry anyone, any age, sex or creed, no questions asked. The ceremony lasts just fifteen minutes and it's fully sanctioned, of course, by the snake god Lothar. We sacrifice a live chicken for you. If you want a goat it's extra. Minions of Lothar are included in your package, and Threlgor, here, will drag your victim to the edge of the snake pit and threaten to throw him or her in." One of the large, painted men smiled and waved. "Mithgar plays the drums. We can give you any atmosphere you want, from portentous to sinister. All weddings are strictly nonconsensual. For a love match, you have to go next door to the Little Temple of Love."

"Oh," said Lorayne, "I thought this whole ziggurat was dedicated to Lothar."

"It is," said the priest. "Same god. Different manifestation. Next door, instead of the snake pit, you get champagne, and Threlgor plays the violin." Conspiratorially, he leaned in and whispered, "The minions are harmless as long as you tip them."

Threlgor smiled and waved again.

"Thank you, Father," said Barbara. "This has been most edifying. We wish to hold vigil, now, until our friend arrives for his wedding, and offer our prayers to the snake god for his . . . felicitations."

The priest beamed. "As you wish. Would you care for some drumming, or incense?"

"Oh, dear, don't go to any trouble on our account," Barbara answered, settling herself into a pew in a worshipful pose.

"Well, then, I'll be next door. We've got a big ceremony over there today. Must prepare." With that, the priest and his minions disappeared.

Hours passed, and the priest reappeared several times, shuffling candles around, throwing food into the snake pit, muttering to himself. When he disappeared again, Lorayne whispered to Barbara and Coedric. "Noon approaches, the most propitious time of day for a wedding under Lothar. Where is he?"

"Perhaps he wishes to marry tomorrow," said Barbara.

"But the bridal suite at Sir Gallahad's Folly . . . ?" Lorayne answered.

"I say we hunt him down. I've had enough of waiting," said Coedric.

"Shhh!" Lorayne hissed. Strains of violin music filtered in from the wedding next door.

They all gasped in horror. "That music! It can't be!"

"Pachelbel's Coemphony?" said Coedric.

"That's *Canon in D*, you uncoevilized clod!" Lorayne said, then slapped a hand over her mouth.

Barbara sucked in a breath. "I've just had a terrible thought," she said. "What if Esmerelda is getting married next door."

"No!" said Coedric.

"It can't be," said Lorayne. "That's some other Lothar worshipper. A happy couple. All non-consensual marriages are conducted here." But even as she said the words, she knew. Suddenly, all the pieces fell into place. "I'll kill her!" shouted Lorayne as she jumped up from the pew.

Rather than going out the way they came, and running around outside the building, Lorayne led the way back behind the snake god and through the narrow, stone-walled hallways to the adjacent Little Temple of Love, following the hypnotic strains of *Canon*.

Bursting out from behind another giant carving of the seven-headed snake god, albeit one gilt with gold and looking friendlier than the previous manifestation, they came upon Lord Guano and Lorayne's sister Esmerelda holding hands in front of a flower strewn alter, with Threlgor playing yet another movement of *Canon* on the violin and accompanied by Mithgar on a pipe organ.

At Lorayne's sudden appearance, Esmerelda squealed. Lord Guano whirled, his tacky silver robes swirling about him. "What is the meaning of this?" he said, on cue.

"What are you doing?" Lorayne demanded. "How can you marry this scumball?"

"What are *you* doing?" Esmerelda shot back. "You weren't invited!"

"You *love* this man? He double-crossed us! I could have died trying to save you."

Esmerelda crossed her arms and pouted. She wore a fluffy white confection of a dress with ruffles and bows all over it that pinched rather unflatteringly at the waist. "What do you think it's like when your *brother* is prettier than you are? You were always the darling of the family. Guano is the only man who ever loved me best."

"What?" said Guano. "She . . . is a *he?*"

Lorayne winked at Guano.

"Lord Guano is a . . . *filthy bastard,*" said Coedric. "Marry him and his bill collectors will be chasing you the rest of your life."

"Coedric!" said Esmerelda. "You have a lot of nerve! You're the worst of the lot, chasing . . . *her*"—Esmerelda pointed at Lorayne—"around like a lovestruck puppy."

Lorayne expected an angry retort from Coedric, but when she looked at him, his face was flushed red.

Sensibly, Barbara Faw took up the argument, sparing Lorayne and Coedric the need to speak further. "My dear, you're young. Why tie your future to this man when a whole life awaits you?"

Lord Guano shouted, "Seize them!"

"Stop!" cried the priest, who was waiting impatiently behind the altar. "There can be no blood shed in the Little Temple of Love. If you must fight, please go next door."

The guards, Lorayne, and Coedric shrugged, and started to turn.

"Wait!" shouted Esmerelda, and the assemblage stood still. "This is *my* choice. I'm here to marry the man I love, and that's Lord Guano. Loris, you can kill all of our guards and carry me off, back home to Mother, but the first chance I get I'm going to run away, and come back to my wuzzy bear." She smiled at Lord Guano, who blushed and smiled back. "You can stay, and help us bless this marriage, or you can be gone, but you can't keep us apart."

Lorayne hesitated. Guano was a terrible match for Esmerelda, and the family would never accept him. She could just see them sitting around the dinner table. *Could* some-one *please pass the rolls*, Dad would say, and Esmerelda would fume and Guano would smile and pass the rolls with a compliment to the cook, and Mom would say *Did I hear someone say something? I thought I heard someone talking, but it sounded like an Evil Overlord, and I'd never have one of those at* my *table.* Of course, Lorayne had to admit, things would improve once the grandchildren started coming. They always did. And Guano would probably hook them up with some nice quality fenced furnishings and draperies and such. She sighed, and said, "Esmerelda, if this is truly what you want, then you have my blessing."

Minutes later, Lorayne stood at Esmerelda's side, her appearance altered with some scarves borrowed from Barbara, one wrapped around her head, and the rest stuffed down the front of her jerkin. Her arms were full of flowers. Coedric stood up for Lord Guano, his coelacanth helm (fetched from the carriage) proud atop his brow, although the groom wasn't entirely comfortable turning his back on the fierce clansman. Mistress Faw sat in the front row, weeping into a handkerchief. The priest of Lothar wrapped the couples' hands with an oily black cord, pronounced them man and wife, and presented them to the congregation. Mithgar appeared with a chilled bottle of champagne. "You two are just the sweetest couple," he said.

As Lord Guano and his new Lady disappeared down the aisle, Barbara Faw muttered, "I give them six months."

Moments later, the priest returned, looking vaguely embarrassed. "There is the small matter of the bill, which I'm afraid Lord Guano forgot to pay in his haste . . ."

Lorayne took out her purse and counted the money into his hand. Mithgar and Threlgor stood nearby, smiling obsequiously. Lorayne dropped a coin into each of their outstretched, black-tattooed palms.

Lorayne sighed and turned to Coedric, who was starting at her intently. "What?" she said.

To her mortification, Coedric dropped to one knee. "Will you marry me, Lorayne?" he said, "Or do I have to drag you next door?"

Lorayne covered her mouth. She didn't know what to say. Coedric half drew his sword, glowering at her.

"Coedric," she said, "you're my dearest friend, and I admit I've had moments where I thought we could be more, but, but . . ."

"But what?" said Coedric.

"I like women," Lorayne admitted, bursting into tears. She buried her face in a scarf.

Coedric stood up, and took her in his arms, pulling her close. "Oh, Lorayne," he said, "There's something I've been afraid to tell you. My true name is not Coedric," he said,

taking a deep breath. "It's Coeleste. I, too, am a transgendered barbarian swordswoman."

Lorayne laughed through her tears and kissed Coedric as
Threlgor began playing the wedding recessional behind them.
"Fabulous," she said, finally, breaking away. *"Coemply fabu-
lous!"*

Over the Hill

Jim C. Hines

Florence bundled her blankets and cloak tighter around her shoulders as she trudged through the snow. "Back when I was younger, I could march half a day without a break. Now I can't go half an hour without stopping to piss."

Millicent Redhand smirked. "Some of us expand with age," she said, patting her own thick trunk. "You shrank, so now you're stuck with a bladder the size of a chipmunk's."

Beside her, Grace the Bloody flashed a toothless scowl. "Less talking, more walking."

Florence rested her weight on her staff. "Don't worry, Grace. We'll get Jacob back."

"I know, Mother," she said. Florence sighed. Grace, two years Florence's senior, had taken to calling her "mother" almost a decade ago. Florence wasn't even sure Grace understood it was her grandson who had been kidnapped.

"Why didn't we hitch a ride with that wine merchant's caravan?" Florence asked. "Wait, I remember. Because *somebody* tried to seduce the driver."

"How was I supposed to know his wife was one of the guards?" asked Millie. "Besides, I was only trying to warm my hands."

Grace glanced back. "Do you need to borrow my mittens?"

Hoofbeats cut off Florence's retort. Millie looked at Florence, who listened for a moment, then said, "Sounds like a single rider."

Both women took up protective positions in front of Grace. Florence relaxed slightly when she saw the rider. The gold and green armor on the Appaloosa mare and her rider marked them as belonging to the Viscount's Guard.

The rider's armor was skimpier than that of her horse. Aside from a few bits of steel and bronze to protect her chest and nether regions, she wore only a long, green cape. Not the most practical uniform, but tradition was tradition. Millie gave a whistle of sympathy. "Folks say Guardswomen don't feel pain. Ha! You try donning cold breast-cups on a crisp midwinter morning and see if you feel anything else for the rest of the day. I used to stuff wool into mine to keep warm."

"You stuffed to keep warm," Florence repeated. "Right."

The rider drew to a halt. Florence could see the goosebumps from here. "Out of the way. I've no time for beggars and grandmothers today."

"Name and rank," Florence barked, loud enough to make Grace jump.

"Lissa, Scout Second Class." She drew her cape around herself. "Who are you, and what are you doing on the road on a morning like this?"

"We *were* heading toward Blind Snake River," Florence snapped. "Now we're arguing with a girl who can't bother to show her elders a bit of respect."

Lissa flushed. "The river is unsafe. Bandits have assailed travelers far better protected than yourselves. There have been robberies, kidnappings. . . ."

"We know. We'll take our chances," said Florence.

Lissa nudged her mount, and the horse trotted past to block the road. "Part of my duty is to protect the people of Adenkar. I'll take you back to town, where it's safe."

"Only if that wine merchant and his caravan have left," Millie muttered.

"We don't have time for this nonsense, girl. Who's your commanding officer?" Florence said.

"Baird Redbeard. And he'd be far less tolerant of your backtalk if he were here."

"Baird . . ." Florence glanced at Millie, who nodded. "Stout fellow? Likes morning stars?"

"You know Baird?" she asked skeptically.

Millie leered. "Who do you think got him into chains, girl? You run along home and tell Baird that if he can't teach his Scouts manners, Millicent Redhand is going to give him the tongue-lashing of his life." She winked. "I may do it anyway, for old times' sake."

Lissa slid smoothly from the saddle, landing on the balls of her feet. "I can't let you pass. For all I know you could be spies for the bandits. I'd prefer not to fight, but I'll truss you up like hogs if that's what it takes."

"I don't think so," Millie said. "I've got nothing against bondage, but you're a bit scrawny for my taste."

Grace crossed her arms. "Want me to take care of her, Mother?" she asked in a voice that might have been threatening if it hadn't been so dry and hoarse.

Lissa patted her sword. "I don't want to use force."

Florence stepped forward, but her boot caught on a rock hidden in the snow. She stumbled, and Lissa reached out to catch her.

Florence's staff jabbed Lissa's sternum. Lissa dropped, gasping. Florence pressed the staff against Lissa's throat while Millie snatched her sword.

"Sorry about that, dear. But those bandits have my friend's grandson. We're going to get him back." She smiled. "And you're going to help."

They put Grace on Lissa's horse, with Millie riding behind. Florence was a better rider, but her hands weren't strong enough to catch Grace if she fell. Florence and Lissa walked alongside. A loop of rope bound Lissa's hands and secured her to the horse's saddle.

"Kidnapping a Guardswoman is a capital crime," Lissa muttered.

"What should I do, send you running back to tell Baird?" Florence said. "He's been trying to catch this band for months. He'd send an entire squad blundering to the river, and we'd never get Jacob back."

"If you were a Guardswoman, you swore an oath to the Viscount. You have a duty to obey Baird's orders."

"I have a duty to save Jacob."

"The Viscount has forbidden anyone to pay ransom to the bandits."

"So you can execute me twice. Besides, I don't plan to pay any ransom."

"You plan to take him by force?" Lissa started to laugh.

Grace scowled and punched a withered fist into her other hand. This caused her to list sideways, and Millie barely managed to keep her from tumbling out of the saddle.

Once Grace was stable, Millie leaned down and whispered, "Careful, girl. Florence whooped *your* pretty behind without breaking a sweat."

"Trickery and deceit." Lissa spat.

Florence shrugged. "And threatening old women is honorable?"

"Who are you calling old?" Grace snapped.

Lissa didn't say another word until they stopped for lunch. Millie gleefully raided the saddlebags, seizing a skin of watered-down wine and a paper-wrapped package of trail rations. She tore off the paper, then grimaced.

"Food hasn't changed since we were in the Guard." She rapped a biscuit against the saddle, then tossed it to Lissa. "I'm not risking the teeth I've got left on *that*."

Grace snatched a bit of jerky and began gumming the corner.

Millie grabbed a small copper pot from Lissa's saddlebags. "Come on, Grace." She snatched the jerky from Grace's hands. "Let's go boil that and get it softened up before you starve."

"You're going to be slaughtered," Lissa said after they had gone. "Give up, and I won't report what you did. The Guard can rescue your friend's grandson."

Florence just smiled as she sliced an apple into small enough pieces to chew. "The Guard couldn't find its arse with a map these days. Don't you worry about us, dear. If all goes well, we'll rescue Jacob and be gone before they know what happened."

"And if things go wrong?"

Florence's smile grew. "Then those bandits had better hope Grace goes easy on them." She took another bite of apple and chewed slowly. "So are you going to help us, or do I have to retie that knot? Don't think I haven't noticed you working it loose."

"If you're lucky, they'll just rob you and leave you to die."

"All the more reason for you to protect us, dear. The way

I see it, you can help us, and maybe you'll learn a thing
or two in the process. Or you can go home and explain
how a couple of grannies waylaid you on the road." She
reached into her cloak and pulled out a knife, which she
used to cut Lissa's bonds.

"You're letting me go?"

"It would be a bit suspicious if we showed up dragging
a bound Guardswoman, don't you think? Now don't tell me
that beneath that bland, duty-bound exterior there's not a
young girl dying for a bit of excitement and adventure."

Lissa stared at her wrists. "I did take an oath to protect
the people," she said slowly.

"Good girl. Now go see what's keeping Millie and Grace,
and let me have some privacy. If I don't pee soon, I'll burst."

⹁ They peered over the hilltop at the river beyond. "What
do you think?" asked Florence.

Millie pointed toward the trees on the far side. "If they're
smart, they'll have men there and there. Archers, if they've
got 'em. And at least one runner in case it's a trap."

Florence nodded in agreement. Thanks to Lissa's horse,
they had made it to the rendezvous only a few hours past
sunrise. The bandits' message said to meet a man in a blue
cap by Farmer's Bridge.

"Does that cap look blue to you?" Florence asked.

"Maybe, if you washed off the grime." She flexed her
shoulders. "How do you want to take him? If he's alone,
I can do him with a sword. If he's got backup . . . It's a
shame these old arms can't manage a bow anymore."

Florence leaned toward Lissa. "When we were in the
Guard, we used to call Millie the queen of the bow-job."

Millie stuck out her tongue. Grace giggled.

"You might be able to take him by surprise," Lissa said.
"But if he has friends, you're dead."

Florence looked at Millie, then cocked her head toward
Lissa. Millie smiled.

"What?" asked Lissa.

"She's young," said Florence. "I imagine that fellow hasn't
seen a pretty girl in quite some time."

"She'll need a bit of work," said Millie. "We need to do
something with that hair . . . and she could use help in the
chest region."

Lissa pulled her cape closed. "I'm *not* going down there to seduce that grimy bandit." She glanced at Millie. "*I'm* not some tramp."

"Excuse me?" Millie said softly.

"But you *are* a tramp," Grace said with a shrug. Millie rolled her eyes.

"And there's nothing wrong with my hair!"

"Nothing at all," Millie agreed. "Except you've got it braided so tight I'm amazed your eyes don't pop out. And try smiling once in a while. You look like a statue from the Temple of Stuck-up Bitches."

Lissa's hand slapped her hip where her sword would have been.

"Enough," Florence snapped. "Lissa's a Guardswoman. A soldier." She turned to Lissa. "And a soldier uses every weapon she's got." She untied Lissa's braid and ran her fingers through the dark hair, fluffing it around her shoulders. "Besides, you're quite pretty. At least you could be, if you'd relax a little."

"Enjoy it now," Millie added. "Before you know it, you'll look like us, all wrinkled and spotted like spoiled fruit."

Lissa glanced at the ground. "You really think I'm pretty?"

Florence shifted Lissa's cape out of the way and tightened her armor.

Lissa squawked. "What are you doing?"

Millie whistled. "Adding bulges, girl. If he's not panting like a dog in two minutes, I'll eat my sword."

"It's all in the attitude," Florence said. "You're more than a soldier. You're a beautiful young woman. Flaunt it. Enjoy it!"

Lissa flushed again. "I'm not sure I can."

"Career soldier?" asked Millie. "Spent your whole life learning to swing a sword, no time for fun, and all that?"

She nodded.

"Ha! You're as bad as Florence was when she signed up. She was as uptight as you. Florence, you remember the first time we dragged you to the Mighty Stallions tavern to see the Sword Swallowers?"

"Hush," scolded Florence. "It's okay, dear. If you're not up for it, we'll just have Millicent here try to seduce him."

✧   ✧   ✧

"You're late," said the scout.

"These legs aren't as quick as they used to be," snapped Florence. "I'm here, aren't I?"

"Who's that?"

She glanced at Lissa. "Jacob's sister. She insisted on coming along."

"I miss him *so* much," Lissa said, simpering ever so slightly—just as Millie had suggested. "I'd do *anything* to get my big brother back."

"Do you have the money?"

"Let me check." Lissa flipped her cape back and began patting herself down.

The bandit folded his arms. "Hurry it up, girl."

Florence stared. Lissa was practically throwing herself at the fellow, but he might as well have had snow running through his veins.

Lissa smiled. "I know it was here somewhere."

"Today, if you don't mind." More than anything, the bandit sounded bored. What was wrong with the boy?

Lissa shot her a worried look. "My poor brother. What have you men done to him?"

"Nothing, yet. Boss wouldn't let us touch him. He put up a good fight, though. Strong fellow, your brother."

Florence's stomach tightened. "He is, isn't he? Good-looking, too."

The bandit sighed. "Ain't that the truth?"

Florence knew that sigh. So much for seducing this one. Lissa didn't have the proper equipment for it.

Lissa caught on a moment later. Turning so her mane of hair hid her face from the bandit, she mouthed, "What now?"

Florence didn't know. She had insisted Lissa leave her weapons behind, so as to appear more helpless and enticing. "We buried the money along the road," she said quickly. "For safekeeping. If you'll come back with us—"

"You don't have it, do you?" asked the bandit. "I'm going to have to take you in."

He reached for Lissa's wrist.

"Lissa, don't—" That was as far as Florence got. A moment later, the bandit was on the ground. Lissa pressed his fingers backward until they almost touched his forearm. Her other hand pressed against his elbow.

An arrow sprouted from the snow between Lissa's feet.

A second bandit saluted from the trees. "You two play nice, you hear? Otherwise somebody's likely to get hurt."

Three men escorted them through the woods. The one with the bow kept smiling at Lissa, who did her best to ignore him.

"Why couldn't *you* have been the one at the rendezvous?" Florence asked him.

"What's that?"

"Never mind." She trudged along as slowly as she could without arousing suspicion. How long would it take the others to follow? Probably ten minutes or so, assuming Millie could convince Grace it was important. Better make it fifteen to be safe.

The bandits had done a good job of camouflage. The tents were white canvas that blended into the snow. She counted eighteen men and a few women sitting around a small campfire. There was probably another handful in the tents. She leaned to Lissa.

"How many do you think you can handle, and be honest?"

Lissa glanced around. "In a fair fight? Maybe four or five."

"A fair fight." Florence patted Lissa's cheek. "That's cute." Raising her voice, she asked, "Who's in charge of this rabble?"

Nobody answered. A good number were staring appreciatively at Lissa. The rest looked to a thin blonde fellow who was eating a plateful of dried fish.

"You there, Blondie!" Florence stomped over and planted the end of her staff between his feet. "Where's Jacob?"

"Where's my money?" He glanced at Lissa. "Or did you bring this pretty young thing as payment?"

"Don't talk with your mouth full," Florence snapped.

"Or what?" He gave Florence a gentle shove. She twisted back, catching her balance with her staff. And then Lissa was there.

Flinging off her cape, Lissa stepped between Florence and Blondie. "I am Lissa Bloodsong of the Guard, and if you lay a finger on this woman again, I'll rip it from your body and feed it to you."

Florence pushed Lissa aside. "If you're so eager to die, why not throw yourself on his sword and get it over with?"

"I was trying to protect you, you stubborn old—"

"I'm fine. He wasn't going to hurt me."

"At your age, a stiff breeze can hurt you!"

Blondie laughed. "Keep an eye on them while I grab the ropes. Looks like we've got some new hostages. Somebody should pay a good sum for the pretty one, at least."

Florence glanced around, searching the woods. Where were Millie and Grace? Both women were more mobile than Florence, and they had Lissa's horse. It wasn't like they had Florence's need for a privy break every half-hour. Except when Millicent . . . oh no.

"Lissa, when you went to get Millie and Grace after lunch, what were they eating?"

"I don't remember."

"Did Millie have a purple pouch with her?"

Lissa's forehead wrinkled. "I think so. . . ."

"Damn the woman. She said she left them behind."

"What was in the pouch?"

"Dried figs. Millie loves them. Always has." But it wasn't until a few years ago that they had begun wreaking havoc on her digestive system. "It could be another hour before they get here."

She stopped talking as Blondie returned. He handed the ropes to two of his men. "So you're a Guardswoman," he said to Lissa. "At least you're easy on the eyes."

The bandit who had escorted them to camp gave Florence an apologetic shrug as he looped the rope over her wrists. The one tying up Lissa just looked smug. It was, Florence realized, the same man who had been eyeing Lissa back on the trail.

"I say we keep this one in my tent, boss," he said.

Lissa used a different throw this time, hooking his leg with her ankle and pushing him to the ground by the throat. Before anyone could move, she grabbed his knife and shouted, "I challenge for leadership of this band!"

Blondie started to laugh. "You plan to use that pigsticker on me?"

"I'll beat you with any weapon you care to name."

"Fine." He snapped his fingers, and one of his men passed a loaded crossbow into his hands. "Use the knife. I'll stick with this baby."

Florence pulled away from her captor. "Oh, for crying out

loud." A lifetime ago, she would have kicked the nearest bandit in the groin, grabbed his weapon, and fought back-to-back with Lissa until they were both free or dead.

Instead, she hobbled over to Lissa and tugged the knife from her hand. "If you want to get yourself killed, that's your business, but if you keep on like this, Jacob and I will likely end up dead as well."

Lissa puffed up, causing several of the bandits to goggle appreciatively. "I was—"

"I know," she said softly. "And I appreciate it. But do it again and I'll brain you myself." She turned to Blondie. "You'll have to forgive Lissa. She's headstrong. But she does *not* want to challenge you."

"I didn't think so." Blondie smiled and set the crossbow on the ground.

Florence smiled right back. "*I* do."

"What?" A half-dozen people said it at once. Florence ignored them as she fumbled out of her blankets and cloaks. The wind bit like cold steel, but she ignored it. Bandits stared in amazement as she shed layer after layer of old wool and faded cotton. When she finished, Florence was clad almost identically to Lissa.

Her tarnished breast-cups were loose against her chest, and her emerald loincloth would have slipped right over her bony hips if she hadn't had the belt taken in last month. Frayed yellow tassels tickled her thighs. Her skin was the color of parchment, and age spots spattered her body like ink. Dark veins and pale scars crisscrossed her arms and legs.

"You can't be serious," said Lissa. "I can't let you do this."

"I was fighting bandits when your daddy was still squealing for your grandma's tit."

"He'll kill you."

Florence sighed. "I'll be seventy years old this summer. You're what, sixteen?"

"Eighteen," Lissa said defiantly.

"Eighteen. Gods protect you, girl. If this jester kills you, he's taking your whole life away. If he kills me . . ." She shrugged. "That's a few less years of eating mushy food and hunting privies."

"That's crazy."

"You said it yourself. I was more likely to get myself killed than to save Jacob. But none of us can afford Blondie's ransom, and it's not like I have much to lose." She smiled. "The most dangerous foe is the one with nothing to lose." Florence poked her staff toward Blondie. "So let's get this over with before I die of old age."

"You've made your point, old woman. I respect your courage, but—"

"Fine." She hobbled toward the tents. "I'm going to free Jacob. If you want to stop me, you'd better do it now."

He gestured at his men. "Troy, tie her up and put her with the other hostage."

Troy turned out to be the blue-capped bandit they had met at the river. Florence jabbed a thin finger into his chest. "Don't you dare. I challenged *him*. Shame on you, doing his dirty work. You sit down and wait until he settles things like a man. Then you can tie me up."

She shook her head sadly. "What's a boy like you doing with this ragtag band, anyway? You're young, healthy, handsome . . . I'm sure it sounded romantic, to live out here surrounded by rugged, outdoorsy men." Troy blushed. "But they're not for you. Find yourself a nice boy and an honest job. There are safer ways to earn a living than following garbage like this." She cocked a thumb at Blondie, who was no longer smiling.

"That's enough," he said.

Florence ignored him. "And *you*," she said, turning toward a bandit with a bald head and a blotchy birthmark on his cheek. "You look like you haven't bathed in a week, and I can smell your breath from here. Nobody's going to respect you if you don't respect yourself, least of all a pretty girl like Lissa here. And if you can't mend the rips in that cloak, just fold it up and leave it. I'll take it when I leave. And I expect to be paid a fair sum for fixing it, understand?"

He nodded dumbly. Some of the others laughed, but Florence had already moved on to a young boy. Blondie barked an order, and the boy drew his sword.

"Give me that." Florence snatched the sword by the blade and plucked it from his hands. "Did he give you this bit of scrap?"

"Yes, ma'am."

She ran a thumb down the blade. "The handle's loose, the balance is horrendous, and it hasn't been properly sharpened since before you were born. A sword like this is a greater danger to you than to your opponent, understand?"

"Yes, ma'am."

"Good. Now, you demand a real sword from this cheap-skate, and if he doesn't give you one, you march right back home to your mama. Otherwise you'll be dead before you're old enough to shave."

Before she could start in on the next bandit, Blondie grabbed her shoulder and pushed her to the ground. The cold earth was hard as brick.

"What's wrong with you?" snapped Florence, once she caught her breath. "Sneaking up on an old woman. Didn't your parents teach you any manners?" Grumbles of agreement spread around the circle.

"Quiet," yelled Blondie. "I'm not going to fight you, but I won't have you talking to my men like that."

"I'm taking Jacob," Florence said, her voice firm. She heard Lissa shifting nervously.

Blondie started to laugh, great gut-wrenching guffaws that echoed through the woods. "I like you. You've got more spunk than any woman I've met, and if you were a century younger . . ." He shook his head.

"If I was that young, I'd take your head to the Viscount as a trophy."

Blondie was still chuckling. "A shame you're no longer young." He raised his voice. "Kill her."

A few of the bandits actually rose. Florence crossed her arms, and they stopped with their weapons half-drawn. "For shame. Next thing you know, you'll be robbing babies. Sit down, all of you."

Nobody spoke. A hawk shrieked in the distance, sounding like laughter. Slowly, the bandits sat.

Florence turned back to Blondie. "You should find another career. You're too dumb to lead bandits. You should have killed me the second I challenged you. Now it's too late."

"Is that so?" he sneered. His hand went to his sword, and then he jumped in surprise. He touched his neck, where a slender black dart protruded from the skin.

"It's so," Florence said.

His lips pulled back, and he drew his sword. The first blow shattered her staff and spun her to the ground. His second swing never connected.

Lissa leapt over Florence's body, and her foot crunched into Blondie's chest. He flew backward, dropping his sword. Lissa grabbed the sword and brought it into a guard position.

Behind her, Blondie staggered to his feet and drew a curved knife. He took one step, then stopped as the jagged end of Florence's staff poked his stomach.

He sneered and snatched the staff. Florence smashed the other half of the broken weapon against his knuckles, and he fell back, howling. His yells faded as the toxins in the dart took effect, and he collapsed into the snow.

Florence rolled over and looked at the trees, where Grace was putting another dart into a slender black tube.

"About time you got here!" Florence yelled.

Millie looked sheepish. Grace simply glared and said, "The next one who threatens my mother gets a dart in the eye."

Jacob was unharmed, if embarrassed. Florence spent ten minutes chewing him out for being so careless as to let a pair of bandits get the jump on him. Then she gave him a hug and a quick kiss and sent him to round up the bandits' horses.

As for the bandits themselves . . . Florence glanced around. More than half had chosen to accompany them back to town. Some clearly didn't want to be around when Blondie woke up. Others were afraid of what would happen when the Guard arrived.

"What will you do from here?" Lissa asked.

"You mean what will *Jacob* do?" Millie piped up.

Lissa flushed and brushed her hair back from her eyes. Florence only smiled. Anyone could see the way those two had been eying each other. She already had a bet with Millie as to how long it would take Lissa to drag the boy into bed. She leaned toward Lissa. "It turns out Jacob's been talking about joining the Guard. The daft boy has never touched a sword in his life."

"If he's never touched a sword, why would he want to—"

Florence gave her a pointed look, and her blush darkened.

"Oh. Well, I could . . . um. I can keep an eye on him. If it would make Grace feel better, I mean."

Millie chuckled. "I'm sure she'd feel much better, knowing you were there to help him master his sword."

"Don't worry, dear," said Florence. "Grace plans to keep an eye on Jacob herself. She's been going on about it all day, how she's going to sign up for another ten-year stint."

"But she's—"

"Too old?" finished Florence. "Grace Shadowsoul can hit a fly at fifty paces with that blowgun. Do you really want to finish that sentence?"

She shook her head. "I just worry what would happen to her."

"Nothing, so long as she's got the right commanding officer." Florence smiled and waited for that to sink in.

Lissa's eyes widened. "You mean *you*? But—"

"Don't finish that sentence either, girl. Besides, it beats sitting by a fireplace crocheting socks and waiting to die. Between Millie, Grace, and myself, we'll get the Guard back into shape."

Lissa's face tightened. "That sounds . . . nice."

Before she could say anything more, Grace and Jacob came thundering up the road on their horse. Grace's gray hair was slick with sweat, and a wide smile wrinkled her face. "Come on, Mother! We'll race you to that hilltop!" She took off again without waiting for an answer.

Florence turned to Lissa and Millie. "Let's catch her before she hurts herself." She stretched her knotted fingers and flicked the reins. Her horse leapt forward, jolting her bones and leaving the others to chase after her. Her joints would ache something fierce tomorrow morning, but that wasn't the worst of it.

As she rode, she muttered to herself, "First thing I do once I'm back in the Guard is requisition a saddle that won't jostle the bladder so badly."

A Sword Called Rhonda

D. S. Moen

"Hey, Karma," Rhonda the sword whined, "I need to go, like, shopping."

She hung from the wall of my small home in what used to be suburban Palo Alto. Being far away didn't help. I could hear her just as clearly as if I'd held her in my hand with her voice coming out the end of the hilt. I'd tried hanging her from my waist at first, but she just yelled loud enough for everyone to hear. Now, I carry her over my shoulder so she talks in my ear.

I hadn't responded, so she yelled. "Are you listening?"

"Yeah, yeah, I hear you," I replied.

Two weeks ago, I bought the sword at the city's disincorporation sale. It was a fine sword, made of good strong steel that could take a beating. At the time, it seemed like a good deal.

For days afterward, my dreams ended in, "Help me, Rhonda!"

One morning, I started singing the old Beach Boys tune.

"I thought no one would ever listen to me!" Rhonda said.

She hasn't left me alone since.

"And you so need me, too. You're a mess! Look at that eyebrow. Don't you ever pluck?"

I rubbed the bridge of my nose. So it had a little hair. Big deal.

"Karma," the sword interrupted with all the charm of a spoiled teenager.

"What!"

"I need to go shopping."

"What did I tell you last time you asked to go shopping?"

"I know there's a mall in Palo Alto, Karma. I want more moisturizer. You promised. I laid that guy open for you, and you said you'd get me some so I wouldn't get all rusty."

"I said I wouldn't let you get rusty. You're not. I've fulfilled my promise. Besides, Crisco will keep you from getting rusty. You don't need moisturizer."

"Crisco! That's disgusting. I'd never put that stuff in me when I was alive. It's just grody. Don't you *dare* wipe it on me."

"I was teasing you. You know I use mineral oil."

Rhonda sniffed. "Disembowelling a hunk like that? It's totally awful. I deserve a reward. A token. Something to keep me from getting all wrinkled."

I chuckled at the thought. What, was she going to turn into a Damascus blade? Right. "Okay, okay, we'll go if it makes you feel better." I had a million things to do, but at least she'd leave me alone. I hoped.

The living room held a shelf of books, a few knickknacks and not much personality. It was so small that I had to keep the surfboard in the attic. I pulled Rhonda's scabbard off the wall and slung it across my back. Then I pulled the poncho off the wall.

"Not the singing," Rhonda said. "Can't we use the surfboard?"

"You're the one who wants to go to the mall, and I'm not walkin', nor am I spending the day at the beach. So you'd better sing with me, because if we don't sing, the poncho's not going anywhere."

"Whatever." I envisioned her flipping her shoulder-length blonde hair.

I laid out the poncho and stood on it. Leaning forward, the scabbard thwapped my kidneys. I stood up straight.

"I have a little Spanish flea," I sang. Rhonda joined in after the first word. The orchestral accompaniment, the original Herb Alpert, emanated softly from the carpet, helping us keep rhythm and pitch.

I hated that I couldn't afford a better ride, like one of the magic carpets or the cheapo magic surfboards so common in Silicon Valley these days. Just a poncho with a love for old Herb Alpert tunes, sold for a song because someone couldn't stand driving to the same tunes all the time. I had a surfboard, a vintage wooden Johnny Rice, but it insisted on going surfing whenever I used it. So, unless I wanted to spend all day out, I used the poncho instead.

As the music continued, the poncho started bouncing. "It holds a little stuff and me." It hovered and glided jauntily out the door, smoothing out when we sang in harmony.

We swooped upward. Rhonda whooped, which made the poncho falter. I sang louder, and it recovered before we dove to the ground.

We flew over burned-out houses and collapsed garages, singing like idiots to that old tune. Fewer than five percent of the Palo Alto suburbs were still standing. Most houses were rubble, the debris pushed into huge piles every few houses. Some people still had gardens. We passed rich guys sitting on hand-tied silk carpets from Stephen Miller's gallery, all powered without sound.

When we arrived at the ruins of the Stanford Shopping Center, Rhonda finally got it. "Where's Nordstrom? And Macy's?"

The multideck parking lot was a complete wreck, but I was unprepared for the carnage to the stores. Entire walls were missing. How, I wondered? And, when we passed Neiman-Marcus, a woman knelt at the one standing wall, sticking a piece of paper in a crevice. Great. The wailing wall of Neiman-Marcus. Who knew?

Bang & Olufsen looked like someone had exploded an electronics factory. Rhonda whimpered over red-satin-nylon-that-would-not-die thongs and push-up bras from Victoria's Secret. No one had touched those.

"Karma, get them for me. I wear a 34B."

I didn't have the heart to point out that she was, maybe, a 4 at present. After all, I was hoping that I could free her from the sword. I scrounged around the rubble and found two bra-and-thong sets in aubergine. I guess no one wanted eggplant-colored undies.

At Rhonda's insistence, we scrounged through the wreckage for clothes. Most of the stuff was too torn or worn to use, but I found a couple of the golden-age sixties outfits and two intact pairs of white go-go boots in my size. Not that I'd wear them, but I might have to if I wore out my other shoes.

"It's just so sad." Rhonda started crying. For the first time, I felt sorry for her. Her world was gone, and she wouldn't really know how to cope in mine. She didn't even like being a sword. Last week, when we'd killed the guy who tried to rob the house, I had whacked off his arm and all she could do was yell, "Gross!"

Finally, the question formed in my head. If she'd been enchanted, maybe she could be unenchanted. Maybe I could have a sword all my own without being pestered about shaving my legs.

"So who put you into a sword anyway?"

"The Duke did."

"The evil wizard?" I asked.

"Wizard, hah. He's a scientist. And a surfer. He so totally hates it when people call him a wizard."

I sighed. "They call him a wizard only because they've heard about the dog."

"That was a failed spell . . . I mean formula."

"See?" I asked. "Even you called it a spell."

"Karma, it was so totally not a spell."

"How do you know?"

"I just know," Rhonda said coldly.

"Then what happened?"

"Like, you know the rest. I didn't stop seeing his apprentice Joe. We'd even exchanged our puka shell necklaces and everything. We were practically married, but hadn't signed the papers. The Duke was totally mad that I wouldn't obey him. Like why would I, you know? Well, he said he'd teach me a lesson. He turned me into a friggin' sword. And then, Joe tried to hug me and sliced his arm up."

"Where's the Duke now?"

"He died the next year, and Joe left for Monterey and I've tried to get there all this time."

Great. So the Duke couldn't undo the spell. "How long have you been a sword?" I knew it couldn't have been too many years; retro sixties had been popular just before the Collapse.

"What year is it?"

I told her.

"So it's been, hmm, my math is rusty. Eight years?"

"Yep." What next? "How about if we take you to someone who might have an idea how to get Joe back?"

"That'd be awesome. I would so totally owe you."

I smiled.

Along El Camino, one of the few places that hadn't been devastated was the Psychic Eye shop in Mountain View. I hovered over on the poncho, singing to the Herb Alpert tune "Casino Royale."

Inside the store, the soft sounds of Enya, the reverb queen, played from a tune crystal.

I approached the counter, asked for a reading. The clerk led me through beaded curtains into a back room.

"I am Elvis; I can read for you," the small waif of a man with a glow-in-the-dark smile said. He wore a gold lamé dinner jacket and sunglasses. "Your question?"

"How can I keep my sword and help Rhonda, who is trapped in the sword, live a happy life?" Okay, I didn't care about the happy life part, but I try to live my life by principles.

He turned over five cards, flashing a pinky ring with each card. Three of rods. Three of swords. Three of pentacles. Three of cups. Magician.

His brow furled, then he said, "Aha!"

"What?"

He leaned back smugly. "Try the elements."

"You mean like oxygen?"

"No, no. Fire, Air, Earth, and Water. In that order."

"Huh?" I looked at the cards: a guy looking out to sea, a breaking heart, a guy working on a church window, and three women hovering over glasses. Didn't seem related to what he was saying.

"You see, all of these are threes, so it's about threes—that part of the journey that's the separation. And the three of swords means separation. So it's about each element. And the Magician card has all the elements. So, that's your answer."

I nodded, realizing he wasn't going to give me anything that made sense. I pulled out the money, but he gestured at a stout ceramic jar.

"I don't touch money myself. It changes my readings."

Whatever. I put the money in the jar. As I left, I looked back and noticed that the jar had writing on it: Mistakes.

This time, since I needed to carry more stuff, I decided to take the Johnny Rice. At least we'd have better music. We sang "Surfer Girl" and other old surfer tunes as we cruised west to Half Moon Bay. We stopped in the mountains to get some wood, because I knew I'd need a fire.

When I got to the beach, I pitched a tent, because I had no idea how long everything would take. I'd want to crash later and I'd be tired.

I dragged some branches out onto the beach and built a fire.

"Karma, what are you doing?"

"Following Elvis's advice."

"I'm afraid of fire. I don't want to get burned."

I sighed, put a potholder on the hilt, and thrust her in anyway.

Before the sword warmed to the touch, she screamed and yelled so much that I couldn't help it. I pulled the sword out. "Do you want out or not?"

"Yes, but Karma, that just totally hurts."

I stuck her back in the fire anyway.

"Karma, stop it. Don't make me scream again."

I felt sorry for her, so I pulled her out.

I thought about the next thing. Air. Well, I could just sit here on the beach and hold her up, I suppose.

So, I settled back in the sand, and held the sword aloft, but all I got was wind-chapped and a sore arm.

"Karma? What are we doing?"

"Holding you into the wind."

"Oh." She paused for a moment. "Why are we doing this again?"

"Sheesh, how many times do I have to remind you?"

I held her aloft in my other arm for a while, but nothing happened.

"Okay, air didn't help."

With the shovel from my pack, I dug a hole in the sand.

I lowered Rhonda into the hole, then started shovelling sand over the sword. She started screaming again.

"What are you doing?"

"I'm using Earth to free you." By this time, I was growling. I was doing this for her, or so I kept trying to convince myself. But no, she just wouldn't cooperate.

"You hate me. Admit it."

At first, I did. The thing was, she was growing on me. I pulled her out and cleaned the sand off. "I'm sorry. I was trying to help."

Exhausted, I sat in front of the smouldering fire and cooked some meat. We went into the tent, and I collapsed, waking in late morning.

After breakfast, I tried Water. I walked out into the waves and dunked her into the ocean.

"You idiot!" Rhonda burbled. "I can't swim!"

"What, a Valley Girl surfer chick who can't swim?" I pulled her back out so I could hear her answer better.

"I don't surf, silly. I just go to the beach to watch bitchin' dudes and work on my tan!"

I shook my head. I should have known. Why the hell had I trusted a psychic named Elvis?

I had to spend the whole next day making up to Rhonda for dunking her in salt water.

We returned to the Psychic Eye. This time, Elvis wore a white leather jumpsuit with fringe.

"How did you fare?" he asked.

"Not well." I catalogued the various things we'd tried.

"Let's try another reading," he said.

What the hell. Worst case, I'd be off on some other wild goose chase.

This time, he dealt three cards. Three of cups. Three of swords. Tower.

"Two of those cards are the same," I say. I wasn't sure he'd remember, but I did.

"Yes. They are clearly more significant."

"Please don't tell me to do the same thing over. I couldn't stand it." Rhonda whimpered, so I knew she agreed.

"Does she love someone?"

"Of course."

"Has he kissed the sword?" He stopped for a second, then looked up. "I'm sorry, I shouldn't have made that assumption."

"It is a he. I don't know that he's kissed the sword, but he did try to hug it."

"Not the brightest bean in the crop, is he?"

I shrugged. "What should I do?"

He looked at me, and I knew. Have her kiss him. Naturally. We hopped off to Monterey, where Joe still had his Surf Shak.

Naturally, we had to take the Johnny Rice. Rhonda *insisted.* Joe looked older than Rhonda had described. She giggled when she saw him. I had to admit, he was the perfect surfer dude: blond curly hair pointing in all directions. Tall, broad-shouldered, tan, looking pretty fine in the tank top. Heck, I could totally see why Rhonda liked him. Totally? Gah. I had to get away from Rhonda. Soon.

"Can I help you?" He looked up and down, recognizing me as Not Of His Tribe. Then he noticed my board. "Gnarly board you have there."

"Yeah, I've got something to show you."

"Oh?" He asked.

I put the surfboard down and pulled out Rhonda. I showed him the sword. He looked up, smiling.

"Rhonda. Is she . . . ?"

"She's fine." I noticed the shell necklace, probably what Rhonda had talked about. And I realized, when I looked in his face, that he'd missed her all this time. "Someone suggested that, if you kissed the sword, she might be able to depart."

He flexed his right arm and I saw the scar from the sword where he'd tried to hug her.

"Just don't kiss the edge, okay?"

He kissed the flat of the blade, but it was just a quick peck.

"No, silly. Kiss her."

He looked embarrassed. Then, on a whim, I kissed it. A nice, long, slow kiss.

"Eeww, that is so gross. I am out of here. I am so out of here!" And a long-haired bleached blonde stepped out of the sword into Joe's arms. She was completely nude, but that didn't bother Joe. It bothered me though. I didn't really want to look.

I turned away to leave.

"Stay for the wedding." Rhonda said. "It'll be awesome!"
"No, you two have a lot of catching up to do. But, I have
a wedding present for you." I gave them both the Johnny
Rice. A surfer couple should have a nice vintage surfboard.

"Dude, that's freakin' awesome, thank you," he said, trying
to cram all the words into a single syllable.

"Oh, Karma, you're just so bitchin'," Rhonda said. She
turned to hug me, but I didn't want to be near her.

The sword? I renamed it when I got home.

Mo. Silent Mo.

Giants in the Earth

Esther M. Friesner

"Have you ever had one of those days where you just can't get a psalm started?" King David sat back on the royal throne of all Israel and drummed his fingers on the gently curving cedar armrests. "The opening line's the hardest part. I've got everything else down pat: rhyme scheme, subject matter, nifty metaphors that do *not* involve sheep, for a change. Sheep! Don't get me started. You grow up as a simple shepherd boy—what the hell else *is* there to do in this country?—and right away you can't write a psalm without everyone picking it apart, looking for hidden references to sheep, sheep, sheep, 'til the cows come home. To say nothing of those so-called 'jokes' the men used to tell about me back in my army days. Soldiers, *feh*! As if *they* never—"

"Your Majesty was saying something about an opening line?" Tirzah asked amiably. As concubine *du jour* she had certain assigned tasks, not the least of which was keeping King David's conversation on track. When a man spends the better part of his youth on the lam from a crazy king like Saul and the rest of his salad days amassing a comfortably *haimish* empire, his body may cease wandering but his mind often does not.

"Oh, right, right, a catchy first line, yes, hmm . . ." The ring-encrusted royal fingers, each adorned with a precious stone the size of the rock that slew Goliath, went back to drumming on the armrest. "Listen, my subjects, and you shall hear . . . When that Goliath with his spears and arrows/ The men of Israel had piercéd to the marrow . . . Whose sling this is, I think I know . . . There once was a giant from Gath . . ."

"Perhaps Your Majesty should work on a different psalm?" Tirzah suggested, popping a grape into her mouth. "I've found that when I reach a point where there doesn't seem to be any solution to the problem at hand, it helps to switch projects entirely."

The king gave her a smarmy smile. "You're a concubine, my dear," he said. "What problems do you face that can't be solved by a new necklace or an extra dollop of myrrh?"

Tirzah opened her mouth to answer, then thought better of it and stopped her gob with a handful of dates. It didn't do for a woman to backtalk the king. She understood that, as a concubine, she had only two career paths: Cling to the king's good side like moss to a stone or spend your days locked up among the women.

Not that there was anything *wrong* with being locked up among the women, but as JHVH was her witness, it was *boring.* The ladies of the royal household seemed able to talk about nothing save clothing, cosmetics, candy, kids, and the king's elusive favor. Those who'd managed to get a colt off the royal stud formed an exclusive clique whose favorite pastimes were sneering at their less fertile colleagues and zealous jockeying/backstabbing in order to get their child in line for the throne.

As much as Tirzah despised the snotty Womb Supremacists, she knew that her only hope for advancement lay thataway, and the more she hung out with David, the better her odds of hitting the royal jism jackpot. All of which was why she swallowed her pride along with a mouthful of chewed-up dates, smiled ever-so-sweetly, and replied:

"Yes, O my beloved king. How silly of me. Your life is much more important than mine, of course. *Me* daring to suggest anything to *you*? Tsk. What *was* I thinking? Can you ever forgive your po' li'l featherheaded Tirzy-wirzy who wuvs 'oo so vewy, vewy much that she just can't wait to get you alone and perform the Babylonian Basket Trick for your intense, unbelievable pleasure?"

"Wuzzah?" Despite Tirzah's almost-never-fail employment of that tempting combination, fulsome baby talk and promised perversity, the king wasn't buying. He'd chided his concubine and gone straight back to wrestling with the uncooperative psalm.

Tirzah frowned and double-checked her breasts. Yes, still firm, still golden as a pair of melons, still exuding rare floral essences imported from Egypt at great expense. When it came down to cases, she had no doubts about her physical attractions; but when the match was Concubine vs. Blank Parchment, best two falls out of three, she was stymied. What was it about the composition of a psalm that managed to gobble up the king's full attention?

"Yes, dear," she muttered under her breath. "You just go back to composing that psalm all about how you slew Goliath, big whoop. I'll be right here when you finally want me. Where else do I have to be?"

"Gath . . . wrath . . . bath . . . Sheba . . . huh?" said the king, blinking as he looked up at her from his labors.

"Nothing," said Tirzah wearily. "I was just thinking about how much I love you. Wildly. Madly. Passion without bounds." Her voice was only a little flatter than her taut young belly, but the king wasn't really paying any attention and she was past caring. "Yea, verily, I would do anything to prove my love for you, yep, sure, you name it, just—"

"Of course you would; it's in your job description. Why the blazes do you have to gabble about it, woman?" King David demanded. He might have said more, but at that moment the calm of a summer's afternoon in the royal court was broken by the abrupt entrance of the king's majordomo. He was an overly excitable Moabite whom the king had hired as lip service to valuing diversity somewhere in the palace besides the royal harem.

"Majesty! Majesty!" he cried, scuttling into the throne room, wringing his hands. "Oh, the unspeakable horror! Oh, the devastation! Oh, that ever this should come to pass!" He threw himself facedown at the king's feet, gurgling prophecies of generic doom.

"What is it?" the king demanded, toeing the Moabite

firmly. "And it had better be good. The last unspeakable horror you reported was a wild donkey that got loose in the marketplace and ate three cabbages. When it ate a fourth you escalated the event to a full-fledged devastation. I hope you're not wasting my time with another four-cabbage disaster, because tomorrow is the anniversary of my battle with the Philistine champion, Goliath of Gath, and if I don't finish this psalm about how I slew him, I'll—"

"But you *didn't* slay him, Majesty!" The trembling Moabite raised his eyes to the king's dire countenance. "He's back. Goliath of Gath is back, he's waiting outside the gates of Jerusalem, and he says he's not leaving until he's got your head on the end of his spear!"

A table had been fetched and King David's council had been summoned into the throne room with such haste that no one had thought to dismiss the concubine. Thus Tirzah found herself wandering around the periphery of the strategic huddle, nibbling a fistful of almonds, and peering over the shoulders of David's most trusted advisors as they discussed the situation in hushed, intense tones.

"But it *can't* be Goliath!" King David protested. "I *killed* him! I killed him *good*. First I whapped him with a rock— POW!—right between the eyes, and when he hit the dirt I took his own sword and I cut his head off. They don't come much deader than that."

"As Your Majesty says," one of David's generals replied soothingly. The royal council was made up of nothing but generals, the Mighty Men of Israel, with a case-by-case visit from the occasional prophet-without-portfolio. "And yet, evidence to the contrary is even now standing without our city gates, single-handedly blocking traffic and interfering with peaceful commerce."

"What I don't understand—" said the king. "What I honestly do *not* understand at all, no matter how hard I try, is *why* in the name of the Unnameable you, my so-called generals, haven't just sent out the army to deal with the, er, impediment to peaceful commerce. Giant or no giant, there's only one of him."

The generals looked sheepish enough to give David bad flashbacks to his boyhood. At length, one of them broke the uneasy silence.

"True, Majesty, that would be the sensible thing to do. But before we could dispatch so much as a patrol of spearmen to confront the giant, he issued . . . the *challenge*."

"The challenge?" David echoed. "What challenge?" He was leaning his fists on the conference table and Tirzah noted how very white his knuckles were turning, coupled with the fine beading of perspiration on his brow. He was also breathing a bit raggedly, all of which indicators led her to believe that he knew damn well *what* challenge.

"The challenge to single combat," General Eliezar said. "The same challenge he gave to King Saul's troops the first time you killed him. The time you *thought* you'd killed him." He was the youngest man on the king's council and as such did not have the brains of a kitten when it came to survival off the battlefield. He simply did not know any better than to assume that when the king asked a question, he wanted an honest answer. His colleagues exchanged looks that were equal parts pity and thankfulness that Eliezar was there, about to take the royal slingstone for the team. Better him than them.

"I . . . *did* . . . kill . . . him." The words only just managed to escape the king's mouth through tightly gritted teeth. "Not for the *first* time; for the *only* time! I cut off his bloody *head*! Don't you know *history*?"

"I know there's more being written every day," Eliezar replied, as obliviously cheerful as ever.

"Good. Then go write some," David snapped. "Get your scrawny butt the hell down to the barracks, pull together a troop of men, and take down that giant!"

"Majesty?" Eliezar raised one eyebrow in bewilderment at his sovereign's orders. "Goliath's challenge wasn't leveled against the army. What he said was—"

"*How many times must I repeat myself?*" King David's bellow shook cedar dust from the throne room rafters. "That is not Goliath! Goliath is *dead*."

"Not according to him. He says he's Goliath, he's got Goliath's armor, and his appearance has attracted a whole bunch of veterans from King Saul's army, all testifying that they recognize him as Goliath. He says he's not leaving until you come out and face him in hand-to-hand combat to the death. No backup troops, just you and your armor-bearer, if you need one. He says you'd *better* wear armor, because he can put a spear through a twenty-five-year-old plane tree at one hundred paces."

"Is that all?" The king's voice had gone very low and growly. It was a warning sign the young general did not seem to recognize or heed.

"Yes. Wait, no: He also says that after all these years you've probably gotten fat." Eliezar smiled radiantly, duty done. He was woefully unaware that the rest of the council were edging away from him as he spoke. Older and wiser, they had no intention of becoming collateral damage when King David finally lost his temper and flattened the lad.

To their surprise, instead of a royal explosion, King David's reaction was merely to sigh deeply and pinch the bridge of his nose. "Bugger," he said. "If he's drawn a crowd of Saul's old army buddies, I'll have to fight him, whoever he is. People are watching. I'll bet drachmas to dromedaries that a whole mob of our foreign trade community is out there too, waiting to see what I'll do. If I don't fight it'll be a *shonda* for the *goyim*."

"A what?" Like many on the council, Eliezar had a hard time understanding his king when David lapsed into the local dialect of his youth.

"Just fetch my armor, dummy. And will someone please clear away that concubine?"

All the good seats for the big rematch were taken. Tirzah tried to squirm her way through the press of women hogging the few windows that had a decent view of the road where the giant awaited King David's appearance, but was firmly rebuffed.

"We outrank you." Leah sniffed disdainfully. She was a skinny creature, relic of David's brief flirtation with the philosophy that Less is More. He'd tired of her bony embraces, but not before she bore him a son. "We are the royal mothers."

"I'll say you are," Tirzah grumbled.

"What was that?" Hulda asked sharply. She'd been a concubine-of-last-resort until she'd lucked out and birthed a baby boy.

"I said that for all you know, *I'll* be a royal mother some day, too, so maybe you should be nicer to me." Tirzah waggled her hips at the women. "I found an old Babylonian bedroom manual last week and it's got plenty of sure-fire tricks to guarantee—"

"Ha!" Hulda was one of those annoying know-it-alls who was likewise a say-it-all. "If our lord David loses this battle—which he won't, unthinkable, JHVH forbid, *p'too-p'too-p'too*, I never so much as suggested the possibility—you'll be nothing. It takes two to make a royal baby. Or didn't your Babylonian smut book mention that?"

Tirzah stared, horrified. The truth of Hulda's words was inescapable. If David fell to Goliath's spear, her life was over too. What happened to concubines when their master died? Those with children of the royal blood would be looked after by the next king, if only so he might keep tabs on potential rivals. Those who were still virgins due to bureaucratic oversights might find employment elsewhere. For those like Tirzah, neither maiden nor mother, the game was over.

Oh no! she thought wildly. *What will become of me? Being a concubine is all I know how to do! That and watching sheep, but I will see myself chopped up and served over couscous before I go back to doing* that *again.*

Memory conjured up the image of her mother on the day Tirzah announced that she was turning in her shepherd girl's rod, staff, sling, and lambing kit in order to audition for the king's harem. "I want to smell of myrrh, not manure," she explained. "Is that such a bad ambition?"

"Fine," Mother said in a way that made it obvious how very far from fine it all was. "Go. Be a concubine. See if I care. Break a mother's heart. All I'm saying is that you could do better. This is an honor, to share the bed of a man old enough to be your father without even he gives you an engagement ring? And why should he? Why buy the sheep when you're getting the sex for free? But don't listen to *me*. Go. Make from this filth a successful life. When I think of what I sacrificed for you—"

She'd gone on in the same vein right up until the minute Tirzah left, which was not a moment too soon. She'd been on the point of seeing whether she could turn her old sling into a suicide weapon rather than listen to one more word from Mother. She could have done it. Tirzah's skill with the shepherd's weapon of choice was a local legend, which was why none of the local boys ever proposed marriage.

They were all put off by the thought of having a wife who was a better shot than they were.

The wise men of Israel and many other lands have often compared the arrival of a revelation to being struck by a thunderbolt. In doing so they overlook the fact that a thunderbolt only does a finite amount of damage, whereas great ideas have the potential to wipe out whole kingdoms. Tirzah's personal thunderbolt struck right in the midst of her not-so-nostalgic musings over her past life and future prospects.

"My sling!" she exclaimed, with the look of someone who has just seen a dull door swing open to reveal a cave full of treasures beyond price. She rushed off to her chamber before any of the other wives could blink.

A quick dive into the small cedarwood chest at the foot of her bed produced Old Wolfbane, as she'd dubbed the faithful weapon that had protected her flock from many a famished predator. The tatty tunic and headcloth she'd worn when she first showed up at the royal palace were there as well, along with her road-scuffed sandals. It said much for Tirzah's beauty, that when she'd arrived thus clad at the palace gates, the harem administrators had seen her employment potential despite such poor packaging.

It was the work of a moment to change clothes, the work of another to grab her sling and dash away in search of the king. She encountered no hindrance to her flight: King David ran a free-range harem. The guards were there to keep other men out, not to keep the women in. Why would they want to leave? They were fed, clothed, and cosseted, and if some smartypants decided she'd have a lover and pass off his child as the king's, well, thwarting such schemes was how the Royal Harem Records-Keeper earned his daily flatbread.

Tirzah found the king in his inmost apartments, fighting to squeeze into his old armor. The armor was winning. It had been years since David had led men into battle. Peace brought prosperity to the land, paunchiness to the ruler thereof. He was in a foul mood.

"All I can say is that after putting me through so much trouble, that jerk out there had *better* be Goliath! If he's not, I'll *kill* him!"

The king's two armor-bearers exchanged a look. Neither

one was about to point out the lack of logic in what His Majesty had just said. David might not fit into his armor, but he could still swing a nasty sword.

"Majesty, a word!" Tirzah cried.

The king turned to face what looked like just another grubby shepherd from the highlands. "Who are you, who let you in here, what do you want, and get out," he said.

Tirzah threw herself facedown on the carpet. "Mighty king, I bring news for your ears alone, words that will destroy the giant at your gates." She did not dare look up until David gave her leave to do so, but she could gauge what was going on when she heard the snap of fingers followed by the sound of two pairs of retreating feet.

"All right, Tirzah," said the king. "You can get up now; they're gone."

She raised her head and stared at him, amazed. "You recognized me?"

"Finally. When I'm not trying to write psalms, I *do* pay attention to you girls." The king wandered over to the wooden stand where his armor-bearers had replaced his helmet, breastplate, and shield before leaving the room. "So, what's on your mind? And why are you dressed like that? Nice sling, by the way."

"Speaking of slings—" Tirzah began, and went on to tell the king her plan. When she was done, he was rendered so stunned that he had to lean against the armor stand for support.

"You're crazy," he gasped. "Insane. You'd never pull it off. I can't allow it. I forbid it."

"Why, Majesty?" she asked. Could it be he loved her?

"Because when you lose and the giant pulls your helmet off—if he doesn't pull your head off with it—everyone will see who you really are. How would that make *me* look? 'King David's such a coward, he has to send a girl to fight his battles for him!' That's just the *start* of what people will say." He slapped the royal shield to emphasize his point.

Tirzah's face hardened. She whipped out Old Wolfbane and dropped something large and hard into the sling. Though she'd had no opportunities to find a proper rock en route to the king's quarters there were plenty of other bits of detritus littering the palace halls. *Whizzz-ZING!* went Old

Wolfbane and *whizzz-CLANG!* went the peach pit some sloppy guardsman had dropped on his lunch break.

It hit the king's shield dead center, lodging itself half an inch deep right between two of David's fingers. His Majesty gaped at the still-vibrating pit, then looked at Tirzah. "Congratulations," he rasped. "You got the job."

King David's armor covered a multitude of sins. No one who saw the small figure that came clanking out of the palace and down to the city gate dreamed that beneath that breastplate were a pair of really impressive breasts, nor that the helmet (with special false beard attachment) concealed a woman's face. Luckily the concubine and her king were more or less of a height. Luckier still, David had never really lost his high tenor voice, a range which overlapped nicely with Tirzah's deep, rich alto.

Tirzah's heart was beating wildly, but not with fear. If truth be told, she found the whole situation incredibly exciting. At her belt she carried her faithful sling and a pouch of stones, specially selected for their perfect balance of killing mass and aerodynamic capabilities. She knew she had the skill to bring the giant down with one shot, and as for the beheading that must follow . . . Well, she'd chop those vertebrae when she came to them.

The Philistine stepped forward at her approach, a spear the size of a weaver's beam in hand. Sunlight glittered on a lavish though ill-tailored set of armor. Just such a helmet had saved Agamemnon's skull at Troy, its heavy nasal and side pieces reducing Goliath's face to a pair of eyes peering through tiny slits and a mass of wild black beard foaming out the bottom.

"At last!" the giant roared, pounding spear against shield. "Come, O king! Come and meet your death!"

"The Lord judge between thee and me who shall live and who shall die!" Tirzah shouted back, loading her sling and gauging her shot. She felt silly spouting such highflown words, but she thought it was something David would say.

The giant made the first move, drawing back one mighty arm, ready to fling the huge spear with all the force of that towering body. For an instant as she stood there, staring with a mix of admiration and alarm at those smooth, muscular arms, that warrior's grace, Tirzah was abruptly aware of the possibility that she might not get out of this combat alive.

The realization froze her where she stood, making her a painfully easy target as the spear took flight, accompanied by the Philistine's great war cry. That thunderous sound proved a blessing in disguise, for it snapped Tirzah out of her perilous trance just as it shook the walls of Jerusalem. But it wasn't the mere volume of that shout which did the trick. As King David would say about psalm-making, *It's not just the music, it's the words.*

The word in this case being: "Whoopsie!"

Whoopsie indeed, for the giant's too-loose mail shirt belled out just enough to divert the spear's course. It flew wild, landing a good ten feet off-target. The Israelites cheered, some for their "king," some for the visible evidence of the Lord's favor, some just to taunt the Philistine.

"Hey, Goliath, you throw like a *girl!*" one wit in the crowd hollered.

"She sure does," Tirzah murmured. The giant's "Whoopsie!" was a sorcerer's eye-opening spell. Now she saw that the Philistine's beard was as bad a fake as her own. To this evidence she added "Goliath's" hairless limbs, the decidedly soprano timbre of her voice in that unguarded moment when the spear misfired, and the fact that no male warrior would cry "Whoopsie" where the more traditional "$*?$#%!" would suffice.

Tirzah wasn't the only one to add two and two. Dawn figuratively broke over Jerusalem.

"That's a woman under all that armor!" someone cried.

"Aye, not Goliath at all!" one of Saul's veterans piped up. He had been the first to swear, loudly and vehemently, that the giant at the gates *was* Goliath, but now that memory somehow eluded him. "I said it from the start. Goliath was much taller, six cubits and a span. She's barely five cubits! But no one ever listens to me."

Meanwhile, curses echoed from within the brazen helmet. "Stupid armor! Stupid beard! Stupid, cheapskate brother! 'Oh, it'll fit you just fine, Asherat!' he says. 'No need to take it to the smithy for a refitting,' he says. 'Just think how good it'll look in the chronicles if you kill David while wearing Dad's old suit of armor,' he says. What a salt-head!"

She reached up and doffed the brass helmet, fake beard

and all. Masses of curly blue-black hair tumbled down her back. Eyes the color of the stormy Middle Sea flashed hatred at the mocking Israelites. Drawing herself up to her full height—which really *was* six cubits and a span, no matter what the blabbermouth veteran claimed—the false Goliath glowered at the phony David and declared: "My name is Asherat of Gath. You killed my father. Prepare to die."

"Bull dung!" shouted one of King David's generals from the safe vantage of the city walls. "You're no Philistine champion; you're a *girl*. The nerve of you, daring to challenge a man to single combat! Well, little missy, we'll soon teach you your proper pla—"

There was a resounding jangle and thud as the ill-fitting armor hit the ground, followed by the sound of a second spear whipping through the air. It lodged itself halfway up the haft in the city battlements just below the mouthy general.

"The next one won't be a warning," said Asherat.

The general peered down over the wall. Gauging where Asherat's spear would have struck him had there been no intervening battlement, the still-vibrating shaft was just this side of obscene. His face turned very red, but he waited until he scampered back into the city before bawling orders for his troops to mass up and sally forth against that unnatural female.

Meanwhile, outside the walls, chaos ruled. Some folks dashed back into the city, more terrified now that they knew the giant warrior was female. Others came streaming out, eager to have a good view of the bloody business when the troops took on Asherat of Gath one-on-fourscore in a fine display of manly courage.

Tirzah looked from the city to the lone woman against whom the full might of the garrison was even then being marshaled. Asherat was out of spears, but had taken up her sword and was bravely awaiting a battle she could never win.

"Son of a *bitch*," said Tirzah, clenching her fists so hard that Old Wolfbane's thongs cut the skin. The unfairness of it all got under her skin like ringworm. Something had to be done. She marched forward to confront the giant.

Asherat hefted her sword, ready for combat, only to behold a wondrous thing. Instead of drawing a blade or swinging that deadly sling, the person she and everyone else still believed to be David stopped a few paces away from her, turned towards Jerusalem, and decreed: "By order of the king, let no man raise any weapon against this woman, upon pain of death! She has my royal protection and is free to go from this place unharmed!"

"Puny worm, I do not seek your charity!" the giant roared down at Tirzah. "Let them come! I will show them how a daughter of the great Goliath dies!"

Tirzah rolled her eyes. She hated stubborn people. "O sweet maiden," she declared, enunciating and projecting every word so that there could be no subsequent doubt among the remaining witnesses as to what she was going to say. "It is not charity that moves me to such speech, but love. Your belly is a heap of wheat, your neck a tower, your breasts are twin does that feed upon the lilies, and you have a very nice personality. Though our peoples be enemies, I would we two were friends. Very *good* friends if you get my drift and I think you do, nudge-nudge, wink-wink. Behold, your bravery has changed my very heart!" Whereat Tirzah sidled just a bit closer to Asherat and pulled the neck of her armor and undertunic out just far enough to give the giant a good, long, indubitable view of what lay beneath.

"Yow!" the Philistine exclaimed. "Those are some big lilies!" While the spectators engaged in a brisk round of *WHAT the Gehennah did she mean by THAT?* comprehension crashed into Asherat's skull with the impact of a pretty big rock. "Uh, what I mean to say is—is— Take me now, you Jewish prince!" She flung her arms wide and fell to her knees before Tirzah. The cheers of the Israelites effectively drowned out the whisper which followed: "I don't know who you really are, lady, but if you can get me out of this mess with a whole skin, you're definitely my new best friend."

In response, Tirzah threw herself dramatically into the giant's embrace, the better to murmur privily in her ear, "Skin, *shmin*. With any luck, we'll both escape with a grubstake big enough to choke Leviathan!"

"I don't need grub; I need new armor," Asherat hissed back. "I was with the Egyptian army until one of my so-called buddies, Hathi the Long-striding, got too chummy. When I gave him the brush-off he wrecked my armor on purpose, while I slept. They call him Hathi the Truncated now. No armor, no job. That's why I went home, hoping my brother would loan me money for a new set. I forgot what a tightfist he is. It was his bright idea for me to challenge David. If I won, I'd reveal myself and the Israelites would pay through the nose to hush up the fact that a woman beat their king and I could buy my own armor. If I lost . . . Well, if I lost, I wouldn't be his problem any more."

"Asherat, you're no one's problem; you're my solution," Tirzah murmured. She pulled herself free of the staged embrace and once more addressed the gawking citizens of Jerusalem. "By my royal command, let a suitable bride-gift of golden ornaments be brought forth from the royal treasury as befits the stature of this woman! Also, much silver. And a picnic lunch. We're going to take a little walk over towards the Mount of Olives to, er, get to know one another better. And anyone who feels like playing Peeping Tobias on us, well, do the words 'pain of death with extreme prejudice' mean anything to you people?"

Apparently so, for it was a good eight hours later, by the palace's imported clepsydra, before the Moabite majordomo informed King David that he was engaged to a giant besides being short several pieces of really good gold jewelry, much silver, a set of armor, a picnic lunch, and one concubine. Fortunately for the concubine in question, David was still too busy trying to finish that pesky psalm to pay heed to his flustered servant. By the time he actually came to care about his losses, Tirzah and Asherat were well and truly out of his royal reach.

"So the Egyptian army hires *women*?" Tirzah asked when they finally paused for lunch.

"Uh-huh. The Hatshepsut Brigade." The giant munched a piece of hummus-laden pita. "We were supposed to be a battlefield diversion, so the regular troops could attack while the enemy was laughing at a bunch of silly girls with swords. Except our slingers never gave anyone the chance to laugh and the rest of us finished the job before the 'real' soldiers got there."

"Slingers?"

"First strike capability slingers are the backbone of the Hatshepsut Brigade. You any good with that thing?" Asherat nodded at Old Wolfbane. "I could put in a word with my sergeant, get you onboard. Good pay, looting privileges, full medical and dental benefits, with a minor out-of-pouch supplement for elective trepanning. Interested?"

Tirzah thought it over. She would be needing a new job eventually; there wasn't much of a market for used concubines and most of the loot they'd gotten from David's treasury would have to pay for a new set of armor.

Two new sets of armor.

Free medical, free dental, a career that depended on her wits instead of her womb, and no sheep? What *wasn't* to like?

"Mom always did say I could do better," she mused. She doodled a sketch of David's face in the dirt, spat an olive pit dead center into the king's brow, and smiled.

Rituals for a New God

Wen Spencer

Madeline was working on her new sculpture, *Struck by God*, when she first sensed the prayer. It spread a disquieting need through her, like hunger. She put down her acetylene torch, peeled off her safety goggles and work gloves to wander out of her barn workshop and into the house.

Her husband looked up from his monitor as she meandered into the kitchen, hand tangled in his hair, tugging absently as he studied manufacturing schematics of his newest patented invention. "What's up?"

"Don't know." She opened the refrigerator, frowned at the contents, closed the door again. "I think I'm going to town."

She went out to her '52 Ford pickup, classic despite the many rust-through patches, parked beside the cinderblocks on which it used to rest. On the first try, the engine groaned as if the battery was dying, but she turned the key again, willing the truck to start. The engine caught, shuddered and settled down to a rough purr.

The prayer was so faint, just a nagging urge to go someplace and perhaps eat, that she could have ignored it if she'd known. It was her first time answering a prayer, though, and thus she didn't recognize it for what it was. So, despite the fact she didn't have any money in her pockets, nor the desire to stand as someone's deity, she went.

As she drove, she pondered her sculpture. What was wrong with it? She had struggled for days now, trying to give form to her inner feelings. She conceived it as a massive gleaming bolt striking a small fragile figure. Somehow it wasn't working; there was no inner identification to the whole or any part of it.

The road, the Ford, and the niggling prayer-borne desire took her south toward Pittsburgh with its sprawling suburbia. Where the farms and stop signs gave way to red lights and custom homes, the burnt offerings snared her tight.

The smoke traced "Please" across her senses. "Protect us" whispered the cooking meat. "Hurry," murmured the spilt wine. She paused overlong at a red light as it turned to green, recognition on her, trying to resist. The blare of the angry horns behind her, and the call of the prayer, turned her off the main road into the maze of artful turns and high priced cul-de-sacs.

When she arrived, however, she wasn't recognized.

She pulled the pickup up to a carefully manicured lawn of a contemporary ranch house. Frost whited the grass to the winter-brown edge. In the asphalt driveway, before his open garage door, a man stood grilling steaks, a bottle of her favorite brandy in hand. He eyed her battered pickup suspiciously.

She turned off the engine, and the old truck rattled and shook before settling down to rest. She sat, listening to the ticking of the cooling engine, wondering what she was doing here. True, she wasn't the most devote Presbyterian. She always viewed organized religions, their rites and rituals, as creations of men, often more interested in controlling their flock than defining God. She believed, though, in the one God, All Mighty, Maker of Heaven and Earth. Believed it to her core. So why was she here? Why was this happening to her?

It occurred to her that perhaps she had caught scent of the grilling meat, followed the smell, and mentally twisted things in some crazed notion that she was summoned. Being crazy certainly was more believable, a natural occurrence which occurred often, and didn't challenge the fabric of reality.

The man glanced in her direction, and poured a dribble of the expensive brandy onto the coals. Flame *woofed* upwards, searing the beef. "Come!" it cried to her, and she was halfway out of the truck before she realized that she was moving.

"Can I help you?" The thirty-something man, worn to premature gray, he seemed caught between embarrassment and wistful hope.

"I felt you calling." She waved a hand toward the grill, the spilt brandy, and the burnt offering. "I think all this is meant for me. Do you need some kind of help?"

"You're one of the new gods?"

She shrugged. "That's what they're calling it."

He took it as a yes. "Really? It worked? Amazing!" He laughed with nervous exhilaration. "Awesome!" He started to hold out his hand, and then checked the motion. "Is it all right to shake hands? It's not sacrilege or anything?"

"No, it's fine." Madeline shook his hand, suddenly conscious of her filthy, patched jeans, unwashed hair, and dirt-smeared face.

"Mac Pierson." He held out the brandy and motioned to the steak. "Do we start with this or do I give it to you later?"

"Let's eat and you can tell me what I'm doing here."

The food gave meaning to the phrase "nectar of the gods." Madeline could barely keep from moaning as Mac Pierson told of his wife falling to a mysterious illness.

"Do you think you can help? I mean, really help? We've tried everything else: X-rays, CAT scans, acupuncture, herbal therapy . . . She's only gotten worse. I figured—I figured it couldn't hurt to try one of you new gods. I sent the kids to school, fired up the grill, and winged the rituals."

And luck of the draw, he had gotten her. "I can try."

He led the way into the house: gleaming wood floors, oriental carpets, Ethan Allen furniture, and the hospital smell of antiseptics. On the living room coffee table, she spotted Pierson's inspiration. "New Gods Walk Among Us" exclaimed the tabloid cover. Always more reserved, the *Time* magazine stated "Mass Miracles or Mass Hysteria?" She had all the same magazines at home, researching her condition, and finding no answers. *Hysteria.* Actually, it would be comforting to believe that was all it was, and nothing more.

"She's in here!" Pierson called from the master bedroom at the end of the hall.

Madeline stopped short at the door.

A creature waited in the master bedroom, something half snake, part cat, part a weird collection of others. Eyes black and cold as onyx marbles regarded Madeline. It sat curled on the chest of an unconscious woman lying in the bed, claws kneading her nightgown-clad breasts.

"My god!" Madeline yelped in surprise. "What's that?"

"This is my wife. Grace."

An oxygen mask shrouded Grace Pierson's face, but did not totally hide her fragile beauty. Even inert, she exuded brilliant warmth. Perhaps Madeline's imagination supplied the impression, wove a complete fabrication from the comfortable elegance of the home and Mac Pierson's devotion to his wife. Perhaps sensing the inherent good in a person was part and parcel of being a god. Regardless of the source, Madeline felt a sudden rage at the injustice.

"Hey! Shoo! Go on!" She tried shooing the creature away like one would scare a cat, with a wave of the arms, and a quick hiss. "Get! Leave her alone!"

The creature flinched, as if her voice pained it, but otherwise sat unmoving. The digital rhythm showing on the heart monitors flickered, and Grace gasped slightly into the oxygen mask. Alarmed, Madeline stepped toward Grace and the creature crouched lower, its spine fur lifting into hackles. It opened its snoutlike mouth, exposing a horde of needle teeth, breath rank as week-old road kill.

Okay, it was braver than she was.

Madeline backed out of the room. A lifetime of farm animals had given her plenty of respect for what a mouthful of teeth like that could do. The next door down was a boy's room, a clutter of sports equipment. The Piersons' son apparently played goalie position on a hockey team: she found a facemask, leg guards and body armor and tugged them on. She picked up a hockey stick, tested its heft, and abandoned it for a baseball bat.

"Um, pardon me, but what are you doing?" Pierson asked.

"I'm not going in there without a weapon and some protection!" Madeline snapped. Maybe she should go out to her truck and get her shotgun.

"A weapon?" He started to edge between her and the

door to the master bedroom. "What do you need a weapon for?"

"You really can't see that?" Madeline pointed at the creature.

Pierson glanced over his shoulder. "What exactly am I suppose to be looking at?"

"Something really ugly." Madeline took a few practice swings with the bat, then steeled herself to step back into the room, bat cocked up over her shoulder. "You're going to have to trust me."

Pierson reluctantly let her pass and then hovered close behind her.

The creature hunched down again, hissing loud as air brakes on a tractor-trailer truck. Madeline inched forward, wanting to make sure her first swing hit. Suddenly the creature sprang, and, yelping in surprise, she swung, fighting the urge to clench shut her eyes. Oak *thunked* into flesh, and through her squinted gaze, she saw the creature fly back across the room to smash into the dresser mirror. The mirror shattered.

"Oh damn!" Madeline cried. "Sorry about that."

"Oh, shit! There *is* something in here!" Pierson bolted away.

The monster scuttled under the bed. Blood seeped through rends in Grace's nightgown and her breath grew fast and light.

"Shit, shit, shit!" Madeline stepped toward Grace, alarmed by the blood and the woman's obvious distress. The creature started growling under the bed; a deep rumble that Madeline could feel in the soles of her feet. The sound, and the sudden image of those teeth locking down on her ankles, checked her. "Okay, get the monster first, then deal with Grace."

Madeline backed up as far as the room allowed and stooped down to peer under the bed. Shadows swallowed the creature and dust bunnies whole. There wasn't even a cat-eye gleam from those cold black eyes. No way she was crawling under the king-sized bed to get it, armor on or not. The bat didn't give her a long enough reach. She considered getting the hockey stick, and then decided even that put her too close to those teeth.

Ideally, she needed a long sharp pole, or a net on a pole, or her head examined.

Pierson came up the hall and stopped just shy of the doorway, armed with the abandoned hockey stick. "I closed all the doors, so it couldn't get into the other rooms—that is if it can't go through wood. Is it still in there? Is Grace okay?"

"It's under the bed. Grace is fine." *For now.* Would her shotgun work? Was this creature like a vampire, where only holy water and sunlight did any harm? Well, the baseball bat connected with it. "Mr. Pierson—Mac, could you do me a favor? Go out to my truck and get my shotgun. The ammo is behind the seat."

She waited with the creature growling and rumbling, wondering yet again: why me? Was this some obtuse, karma-incurred lesson brought on by believing that God didn't concern himself in the day-to-day life of his creations? Was it because the Feng Shui of her house was better than she thought, somehow tapping extraordinary powers and fun-neling it into her? Or was the Wiccan purification ritual her best friend performed on her workshop somehow respon-sible?

Pierson returned, carrying her shotgun gingerly, as if he expected it to go off accidentally. He startled her by ask-ing, "So what do you think?"

"Pardon?"

"Is it a demon?"

"The hell if I know." She loaded the shotgun full, unsure how many shots it would take but certainly not wanting to be caught short once the action started.

"I thought—I thought you would know everything, that it went along with being a god."

"Apparently I'm not that type of god." She didn't actu-ally believe she was any type of god. But if she *was* going to start shooting up this man's house, it would be best if he thought it was holy intervention.

She chambered a shell, warned him to stay back, and mindful of the woman on the bed, got down as low and as close to the bed as she dared.

She had never fired a shotgun inside before. The noise was like a cannon, a deafening bark followed by endless ringing in her ears. In the muzzle flare, she saw that she nearly missed the beast entirely, catching it only in its back haunch. Still, the shot slammed the creature out from under the bed and into the far wall. It left a stain of mucous yellow on the wallpaper when it hit, and then careened madly about the room.

Madeline leapt onto the corner of the bed to get out of the creature's path. It bowled over Pierson in the doorway, clawing him up as it climbed over him, and escaped down the hall. Pierson scrambled in the opposite direction, leaving a smear of blood on the wood floor. His mouth moved, but she could only hear the ghost ringing from the gun's report. Madeline bound into the hall, saw the creature corner into the kitchen, and followed.

It crouched under the kitchen table, hissing. The haunch wound, bleeding like a kid's snot nose, seemed smaller than she initially thought. Chambering a shell, she took careful aim between those black eyes, and fired. The buckshot slammed the creature against the wall. As it went limp, it lost form. Smoke, black as the creature's eyes, roiled upward and then dissipated.

She found Pierson guarding his wife, the baseball bat in hand. Blood slicked the front of his shirt to his chest. "It's dead!" She shouted over the ringing in her ears. Sticking her fingers into her ears, she willed the ringing to stop, and the noise vanished. "Let me look at those cuts."

He gestured helplessly at his wife. "She's dying! She moaned when you fired the second shot and then her heart started fibrillating. Oh, God! Oh, God! Do something!"

Grace Pierson lay deathly still except for her shallow, faltering breathing. Blood seeped from the claw wounds on her chest. Where Madeline touched her, the flesh healed cleanly. Health flooded Grace's ash pale skin, only to drain away again. The monitor showed only a momentary slowing of the frantic pulse. Mac knelt beside the bed, clutched his wife's hand, and whispered a soft mantra of "Oh please, oh please."

Madeline clung to Grace's other cold hand, willing her to live. *Why wasn't it working?* Irony struck her, and she fought the sudden desire to laugh. Deny it all she wanted, but she believed in herself. She didn't know why her, and she certainly did not rate her powers equal to God, the Father, but she *knew* that she had the power to heal Grace. The smooth skin of Grace's breast stood testament that her powers worked. All the health that she willed into Grace, though, continued to sieve away.

"Why is she losing everything I give her?"

Pierson glanced about the room. "Is the monster back?"

Madeline opened her mouth to say she had killed it, and stopped. What if dissipating the creature hadn't killed it? Every time she had damaged the creature, Grace had worsened. What if it had been healing itself with Grace's vitality? If she hadn't killed it, it could still be feeding on Grace.

But if it no longer had a form, how could she stop it? Perhaps there was a physical link between woman and monster she could break.

She ran her hands over Grace's slender arms, searched her glossy black hair, and pulled down the blankets. Sticky, fibrous black strands wove like grapevines through Grace's toes, wrapped about her foot, and crawled up her right leg to midcalf.

"Oh, ick!" She tried using the corner of the blanket to scrub away the strands without touching them directly. Skin and muscle shifted under the cloth, giving no hint the strands actually existed. "Christ on a donkey." She muttered as she realized that she actually had to touch the growth with her bare hands. "Could you get me a bucket or something to put this stuff in?"

Pierson looked mystified but scurried off without a question. She stripped off the hockey equipment. He returned with a galvanized steel bucket in hand. This was going to be so creepy. Thoughts of the stuff growing on *her* already had her skin crawling and, as the last places she wanted to touch with contaminated hands, her eyes and nose itching.

The strands felt like cords of thick, damp, greasy snot. As she pried them off, it seemed that they thrummed with deep anger. Tiny hairs bristled the ends, and occasionally a longer hair thinned to spider-silk fine and trailed off toward the kitchen. After great inner debate, she snapped these off short. All the while, she willed Grace to be better, that the creature would find no refuge in the house, that everything would be good and right. With a sound like ice quick-chilling a glass, the mirror knit itself whole again.

They burned the strands on the grill, which Mac promised to take to the dump once the ashes cooled. Madeline scrubbed her hands with bleach and ammonia before feeling clean again.

Grace Pierson, who had lain like the dead during the whole struggle for her life and possibly her soul, woke when Madeline shook her shoulder. Like a butterfly, she struggled out of her cocoon of oxygen tubes, IV drips, electrode lead wires, and catheter, slipped into a bright dress, and fluttered about the room, laughing over how good she felt.

"Thank you," Grace lighted briefly in a warm hug, smelling of sunshine and clean sky. "I don't know how you did it, but thank you."

Mac Pierson followed Madeline out into the kitchen, with awe in his eyes. "You're really a god!"

Madeline collected her shotgun from the kitchen table. "I guess so. I wasn't like this before."

"What was it like?" He asked. "Did you just wake up one morning, changed, or did it hit you, like lightning?"

Madeline shrugged, thoughtfully unloading her shotgun. Once she considered it, quiet miracles filled her life. "Things have always had weird ways of working out. Like once I was downsized from a machinist job. I spent a week without sleep to finish all my works in progress, and then found an upscale art gallery that would give me space. Only, the owner copied down the prices wrong, and sold them all for a hundred times more than what I wanted."

He didn't see the magic of it, so she said that it was like being hit by lightning.

The late-winter frost was gone from the yard. Green buds of spring flowers dimpled the flowerbeds. The rust was all gone from the front right fender of her Ford. She supposed it was difficult to compare those old mundane miracles to these new ones.

Starting the Ford's engine, though, she remembered how, just a day after telling her husband how she always wanted a classic old pickup truck, they found it rusting away in the yard of their dream home. Two for one, her husband quipped, surely a sign that they controlled the universe. What if there lay a germ of truth in that joke? What if the simple answer to "why her" was because she believed in herself? Like a Buddhist finding nirvana, had she simply found a new level of self-empowerment?

Wen Spencer

On the heels of this thought, came the solution to her sculpture, *Struck by God*. She should invert the piece. Instead of gold, the bolt would now be a wedge of graduated blue, like the layers of water of a deep clear lake. At the apex would be a gleaming figure. She had broken the surface of the ordinary world, and crawled out of the lake to stand on an unfamiliar shore. And if the newspapers read true, there were others gathering there with her.

I Look Good

Selina Rosen

The seeds of rebellion were planted on the morning I woke
up leaning against a tree covered in cold dew, with my left
nipple screaming in pain.

I had fallen asleep at my post, and why not? I hadn't
had a decent night's sleep in weeks. I straightened up quickly
and pulled at the chain mail till my nipple was free.

That's all a damn chain mail bra is good for. If you don't
believe it, look at my poor body.

As armor goes, a chain mail bra and loincloth doesn't offer
much protection. See, very few fighters actually aim for your
boobs or your crotch. They're way too busy swinging at the
more obvious targets—like your head and your bare arms,
stomach and thighs. In fact, you might as well paint the
uncovered parts with bull's-eyes and be done with it.

I guess it happened for me the way it happens for so many
other young people who wind up in the employ of an evil
sorcerer. You're just standing around your village one day
wondering if the turnip crop is going to be a good one, and
in ride the evil sorcerer's minions looking for recruits. If you
still have all your teeth and look good, you're in. If you
can hold a sword without tripping over it and ride a horse,
you move right up the ranks.

Now I know what you're thinking. Why would anyone willingly join the minions of an evil sorcerer? And yet, you show me an evil sorcerer, and I'll show you hundreds of loyal minions, all willing to throw themselves on pikes to save the wizened old creep.

The answer is as old as time itself. It's all about the money. You see, evil guys have no morals or ethics, and so they have buckets, caves, castles, dungeons full of ill-gotten treasure. Even the most lowly evil sorcerer's minion will earn more in a week than a turnip-grubbing wretch can make in a year, and that's if the crop comes in good. Evil sorcerers aren't stupid; they know not all things can be bought. However, loyalty isn't always one of those things.

Most evil sorcerers throw in great health benefits—as many of them have the power to heal you—and a retirement package to die for, not to mention overtime and hazard pay. The recruiters promised we'd see strange lands, and meet exciting new people, then plunder the land and kill the people and take everything for ourselves.

It was a deal that would be hard for any starry-eyed youth who dreamed of a better life to walk away from.

Of course, the big deal maker for me had been the uniform. At twenty I had looked amazing in my armor—the long, flowing, blood-red cloak that was the uniform worn by the minions of Ikious the Terrible. The armor had shown off my well-defined body. The color of the cloak had complemented my dark hair and eyes. The gold-handled long sword I wore strapped to my side set off my bronze skin, and *damn* I looked good!

I had risen up the ranks quickly till I had the job of Ikious' captain of the guards—his personal protector. I'd held the post for many years and served him well. For the most part it had been a great job. I pretty much just stood around wherever he was, looking menacing and sexy, as he worked his evil magic spells and made his evil potions. Occasionally he'd hold court of sorts. Some paladin or other white knight type would be drug before him as he sat on his throne of human skulls. I'd stand to his right side with my hand on my sword hilt and just the right combination of snarl and smile on my lips as my employer would "question" the good guy. Then when he'd gotten all he could from him sometimes he'd even let me cut the guy's head off.

Yes, those had been high times. But then I had looked good in the outfit, and at thirty-eight I wasn't so hot in it any more. My once flawless body was now a testament to the ineffectiveness of the armor we warrior-type minions wore. With age I had developed a bit of a paunch, and from wearing heavy metal as my only support, my breasts now hung almost to the top of my belt which—if I was looking on the bright side—at least afforded a little more protection for my stomach, but looked sort of like two cannon balls fighting over the same space when I walked. In fact, I often joked that if I could learn to maneuver them correctly without bouncing them into one another, that I could probably successfully knock out two opponents at once.

I had started moving slower in the last few years because my joints often ached. No doubt from years spent freezing my nether regions off. See, though an all-enveloping cloak should afford a certain amount of warmth, it isn't worth what a horse leaves behind him when you're wearing nothing underneath but cold metal and it's snowing and the wind's blowing. In fact, I've often said I'd be better off naked.

Which is exactly how I felt on that morning when I woke in pain, frozen to the bone from the all-night vigil I had been ordered to keep while the evil sorcerer Ikious the Terrible and my replacement slept warmly in his tent.

Some of the other girls had suggested that I was just jealous, and I admit I was mad as hell about losing my position to some young upstart. But I was in no way jealous of her relationship with Ikious. I slept with him because it was part of the job, not because it was particularly enjoyable.

Let's face it, evil guys are selfish in bed.

She had gotten my job. A job I'd done well and loyally for many years. It wasn't my fault I didn't look as good or move as well. It was all the fault of the uniform. A uniform that Ikious had hand-picked.

On that morning as I stood in the woods with my flesh nearly blue, my knees barely functioning, and my nipple throbbing, I decided I was sick of that damn uniform.

❖　　❖　　❖

We were on a quest for the Great All-knowing Cumquat, a fruit that when you ate it was supposed to give you the Knowledge of All Things.

Evil sorcerers are always going on quests for things to make them even more powerful. No doubt so their under-clothed, under-armored minions can risk their lives and frostbite trying to find them.

We were close to the cave entrance. The cave wherein we would supposedly find the tree which bore fruit only on the twelfth day, of the twelfth month, of the one hundred and twelfth year, at the exact moment that the moon hit its zenith. When the correct incantation was spoken, the one and only Great All-knowing Cumquat would start to glow, and at that moment it had to be picked and shortly after consumed or the power would be lost forever.

I don't make the rules.

I stayed loyally at my post till Ikious strolled from his tent and stated that we were by his calculations half a day away from the mouth of the cave. Further, he said that even when we had fought all the creatures guarding the tree we should have plenty of time to retrieve the Cumquat and for him to become even more powerful, which would mean hazard pay and bonuses for all of us. We all cheered of course, though I have to admit myself less than enthusiastically.

For some reason any sorcerer, evil or otherwise, always finds it necessary when going on a quest to cut it to the very last minute. That's one of the downsides to working for an evil sorcerer. When they fail and lose a magic item they want very badly, they get really testy and kill from one to ten minions. Up till this time I'd been among the not-to-be-fragged minions, but I wasn't any more. That, as much as the fact that marching fast kept me warmer, had moved me to the front of the ranks. See, if Ikious saw me kicking a little creature gluteus maximus, he might just decide I didn't deserve fragging.

So I was in the very front when we ran upon the huge troll guarding the entryway to the cave. He slung an enormous war hammer at me that I easily jumped away from, but which crushed the warrior standing to my left. That was the thing Ikious had forgotten; you didn't get to be an *old* minion unless you were also a *smart* minion.

With the troll's weapon temporarily held in a suction to the ground by warrior goo, I jumped up and planted my sword easily in his heart. Then I jumped out of the way before he could fall on me. I was thinking I had just successfully moved back into the not-to-be-fragged pile, when much to my dismay, the bastard toppled over backwards— successfully blocking the cave entrance.

Ikious walked up to me, his face a mask of anger, and yelled, "Oh, great going, Helgar! Now I'll have to waste a Move the Giant Troll spell."

"We could move him, Master," I suggested. After all, he was just a troll, not a giant or a cyclops. I just didn't get why he was making such a big deal, and I was thinking that I was definitely in the to-be-fragged pile if we didn't get him that damn Cumquat now.

"We could move him, Master," Ikious mocked me, and then with a simple whispered word the troll flew out of the opening. "Why don't you go first, Helgar?" he suggested.

Which of course meant I had just been relegated to the position of cannon fodder. I walked into the cave, and the other minions followed. Ikious did a light spell to guide us— which in my opinion was more or less a way to let anything that was supposed to be keeping us out know that we were coming.

I always wondered why he didn't try something like a Make Everyone See In the Dark spell. Makes more sense to me. It would be a damn sight more stealthy.

We walked for a long time without running into anything, which made me believe that either Ikious' calculations were incorrect, and we had turned the wrong way three or four turns back, or we were getting ready to run into something incredibly nasty.

Enter the medium-sized, three-headed weasel.

Now I know it doesn't sound all that terrifying, but I assure you this was one deadly beast. A third of the minions lay dead before the last of the weasel heads had been severed. I had yet another cut on my stomach, which was no doubt going to leave a scar, and Ikious was bitching that we had wasted too much time. It was then that I charged on ahead even faster than I had before, forcing the minions and Ikious to either keep up or be left behind. Turns out I ran right by the herd of small but very poisonous spiders which fell upon the group of minions just behind me. Instead of turning around to help them fight them, I just moved further ahead of the group. I heard Ikious spout an incantation to dispatch the spiders. I don't think he even noticed then that I had left them behind. He might have even figured I was dead. I increased my pace even more.

Now here's something to think about. Why would a god or sorcerer—or anyone else who makes magic crap—create something so dangerous that you have to hide it and put creatures to guard it to keep it from falling into the wrong hands? And if you did it accidentally, why wouldn't you then destroy it? And if you couldn't destroy it, why not blow up the entire cave you put it into? I don't care how determined you are, you aren't going to pick through thousands of feet of rock. Even hundreds of loyal minions aren't going to be able to move ten miles of rubble.

I could feel it. The moon was rising; we were running out of time. You see, in all those years I had worked close to Ikious I had listened carefully to everything he'd ever said. I'd slowly, carefully, learned every spell in his book, every incantation. Looks fade, your health fails you. You can't be a warrior minion of an evil sorcerer your whole life. Eventually you have to find something that isn't so physical.

I ran into the main room of the cave, and there it was— the tree of the Great All-knowing Cumquat—and between it and me a moat of bubbling acid.

No problem.

Ikious and his few remaining minions skidded to a halt on the other side of the moat of acid.

"Helgar . . . how?" Ikious asked, looking at me across the acid and then at the tree behind me.

"Simple," I said with a shrug and held the glowing fruit up in front of me. "I walked across." I waved my hand dismissively in front of me, and the moat of acid seemed to disappear.

"Helgar . . . give me that fruit, and . . ." The moat was still there; it was just a simple glamour. Ikious and his new captain of the guard fell right in.

See, it's a well-known fact that when evil sorcerers are faced with losing a magic item they want really badly, they go temporarily insane. If he had been up to his full game, he never would have fallen for such a simple trick.

I looked at the minions who stood staring in disbelief as Ikious melted in the acid, and I ate the Great All-knowing Cumquat.

It was actually very disappointing. See, it would have more accurately been titled the Cumquat of the Knowledge of How to Cure Ailments of the Foot. Why the god or sorcerer or other thing that creates such items had thought it necessary to hide it so well and put all the creatures there to guard it, I have no idea.

Maybe it was all an elaborate joke. Whatever the case, I found no need to tell the remaining minions. I let them all go with severance pay.

So, now I'm in the evil sorceress business, with my own scantily clad minions of well-built men. But when we go on quests to get great evil stuff, I let them dress warmer, in the hopes of keeping their loyalty.

These days I wear long, flowing, loosely-fitting, luxurious robes of purple and blue velvet. I'm warm and comfortable, and *damn*, I look good.

Combat Shopping

Lee Martindale

Horatia waited until the battle was over before trying to dismember the mage.

That she was a professional accounted for a portion of her patience. That she was a trifle busy staying alive accounted for the rest. That the spell which dissolved her armor into a heap of unrecoverable slag around her ankles had come from the hand of a mage *supposedly* on Horatia's side of the conflict accounted for the warrior's less-than-collegial attitude.

Horatia had been dubbed "the Heroic" as much for her impressive dimensions as for her considerable prowess in battle. One look at those heroic, near-naked proportions moving toward her with deadly intent was enough to send the dainty mage scrambling up the nearest hairy, sweat-drenched warrior. Asaria made it to his shoulders and was seeking purchase on his head when Horatia peeled her off. Asaria managed one unladylike squawk before a sword-hardened hand closed around her throat and the arm to which it was attached held her eye-to-eye-level with the considerably taller battle-maid.

As her comrades alternated between laughing at the situation and admiring portions of the warrior they didn't

157

normally see, Horatia glared. Then she growled, "Give me one reason, *bann seighe* bait, why I shouldn't scatter little bits of you from here to the borders of Keldaough."

The dangling mage opened her mouth to speak—whether spell or supplication is not known. But speech requires breath and taking one proved to be problematic. Next she balled delicate hands into delicate fists and beat an equally delicate—and ineffectual—tattoo against the arm that held her. She was starting to go limp, her usually ruby lips turning an unflattering shade of blue, when the company's commander arrived and bellowed at Horatia to "put that spellcaster down this minute!" Horatia blinked, came to attention, opened her hand and complied.

An hour later Horatia arrived at the commander's tent, wearing tunic and breeches and the wary demeanor of a mouse suddenly deposited into a loft full of cats. Asaria arrived shortly thereafter, moving stiffly from the bruises to the underpadded portion of her anatomy on which she'd landed. Both declined the seats offered by the commander.

"Then let us get right to the matter. As I understand it, the attempt by Horatia the Heroic to throttle Asaria Katri a short while ago was precipitated by the destruction of the former's armor by a misfired spell from the hand of the latter. Is that the way of it?"

"Aye, sir," Horatia answered, glaring at the other woman.

"I'm not sure what you mean by 'misfire,' Commander," Asaria began, her usually sweet voice hoarse and with an upper-register harmonic that made the others wince, "but I can assure you that no ill will was intended. These things happen occasionally; my apprentice has been chastised for his error in calculation. And now that we have that cleared up . . ."

"Not so fast, madam," the commander barked. He glanced at Horatia with a look clearly meant to nail her in place, then turned back toward the mage. "The cause may be identified, but the effects still remain to be put right. To a warrior, armor is as necessary a tool of the trade as sword or pike or war hammer. Deprive one of my best warriors of her armor, and you deprive *me* of one of my best warriors . . . a situation to which I don't take kindly. Therefore, it is my order that you, Asaria Katri, will make generous restitution to Horatia the Heroic, in an amount sufficient to replace what has been destroyed with as good or better than she had." Asaria began to sputter, but the commander ignored it as he continued, "Plus an amount sufficient to serve as recompense for the time she'll have to take to find that armor or have it made, and the time spent away from my army. All told . . . I'm thinking a sum of two thousand gold pieces to be a fair one."

"Two *thousand* . . . ?" the mage's protest came in a voice that was entirely within that annoying upper register.

"Make that three thousand," the commander cut in, "and more if you continue to ignore the value of swift compliance."

Asaria's normally beautiful face twisted into an unflattering mask of rage, but in the end, under the commander's cool gaze and Horatia's hot glare, she signaled her begrudging acceptance of the order. The commander turned to Horatia. "And what say you?"

"Begging the commander's pardon, would that be real earth-drawn gold or spell-spun stuff?"

Asaria started sputtering again and appeared to be at the very beginning of an impressive round of hysterics. The commander cut her off. "Real gold. Four thousand, Asaria?" The mage took a deep, obviously painful, breath and nodded.

"Very well. You will deliver three thousand pieces of non-magical gold to Horatia at first light, along with your personal and *sincere* apologies. This matter is concluded."

"And what of her attack on me?" Asaria fairly screamed. "What punishment do you give for her laying rough hands on me, for trying to kill me?"

The commander raised one eyebrow and looked sternly at Horatia. "She has a point. You are fined one copper piece for losing your temper."

Riding into Forgecroft was like entering the afterlife awarded heroes in the tales on which Horatia had been raised. From all directions came the delicate music of small hammers working chain, the flat chime of larger hammers working plate. Everywhere she looked, she saw the spark and glow of the metalworkers' forges and the glint of sunlight off the finished products of the armorer's art. The smile that came to the warrior's lips was one of joy and anticipation.

The commander had given her the name of an inn he

favored, along with directions, and in very short order she was installed in one of the private rooms above it. A word with the innkeeper made arrangements for her evening meal, and then it was off to the first name on her list.

AMBYRCRYFFYE Y FYRCCHE, the sign proclaimed, PURVEYOR OF FINE ARMOR SINCE THE THIRD YEAR OF THE REIGN OF KING CRYDDWHELAN THE MANLY. Whomever and whenever that might have been. But it was, indeed, fine, if the vastness of the space and the quality of the wares on display were any indication. Row after row of spangenhelms, spaulders, chausses and besagues, gorgets and gauntlets and greaves, polished to a mirror's sheen or covered with intricate engraved decoration. Rack upon rack of mail shirts and coifs and bishop's collars, supple as linen and dense enough to turn the thinnest bladepoint.

A polite cough behind her caught Horatia's attention, and she heard a voice say, "Good day to you, my lord, and welcome. May we be of assistance?"

"Yes, indeed," she replied as she began to turn, "I'm looking . . ."

The man blinked and looked flustered when presented with unmistakable evidence of his misidentification of Horatia's gender. But he quickly recovered. "My humble apologies, my lady. How may we serve?"

"I understand you're the best armorer in town."

The salesman beamed. "Indeed so, my lady. Voted so in the *Forgecroft Observer* five years' running. May I say you've come to the right place for a gift for your noble spouse."

"I'm not married."

"For your handsome betrothed then."

"Don't have one of those either."

"Then it's your brother being so honored?"

"I probably have a few running about, but so far, none have made themselves known to me."

The man was reaching the end of both experience and imagination. Then a thought crossed his mind and he smiled solicitously. "Of course. A tribute of fine armor from a dutiful daughter to her beloved father."

Horatia barked a laugh. "That would assume I knew who he was. No, the armor I'm looking for is for me."

The man's face went the color of milk from which the cream had been skimmed. From his mouth, which had dropped open, came a short series of unintelligible sounds, and his eyes, holding an unreadable mixture of expressions, had returned to Horatia's impressive bosom. "But . . . you're . . . you're . . . female!"

"I thought we'd already established that. So can you help me or not?"

"My lady, I am so terribly sorry, but we cannot. *Ambyr-cryffye y Fyrcche* is an armorer of *gentlemen*."

Horatia pointed to a large yet tasteful sign on one wall of the shop. "It says right there, and on one out front, that you specialize in custom work. I assure you I can pay for it."

"Indeed we do," came the reply, "and I'm sure you can, but . . ." There was a pause as he cast through his mind for an acceptable comeback. The patent smile returned, and he continued smoothly. "None of our designs and patterns would take into account your . . . huh . . . unique dimensional challenges." He seemed rather pleased with his delicate turn of phrase. He seemed even more pleased when another idea struck him. In short order, Horatia had been given the name and location of someone who worked exclusively in "designs for women."

Horatia double-checked the address she'd been given; *Feddoricce GroveHoly's* looked like many things, but an armorer wasn't one of them. And the "armor" on display in front of the shop looked like nothing the warrior had ever seen on the battlefield, in either configuration or color.

Take the item identified as a "breastplate," an intricate interspiraling of what appeared to be hammered gold and silver, displaying fine craftsmanship and an engineer's eye for cantilevering. But it was plate armor by only the thinnest definition of the term and left more of the titular anatomy exposed than it protected. The idea of having anyone see her in it made Horatia blush; the thought of facing a bare blade with nothing but it between the blade and her was one she put aside quickly.

On the other side of the entrance was something that covered a great deal more of the torso and was made of leather, although she knew of no natural animal that courted predatory attention with a pelt of such a color. It also appeared to be so small in the waist that one would be hard-pressed to breathe in it, much less fight. As to the functionality of the four dangling straps at the bottom, she had not a clue.

She was examining a bit of mail—two bits, actually, tiny triangles of iridescent links strung on a thin chain—when a female voice behind her said, "That doesn't come in your size." At first glance, Horatia wondered where the woman who had spoken was hiding. The person she'd turned to face looked like an undernourished preadolescent boy, although why a boy would be wearing a spirally breastplate and a microscopic breechclout that matched the mail in her hands, she couldn't guess.

She wasn't given time to try; the hanger was plucked out of her hands and returned to the rack as the woman said, "Actually, you'll find *nothing* here in your size. Our artisans design for an elite clientele and," she looked Horatia up and down, pursed her lips and snorted derisively, "that clientele does *not* include *oversized* women."

"Over *whose* size?" Horatia queried as she returned the up-and-down appraisal with a raised eyebrow. "From the looks of it, your artisans don't design for women at all. And they sure don't design armor, which is what I'm looking for. Any suggestions?"

Horatia next found herself looking at full-length wall-portraits of willowy maidens and signs announcing BREAST-BINDINGS SALE! BUY TWO, GET THE THIRD FREE! and wondering if she'd misremembered the street address. Then she spotted another sign that read, ON YOUR WAY TO YOUR IDEAL SIZE? WEAR LLAENE BRIANT ON YOUR WAY DOWN!. And the saleswoman approaching her was considerably more substantial than the women in the portraits. This must be the place.

"Right this way," the woman replied brightly when Horatia told her what she was looking for. Horatia began to feel hope. It didn't last long.

Oh, there was plenty of armor there, neat piles of mail shirts, rows of breastplates, stacks of greaves, and racks of helmets. And every single one of them had been painted black, dark brown or olive. It was, to Horatia's eye, decidedly drab, and so odd that she asked the woman about it.

"Isn't it wonderful?" came the bubbly reply. "Dark colors are *so* slimming, don't you think? A *Llaene Briant* exclusive, guaranteed to take twenty pounds off your appearance."

And add twenty gold pieces to the price, Horatia retorted
mentally, *not to mention making it nearly impossible to tell
anything about the metal and workmanship involved.* But
this was, so far, the closest she'd come to finding what she
needed. Which brought her nosefirst into the next obstacle:
the question of sizes.

"Another exclusive," the saleswoman informed her brightly.
"Our sizing charts are formulated to promote self-esteem
among our customers. For example, a woman who wears
Forgecroft Standard 16 is a Size 8 here. And no nasty
numbers like 20 or 22; we have 1X. All the way up," and
here she almost squealed in delight, "to *3X!*"

Having determined that she had absolutely no idea what
size she took in either system, Horatia submitted herself to
the saleswoman's measuring string. Her patience, already
weakened, slipped even further as the woman commented
on each measurement she took, first with clucking noises,
then with a running commentary about the Wizard Sim-
monius and how his Diminishing Spells would work wonders on the warrior's "overplump" physique. "Overplump
for what?" snapped Horatia.

After much tag-looking and stock-shuffling, Horatia was
handed a mail shirt to try on. The shirt's tail had barely
settled around her ankles when the saleswoman trilled,
"Ooooh, that looks *wonderful* on you!" For Horatia, it was
the last straw.

"Were you born a twit or was it something for which you
had to study? What this looks like is something proportioned
for someone at least eight hands taller than me with no
bosom and even less muscle. It's so narrow in the shoulders that raising my sword arm will cut off the circulation
to my head. That is, if the shabby materials and shoddy
workmanship don't part like a bargirl's virtue. Don't you
have any pride in what you offer for sale?"

"I don't know how it is in whatever barbarous land from
which you come, but around here, we big girls have to settle
for what we can get. We should feel lucky there's anything
at all like this in our sizes."

"Where I come from," Horatia said as she peeled chain
mail over her head, "we *big girls* are called *women*, and
the only *luck* involving this trash would be in it not getting me killed."

✧　　✧　　✧

So it was that the evening found Horatia in the common room of her lodgings, nursing a tankard of ale and a bad attitude. The innkeeper's hearty dinner and commiserations over her plight had had some restorative effects, but she was still thoroughly disgusted, not to mention frustrated, angry and tired, more or less in that order. And a disgusted Horatia the Heroic, not to mention one who was frustrated, angry and tired, more or less in that order, was not a woman to be approached with trivial matters. The one lothario to do so had been shown the error of his ways in devastatingly short order, and the rest had, apparently, taken notes.

Or perhaps not. "Mind if I join you?" asked a deep baritone voice as two tankards slid onto the table.

Horatia looked around and drew breath to say, "Yes, I do mind. Move along." And was stopped by the merriest blue eyes she'd ever seen. That they were even with her own caused her to refocus and look again. Horatia had heard of people born normal-sized from the waist up and small from the waist down, but until now she'd never seen one.

"I'm Siorce. And I think I may be the solution to the problem the innkeep tells me you have. Your next ale is on me while I tell you how."

Siorce Halfleg claimed to be an armorer, a claim that Horatia could almost believe. The calloused hands, the muscles in the arms and shoulders, the heat-creased face were, indeed, those of someone who worked with fire and forge. And the story he told wasn't all that farfetched, either.

Born the only son of a crafter of armor and arms, Siorce's father had decided to teach him the trade despite his "deformity." He'd been well into his training, the equivalent of guild-standard journeyman, when slavers had taken him far from his homeland and sold him as a novelty to a nobleman's retinue. By the time that nobleman had visited Forgecroft, the novelty had worn off, and Siorce was sold again, this time to a blacksmith and farrier who put his background to limited use. With that master's death had come his freedom, the shop and a decent living. But not the one thing he wanted: the right to call himself a Master Armorer and ply the trade to which his father had trained him.

"For that," Siorce continued, "I need a thousand gold for

the fee and a project so unique, so innovative, that *not* considering it a masterwork would be unthinkable. And you, madam warrior, are that project."

The next morning, Horatia moved out of the inn and into a tiny but comfortable room behind Siorce's shop. The armorer wanted her available for fittings and adjustments and offered her room and meals in exchange. And avail he did, frequently and at all hours that he worked, which was— during the next two and a half weeks—closely akin to all hours.

Not that Horatia really minded. Siorce's wife, a pleasant and intelligent young woman who was nearly as deft a hand at knitting mail as her husband, set a fine table. And the pleasure of watching Siorce measure, mold, fit, adjust, tweak and otherwise sculpt each piece was well worth being nudged out of bed, however frequently.

So it was that on a morning not quite three weeks from her arrival in Forgecroft, Horatia the Heroic went before the Guild Elders wearing armor worthy of her name, armor that fit her like a second skin and felt as strong as dragonscale of legend. Armor that added to the impact of her leaning over the High Table and asking, in a deceptively quiet voice, what *exactly* it was about the work of Siorce Halfleg that made it ineligible for consideration for Master status. Armor that stood up to the subsequent and remarkably rigorous inspection.

And so it was that Horatia rode out of Forgecroft the following morning with a purse considerably—and voluntarily— lightened and a head hosting a hangover worthy of the celebration she'd enjoyed the night before. Siorce and his wife had been insistent that she owed them no more than the thousand gold pieces paid as fee to the Guild. Only sweet reason—and the steady application of equal parts peatliquor and good-natured threats—had convinced them to take an additional fifteen hundred. As far as Horatia was concerned, she'd gotten the far better of the deal.

One other thing did Horatia carry: a promise to herself and the gods of what would happen to Asaria should anything happen to *this* armor.

Battle Ready

J. Ardian Lee

Guard duty. It was just past sunset, and the edge was gone from the heat of the day, leaving the warm scents of live oak, grasses and earth. Private Deal stood at her post, a sharp ear turned not to the perimeter but rather toward the bivouac tents. The moon laid silver across the landscape, but here among the trees was near complete darkness. Her pulse thudded, for she knew the plan was risky. Here in the heart of Texas, Daryl Deal was flirting with danger.

Finally there was a tiny sound of rustling leaves behind her, and she turned. It was Peter, his shadow distinct among the trees. "Where have you been? You told me 2130 hours." She ran her hands over the sergeant's breast pockets as he held her by the waist and guided her to a spot between two trees. They were already out of sight of the rest of their unit, but it was good to have more line-of-sight obstacles. They leaned their rifles against a thick, gnarled oak, dark shapes against the shadowed tree.

"Sorry, unavoidable," was all he said, then she found his mouth with hers and kissed him with all she had.

"Oh, Peter." There was little time to waste. The watch would change soon and some other soldier would expect to occupy this spot. Peter was very late. Daryl's fingers went to unbutton his shirt. His went to the buttons of her fatigue shirt. Maintaining lip-lock was probably not the most time-effective strategy for clothing removal, but she couldn't bear to let go. They sank to the thick, dry grass at the foot of the tree. He pressed himself to her, hard. Well-named, he was, yes indeed. A low moan rose to the back of her throat.

Her fatigue shirt open, Peter slipped his hand under her skivvy shirt to reach the clasp of her bra. She waited for it to snap open.

And waited.

"Dang," he said as he tugged. Her torso twisted and air heaved from her with each pull. "How does this thing release?"

"It's a little complicated. Push down at the left, twist, and then . . ."

He grunted, then rolled her over a bit so he could untuck both shirts and see. "What in the world . . . ?"

Peter drew up the shirts to expose the bra cups underneath. "What *is* this?"

Her chin pressed to the wad of cotton he held as she tried to see. "They issued it yesterday. They called it a 'battle bra.' It's supposed to be a specially designed bra just for the army."

"I thought that was a Canadian thing." He picked around the edges of the cup.

She shook her head. "I think ours are a little different." She knocked her knuckles against the olive drab cup and it gave a hard thud of cotton over metal. "I mean, that's steel under there."

Peter knocked on her breast, too. "Oh. I thought that was you. Lemme see this thing." He picked at the edges of the cotton-upholstered support device, then squeezed the cup. "No wonder they're huge." He poked the embroidered rose between her breasts.

"Don't—"

There was a click, and a hiss as smoke shot from under Daryl's armpits. They waved and coughed, but soon they were surrounded by an oily mist. "Smoke screen," she gagged, trying not to cough too loudly.

He choked, "Sounds perfectly useful if you can get the bra off to leave it behind. Whose bright idea was this?"

"Well, you know the Pentagon." The smoke drifted around

them, and Daryl hoped nobody in camp would smell it. With any luck, everyone but the other guards would be asleep by now.

As the smoke cleared, Peter sighed and slipped his arms around her again. "Do you think it's shot its wad now?" The smile returned to his voice, and he settled his hips against hers. Dead leaves crunched beneath them and a clump of grass pressed against her back.

"I hope so." She leaned up on an elbow and pressed her mouth to his, sucking on his lower lip. Forget the bra, she wanted out of her pants, and him out of his. With deft fingers she unbuckled his belt and pulled open his fly.

But apparently Peter saw a challenge and rose to it. His hand went beneath her shirt again to the bra clasp. "Roll over and let me get this thing undone." She obliged and turned onto her side to let him fiddle with the clasp. He grunted and tugged and twisted and yanked, and with the final yank there was another click.

"Yikes!" Flame shot out the tip of each cup and sent up the grass in front of her. Peter jerked back his hand, and it stopped. They both whipped their shirts off to smother the burning grass, and quickly stopped the fire from spreading.

Once safe again, they sat back to catch their wind. "That was close," she panted. Small, round charred spots now graced the tips of each breast.

"That was . . . weird." Nevertheless, as he watched her chest heave, the light of lust returned to his eyes. He crawled to her and onto her, and eased her back onto the grass with a tongue deep in her mouth. He pressed himself against her, hard, and reached for her belt. She spread her knees so he could settle between her thighs, and once the belt and zipper were loose he slipped his hand down the back of her pants to ease them off. When he looked down at her chest again, a cheerful smile lit his face. "Oh, here. The clasp is in front." As he spoke he reached for her bra again.

"NO!"

Another click, and a calm woman's voice emanated from the steel undergarment. "Warning. This unit's self-destruct sequence has been activated. You have thirty seconds to enter the abort code. Warning . . ."

Peter uttered an incoherent noise, and Daryl plundered

her brain for the code. "Left, no, right strap, center, left strap, right strap, left." As she spoke, she touched the pressure pads in each spot. The voice then stopped.

The sergeant, face pale, stood to button his shirt, tuck it in, and secure his fly and belt. "I think I'd better get out of here before the next watch comes."

"Peter . . ."

"Gotta go." He then picked up his rifle and disappeared into the darkness.

Daryl sighed and restored her clothing. Her shirt had a hole burned in it, which she would have to explain to the lieutenant in the morning. She sighed again, adjusted her bra straps, and wondered what this thing was supposed to protect her against, anyway.

A Woman's Armor

Lesley McBain

No one ever knew what had happened between The Mac-Diarmid and the foreigner out in the fields. Some said it was a devil's bargain coming home—those who said *that* promptly measured their length on the ground when one of the MacDiarmid clan heard, however. Some said it involved sheep. (Some *always* said it involved sheep.) Some said the foreigner had tried to rob The MacDiarmid of his claymore. But all versions ended with The MacDiarmid's lifeblood soaking into the heather.

Five-year-old Ian swore he'd have revenge if he had to track the murdering foreigner over hill and over dale and across the sea and on *top* of the sea if it came to that. Being just girls who couldn't wear armor and fight like men, he said, his little sisters couldn't help.

To give him credit, Ian *did* leave home at a young age in search of revenge and *did* eventually kill the foreigner. By then he'd become so enamored of the adventurer's life he didn't want to come home. Thus many tales of Ian's exploits filtered back, slowly but surely, to the mountains of his home. Said exploits involved kidnapped maidens, duels, treachery, wondrous gifts, and the like—which were cordially half-believed because "well, Ian *would* be the one to get himself into that sort of trouble, wouldn't he."

What was worse, for his sisters at least, was that the stories always had to mention the idiotic phrase "For the blood and brawn and glory of The MacDiarmid!" Ian bellowed it *every* time he performed some dashing deed. The phrase had to do with the glory of their clan and their father, so his sisters couldn't disavow it publicly. But in private they called it That Phrase and rued the day Ian'd come up with it.

No one had had the heart—or the gall—to claim leadership of the town after The MacDiarmid's murder. The Widow MacDiarmid declined overtures to take up her husband's place. Her daughters weren't old enough to be consulted. Eventually town leadership fell to three people: the innkeeper, Robbie Burnside; the priest, Father Doonan; and the Widow Robertson, who'd come with the original settlers and buried three husbands on the mountaintop since then.

So the three daughters of The MacDiarmid grew up hearing their mother remind them "a woman's armor is her virtue." The original phrase was "a woman's armor is her beauty," but even doting Widow MacDiarmid couldn't really apply it to her daughters.

Deirdre, the oldest, had taken over the forgework once she grew tall enough. Now she stood six foot four and had the forge-toned brawn to match her height. She kept her copper-colored hair sensibly cropped; the shade took after her father's long-dead cousins' coloring, her mother said wistfully. Deirdre could swing a claymore with ease if she wanted to. Usually she used her fists to settle arguments.

Fiona, the youngest . . . Fiona was a handful. She was wiry and thin as the forge cat and wore short the coal-black hair she'd inherited from her mother. Her blue eyes were cold and piercing as The MacDiarmid's own hazel eyes had been.

Fiona was always where she wasn't supposed to be. In addition—which irritated her sisters more than anything—she'd managed to perfect disappearing in plain sight better than the forge cat. "A woman's armor is not getting caught," she gently mocked her mother.

But never in her mother's hearing.

And then there was Maeve, the middle daughter. She was

small for a MacDiarmid and didn't have Deirdre's strength or Fiona's cunning. Men generally didn't look above her chin. She had an angel's voice and an angel's disposition, her mother said. Maeve didn't know what an angel sang like. And singing around the house—as much as her mother loved it when Maeve did—hardly qualified for some celestial choir to Maeve. She *knew* she didn't have an angel's disposition. So she did the chores Deirdre forgot or Fiona skipped out on, cut Fiona's hair into something approaching evenness when Fiona held still enough to let her, sang to herself, and kept to herself. It wasn't that her sisters didn't love her fiercely; she was just . . . Maeve.

Ian had performed some deed of derring-do no one could quite figure out from the exhausted messenger's garbled account, but (stupidly, Fiona muttered to herself) had stuck around long enough to shout That Phrase and gotten himself caught. Since Ian proudly admitted to many of what some would call crimes over the years—and, more to the point, since the last person he'd lopped in half with his claymore had been "some bloody foreign nobleman or other" related to the land's prince and nominal ruler—he was deemed incorrigible.

And thus scheduled to hang.

Robbie Burnside's inn seethed with angry townsfolk. Much drink was taken to aid thought. Mad rescue plans were made and rejected. Yes, Ian was one of their own, and they could muster all the town's men and boys to his aid, but what could anyone really do? Wasn't it true Ian had been clapped in the strongest prison? And wasn't the executioner bigger even than Ian and The MacDiarmid, lord rest his soul, put together?

Meanwhile, the three sisters sat in their cottage and looked at each other. Maeve had given the Widow MacDiarmid a hefty slug or three of the Widow Robertson's home brew to ease the shock of the news. So their mother was sleeping like a babe (a snoring babe) in her own room.

"We've got to do something," Fiona said, brushing stray bangs out of her eyes. "We can't let those bloody foreigners hang Ian, even if he is a bloody idiot for standing around like some hero in a fairy tale instead of making his escape like any sensible person would."

Deirdre stretched. Her chair creaked. "I'd try breaking him out, myself. It's better than sitting around here doing nothing. What would Da say if we didn't at least try and save our only brother?"

"What would Da say to us abandoning Mother?" Maeve shot back. "Who's going to help *her* if we all go off and get ourselves killed?"

Her sisters stared. "We?" Deirdre echoed in disbelief.

"Maevie," Fiona said impatiently, "what makes you think *you* can help us break Ian out of prison? Somebody's got to take care of Mother."

For the first time in her life, Maeve raised a hand to someone. Her hand hit Fiona's cheek with a satisfying smack. Not as hard as Deirdre could slap, to be sure, but it would do. "How *dare* you talk to me that way! You think Ian's not my brother too? You think you two can just go off and get yourselves in trouble the same way Ian did and expect me to stay at home? Who do you think's done all your chores over the years when you were off running wild, who do you think's covered for both of you to Mother and even Father Doonan when it came to that, who's stitched up your wounds and your clothes and thought ahead when all you two could think of was yourselves?"

Fiona pressed one hand to her cheek and looked wide-eyed at Maeve. "You *hit* me, Maevie."

"And do I have to do it again to slap some sense into you?"

Silence held for some moments after Maeve's challenge. Fiona stared at Maeve as if she were a stranger. Deirdre opened her mouth several times but closed it without speaking.

Maeve sighed. "*Think* about the problem, Fi. We don't have enough money to bribe Ian out of prison; we don't have anything else to offer. We don't even know where the prison *is.* And since we're *all* going," she said with a look that dared her sisters to contradict her, "who's going to help Mother if we end up getting ourselves killed or thrown in prison?"

Fiona snickered. "Robbie Burnside, and you know it as well as I do, Maevie."

Maeve blushed slightly. "Well . . ."

"The town would help her," Deirdre said firmly. "That we know. And that messenger can help us find the prison if I have to turn him upside down and shake him."

"Ah, Dee," Fiona murmured, "so subtle." She ducked as Deirdre mock-swung on her, then stuck her tongue out at her oldest sister.

"Both of you stop," Maeve snapped as Deirdre drew back her arm for another swing. Her sisters stopped . . . which gave Maeve a heady sense of power she quickly dismissed. "We're not going to help Ian any if you two start bickering. Finding the prison is only part of it. We don't have weapons, we don't have armor—"

Fiona held up a long, slender hand. "Wait a minute. I think I know where we can get some weapons at least." She smiled mysteriously. "Go on, Maevie."

Maeve and Deirdre looked suspiciously at Fiona. "Even if we *did* get those," Maeve said slowly, "and even if we used all the money Ian remembered to send home over the years when he *wasn't* in his cups, we'd have to get him out of prison and find somewhere to hide him. You know they'd come here looking for him first thing."

"I wish them joy of that," Deirdre muttered under her breath. "Send them up to the thorny heather fields. Maybe the sheep'll gore them for good measure."

The corners of Maeve's mouth quirked. "Maybe they will. But . . . we need more advice."

"Advice?" Deirdre snorted. "We need a miracle."

"Let's go seek advice from Father Doonan," Fiona said with an even more mysterious smile. Father Doonan—tall, white-haired, craggy-jawed—hadn't always been a man of the cloth. He had a Past. But in the mountains, everyone's family had a Past to some degree, so no one much bothered remembering.

Except for Fiona.

"Why do *I* have to wear *armor?*" Deirdre protested as Father Doonan held up a buckled piece and measured it by eye against Deirdre's shoulders.

"Because," Father Doonan said patiently, "you're going to rescue your brother. It wouldn't be fitting for me to let you go rescue your brother without all the gifts I can offer. Spiritual *and* practical."

Fiona sat cross-legged, sharpening her knife. "Told you so."

"Fiona, hush," Maeve chided.

"I'll *not* hush. Dee, you're the biggest of us three. You're the one anybody's going to swing on first *because* you're the biggest. Odds are they're going to be swinging bloody *swords*, not just fists. Would you stop wasting time arguing and put the bloody thing *on* already?"

"Deirdre, your reluctance to don armor does you credit, *as* does your refraining from foul language. *Unlike* your sister, who knows better and ought to be ashamed of herself for using it in front of me," Father Doonan said, raising his voice over Deirdre's attempted reply and Fiona's yelp as Maeve pinched her. "But I'm asking you as a personal favor to wear it. I don't want to have to explain to your mother why I let you go off without armor."

"She'd say Dee wouldn't need it because 'a woman's armor is her virtue,'" Fiona whispered loudly to Maeve. This sent them into nervous giggles. Even Deirdre managed to smile. Father Doonan's mouth twitched.

"Your mother's right. A woman's armor is her virtue *and* her faith. However, under some circumstances, additional armor of mail never hurts."

"If it fits," Deirdre said breathlessly, tugging and pulling. "But . . . uh . . ."

Maeve saw just *where* it didn't fit Deirdre. "Can you do something with it in the forge, Deirdre?" she asked briskly. "Lengthen the straps or whatever you call them so it buckles right?"

"Now that's a good idea, Maeve," Father Doonan said, looking a bit embarrassed and quickly helping Deirdre extricate herself.

Deirdre eyed the armor balefully. "Let me see what I can do. Let's leave the rest of this here for now." She gave the well-used longsword in the open chest a look that suggested she'd rather leave it there for good.

After a hurried visit to the forge—Deirdre swearing worse than Fiona as she rigged the armor as fast as she could to fit a woman—while Maeve checked on their still-sleeping mother and Fiona helped Deirdre, the three went quickly

back to Father Doonan's cottage. Deirdre even agreed to
some hasty lessons in longsword from Father Doonan.

Deirdre could even pass for a man in the armor. Which,
as Father Doonan said matter-of-factly, was best under the
circumstances.

"Won't someone be more likely to attack two women
traveling with one man instead of three women—even if the
man isn't really a man, but just *looks* like one? Since it'd
look like only one 'man' was there to protect the two
women?" Maeve asked him, brow furrowed.

"Well . . . perhaps."

"Fi looks like a boy as it is," Deirdre put in. "No one
will notice if she dresses like one." Fiona opened her mouth
to retort. Father Doonan's frown kept her quiet.

"What about me?" Maeve said.

"Begging the Father's pardon," Fiona said, "strap 'em
down, Maevie, and cut your hair."

"Cut my *hair*?" Maeve's dulcet voice cracked. Her long
russet hair was her one pride.

"We'll think about that later," Deirdre said hurriedly.
"Father, thank you for your help. Do I *really* have to take
the sword?"

"Yes, Deirdre. I pray you won't have to use it."

"Now we've . . . well, I've . . . got weapons and armor,
what's the rest of the plan?" Deirdre said. It broke the silence
as they walked—Deirdre more slowly than the others, getting used to the armor and swinging the sword for practice—
down the back path leading away from the town and the
chapel both. Gloomy thickets pressed in on either side of
the moon-silvered path.

A muffled scream sounded to their left.

Deirdre, armored against thorns and sharp-edged grasses
and using the sword in her hand to slash a path, made the
best time battering through the thickets toward the scream.
When she plunged into a clearing she saw an unfamiliar
pair wrestling on the ground. Not in a friendly manner.

Deirdre charged. The armor-clad man rolled off the girl
and to his feet. In one easy motion, he drew a sword of
his own. Deirdre swung her sword with all her might. The
two blades clanged together, sending the armor-clad man
staggering. He recovered quickly. And Deirdre found herself

trying to remember ten minutes' worth of swordplay lessons as blow after blow fell on her armor.

Ah, to hell with it, she thought. Use what you know, Da always said.

Deirdre dove as far under the man's swing as she could the next chance she had, tackling him and knocking him onto his back. She felt the mail coif tear as she did. Sharp pain blossomed on her scalp. Her fury masked the pain. She began punching and kicking the man with forge-hardened strength before he could get to his feet.

Her sisters dove into the fray a few seconds later. Fiona stamped as hard as she could on the man's sword hand. Maeve clawed his face with her nails. Deirdre finally banged the man's head against the ground hard enough to render him unconscious.

"Dee, you're bleeding," Maeve gasped as the three caught their breath. Fiona tossed the man's sword aside and held his knife to his throat in case he stirred.

Deirdre put her hand to her scalp, then her forehead. It came away bloody. "So . . . I . . . am." She sagged to the ground.

Maeve bandaged Deirdre's scalp and stopped the blood flow from her forehead before Deirdre regained consciousness. It looked as though the stranger's sword pommel had caught Deirdre on the scalp and forehead as she dove at him, but it had all been a blur to Maeve. Then Maeve talked Fiona out of cutting the badly battered stranger's throat. Fiona settled for stripping him and binding him with sharp-edged vines. Both of them whirled at the sound of muffled crying.

The girl huddled at the edge of the clearing, trying to hold her torn clothing together without much success.

"Fi, stay there." Maeve stood up slowly. In her gentlest voice, she said, "My name's Maeve, of the MacDiarmids. No one's going to hurt you." The girl darted a glance at her but didn't shrink away.

Inching her way forward across the clearing, Maeve kept talking in her most soothing tones. Finally, the girl choked out, "You're a MacDiarmid? You know my Ian?"

"Huh?" Deirdre said, half-conscious. "Ian? *Her* Ian? He's *our* Ian."

"Ssh, Dee," Fiona soothed.

"I'm Maeve, Ian's sister," Maeve said, almost within reach of the girl. "These two are my sisters."

"They're *women*?"

"Thank you ever *so* bloody much," Fiona said under her breath, but gently.

"You know Ian?" Maeve asked.

"Ian said to tell . . . he needed help . . . I tried to follow his directions, but I got lost . . ." The girl stood as Maeve took the last step to her side. Maeve slowly removed her cloak—grimy and torn, but better than the girl's shredded gown—and folded it around the girl's shoulders.

"Fiona's over there, next to Deirdre, the one lying on the ground with the armor on. What's your name?"

"Raina." With moonlight masking some of Raina's bruises and scrapes, Maeve could see what Ian had fallen for: Raina's long silvery-blonde hair and wide green eyes and heart-shaped face. She suppressed a wistful sigh.

"Who's *this*, then?" Fiona jerked a thumb at the assailant.

The girl blanched. "My husband's brother. My *late* husband's brother. Ian rescued me . . . my husband was a foul creature . . . his brother's no better . . ."

Deirdre sat up slowly, groaning.

"*Now* what do we do?" Fiona said. "Dee's hurt, we've got this girl to take care of, that scum on the ground over there, and we haven't even gotten out of *town*."

Maeve supported Raina as she swayed. "There's only one place to go."

The Widow Robertson opened her cottage door. "About time you got here. Your mother never had a head for my home brew."

"We were . . . delayed," Maeve said as Fiona and Deirdre staggered up with their burden. "This is Raina. She's hurt."

"So she is, and so're your sisters, and so're you. I assume you stripped that one and bound him with prickly poison-weed for good reason?"

"Prickly *poisonweed*?" Maeve said, turning her head to stare at Fiona.

"Fi's not 'lergic . . . to it . . . neither . . . am . . . I," Deirdre said, panting. "I always . . . forget . . . what it looks like."

"You weren't *conscious*, Deirdre. Fiona did the stripping and binding and she *knows* what it looks like."

"Oops," Fiona said.

"Come in, come in," the Widow interrupted. "You too, Raina of Evendor, cousin to our ruler." Raina gasped. The Widow nodded. "I told your mother that second husband of hers would poison her sure as you're standing here, but she thought she was in love, the sweet little fool. You're her spitting image. Come on, you're wasting time standing there with your mouths gaping open. Wash up, sit down, eat. I'll deal with that one. Leave him outside."

Dumbfounded, the four did as they were told. The Widow stayed outside a long time. The first thing she did upon coming in was wash her hands thoroughly in the deep sink. Then she gathered an assortment of bottles and bandages from her corner cabinet and put them down on the table the four sat around. "You found the scones, I see, and you've all had tea. Let's get you bandaged some more and poulticed."

Later, the Widow said between sips of home brew, "Ian MacDiarmid is a bloody romantic fool. But I'm still not going to let some bloody foreigners hang him; that's for his own to do."

"We've only got armor and weapons for one person," Maeve said thoughtfully. "Fighting our way in isn't going to work."

"I don't need armor," Fiona said quickly. "It slows me down."

"I don't know how to use weapons," Raina admitted to no one's surprise as she continued working the tangles out of her hair.

"Is your cousin—the prince—a reasonable man?" Maeve asked Raina.

Raina frowned. "He was when we were growing up . . . we used to be good friends . . . but my husband was an awful influence on him." The hand holding the brush trembled.

"Could you ask for pardon?"

"*She* couldn't," the Widow said. "*You* could. And your sisters could be breaking Ian out of prison—or trying to— at the same time. That way there's more chance of success. Especially since the prince loves music." She met Maeve's shocked look without blinking. "I've heard you sing when you thought no one could hear you, Maeve. Isn't it about time you used your gift for something important?"

"You want me to wear *that*?" Maeve all but shrieked.

The Widow held the slithery wisp of sapphire-blue silk dress carefully, appraising Maeve. "Do you want to see your brother hanged?"

"But . . . but . . . I'll look like a . . ."

"Temptress," the Widow said imperturbably. "That's the idea. *As* I explained. The prince has an eye for beauty *and* an ear for music. Raina will present you to him; you and she will distract him while Deirdre and Fiona rescue Ian."

"But what if he . . ." Maeve blushed.

The Widow smiled secretively. "He'll be too bewitched by your voice to do anything else. Once I teach you a few songs."

Raina's bribes—all she could raise—had only bought Ian housing in the best part of the dungeon. She could, however, get everyone through the gate without questions given makeup to cover her bruises and new clothing the Widow provided.

Maeve's russet hair, unbound, rippled in the breeze. Her black silk cloak barely masked the curves displayed by the clinging sapphire silk dress. The gate guard leered at her as she and Raina entered the gate. Deirdre and Fiona brought up the rear long enough to get through the gate into the city streets. Deirdre—bruises fading and hair cropped shorter—looked masculine in her armor. Fiona was dressed as a boy, and looked like one.

Raina led Maeve up a set of stairs within the gatehouse, down a twisting and turning interior hallway, and to a door guarded by one well-armored man. "Raina of Evendor and her . . . discovery . . . for the prince," she murmured to the man. Maeve, on cue, fanned herself slightly, as if hot, and undid her cloak.

Black silk slipped off Maeve's bare shoulders. Raina arched a perfectly shaped eyebrow at the guard. "We *are* expected, are we not? I sent word . . ."

"Yes, madam." He opened the door.

Deirdre kept watch in the grimy alley as Fiona fiddled with the lock of the disused dungeon side door using a set of wires and picks. "Where'd you get those?"

"You're not the only one who can make things out of metal. Now hush. I have to concentrate."

Finally, after a seeming eternity, the lock gave. Down a winding set of stairs the two went. They paused at the final turn of stairs leading to a dim and dank-smelling dungeon. A bored-looking guard sat at a table in the center of the aisle, playing solitaire by the light of a flickering lantern. The five cells on their left and four of the five cells on their right were empty.

"This was the *best* she could do?" Fiona breathed almost inaudibly.

"One guard, no cellmates," whispered Deirdre. "*Perfect.*"

The fifth cell on the right held Ian.

He was repeating That Phrase. So loudly it masked any noise from his sisters slipping down the stairs. The two forgave him for it given the circumstances. "But if he says it later," Deirdre vowed silently, "I'll lay him out myself."

Fiona slithered into the shadows, reappearing just long enough to cosh the guard on the back of the head.

Ian stopped mid-Phrase. "What was that? A ghost? Da?"

Deirdre bound and gagged the guard. Fiona pocketed the guard's purse and took the keys off his belt. "No, you bloody idiot, it's me and Dee come to get you."

"Raina . . . she found you? Where is she, Fi? What are you doing in armor, Dee?" Ian sputtered as Fiona unlocked his cell. "And where's Maevie? Not *with* you, I hope . . . Maevie's got no head for this sort of thing."

Maeve, meanwhile, was almost enjoying herself. Singing publicly for the first time—especially to a rapt audience of one rather handsome prince—was new and intoxicating in addition to being nervewracking. Raina had been relegated to a corner after pouring the prince wine. Maeve sang two long songs the Widow Robertson had taught her and two she'd learned in the inn but never dared sing at home. As she was about to begin another song the Widow had taught her, the prince beckoned. "Come here, my dear."

He motioned to an ottoman beside him. Maeve sank gingerly down on it. He brushed back her hair in order to see her more clearly, fingers skimming over her bare shoulder. "You've pleased me. That's rare these days."

"I'm . . . glad. That I've pleased you, I mean," Maeve said, unable to look away from the prince's dark eyes. He seemed sincere, which made her feel guilty for deceiving him. She hoped Fiona and Deirdre had gotten Ian safely away. If they hadn't—she pushed the thought aside.

"So . . . I'm in the mood to grant you one wish. Not too expensive a wish. But try not to bore me with it, my dear songbird. I hate being bored."

Maeve took a deep breath. "My brother's life."

The prince stared down at her. He did have a nice face, Maeve thought. "I'm not bored yet. Is your brother anyone I know?"

"Not by name, I don't think." Maeve gritted her teeth and repeated That Phrase. "It's his . . . signature."

The prince grimaced. "You're related to *him*?"

"Please, I'll make sure he never causes you more trouble . . ."

"My dear songbird, he cut a royal—all right, a royal by marriage—in half. That qualifies as trouble even if he hadn't done anything *else*."

"The man was a monster," Raina murmured from her corner.

"Alas, I think you're right. Pity I didn't see it earlier." He toyed with a lock of Maeve's hair. "Such lovely hair. Such a lovely voice. Such lovely naivete, despite your songs. I could change that."

Maeve sat very still. A woman's armor is her virtue, her mother's voice said in her head.

"I have a dilemma you've complicated. The public loves hangings. But the public hated my cousin's late husband. So they love your brother and don't want to see him hanged no matter how much they love hangings. And for some reason they love . . . that phrase."

Maeve shuddered in sympathy.

"They've taken to chanting it in the streets. Which is why you've cheered me so. I stopped hearing it for a little while. And you're the loveliest songbird anyone's *ever* brought me."

He stopped stroking her hair and picked up his wine. "But if I keep you as my songbird in exchange for your brother's life, I'll *never* get rid of your brother *or* that phrase. I know that type of brother. If *I* were your brother, I might even *be* that type of brother. He'll storm the gates yelling it until he gets himself killed. Then you'd be my unhappy songbird. Which would displease me."

He sighed. "I don't suppose you'd marry me, would you?"

Maeve blinked. "*Excuse* me?"

"Marriage. You *do* know the word?"

"Of course I do," Maeve snapped, nerves and temper frayed beyond endurance. "But what makes you think I'd marry a bloody foreigner—prince or no bloody prince—even to save my only brother?"

The prince choked on his wine, set the goblet down with a crash, and began to cough. When he recovered he started laughing. Maeve realized he couldn't be more than her age despite the jaded air he'd been affecting. Finally he stopped and wiped his eyes. "How about a long engagement? I'll make it a year and a day, which should give you enough time to pack your brother off somewhere *very* far away and come back. If at the end of a year and a day you still think I'm a bloody foreigner, we'll renegotiate assuming your brother stays far away. I promise to be a gentleman; dress as you please and sing what you like. Deal?" He held out his hand.

Maeve thought, then put out her hand. "Make it two years and two days to give me time to penetrate my brother's thick skull, don't ask how my brother gets packed away in the meantime, and you have a deal."

Days later—after battles along the way with rogue horned sheep and roaming cutthroats and Deirdre keeping her vow to lay Ian out when he used That Phrase—the travel-worn group returned to Father Doonan's cottage. Their mother waited there with Father Doonan and the Widow Robertson. Fiona reluctantly surrendered her skean dhu; Deirdre quickly surrendered her armor. Maeve took a long slug of home brew for courage before announcing the deal she'd made.

The Widow Robertson smiled enigmatically throughout the ensuing uproar. "I told you he had an eye for beauty and an ear for music," she said once everyone else had shouted themselves hoarse at Maeve.

"You *approve*?" Father Doonan asked for the group.

"Maeve made a very clever deal." The Widow rocked back in her chair. "I always approve of clever deals. Now, Ian, much has happened since you left. . . ."

Telling Ian all that had happened and explaining who was who to Raina and so forth took hours. By the time the stories finished, the moon stood high in the night sky. The Widow Robertson'd kept pouring home brew with a free hand. Ian slept with his head on the table after consuming ten bottles by himself.

"A woman's armor," the Widow MacDiarmid pronounced in a somewhat slurred voice, glancing at Maeve as she did so, "is—"

"Anything she wants it to be!" the other women cried out in unison.

Hallah Iron-Thighs and the Hall of the Puppet King

K.D. Wentworth

It was early summer, which meant the annual Bandit Holiday had rolled around again, when the local criminals all headed for the seaside and a bit of sun on their pale, scrawny, pox-ridden bodies. For the next two weeks anyone could travel the mountains in perfect safety. No one would need hired protection until those lazy, good-for-nothing thieves quit gallivanting about and returned to their mountain haunts where they belonged.

As happened this time every year, I, Hallah Iron-Thighs, master swordswoman and mercenary, was depressed. How a girl is supposed to make a decent living under such conditions is beyond me. Those wretched bandits simply have no sense of responsibility about upholding the social contract.

My partner, Gerta, and I were attempting to drown our sorrows with the last of our funds that morning down at the dingy Inn of the Crafty Marmot when an envoy arrived, resplendent in purple silk. A grim fellow with ears like pot handles, he looked as though he'd never drunk an ounce of ale in his entire life.

His nose twitched above a silly curled beard as he

surveyed the odorous establishment. "I seek the Lady Hallah Iron-Thighs and her boon companion, Gerta!" he proclaimed in ringing tones. "Can either of you lowly creatures tell me where they might abide?"

Gerta, who had soothed her blues rather thoroughly at that point, fell off her chair with a clink of chain mail and sprawled at his feet. "*Lady!*" Convulsed with laughter, she pounded the floor with her fist. "Hallah, he called you a '*lady*'!"

I drew my dagger and let the light from the inn's single lamp gleam along its serrated edge. "I'm Hallah Iron-Thighs."

"I—see." He produced a scroll tied with purple ribbon. "I am Hermus Zimbolini, Prime Counselor of Bamffle, charged by King Jonquil the Shy to deliver this royal summons."

"Bamffle?" Gerta dabbed laugh-tears from her eyes.

We'd never worked that far west, but fellow mercenaries described Bamffle as a prosperous mountain kingdom of agonizingly small troubles where men fussed over the inadequate size of their buttons and insisted their mothers-in-law should visit more often.

Bamfflian women, our friends had added sourly, worried only that their children were too well behaved, and their daughters might marry above their stations, thereby losing the opportunity to fully develop their characters by overcoming adversity. It was a realm of tea parties and knitting socials, not exactly the sort of place to require a pair of strong sword arms.

We followed the fellow outside, where Gerta unrolled the summons in the sunlight. The parchment was thick and creamy, the border bright gold. She squinted suspiciously. "It has too many letters on it." Of course, any amount of letters always proved "too many" for Gerta.

The messenger eased the summons out of her hand, turned it right side up, then gave it back. He cleared his throat. "His Majesty King Jonquil the Shy wishes you to escort his aunt, the Princess Abyssmina, to her upcoming matrimonial in Hagrishia."

I took the parchment. There were indeed many elegantly scripted letters dancing across the page, a veritable flood of them, but I couldn't make out any *numbers*. "What about payment?"

"I'm certain you'll be handsomely paid," he said.

"Just exactly how handsomely?" I asked, my forefinger tracing the embossed elephant's head on my sword Esmeralda's hilt.

His eyes were flinty. "I assure you that our good King Jonquil is known far and wide for his generosity."

Like we hadn't heard *that* before. "All right," I said. "As we're short on funds with no other offers, we'll bite."

Zimbolini looked pained. It wasn't the last time.

Unfortunately, the journey to Bamffle proved endless. Mounted on a placid mule, Prime Counselor Zimbolini seemed to have no sense of direction at all, leading us first up one road, then down another, so that we kept crisscrossing the countryside.

The fourth time we forded the River Vallat, Gerta balked and jumped off her gray gelding, Slasher. "I think you're just trying to get us alone so you can have your way with us," she told Zimbolini, then grinned ferally and drew her dagger. "Well, come ahead! It might just be your lucky day!"

He paled, then patted his forehead with a white lawn handkerchief. "Nothing could be farther from my mind."

Gerta looked baffled and her dagger sagged.

I crossed my hands on the pommel of my saddle. "You know," I said, "I don't think the Prime Counselor finds us appealing."

Her blue eyes widened. "You mean he's a *sissy?*"

"Got it right the first time." I winked at Zimbolini.

Rigid with indignation, he kicked his mule into a plod.

"Let's kill him," Gerta said that evening as Zimbolini laid out his red satin bedroll, then tied his beard up in curling papers. "I haven't killed anyone all week, and I don't believe he knows the route anyway. He keeps muttering 'it has to be around here somewhere.' We could say bandits did him in."

"There aren't any bandits," I said. "They're all down at the seaside right now, plotting out ambush scenarios in the sand."

"The king doesn't know that," she said, "or he wouldn't have hired us."

She had a point, but I refused—for the moment. There might, after all, be some gold in this deal, and the Mercenary Code recommends that you never kill a client before he pays.

The next morning, when I roused Gerta, she sat up and blinked groggily at the tree line. The sun was just rising and the sky was an annoyingly cheerful orange-pink. She pinched the bridge of her nose. "That mountain wasn't there yesterday."

I glanced at a single majestic peak in the distance, grey granite interspersed with alpine meadows, the odd stream cascading off the rocks here and there. I must have been more tired than I thought the night before. I hadn't noticed the damned thing either. "Oh, so I suppose it's following us."

"Not necessarily," she said. Her face brightened. "Maybe we're going in circles."

"Never mind," I said. "I'll watch the trail. You just keep an eye on that mountain. It's probably up to no good."

The curling papers in the royal messenger's beard crinkled as he turned over in his bedroll, groaned, then sat up and gazed fixedly over our shoulders. "Well, finally!"

"What?"

"Mount Bleer." He pulled the papers out of his beard. "The ancestral seat of Bamfflian royalty. Keep your voice down or—"

Gerta frowned. "Or what, squishy little toad-man?"

His voice dropped to a whisper. "Or it will get away."

My hand went to Esmeralda's hilt. "Are you having us on?"

"No, I swear!" He bit his lip. "Due to certain extenuating circumstances, Mount Bleer is quite—elusive these days."

I stared moodily at the mountain. It seemed farther away than just a few minutes ago.

"See?" he said. "It's heard us. We'd better hurry!"

"Let me get this straight," I said, as Gerta buckled on her sword. "We're chasing a sodding *mountain*?"

"I'm afraid so," Zimbolini said as he saddled his mule. "Our court magician is quite incompetent. His spells rarely go right, such as this one, which was supposed to protect us from invasion. The wretch caused our beloved mountain home to flee potential invaders, not the same thing at all. At the moment, the only way to reach Bamffle is to be escorted by a native."

While he was explaining, the wayward mountain had drifted closer and now loomed at our backs as though eavesdropping.

"Quick!" He leaped onto his mule. "Before it gets away!"

Gerta and I followed. The mountain lumbered backwards, but not before we made it onto one of its winding trails. We rode upward the rest of the day without incident, finally rounding the last bend at dusk when the castle came into sight.

"Oh, my," Gerta said. She stood in her stirrups and stared.

Oh, my, indeed. I sat back in the saddle and studied the scene. The whole construct, portcullis, curtain walls, even the privy tower, was *dancing*. Mortar dribbled from between the stones with every awkward jiggle so it looked like a demented Morris dancer. Zimbolini pulled his mule up beside us and sighed. "Not again. The court magician cast a spell to make it self-cleaning several months ago and now it's always tidying up."

He stood in his stirrups and pointed an accusatory finger. "Bad castle, bad! In the name of the King, I demand you desist!"

With a rumble, the stones settled back to a more appropriate resting state, only slightly out of alignment. "You just have to be firm with it," he said. "It doesn't really mean to misbehave."

"I'll remember that," I said. We followed him into the castle, leaving our horses with a stableboy in the foregate.

In the great hall, tapestries depicting puppet shows covered every wall. The courtiers, all dressed in shades of red and purple, stared as we entered, then went back to gossiping among themselves. They had strings tied to their wrists and ankles, and moved with strange, jerky motions as though performing some bizarre local dance.

An ornate throne stood back by the far wall, next to an ugly floor lamp. A ten year old boy, dressed in grimy blue, sprawled on his stomach at its foot, busy pulling the legs off a set of tin soldiers. He looked up as we approached. "Wow, are you pirates? I've always wanted to be robbed!"

Gerta turned to me, puzzled. "Is that what passes for a serving lad in these parts?"

"Indeed it is not!" Zimbolini quivered with indignation. "That is Princess Abyssmina's intended, Prince Vigal the Simply Smashing, Heir Apparent of Hagrishia, whom you will escort home."

Vigal eyed Gerta's sword. "Have you ever killed anyone?"

She backed away, her hand automatically going for her dagger. I could tell she was confused, which is never safe for anyone within sword range.

He scrambled to his feet, downy cheeks flushed with excitement. "Would you kill someone now so I can watch?"

Zimbolini straightened his travel-stained tunic, then pulled from his pocket a sock tricked out with button eyes and a thread mouth, slid it onto his right hand, and bowed. "Your Majesty," he said, moving his fingers inside the sock so the thread mouth "spoke," "may I present Hallah Iron-Thighs and Gerta Derschnitzel, mighty swordswomen of the lower reaches."

"What do they want?" asked a peevish voice.

"You sent for them, sire, to escort the princess and her betrothed to Hagrishia. As you may remember, she is required to arrive in the capital by Wednesday or the wedding is off." Zimbolini turned to us. "May I present King Jonquil the Shy, Protector of Bamffle, Lord of the Wild Marches of Eastern Nimrod, and Holder of the Avenue of Immediate Availability in Mershorn, capital city of mighty Hagrishia herself!"

"He's king of an avenue?" Gerta smothered a snicker.

A puppet popped up from behind the throne and regarded Gerta malevolently. It was clad in pink and purple robes with a bent tin foil crown perched on its tiny head. "That avenue was presented in honor of my aunt's wedding!"

"Bet you wanted something more useful." Gerta elbowed Zimbolini. "Like a set of saucy pictures!" Gerta has always been a huge fan of saucy pictures.

"Actually," Zimbolini said, "it's quite a nice avenue. All the best, um, *gentleman's* clubs, are located on that street."

I scowled. This was a bizarre setup, but we'd seen worse. "So, King Jonquil—"

The puppet promptly retreated out of sight behind the throne.

Zimbolini sighed. "You have to follow court protocol." He pulled out two more sock puppets, one pink, the other purple.

"You've got to be kidding," I said.

"Oh, I love plays!" Gerta took the purple puppet and her voice rose to a wrenching falsetto. "Hello, Hallah. Is that a sword under your friend's robes, or is he just glad to see me?"

The king puppet reemerged to conduct our audience. Feeling like an idiot, I slid the pink sock puppet onto my hand. "All right. Where is this princess who needs escorting?" The puppet turned to the ugly lamp. "There." I examined the floor beside the throne. There wasn't even room for a royal mouse to hide, much less a princess. "Where?"

"You're not fooling anyone, Aunt Abyssmina!" the king puppet said. "Come out and take your betrothal like a royal." The lamp dissolved into a fortyish female in long pea-green robes. "I'm not betrothed!" She glared at him over an exceedingly crooked nose. "Of course, I don't know why I expected anything better from you!" She sniffed. "You were a nasty little boy, always disemboweling your sisters' dolls."

"Go away, you stupid old lady!" Prince Vigal crossed his spindly arms. "These are *my* pirates!"

"Don't even speak to me, you little worm!" She backed away. "I'm not marrying anyone but Merval!"

Jeez, this play had way more characters than plot. "Merval?"

Zimbolini sighed. "The court magician."

"Not the one who misenchanted the whole kingdom?"

"It wasn't the *whole* kingdom," came a voice from the hall's edge. "Just the royal seat." A tall young man with strapping shoulders and curly black hair stepped into view. "Well, and the Avenue of Immediate Availability in Hagrishia's capital city, but I don't think anyone's noticed it's gone missing just yet. I am working on a counterspell." His eyebrows quirked in the most appealing way. "Do you know a rhyme for 'breast?' "

"Merval!" Aunt Abyssmina flushed an almost maidenly pink. "My pet! Let's elope! I've packed my thong—"

"I'm sorry, Princess," he said, "but I have no time for socializing." He looked wistful. "I do keep telling you that. Besides, weren't you planning to run off with the royal plumber, the one with all the muscles?"

"Oh, that was last week," she said crossly. "I've grown spiritually since then. It's all quite clear to me now. You're the one I want."

"That's very flattering, I'm sure," he said, "but we all know you have to do your royal duty."

"No, I don't!" she cried. "Just tell me what you want!

I can transform myself into ninety-six useful household items!"

"This is all your father's fault," the king puppet said crossly to Merval. "If he hadn't taught my aunt transformation spells when she was a girl, she'd have been safely married years ago."

Merval donned a red puppet. "Yes, it was rather short-sighted of Papà. Mamà always said no good would come of it."

"I can be a spinning wheel," Abyssmina said, "or a spanner. How do you feel about spanners? They're very useful."

"No spanners," I said firmly. "We have to get on the road."

"Can't you do something?" the king puppet said irritably to Merval. "Perhaps cast a spell to make her love the little wretch instead of you? We would consider it a fitting wedding present."

"Of course, sire." Merval pulled out a wand that resembled a bent fireplace poker and closed his eyes.

Remembering the wayward kingdom and the dancing castle, I turned to Zimbolini. "Wait a minute—"

"Blood is red, sky is blue." Merval's arms waved theatrically. "Love the next man you see, if you know what's good for—"

"Can you do a currycomb?" Gerta stepped in front of Abyssmina. "I lost mine last week and—"

"—you!" Merval waved the poker. The air shimmered pink, then fell to the floor in little sparks. The throne room reeked of bay rum.

Gerta looked up, pink sparkles dancing in her hair and eyes. Her brow wrinkled, as it always did when she was trying to puzzle something out. "Merval—darling?"

The magician's eyes flew open. "Blast!"

Gerta tackled him with a flying leap. A breath later, he lay spread-eagled in the middle of the floor, Gerta on his chest. She drew her dagger as I approached. "He's mine, Hallah! Go find your own!" She took a fistful of his hair. "Hold still so I can notch your ear with my family's matrimonial mark!"

He squirmed. "We're not getting married!"

"Having a good time, are we?" I hunkered down beside them.

"We will," she said, "just as soon as he starts being reasonable."

"You could lop off his head," I said. "I bet he would see reason then."

He screeched as she steadied his ear for the first cut. "He is completely spineless. I'm seriously put out that I want him."

"It's not my fault!" Merval bucked against Gerta's weight to no avail. "You got in the way!"

I shook my head. "Just slit his throat, then we'll conduct the princess to her wedding. The king will pay us—how many gold pieces?" I turned to the puppet.

"Three," it said haughtily.

"I was thinking more along the lines of twenty," I said, "or we could just leave you to work this out yourself."

"Ten," it said, "but you have to take Merval too."

"Fifteen," I said, "and we'll take Merval, but what we do with him is our own business."

"Done." It regarded us. "But I want the avenue put back."

Gerta got to her feet, dagger in hand, brow furrowed. She has never been what you would call a deep thinker. Logic in any form, in fact, has always come very hard to her. I knew it was going to take her a few minutes to work this out.

"You stay away from Merval," Princess Abyssmina said. She pushed her sleeves up. "He's a sweet boy and I saw him first!"

"How about this?" Gerta said. "You can light his funeral pyre after the ceremony, if you like." She seized Merval by the collar and held him up like a transgressing puppy. "I'm taking this wretch home to meet my mother," she said to me over her shoulder, "then I'm slitting his throat. Want to come?"

"Can we go by way of Hagrishia?" I asked. "There still is that little matter of dropping the princess and her intended off for their nuptials."

Merval wriggled free and took out his poker/wand, his eyes narrow and determined.

"Oh, no, you don't!" I drew my magnificent sword Esmeralda and advanced on him. "Drop that or I'll lop your arm off!"

"No, it's all right," he said. "I'm just going to remove the love spell." The air shimmered blue and yellow.

I tasted spoiled wine on the back of my throat. The tiny elephant's head on Esmeralda's hilt trumpeted as the hilt twisted out of my hand and fell to the floor. "Leave that boy alone!" it cried.

Hands on her knees, Gerta bent down to look closer. "I didn't know your sword could talk."

"It can't," I said grimly and reached to pick it up.

Esmeralda's trunk slapped my fingers. "Unhand me, you overdeveloped, muscle-bound bimbo!"

I snatched my hand back. "Don't get smart-mouthed with me," I said, "or I'll have you melted down for a doorstop!"

"Like I would care!" Esmeralda turned her elephant face away in a teeny snit.

My hands balled into fists as I rounded on the inept magician. "Some things are sacred, you know!"

"*I* was forged for the hand of a king." Esmeralda preened her hilt with her trunk. "At the very least, I should be on display in a museum, held in trust for future generations! Instead, I've been dragged through one gritty tavern after another, fondled by sticky-fingered serving boys, jolted about on a sweating horse—"

I muffled the tiny mouth with my right hand and shoved the sword back into its scabbard with my left. The trunk flailed beneath my fingers. "Now, then," I said, "where was I? Oh, yes, killing Merval."

"He is a sniveling little wretch," Gerta observed as Merval fled into the farthest corner. "I don't understand why I feel as though he and I ought to pick out a china pattern."

"Gerta, you idiot, he's magicked you," I said. "You're going to have to use some self-control until it wears off."

"I see." She scratched her forehead. "Do you think they can make the wedding cake rum flavor instead of chocolate?"

"Look," I said, "no one is getting married except the princess!"

The king puppet swiveled. "Farewell, Aunt Abyssmina. Rule well in Hagrishia."

But Aunt Abyssmina had already taken her leave. In her place lay an elegant tortoiseshell currycomb.

"Mine!" Prince Vigal cried and snatched it up.

"Well," I said, "that should cut arguments to a minimum."

✧   ✧   ✧

We managed to get down the mountain without Merval enchanting anything else only because I forcibly relieved him of his poker. Gerta was still planning both their wedding and his subsequent funeral, and I didn't trust him to restrain himself.

Of course, once we had left the wandering kingdom of Bamffle, and it was rumbling off into the distance, we had to ascertain just exactly where in the blue blazes we were. A series of grey granite peaks stood before us, wreathed with clouds at the top.

"That's the eastern slope of the Jamplit Mountains," Gerta said. "I recognize that cliff. It's shaped just like a nose."

Then Hagrishia lay on the other side. We would have to cross the pass in order to deliver the prince and his intended.

"Do you think the bandits are back from holiday?" Gerta asked. "I could do with a bit of mayhem."

Back on his fat dun pony, Prince Vigal sighed. He had dressed his currycomb "bride" up in a bit of handkerchief, as though she were wearing a crown, and taken to talking to it. "Princess, we're going to cross the mountains!" he said. "Maybe we'll be robbed by real pirates! Won't that be fun?" He made the currycomb dance in ecstatic agreement.

I sighed. That boy had obviously been too long in King Jonquil's court.

Esmeralda kept making snide comments and I finally gagged her with a bit of rag. What would happen if it actually came to combat, I didn't like to think about.

When we reached the notorious Yarmly Defile, scene of a thousand ambushes, Gerta stood in her stirrups and scanned the heights. Striated cliffs loomed on either side and a strong wind made pebbles tick against the rock. She urged her gelding onto the narrow trail and we followed one at a time, Merval bringing up the rear.

"In my country, the bride and groom fight a ritual battle the night before the wedding," she said over her shoulder. "Their scars prove their undying love."

"Charming," I said.

Merval looked green. "Can't you just give me back my wand? I'm pretty sure I can remove that confounded spell—"

"No can do, sonny boy," I said cheerfully. "You made this marriage bed. Now, you're just going to have to lie in it."

"But—"

"Shh!" Gerta reined Slasher to a stop and the gelding's ears flickered back and forth. "I hear something."

"Hey, down there!" cried a voice from above. "Do you have a spare bottle of suntan lotion? We're fresh out."

Gerta drew her sword and sported a fierce, joyous grin as she scanned the rocks.

"Is that a pirate?" Prince Vigal's lower lip quivered. "I didn't bring any suntan lotion. Does this mean we can't be robbed?"

"There, there, little fellow," Merval said soothingly. "Don't worry. They can still take our horses and clothes—"

"Both of you shut up!" I wheeled Corpsemaker in a tight circle, all the trail would allow. "We're armed!" I called up to our unseen attackers. "Come down if you want to die!"

"Sorry." A face adorned with a magnificent blond beard appeared above the rim. "We're not on duty yet, so no one's getting robbed today. Could you possibly pop round tomorrow?"

"Oh, please!" Vigal had tears in his squinty little eyes. "We've never been to a robbery before!" He held up his currycomb "bride." "Have we?"

The currycomb shook its toothed "head" solemnly.

"Aha!" Merval said from behind. I turned to find him digging in my saddlebag. "Here it is!" He held up his poker/wand with a triumphant flourish.

"Put that thing down before you turn us all into salt cellars!" I said.

His eyes closed as he began muttering a spell. I heard something about "pest," "dressed," and "messed." "Cut that out," I called, "or I'll part your hair with an ax!"

The air shimmered puce. There was a cry of protest from above. I snatched the poker. "What have you done?"

"I turned them all into rutabagas!" He made a grab for his "wand." "Be careful with that!"

"Hey!" The bandit's head reappeared above the rim. He threw a deflated beach ball at my head. "That would have cost a whole copper piece!" His voice was aggrieved. "If I'd paid for it, of course."

"In case you haven't noticed," I said, "this isn't exactly Free Nachos Night at the Inn of the One-Handed Virgin."

"Not so fast!" A fist-sized rock sailed down and brained Merval. "You've got to make restitution!"

The magician slumped over the neck of his horse, then the currycomb in Vigal's plump little hand shimmered, becoming the not-so-blushing bride. She pried herself free. "Merval!"

A rope was thrown over the cliff, then a trio of bandits, all looking rested and tan from their holiday, not to mention extremely peeved, climbed down.

In a fury, Abyssmina began transforming from shape to shape in the hopes of achieving something lethal with which to attack—scullery brush, stew pot, hoof pick, shoe tree—

"Hold on," said one of them. He eyed the shoe tree with interest. "What have we got here?"

—toothbrush, rake, mounting stand, road map—

I drew Esmeralda, but the rag binding her mouth slipped and she shrieked, "Unhand me, you overgrown ape!"

The head bandit, who was very golden-headed and very tan, grinned. "Having a spot of trouble with your sword?"

I muffled Esmeralda with my free hand. The tiny trunk writhed beneath my fingers and I held on grimly. "Certainly— not."

—broom, writing quill, washboard, rug beater—

"Amazing!" The blond bandit snatched the rug beater before it could change and held it up in wonder.

Abyssmina reverted to her true womanly form and slapped his face. "Unhand me, you dog!"

"You're a feisty bit of baggage, aren't you?" The bandit caught Abyssmina's hand before she could swop him again and eyed her appreciatively. "And you've got a bit of meat on your bones, not like those silly girls who always moan about their weight."

She flushed prettily. "Well—"

He pulled her nose to nose. "Have you ever thought of taking up banditry? We're short on females at the moment, *and* we have an excellent holiday plan. We only work when we feel like it, and we go to the seaside every summer."

She looked intrigued. "I've never been to the beach."

"Princess?" Merval raised his head and blinked groggily.

Gerta edged along the narrow defile toward us. "Who wants to die first?"

Well, you could put me out of my misery, I thought crossly, but didn't say it. Gerta can be so literal sometimes.

"Sorry," the bandit said as Gerta closed in on him, sword raised. "We're off the clock right now. No fighting allowed."

Baffled, her brows knit. "But—"

"No," he said firmly. "We came back early because we heard about this magical street appearing up here lined with posh gentlemen's clubs, but every time we get close, it slips away."

"A street?" Groggily, Merval pushed himself up from the horse's neck. "Did you notice the name?"

"Didn't see no signpost, mate," the bandit said, "but all the ladies had these really momentous—" His hands cupped.

"That's it!" A hint of color crept back into Merval's face. "The Avenue of Immediate Availability. Now, if we could just find it long enough for me to remove that spell—"

"No more spells!" I said and snatched up the poker from where he'd dropped it on the ground. "If you so much as look at this thing cross-eyed, I'll splatter your brain all over these rocks!"

"But then the avenue will just wander forever," he said.

Abyssmina was gazing from under lowered lashes at her new bandit friend. "Can you do a beach towel?" he said, then smiled broadly as she transformed into a swath of bright orange fabric. "Oh, well done! How about a sandwich case?"

The rock cliffs shimmered and then in the distance I could just make out a street with gaily-painted houses populated by scantily clad females. Wild strains of music quavered on the air and I smelled patchouli.

"There it is!" the bandits all cried.

"Let me get this straight," I said to Merval. "Now that Bamffle is enspelled, only natives can find it."

"Yes," he said.

"And this avenue is part of Hagrishia, so I'm betting only Hagrishians can enter?"

"You know," he said, "that's entirely possible."

I turned to Gerta. "And we are contracted to escort Abyssmina and her intended, a native Hagrishian, home."

She nodded.

"And conveniently that happens to *be* Hagrishia," I said, "or at least a part of it. So, the contract is fulfilled!"

"But—" Gerta tried to work it out.

I motioned to Vigal. "Would you like to be kidnapped?"

"Yes, please!" He was bouncing on his toes.

"More than you want to be married to Abyssmina?"

"Oh, lots!" He was very enthusiastic. Smart kid. He might go far, for a prince.

I motioned to the bandits. "I think it's just possible young Vigal here can get you onto that avenue."

"You want us to baby-sit that brat?" The blond one sneered. "Not bloody likely!"

I took up my mare's reins. "And, then, of course, once the avenue regards you as natives, so you can come and go as you wish, you can ransom the little bugger." I shoved Esmeralda deep into her scabbard to mute her protests. "If you were ever, say, to find yourselves short of cash for a few necessities."

The bandits looked at each other. "So, lad—" The oldest winked at Vigal over a gap-toothed grin. "Like to steal?"

"Quick," I said, "the avenue's going fuzzy!"

With a whoop, the bandits snatched up Abyssmina and Vigal and loped toward the elusive street. The ladies-in-residence, all fetchingly half-clad, waved and shouted encouragements.

"But that's a street of high-priced courtesans," Merval said as the avenue wavered, then disappeared with all concerned, bound for sunnier climes, no doubt. "They'll have to pay for the ladies', um, favors. They don't give free *samples*."

I smiled. "No, indeed, and when they run out of gold, which I'm betting will be sooner rather than later, the management will not be cooperative. I just wish I could be there to watch."

"That's very bloody minded," Merval said.

"Yes, it is," I said and felt better than I had in days. Even Esmeralda muttering down in her scabbard didn't put me off.

Gerta frowned. "But what about my wedding?"

"Well, you should just go ahead and marry this wretch," I said. "Give in to the spell since you can't fight it."

"I will kill him right after," she said, as if that helped.

I nodded. "Even so, everyone for ten kingdoms will know you were spelled into unwilling matrimony, but just don't pay any attention when they all fall on the ground laughing."

Gerta's eyes flashed. "No one makes Gerta Derschnitzel do anything against her will!" The rocks reverberated in echo.

"Except this." I swung up into Corpsemaker's saddle. At least my mare wasn't talking back to me—yet.

"No, I don't want to marry him." Gerta bit her lip. "Do I?"

"You can if you want," I said.

"I'm almost certain I don't," she said, "but I was really looking forward to my wedding scars. My brother's wife got a *slit nose!*" She smiled in fond remembrance.

"Gee, some people do have all the luck," I said.

White-faced, Merval wrenched his horse's head around and clattered back down the trail with a spray of gravel.

"Oh, no." I studied my nails. "He's getting away."

Gerta urged her gelding into a halfhearted trot. I followed, soothed by the clink of Bamfflian gold in my purse.

We never did catch up with Merval, though we eventually found his horse wandering loose. He must have gone to ground in a cave, the prospect of being doomed to a diet of lichen and snow apparently more alluring than a slit nose and connubial bliss with Gerta.

The next day, the bandits returned to their posts, once again robbing with impunity, so now we have all the work we can handle. I had Merval's wand melted down into a chamber pot, but Gerta is still planning her wedding and has ordered white mail trimmed in ermine in honor of the occasion, should it ever come to pass. As for Esmeralda, she and I have come to an uneasy truce, neither speaking to the other. She does mutter a lot, though, when she thinks I'm not listening.

Sometimes, when we're crossing one of the passes and the wind is right, I hear laughter and wild music and know that somewhere in the mountains, the Avenue of Immediate Availability has once again manifested and bandits are making merry out of season. There's no reason why it should cheer me, and yet it always does.

Go figure.

Princess Injera Versus the Spanakopita of Doom

Robin Wayne Bailey

She woke on the beach. The cool surf still licked her toes, and the relentless afternoon sun beat down. Her ebon skin itched with a miserable combination of sea salt and sand and sunburn. Though too weak to rise, she managed to lift a dark-skinned hand and brush back the matted lock of curls that covered her face and blocked her vision. Even that small effort caused her pain. She ached all over.

A fat crab stared her in the eye, mere inches from her face. With one menacing claw upraised, it scuttled sideways a few steps and stopped again to regard her from another angle, as if wondering if she were edible.

In that regard, she had the advantage, for she knew it was, and she was famished. Hunger overcame her fatigue. She lashed out with her right fist, smashing downward, cracking the crab's shell with her first blow. It squealed and tried to back away on its broken legs. Springing to her hands and knees, she smashed it again. Then seizing the still-wriggling creature, she twisted and ripped the shattered claw, dug her well-manicured fingers into the pieces of the shell, and split it completely open.

As she sucked out the raw white meat and savored its sweetness, the juices of the creature's innards streamed over her parched lips and down her chin. She was too hungry to be delicate. In no time at all she licked the shell clean and started on the still-twitching crab legs. "What I wouldn't give for some melted butter!" she said to herself between bites, "with some ginger, parsley, atjar, raisins, almonds, and peppers, and an oven to bake you in, and a nice wine to wash you down!"

However, the raw crab refreshed her and replenished her strength. Rising to her feet, she looked around. The piece of ship's wreckage to which she'd clung through the night and upon which she'd floated ashore lay on the beach just a few paces away. Her armor was still securely bound to one of the boards with her belt, but as she trudged toward it she cursed.

The scabbard on the belt was empty. Her favorite cutlass was gone, lost on the bottom of the sea. She kicked at the sand in disgust, then put it out of her mind. Without that lucky bit of flotsam, she'd be at the bottom of the sea with her weapon.

Leaving her sandals on the beach, she waded back into the sea to rinse the sand from her garments and the tangles from her curls. As she did so she scanned the watery horizon and gazed up and down the shimmering shoreline for any trace of her ship, its wreckage, or any survivors from her crew, but she saw nothing. She was stranded, alone, and far from African shores.

Still things weren't all bad. She wasn't cut or bruised. Nothing was broken. She ran her hands over the softly clinging leopard-skin furs she wore, gingerly exploring the swells of her breasts, the curves of her hips. In fact, she admitted to herself, for a ship-wrecked castaway she looked good! She drew a deep breath and tossed her wet black mane. As she stretched, she imagined she heard the throbbing drums of her homeland.

Boom, tee-dee boom! Tee-dee boom! Tee-dee boom!

A voice spoke from the shore behind her. "The jungle cat that sacrificed itself to make that outfit did mankind a wonderful service, Injera."

She whirled, splashing water, one hand automatically going to her left hip for the cutlass that wasn't there. Bending quickly, she scooped up the only weapon available—a handful of sandy mud. She held it ready.

Near the water's edge a man grinned at her from astride the bare back of a dun mare. His skin was pale, lightly olive-colored, smooth. A finely trimmed beard emphasized the chiseled line of his jaw, and a slight breeze brushed through the straight locks of his dark hair. He wore a plain white chiton over one shoulder and a broad leather belt to hold it in place. His leather sandals were expensively made.

"*Princess* Injera," she shot back with a defiant lift of her head, "of the Gojjam people . . ."

The man interrupted with a sharp laugh. "Princess? You underrate yourself! You're the dread pirate, Injera, queen of the raider ship *Yeshimbra Assa.*" He threw one leg over his horse's head and dropped to the sand. "You see I know you, my fiery little pepper. For days I've tasted the flavor of you as your ship sailed near. I've inhaled your essence and your aroma."

Injera raised one arm uncertainly and sniffed her pit. Then she glared and prepared to launch the handful of mud. "Take that back!" she warned. "I don't have any aroma! And who the hell do you think you are?"

That maddening grin spread wider upon his face, revealing perfect teeth. With one hand he clung to the reins of his horse's bridle. In the other he carried a coiled leather lash. "Just a figure of speech, my sweet potato," he said. "No offense intended. My name is Gyro."

It was Injera's turn to laugh. "Hero?" She ran a dubious eye over his not-unappetizing form. "Maybe you're overrating yourself? You don't even have a sword!"

"*Yee-row,*" he repeated, correcting her pronunciation. "And long pointy things have never held much attraction for me, at least not metal ones." He raised the whip and winked at her through the coils. "I'm rather good with this, though."

Injera's gaze narrowed. Was he threatening her? She lifted her head higher still and thrust out her leopard-spotted chest. She didn't take well to threats, and his puny leather lash didn't frighten her. To show that she wasn't afraid of him she rinsed the mud from her hand and waded back toward the shore.

"Look, I'm perfectly willing to beat the nutty stuffing out of you if you try to hit me with that," she told him, "but

I'm hot and tired and thirsty. So why not just point me toward the nearest village? It must be suppertime somewhere."

Gyro pushed at a piece of crab shell with his toe. "Still hungry?" He dropped the reins of his mount and shooed the animal a few paces up the beach. "Safer for her," he laughed as he turned back to Injera. "I'll bet you could eat a horse."

Injera snarled and clenched her fists. If this stranger intended to give her trouble, she'd accommodate him. She could outfight and outwrestle any man she'd ever met, and this one, pretty as he was, didn't look like much of a challenge.

However, now that he'd mentioned it, the dun mare did look pretty tasty. A bit on the lean side, perhaps, but a girl had to watch her figure. That still left the problem of drink. She licked her lips and wondered what kind of wine went best with horsemeat.

A nasty grin turned up the corners of her lips. *Equine, of course.*

Gyro took a step back and raised a hand to forestall her advance. "She's much too stringy," he said, as if he'd read Injera's mind. "Why not let me whip you up something more to your taste!"

The whip uncoiled as he swung it above his head. Injera flung up her hands and jumped back out of range, then watched, gape-jawed. The leather seemed to glow and shimmer, to throw off streamers of color, sparks of radiance. Suddenly the air split with a sharp crack and a flash of light.

A clean white tablecloth lay spread over the sand at Injera's feet, and upon it was a platter of *doro wat*, which was roast chicken served in red pepper sauce. Rich aromas of onion, fenugreek, nutmeg, and cardamon hung over it like a steamy cloud. Scattered around the chicken were seasoned, hard-cooked eggs, steamed lentils, and collard greens.

A second steaming platter held beef *tibs* and raw beef *kitfo* with shallots and chilies and yams. Still a third platter held stuffed whole honeycomb tripe with spiced rice and turmeric sauce. And fish *imojo*!

Along the edges of the tablecloth were smaller bowls with *dabo kolo* biscuits, *chiko* cakes, and lamb *alechas*. And at the center of it all were two tall bottles of the honey wine called *tej*!

Draping the whip over his right forearm, Gyro bowed from the waist and made a sweeping gesture. "Wands are so ordinary," he said with that ever-present grin. "Can I cook, or can I cook?"

"All my favorites!" Injera exclaimed, her mouth watering as she clapped her hands in delight. Half intoxicated by the smells, she threw herself down on her knees and seized a saucy chicken leg. She glanced around for the beer she liked best. It wasn't there. "But you forgot the *talla*."

"Be grateful!" Gyro chuckled. "You don't serve *talla* with such a complexity of flavors."

"Whatever you say," Injera agreed as she devoured the chicken leg and cast the bone away. She shoved her fingers into the spicy beef *tibs* and raised a mouthful to her lips. "I owe you anything you want for all this!" she sputtered as she chewed. "It's delicious! Wonderful! However you pronounce your name you're certainly my hero now!" She stuffed an egg into her mouth and shot an inviting look at her provider. "Please, won't you join me?"

He smiled as he watched her eat. "I prefer Greek."

Injera shrugged and gave her full attention to her meal. She didn't question where the food came from. It was real enough. It filled her stomach and pleased her tongue, and the *tej* wine tasted better than any she'd drunk in her own homeland. Gyro was a sorcerer, more skilled certainly than the *shamans* of Gojjam, but she knew the type, and she knew also that sooner or later, like all sorcerers, he'd ask some price.

For now, though, she was enjoying the best meal of her life on a beautiful beach, beside a blue ocean under a gloriously brilliant sunset with a handsome man at her side. It was almost romantic, and she forgot about her lost ship and crew, her cutlass somewhere at the bottom of the sea, and the coastal city she had sacked and burned the day before. One by one, she emptied the platters and the bowls, and one of the bottles of honey wine, and she tossed them into the water where the tide deposited them on the beach again.

Mindful of the sorcerer's price, Injera saved one bottle of *tej*. As the sky grew darker and the first stars began to appear, she smoothed the tablecloth and stretched out upon it in seductive fashion. With one hand she loosened a strap of her leopard-skin halter. Then she gazed up at Gyro and extended the same hand.

Her voice turned throaty. "Now make me *your* banquet!" she said with a wink. "Even Greek, if you prefer that."

Gyro stood looking out to sea with folded arms. The coiled whip hung from a loop on his belt, and the rising sea breeze stirred the folds of the brief chiton he wore, giving her an interesting view from where she lay. His bare thighs and shoulders, nicely muscled, awoke a different appetite in Injera. He turned toward her, and of course he smiled.

"You must be joking," he said. "I wouldn't have thought you had such a sense of humor!"

Injera bristled and sat up. "It's the traditional way a woman repays a man for a lavish dinner!" she snapped. Her eyes narrowed with warning. "You don't want to go against tradition, do you?"

Gyro shrugged and moved a step away. "That may be the tradition among the Ethiopes, Your Highness," he said with more than a hint of mockery. "But this is Hellas, called Greece by some, and we do things differently." He whistled for his horse, and the dun mare walked across the sand to his side. "There is something you can do for me, however."

Injera sat up and crossed her legs, and her gaze turned wary. The handsome sorcerer before her suddenly seemed too handsome, his arrival too opportune. What was he really doing here on this isolated stretch of beach? Why his ostentatious display of magic if not to impress her? Not that she objected to that, for the food had completely restored her strength. Yet there was an unsettling tone in his voice that she hadn't noticed before.

"The trouble on the *Yeshimbra Assa* began with a fire," she said suspiciously, "in the galley."

"You were leagues from the coast, but I smelled the spicy *metin shuro* stew your cook was preparing," Gyro acknowledged. "I caused it to flame up and spill over the deck."

Injera couldn't hide her shock and outrage. Gyro grinned. "What? You expected windstorms? Giant waves? All that unimaginative fairy-tale stuff?"

"You burned my ship!" she cried.

Gyro gave her a scolding look. "Nonsense! I've never burned anything! I have a reputation!" He looked thoughtful for a moment, then inclined his head, and that annoying grin returned. "Let's say that I grilled it, or given the fat on some of your crew, that I braised it."

Injera sprang upward like a cat, and her hands closed around Gyro's throat. They both fell back struggling on the sand. "Then I'm only kneading your doughy little neck!" she shouted, her face close to his as she straddled his chest. "I'm only tenderizing your scrawny windpipe!" She banged his head on the ground as she squeezed the breath out of him. "Now who's cooking?"

The dun mare, docile until now, gave an angry whinny, charged, and struck Injera with a powerful toss of its head. The blow sent her tumbling. Unharmed, she rolled to her feet with wiry grace and spun to face the sorcerer again, but the horse stood between them, its eyes blazing.

Gyro took the mare's reins in one hand, and after a moment of standoff, he offered them to Injera. "If you help me, Princess, I'm prepared to send you home again. As your reward, I'll obtain a new ship for you, better than your last one, and a new crew."

Injera spoke through clenched teeth. She didn't really care about her crew. Pirates and privateers were cheap meat. But the *Yeshimbra Assa* had been a good ship, and no Greek vessel would ever adequately replace it. "What do you want of me?" she demanded.

"Like myself, you have a reputation," he answered. "Your daring and fighting skills are renowned and feared along the coasts of many nations." He looked her up and down from the far side of his horse, then winked again. "And I might add, so is your beauty, although personally, I think you should eat more. You're much too thin."

Injera glowered. "So much butter. You'll spoil the soup with that kind of flattery."

"A pinch of sugar, a pinch of salt," Gyro replied in an off-handed manner as he stroked the mare along the withers. "I appreciate a full-bodied flavor,"

She didn't like the sound of that, nor did she care for the way he looked at her sometimes as if she were a tidbit or a piece of dessert. Her distrust for him grew with every word he uttered. However her curiosity grew with it, for as he'd said, she had a reputation. What could be worth so much that he would risk her displeasure?

Gyro anticipated her question. "Not far inland from here you'll find a structure. A temple, actually. On an altar in one of the chambers lies a box, ornately carved and locked with locks on the three unhinged sides."

"A bread box?" Injera interrupted, flashing her own sarcastic grin. She turned serious again "What's inside it, and what's the catch? Why don't you just go get it yourself?"

"The contents are unimportant and without value to anyone but me," he answered with such crispness that Injera knew he was lying. "The catch, as you say, is that it's guarded day and night by a society of hideous creatures that call themselves . . ." He hesitated, trembling, and for a moment he seemed almost unable to speak. " . . . the *Spanakopita of Doom.*"

Injera looked from Gyro's face to the coiled whip hanging from the loop on his wide leather belt. The sorcerer seemed to have no other weapons, and she wondered if it possessed abilities beyond those that he'd demonstrated. It reminded her that she had no weapon of her own.

"I'm not equipped for such a caper," she said, making a gesture with her empty hands. "Thanks to you, my sword lies rusting at the bottom of the sea."

"You have courage and resourcefulness," he informed her. "I'm sure you'll be able to provide for yourself." His apparent fear gone, he once again gave her that hungry, up-and-down look, and when he licked his lips with the pink tip of his tongue, it made her skin crawl. "Remember," he added, "if the risk is great, so is the reward—a new crew and a new ship to resume your journey homeward."

Injera considered her options. She could just walk away, head up or down the beach until she came to a village, and forget this dubious encounter. She owed Gyro nothing. She'd offered to pay for her meal in the manner she knew best, and he'd declined.

Still, she was an adventurer at heart. The same impulse that impelled her to leave the soft life with her royal parents in Gojjam and trade the crown of a princess for the title of raider-queen compelled her now to accept Gyro's challenge. Curiosity was a powerful force.

Greed, even more so. She thought about the box Gyro

desired. Not for a moment did she believe his declaration that it contained nothing of importance. She envisioned jewels, pearls, perhaps gold. The holds of the *Yeshimbra Assa* had brimmed with treasure, and it all lay at the bottom of the sea now. Her dark brows knitted together as she relished the idea of taking Gyro's treasure from him as he had taken hers.

"A new ship and a crew," she repeated, but it would never do to let Gyro dictate all the terms to her. She was a princess, after all. "The box you desire will be yours, but only that. I keep anything else I carry back. And when I return I'll be hungry, so you'll provide me with one more meal as grand as the one I just consumed."

"You show a lot of crust trying to haggle with me," Gyro said. He nodded with new appreciation as he touched the whip on his belt and stroked it lightly with his fingertips. "I accept your terms." He offered the mare's reins once more. "Take my horse. She knows the way."

But Injera wasn't ready to leave until she'd retrieved her armor. While Gyro watched, she adjusted the straps of her sandals and then fastened her greaves into place on her shins. Next, she strapped bracers on each of her forearms. "Don't just stand there," she told Gyro as she held out her breastplate. "Help me with this!"

"Never was a piece of metal so aptly named," he said as he took the breastplate and fitted it on her body. Injera gave a quick shudder while he fumbled with the straps and buckles for the leather padding inside the breastplate was still wet and cold. "You look positively Greek!" he added, stepping away when he was done.

"So did the man I took it from," she answered sharply. She picked up the belt with the empty scabbard, scowled at it, then tossed it aside. As ready as she could be, she grabbed a handful of the dun mare's mane and swung up astride its back and wrapped the reins around one hand. With her other, she pointed to the tablecloth on the sand. The remaining bottle of *tej* still lay there. "Give me that," she demanded. When Gyro complied, she pulled out the cork with her teeth, put the bottle to her lips, and upended it. She gulped loudly, making a show of her drinking skill, then with a casual flip of her arm, tossed the empty vessel into the waves.

"All right, horse," she said as she wiped her lips with the back of her hand. "Earn your oats." She beat her heels on the dun mare's flanks, and the animal took off across the beach at a gentle canter and headed inland.

Even in the dark of night the horse knew its way. Injera had no choice but to trust the mare, so she observed the sky and the landscape as well as she could perceive it. Black, jagged mountains loomed in the east. The sharp peaks pricked a star-flecked and cloudless sky. She noted familiar constellations and tried to approximate her location. The *Yeshimbra Assa* had gone down in the Ionian Sea off the coast of the Peloponnesos. She guessed she was somewhere south of Patras, but how far south she couldn't tell.

With the sand and the sea far behind, the ground turned rocky. Her bare thighs began to chafe. Her leopard-skin costume wasn't really suited for riding, and she wondered how Gyro in his chiton managed it. But she ignored the discomfort and focused her thoughts again on the contents of Gyro's mysterious box. Fantasies of treasure filled her head, rings for her fingers, necklaces for her ebon throat, diamonds and emeralds for her earlobes!

Gyro was a coward! Too weak and too afraid to do his own thieving, he was sending a woman to do it for him. Whatever the treasure, why should she share anything with him?

The landscape changed again. The mare carried her into low foothills and along grassy slopes. Olive trees grew wild and twisted. Injera lifted her nose to the breeze. A subtle mixture of scents—lemon balm, fennel and dill—filled the air. As she descended into a valley, she detected faint whiffs of still other odors, fragrances she could not identify, but which made her mouth water.

Damn! she thought as she ran her tongue over her lips. *This riding is hard work! I'm hungry again!*

In the black of night Injera still could see no discernible path, but up the far side of the valley the mare unerringly carried her. It didn't matter how Injera tugged the reins; it knew its own way, and whether by magic or nature, Injera couldn't guess. She knew, however, that they were near their destination when the mare reached the top of the hill and stopped.

Injera stretched as she looked around. There was nothing

at the top of the hill but grass and wildflowers. She snapped
the reins, urging the mare forward, but it refused to move.
She drummed her heels on its flanks with the same result.
She cursed the stubborn beast in a variety of languages. The
mare flicked its tail and lashed her bare back once, but
otherwise remained still.

Then, almost by accident, Injera saw what the mare
wanted her to see. As she raised her hand to slap the horse's
neck, from the corner of her eye she caught a glimpse of
a strange structure, not on the hilltop where she found
herself, but on the next, higher hilltop.

It sat nestled in the very shadow of the mountains. Even
in daylight, Injera guessed, it would be nearly invisible. Only
a trick of starlight and the mare's steadfast and unyield-
ing gaze had revealed it to her. Again she snapped the reins
and drummed her heels, but the mare would go no farther.

Injera dropped to the ground, nearly stumbling as her feet
touched the grass. Her legs were half-numbed from the long
ride. She rubbed her thighs, sure that they were raw and
that it would take a week of milk-bathing to soothe them.
Almost as irritating, her breastplate slipped down, and the
damp leather padding dragged her leopard-skin top with it.
She cursed Gyro for not getting all the snaps and buckles
fastened properly and readjusted everything herself.

"If you're not waiting when I get back," she groused at
the mare, "I'll skewer your stringy carcass."

Wishing for her cutlass, or any weapon, she started down
the hill and up the next one. She could no longer see the
structure. Darkness had swallowed it again, but she knew
well enough where to find it.

Gyro had called it a temple. If so, she wondered to what
god. She achieved the summit of the hill to find herself upon
a small plateau. A large copper moon just rising into the
sky shone through a gap in the mountains. Its peculiar light
illuminated an elaborate colonnade supporting an entablature like none she'd ever seen. Careful to remain in shadow,
she stole closer.

The frieze above the entablature was decorated, not with
scenes of battle or deeds of glory as were so many Greek
temples, nor with images of their gods and goddesses.
Instead, Injera noted a procession of scenes from a common kitchen: a figure making bread, another leaning over

a cookfire, a fowl roasting on a spit, a woman wiping her hands in an apron.

I don't know if I need a cutlass or a spoon, she thought to herself as she crept forward.

A cascade of steps led upward to the entrance. The colonnade and the entablature were little more than a facade. The actual temple extended cavelike deep into the mountain against which it was set. As she stood on the threshold, the smells of lemon balm, dill, and fennel swirled around her. The smells of nutmeg and cumin were just as strong. For a moment she thought she would sneeze and give herself away, but pinching her nose shut, she ventured inside.

A red, flickering light deep within the cave drew her forward. She moved soundlessly, alert for any danger, testing each footstep before putting her full weight upon it, wary of traps. She couldn't see a ceiling, nor any walls to left or right, yet the space was as warm as an oven!

She glanced nervously behind her. Beyond the open entrance the rising moon poured its oily light on the hillside. Licking her lips, she turned toward the flickering light at the back of the cave again.

A small voice inside her head warned her, *Don't go toward the light.*

Small voice, she answered silently, *shut the hell up*. She'd come for a box full of jewels, and she wasn't leaving without it.

But where were the dreaded *Spanakopita*, the fierce warrior guardians of the box, that Gyro so feared? She'd seen no sentries outside the temple, nor at the entrance. What if they'd abandoned this place and taken the box with them? Yet there was the fireglow ahead, so someone was home.

With catlike stealth she crept forward. She'd never been in a cave before, and the darkness impressed her. Nor was she quite convinced she actually was in a cave. The floors were smooth, and no dampness tainted the air, only warmth and the heady aroma of exotic spices.

Abruptly, the walls closed in. Injera's heart pounded. Putting a hand out before her, she felt the warm stone and found reassurance. The walls were not moving, as she had first thought. She had only reached the far side of a round chamber. She stood at the beginning of a long tunnel, no natural formation, at the end of which burned the firelight she'd been moving toward.

Her stomach rumbled. All the yummy smells were increasing her hunger. She tried to keep her mind on the task at hand, but food fantasies and the promise of her next meal stole through her thoughts. She licked her lips and tasted the salt of her own sweat. When she reached the end of the tunnel, Injera gave a loud gasp. Her gaze roamed around another large chamber, but unlike the outer chamber this one was richly furnished. A huge hearth stood at one end, and in it burned the fire that had guided her. A heavy black cauldron hanging above the flames steamed and bubbled. From this cauldron issued the many herb-and-spice odors that filled the temple and drifted on the night beyond even into the hills and valleys.

Marble tiles made the floor, each polished to such a sheen that she could see her image multiplied dozens of times. She hesitated, barely recognizing her reflection. In the red, dancing fireglow she looked wild and feral, not a princess at all. Her frown disappeared, though, as she turned her gaze toward the dining table that occupied the center of the room. Upon a tablecloth of fine Athenian lace lay plates and bowls and cups seemingly of glittering gold!

Injera dashed across the floor and seized a plate. Indeed, it was gold! She quickly took stock. Thirteen full place settings artfully embossed, with napkins of red silk and utensils of silver! And jewel-encrusted oil lamps at either end of the table! Injera felt like shouting. She was rich once more!

Then her gaze fell upon a box at the center of the table. Among all the splendor and wealth it would have been easy to overlook for it was plain wood, no longer than her forearm and no deeper than the width of her hand, unadorned but for the iron bands and three thumb-sized iron locks.

She eyed the box uncertainly. She'd envisioned something larger—a cask, perhaps, or something more distinguished. Still, it might make a lady's jewelry box. Or—and this was a troubling thought—maybe Gyro had spoken truthfully when he said it contained nothing of value.

There was only one way to find out. Injera rubbed a hand absently over her growling tummy, then leaned across the table and picked up the box. It wasn't particularly heavy. She held it close to her ear and shook it. Nothing rattled inside. Frowning, she studied the rough wood and the old locks, and picked up a table knife. Maybe she could pry it open.

At the far side of the room, the fire in the hearth flared, and the cauldron began to bubble noisily. Clouds of steam roiled into the air. Potent fumes of scallions and leeks suddenly stung Injera's eyes. Waves of heat seared her skin. Clutching the box to her breast, she stumbled back and knocked over a goblet. It fell to the floor with a clatter.

At the burning center of the hearth fire amid the hottest flames, a shape appeared and pointed an accusing finger. An angry voice boomed through the room. "Let any hungry soul come to our table and eat!" A second shape appeared behind the first, then a third and a fourth. "But whosoever would steal from us must die!"

For a moment, Injera's courage deserted her, and she screamed as the shapes walked out of the flames. More than four! Six! Ten! Twelve! One for each place setting at the table—plus a guest! Gyro had called them hideous. It was no exaggeration! They were tall with thin, lanky arms and legs and dark featureless faces, and their skin—if truly it was skin—gleamed with the cooked green color of spinach!

With arms outreaching, they advanced toward her, spreading around the room to block her escape. Injera gave another short scream. She grabbed a plate and flung it at the nearest figure. The metal edge stuck in its chest with a wet sound but no visible effect.

Injera shot a desperate glance toward the tunnel as a long arm reached for her. Steam poured off the creature's flesh, and she could feel the heat radiating from it. She barely ducked in time to avoid its grasping, claw-shaped hands. Flinging herself back against the table, she kicked out with both bare feet and sent the monster reeling into one of its companions. A green smear marked the floor where they fell, but both rose again unharmed.

With little room to run, Injera leaped upon the table. With the box in her left hand she grabbed a knife in her right. The *Spanakopita* ringed the table. An arm reached for her from the left side, and she batted it away with the box. A hand closed on her right ankle. She cried out at its steaming touch, bent, and slashed with the knife. The hand went flying and struck the floor like a spoonful of collard greens.

"I'll never be able to eat my vegetables again!" Injera muttered under her breath as she watched a new hand instantly take form at the end of the wounded creature's arm.

A strange rasping chant began to rise on the air as the creatures pressed around her. *Spanakopita! Spanakopita! Spanakopita!* Injera wasn't sure if it came from the monsters or from some other source. It sounded like hundreds of voices all whispering, hissing, demanding in terrible unison. She tried to shut it out as she shoved a spoon into a featureless face, slammed a bowl over a head that squished flat and reformed, drove a table knife through a lipless mouth.

She threw plates, cups, silverware, and still the monsters reached for her. One of them started to climb upon the table with her. With all her strength she swung the flat box, knocking its head sideways. Again and again she beat the creature, all the while kicking at hands that tried to seize her legs and ankles, until it toppled off. And still it got back up.

With an enraged cry, she flung the box at the stubborn monster.

Eyes stinging, choking on the spices that filled the air, Injera bent down and grabbed the tablecloth. The few dishes and pieces of silverware still on the table went flying as she straightened again. With a desperate effort, she swept the lace around her head and flung it. It spread like a net as she let it go and ensnared a trio of monsters at the end of the table. It wouldn't hold them long, but it gave her the only opening in the fight. Heart hammering, she ran the length of the board, somersaulted over their heads, and landed in a crouch on the floor.

"Hah!" She paused long enough to spit on the polished marble tile and to shove her breastplate back into place, for the straps had slipped again. Then she dashed for the tunnel. But three steps into it, she tripped and fell flat on her face. Cursing, wide-eyed with fear that the monsters had caught her, she sprang up again and looked back. Gyro's box lay at her feet! So did a gold table knife!

She wasn't going to leave empty-handed, after all!

As the monsters shambled after her, Injera scooped up her treasures and ran as fast as she could through the tunnel, through the warm outer chamber, and into the night. On the steps beneath the colonnade she paused to gulp deep, ragged breaths and look back over her shoulder. She couldn't see the monsters behind her!

Her right big toe throbbed, but she wasn't taking any more chances. Wincing with every step, she ran down the slope and up the next. By the time she made it to the summit of the hill where the dun mare waited, she was hopping and hobbling, but she wanted still more distance between herself and that damnable temple.

The mare accommodated her. Once she was astride its back with the box under her arm it took off at a mad gallop.

"You got it!" Gyro hadn't left his place on the beach. He leaped up excitedly from where he'd been sitting on the white tablecloth. A half-finished sandcastle stood nearby. "You actually did it! I knew you were the woman for the job!" He thrust out a hand even before she dismounted. "Give it to me!"

Dazed and aching from her frantic return, Injera tossed the box down to him. "Whatever's inside that thing damned well better be worth it," she warned. "I'm starved, and I've been through hell, and every bone in my body aches, and my thighs are completely raw!" She slid down from the dun mare's back and winced in pain. "And I've broken my toe!"

"But you beat the *Spanakopita of Doom*!" Gyro cried as he turned the box over and over in his hands. His eyes gleamed, and he trembled with anticipation. Nervously, he fumbled inside his belt, drew out a key, and held it up to the moonlight. "You have no idea how many heroes . . ."—he pronounced the word very carefully for her benefit—" . . . I've tricked, I mean, sent to that temple for the contents of this box."

Injera clenched one fist as she hobbled closer for a better look. Her other fist closed on the gold table knife she wore behind her back in the waistband of her leopard skins. If there really was anything of value inside that box, she intended to share in it. "Where'd you get the key?" she asked suspiciously. "And what were those monsters?"

Gyro shrugged, as he inserted the key into the second lock. "Every cook experiments," he answered. "They were an experiment that went wrong. I think I got some ingredients mixed up."

Injera grabbed a handful of his hair and jerked his head back sharply. "You made those things?" She flung him onto his back, disgusted.

Gyro scrambled to recover the key he'd dropped, then flashed her a brief smile. "I wanted a perfect kitchen," he explained as he inserted the key and popped open the second lock. "A place where every man could come and eat his fill. Of course, a perfect kitchen requires a perfectly trained staff!"

"They turned on you and drove you out." Her eyes lit up suddenly. "You tried to take something." She pointed to the box as he opened the third lock. "You tried to take that!"

"My recipes!" he shouted with a laugh as he threw open the lid.

Injera stared with disbelieving eyes. "It's—it's a cookbook!"

Gyro shot her an offended look, and his eyes burned with an angry fire. "Not just any cookbook, you stupid woman!" He clutched the book to his heart. "This is the cookbook of the gods. You can't imagine what I can whip up with this!"

Injera drew her knife. "You're mad!" she shouted. "I should . . . !"

Gyro ignored her and opened the book, thumbed through its first few pages, then stopped. The fire in his eyes died suddenly as a powerful odor of dill and fennel and nutmeg rose from the pages. Too late, he tried to slam the book shut, but a dark, wetly green hand thrust up from between the covers and clamped with ferocious strength around his throat.

Horrified, Injera fell back on the sand and crawled away, unable to take her eyes from Gyro's face or the too-familiar hand that choked the life from him. The sorcerer gurgled and gasped, and his eyes rolled up inside his head, and then his tongue lolled. When he was finally dead, the hand released him and withdrew into the book again.

The wind made an eerie sound as it rustled briefly through the pages. *Spanakopita! Spanakopita! Spanokopita!* Then, of their own accord, the covers closed.

After a while, as the moon began its westward descent, Injera got to her feet. Regaining her courage, she flung book and box as far into the sea as she could and sat for a long time thinking and staring at her gold knife, and eventually she made a fire. She was still hungry. Immensely so. When she couldn't make the whip work, she flung it after the book and box and sat down to think some more and to stare into her fire, and slowly she smiled.

Gyro had promised her a good meal.

By dawn, he had delivered.

And as for his dun mare? It was truly done—well done. Like Gyro.

Brunhilde's Bra

Laura J. Underwood

"Psst! Hey, lady . . ."

"Who are you calling a lady?" Gerda retorted to the seedy little man who slipped into her booth. He was swaddled in several layers of cloak and robes, leading her to suspect that he was even smaller than his lack of height indicated.

"Well, I don't dare call you *sister* because I suspect you would smack the holy hog out of me," he said cheerfully.

"What do you want?" She glared over the top of her tankard, hoping the stern look would hasten his desire to leave. But he pushed back his hood, revealing a face that even a mother would cover. And when he grinned, the effect was all the more bizarre.

"The name's Sigurd," he said. "I'm a man of the road, and I procure rare items which I sell . . . and when I came into the tavern and saw you sitting here, I said to myself, now there is a woman of warrior proportions. . . ."

"Don't get cheeky!" Gerda said. "Or I'll add another smile under that phony one you're wearing." She put a hand to the hilt of her sword. The seedy little man drew back mere inches.

"No offense, but I have an item for sale that I suspect a woman of your . . . profession would find useful," he said.

"What?"

He reached into his cloak. Gerda heard a metallic clank. Then he drew out a moderate-sized parcel wrapped in old burlap. Drawing back the edges, he revealed what looked like a pair of large metal platters bound together with strips of leather.

"What in the name of the All Father is that?" Gerda asked.

"Brunhilde's Breastplate," Sigurd said.

"Looks more like Brunhilde's bra," she retorted.

"No, it's her breastplate. . . . You think I'd be stupid enough to consider selling a mere bra to a woman with arms like yours?"

"What's wrong with my arms?" Gerda said.

"Nothing. They're good strong arms, more than capable of breaking my neck."

"Well, as long as you realize that," Gerda said sourly. "So where'd you get the . . . breastplates?"

"Off a Valkyrie," he said. Gerda started to open her mouth. "Oh, don't worry. She was sleeping in some magic ring of fire and isn't likely to wake up for a while."

"And you just took her bra?" Gerda said. "What sort of little pervert are you?"

"I'm not a pervert," he protested. "And it was obvious that she didn't need it. And anyway, it was silly of her to wear metal while sleeping in the middle of a magic fire. Think of the blisters. . . ."

Gerda frowned. "Let me get this straight," she said. "You crossed a magic ring of fire built by Odin himself just to claim Brunhilde's bra. . . ."

"Breastplate," he corrected. "And no it wasn't easy. Burned my bum just leaping over it."

"You leapt over Odin's fire?" Gerda couldn't help but sound impressed.

"Pole-vaulted, actually—learned it from the Romans. It's how they get on horses without any stirrups, you know. A man of my stature has to grab every advantage he can, you know."

Gerda rolled her eyes. She had no doubt that there were other advantages he'd like to grab. "So you vaulted over the magic fire, fondled the breasts of Odin's daughter while stealing her bra, and now you want to sell it to me?"

"Well, I didn't exactly fondle her breasts," Sigurd said,

looking a little agitated by the accusation. "But that is pretty much the gist of it all."

"Why?"

"Why what?"

"Why should I buy a used metal bra that looks two cup sizes too big and will probably chafe like everything?" Gerda said.

Sigurd leaned closer as though not wanting to share what he had to say with the whole room. "It's got magic powers," he said. "But it only works for women."

"What sort of magic powers?" Gerda leaned over so she was practically nose-to-nose with him, then drew back again when his breath assailed her. Smelled like he'd been sucking Brunhilde's socks.

"Picture yourself on the battlefield swinging your ax—"

"Sword," Gerda corrected. "Can't abide an ax."

"Okay, sword," Sigurd said. "You're surrounded by the enemy, and they decide to rush you at once because they figure you're a helpless woman. Only when they come at you, swinging their axes and war hammers, they discover to their dismay that you are invincible!"

"Invincible?" Gerda repeated.

"Exactly!" Sigurd said. "The magic in this breastplate will make you impervious to ax, sword, slings and arrows and anything else the enemy throws at you."

Gerda cocked her head. "Okay, how much?"

"What can you spare?"

She thought about it. All she had on her was two gold coins and a ruby she won in a poker game with a troll. And the tavern bill wasn't paid. Still, if the breastplate did what he said it did, she wouldn't have to worry about money any more. She would be the most invincible woman warrior in the land. That reputation alone could earn her more gold than she had ever seen in her life. Mercenary wenches were all the rage these days. Gerda needed an angle that would put her ahead of the other women, and this bra might just do the trick. Slowly, she reached into her belt pouch and tossed the coins and the jewel on the table. "That's everything I own, except for my sword and my horse, and you're not getting those." Especially, she thought, since she didn't really own the horse. It was a loaner from King Braggart the Weary in whose service she fought.

Sigurd looked at the offering and sighed. "Well, it's not as much as I had hoped . . . I've got this dragon of a bill collector on my tail."

"It's all I've got!" she snapped.

"Okay, okay. It'll have to do."

He pushed the parcel towards her and scooped up the ruby and the gold.

"Oh, one other thing," he said.

"What?"

"Word is there's a curse on the breastplate."

"What sort of curse?" Gerda asked with a glower of suspicion.

"Well, if I remember rightly, if you die, you become a Valkyrie."

"But how can I be killed if the breastplate makes me invincible?"

Sigurd shrugged. "Beats me," he said.

Before she could offer to do just that, he was gone.

Gerda looked hard at the breastplate. The damned thing had better work, or she would go looking for Sigurd and use him to practice tying knots. She picked the breastplate up and headed for the stairs to find some place private to put it on.

Well, it did fit better than Gerda expected, but that was because the moment she buckled it on, the plates shrank to cover her breasts in cold metal. *Damn,* she thought. She should have put it *over* the shirt. She tried to reach around and unbuckle it to correct the problem, but in shrinking to fit her girth, it had put the buckles out of reach. And her muscled arms were not as flexible as she would have liked. One of the reasons she had given up swinging an ax was that her deltoids and trapezium were too big to allow her to bend her arms all the way around behind her.

Double damn. Now she would have to get someone to unbuckle it for her, and that was not a good idea in a tavern full of drunken soldiers who would likely misconstrue her need into a proposition. The barmaid then. She might help. Or not. Considering that Gerda owed a tab that she had no way of paying at the moment . . .

So, I'll just wear it, she thought. Surely, it would warm to her skin . . . hopefully. But in the meantime, it was chilling her breasts and mashing them flat, and it was starting to chafe as well. She hauled her shirt and her cloak over it, stepped out of the lavatory—which was really a closet with a chamberpot—and decided to look for an exit to the tavern. Hopefully, she could get back to camp before the tavern keeper noticed she was gone.

Luck had it, however, that the tavern keeper had noticed her absence. Gerda heard him on the stairs, asking the barmaid if "that big-armed wench with the sword" had paid her tab yet. *Triple damn.* Gerda should have kept one of the gold coins. That weasel Sigurd would probably have taken one gold piece and the jewel. She looked back and forth, then chose a door and pushed it open.

The room into which she stumbled was dark, but not so much that she did not see the sleeping young man— who didn't stay asleep for very long. He opened a pair of melt-your-heart blue eyes and squinted as he tried to focus on her. "Whuh . . ." His face reminded her of a hero she'd once seen on the battlefield. Or one of her commanding officers . . .

Gerda decked him hard and fast before he could recognize her. He flopped back down on the pallet unconscious. That problem taken care of, she made for the window. A medium drop awaited her, but there was a wagon full of hay conveniently there. She jumped, landed and felt the wagon lurch as one of the axles broke. A dog started to bark as she rolled out of the hay and hit the cobbles. Not waiting to see who might come out, she bolted for the gate and was quickly charging down the road at a pace that would have made a Valkyrie jealous. That was when she remembered that she had left her horse at the inn.

Quadruple damn. She couldn't go back now. Oh, well, maybe the tavern keeper would return it to the camp . . . or not, since she still owed him a tab.

Gerda continued down the road at a fast trot. Better to get back to camp tonight. She could look for another horse tomorrow.

Gerda managed to bed down in one of the spare barrack tents without going through a lot of trouble. In fact, the guards at the camp asked no more than the password before letting her go on. They looked as sleepy as she felt.

Come morning, she rolled off her back because the buckle was cutting into her flesh, only to have the metal cups of Brunhilde's bra bite into her flesh.

Damn, damn, triple damn, she thought. The blasted things were still as cold as ice and pinched like her uncle's hand. She rolled a bit more, trying to get at the buckles, but they were still out of reach. Cursing, she crawled to her knees and staggered to her feet. Then walking out of the tent over to the horse trough, she ducked her head. The chilly water cleared her thoughts and her sinuses.

Her next stop was the camp latrine where she cleared her nature and contemplated asking one of the other women in the troop to unbuckle the breastplate. Then again, they might think she was making a play for one of them. One never knew these days. With a sigh, she finished up and headed for the mess. Breakfast was being served, a ration of bread and cheese and ale. She snagged her share and claimed a seat, and was just about half finished with the food when the horns sounded. *Twice time triple damn,* she thought. Men and women alike lurched to their feet. Someone shouted that enemy long ships had landed on the southern shore, and there was a call to arms. Gerda made sure her sword was strapped on tight and charged out into the misty morning. Beyond the rise were sea cliffs, and she could hear the mad shouts of the warriors who had already beached.

Gerda and the warriors of her troop charged down the narrow paths that ravaged the craggy face of the cliffs. Their archers shot arrows from above while their horsemen sought a less risky path. The idea was to keep the invaders from reaching the cliffs, though whose idea was questionable at this point. Gerda was not afraid. She had known enough battles, but it seemed like a thousand invaders had poured out of those long ships. And though the breastplates did their job—neither sword nor ax nor hammer touched her— she swiftly tired of the conflict. Too bad the breastplates didn't gift her with strength as well. She could have used the help. There were just too many invaders trying to hack off her head or disembowel her. She still managed to make a good account of herself, but as soon as she wounded one man, another—no two others—took his place. She slashed and hacked and managed to reave her way through a number of men before she stopped at the surf. There she turned and looked back to survey the swath she had cut through their numbers.That was when she spotted the four women on flying horses. They floated in the air, looks of anger on their faces. By the All Father's beard, were those . . . was she?

"You know, Brun, Daddy is *not* going to like finding you outside the magic fire," one of them said.

"What?" Gerda waved her sword. "Begone, Valkyries, I am not dead!"

"No, but when Daddy Odin finds out you escaped without the hero, he's gonna be mighty peeved," a second one said.

"What . . . are you nearsighted or something? I am not who you think. I am Gerda of Grimgeld."

"Right," the third one said, "and I am Penelope of Pretoria. Let's grab her, girls. Daddy Odin will want to handle this one personally."

They dove at her. Gerda tried to duck, but horse hooves clipped her in the back of the head and drove her facedown into the sand and darkness. *So much for magical invincibility* was her last thought.

Gerda's head was ringing like an opera hall, and as she opened her eyes, she discovered that she was indeed in some sort of hall. No ordinary one, to be sure. The carvings were of gods and monsters and all sorts of strange shapes interwoven in some sort of orgy of wood. Around her, she heard laughter, and when she glanced up, she saw rows of tables occupied by men and women who looked like they had seen some hacking and slashing in their days. Pale and pasty-faced as they were, they appeared to be having quite a good time.

With a moan, Gerda rolled over. The breastplate clanged against the stone floor with an unusually loud clamor. She yipped as it pinched her. *Damn, triple damn, triple damn,* she thought and struggled to get to her feet.

A tall man on a throne sat before her. Two ravens occupied the posts of his chair. He looked at her with only one eye.

"Brunhilde, you've lost weight," he said.

"The name's Gerda, not Brunhilde," she said. "Where am I?"

"In Valhalla," he said. "And what do you mean, your name is Gerda? I didn't name you Gerda."

"Oh, and just who are you?" she said.

"Brunhilde, I am your father," he said leaning close.

There was fire in the one eye. Gerda gulped. "All Father," she muttered.

He smiled. "See, I knew they couldn't have hit you *that* hard. Now tell me, my daughter. Why are you here?"

"Because they kidnapped me," Gerda said, pointing to the Valkyries who were flitting around the upper reaches of the hall on their flying horses. Now and again, one of those airy equines would lift its tail. A resounding plop would follow. Made Gerda wish she had a shield . . . or a tent.

"Your sisters did not kidnap you, Brunhilde. They brought you back to me because you've been naughty."

Gerda frowned. "Look, maybe you better ask for a new eye because the one you've got isn't working well. I am not Brunhilde. I am Gerda of Grimgeld, daughter of Ortho the Grey and Fredda the Pink, a mercenary in service to King Braggart the Weary."

Odin, All Father reared back, looking perturbed. "But you are wearing the Breastplates of Brunhilde," he said. "And they fit you like a glove . . ."

"Yeah, well, you know, I just bought the thing from this weasel of a little guy named Sigurd who says he leaped over the magic fire and ripped it off your sleeping daughter."

Odin's eye darkened. "Sigurd! But how could *he* have crossed the magic fire? Only a hero who is pure of heart can set my beloved Brunhilde free."

"Yeah, well, he made it, and he sold me this set of tin tits, and I want them off!"

Gerda wrestled with the breastplate a little more.

"Oh, here, let me help you," Odin said. He stepped down from his throne and knelt, which still had him leaning over Gerda. A few quick flicks of his fingers, and he had unhooked the buckles. The breastplate fell from Gerda, clanging to the floor and leaving her half naked. *Double qua-druple damn,* she cursed and clapped hands over her breasts as several dozen pairs of dead eyes turned. Their tongues dangled in delight. "Hey . . . where did this mortal woman come from?" Odin said as he lurched back.

Gerda turned to find Odin staring at her balefully. "Only

the dead may enter Valhalla—or one of my daughters," he said. "And you are neither!"

"I have been trying to tell you that," Gerda said.

"Valkyries! Rid me of this woman's presence."

"Hold on! Just tell me where the door is," Gerda said. But Odin was standing now, rearing over her in All Father godly glory. Behind him rose a host of other gods. All tall and looking rather disturbed to see her. Gerda decided that this was one party she didn't want a part of. She turned and ran, heedless of the cold that left a chill on her skin and raised gooseflesh. All she wanted was out of this place as fast as possible.

There was a screech, and one of the Valkyries came soaring at Gerda. Gerda ducked under the sword that tried to cut off her head and rolled to one side. Her body slammed into a table so that it was upset, and several goblets and platters of purest gold tumbled and clattered to the floor. Clutching one of those large platters like a shield, Gerda snatched up a goblet as well. As ranks closed, she hammered away with the goblet, backing towards the door.

They opened and let a blast of cold icy wind in. The bracing wind smacked at Gerda's back, and blew the Valkyrie off her horse. The creature landed, and Gerda dropped the goblet to grab a handful of mane and vault onto the horse's back. She rammed heels into its side and with a whinny the horse plunged through the door.

"Hey, that's *my* horse!" the Valkyrie whined. "Daddy!"

Gerda ignored them. She had never ridden a flying horse before, and certainly would have been grateful for a saddle and some stirrups, but beggars couldn't be choosers, she told herself. So with one hand still clinging to the mane, she whacked the horse on the rump with the shield. It surged over the rainbow bridge, nearly knocking Heimdall down as he raised his horn. And suddenly, it was plunging towards the earth, shrieking madly. Gerda was shrieking too—with terror—for she felt certain the beast was going to drop her over its head as it left her stomach behind.

But the sudden drop stopped, and the horse landed on the beach.

Men were still engaged in battle. The invaders looked up at the half-naked woman on the flying horse with the golden shield. With shouts of fear, they pointed and fled for their ships. Behind Gerda, the troops of King Braggart the Weary cheered.

Gerda jumped off the horse. She staggered over to where one of the fallen lay, and ripping his cloak free, she dragged it about her shoulders.

"Are you not going to take him to Valhalla?" one of the warriors asked with a frown.

Gerda decked him and marched off the field, still clutching her golden platter.

A moon passed since that fateful day. Gerda sold the platter and made herself quite a bundle. She would have sold the horse, but it flew away. Just as well. She didn't really need a flying horse that only knew the way from Midgard to Valhalla and back. So she bought herself a nice earthbound beast, purchased some new armor and went back to war to make a name for herself. Heck, the captain she had knocked out in the tavern that ill-fated night had no clue as to who decked him. He made her a sergeant.

Gerda was sitting in the same tavern one evening, about to quaff a tankard of the finest ale the landlord had to offer, when a familiar figure scuttled into the seat across from her. "Sigurd, you little turnip," she said and grinned like a wolf.

"Hey, Gerda! I've been hearing all sorts of grand tales about you."

"Such as?"

"They say you went to Valhalla and came back a Valkyrie. . . ."

"Well, not quite," Gerda said. "So what brings you out from under your rock, you thieving little toad?"

Sigurd touched his chest. "Why, Gerda, I'm hurt to think you would speak so to me . . . after all, if I hadn't sold you Brunhilde's Breastplate, you would never have made it to Valhalla and gotten rich . . ."

"You're right," she said. "But you know, that bra caused me more trouble than it was worth, and I swore that if I ever saw you again, I'd send you straight to Muspelheim . . ."

"Now, now," Sigurd said. "Kill me and I won't be able to share this really great bargain with you . . ."

"What sort of bargain?" she said with a frown.

"Well, I was out in the forest a few days ago, and who

should I happen upon but old Thor, and he was taking a nap under a tree . . . so I lifted his hammer . . ."

He reached under his robes and drew out a short stick with two knobby wads of metal on one end that vaguely resembled the hammer amulet some of the warriors wore. It also resembled something else in Gerda's mind, but she was too polite to say so. Sigurd pushed it across the table.

"So how much will you give me for it?" he asked.

Gerda arched one eyebrow. "Five," she said.

"Five?" Sigurd smiled. "Five golds?"

Gerda set her tankard aside and seized up the hammer. "No . . . five lumps, you lousy little thief . . ."

And with that, she proceeded to beat the snot out of Sigurd with the hammer of Thor.

Smoke and Mirrors

Steven Piziks

"I don't want to wait," Crystamel said. "I want a new body *now*."

Dagmar rolled her eyes at Ramdane, who simply shrugged. Overhead, the sky was a cloudless blue and a crisp fall breeze brushed through a crazy quilt of forest leaves. The sun was sliding toward the horizon, and Dagmar's mail shirt chafed annoyingly as she raised a rock to pound the last tent stake into place. Ramdane had lost the stake hammer. Normally Dagmar would have made her forgetful brother put up the tent, but that would probably mean fighting their way out of a collapsed tangle of canvas at some point during the night. After a curious chipmunk sniffed at one of the stakes, say.

"This isn't fair," Crystamel groused from her perch on an old stump. "You two always have nice bodies, but I have to put up with this. Look at this—I'm wearing out." She shook her bedraggled brown feathers to prove her point. Two pinions fluttered away, then plunged straight down and clattered against the hard oak roots. Ramdane sighed and picked them up. Both had changed into solid stone. In addition to the feather problem, Crystamel was missing an eye and her beak was chipped. She looked less like a falcon and more like a battered stuffed toy.

"What do you think, Mar?" Ramdane reached into his backpack to pull out a small stone cat and a hammer. "A transfer won't take a minute."

"Oooh!" said Crystamel. "I haven't been a cat in ages!"

The rock skinned Dagmar's knuckles. She yelped and shoved her fingers into her mouth. "Mofe," she growled. "Afomufwy mot."

"What?"

A popping noise as Dagmar freed her fingers. She was a tall, stocky woman with ash-blond hair and a face that was pretty if the light was right and you couldn't see the scars.

"No," she repeated. "Absolutely not. It isn't safe. And gimme that hammer. You said you'd lost it."

"Aw, come on." Ramdane set the little cat next to Crystamel on the stump. He was shorter than his sister, with a whipcord build and curly brown hair above blue eyes. Talismans clacked and clattered at his belt, marking him a talismonger just as Dagmar's sword marked her a warrior. "The campaign's over. The enemy guys are dead or fled. It won't take but a minute. Just stand guard, all right?"

Before Dagmar could answer, he started chanting. Crystamel stiffened. Ramdane raised the hammer and brought it down hard on the falcon. It shattered into rocky rubble. Ramdane continued to chant. A silver mist seeped out of the crumbled rock and tried to dissipate, but Ramdane's spell caught it and pulled it back. The mist drifted toward the little cat. Dagmar shuddered. This part never failed to creep her out. The mist, she knew, was a part of her younger brother's soul, and if he focused it into a properly-prepared talisman, it would bring the talisman to life as a familiar. If Ramdane made a mistake, however, and the soul fragment didn't make it into its new home—

Dagmar's ears caught the sound of crackling brush. Something shiny glinted in the sunlight.

"Ramdane!" she hissed, but Ramdane, caught up in his spell, didn't hear her.

The bushes abruptly parted, revealing a greasy-looking man wearing a tattered red robe and holding a hand mirror. He spoke a single sharp word, and the silver mist was sucked away from the cat. It vanished into the mirror. Ramdane cried out and collapsed to the ground as Dagmar whipped her knife from its sheath. Her sword was on the other side of their camp, a fact Ramdane hadn't bothered to check before he started his spell.

I knew it, Dagmar thought fiercely. *I just knew it. Do the right thing a hundred times and nothing happens. Do the wrong thing even once and it bites you in the ass.*

"I wouldn't throw that knife," the stranger said. He had dark hair that clung to his skull from lack of washing, a wispy beard, and a thin, hungry face. Two bird skulls, a dried worm tied into a knot, and a dead snake with its tail stuffed into its mouth hung from his belt—a paltry collection of talismans. "If I got hurt, I just might drop this mirror, and wouldn't that be a shame?"

Dagmar shot Ramdane a glance. He was on his hands and knees, retching.

"What do you want?" she asked, not lowering the knife.

The man smiled, revealing perfect, white teeth that contrasted sharply with the rest of his appearance. "You killed my employer."

"Prepare to die?" Dagmar asked.

The man looked confused. "I'm the one holding the magic mirror. *You* prepare to die."

"I didn't—never mind," Dagmar said. "Look, a lot of people were mad at your employer. It was probably the altar and all those children. And the sharp, shiny knives."

"He paid his retainers on time," the man snapped.

"They do say no one can be all bad."

"Don't get smart. You're not in charge here."

Dagmar's heart was pounding, but she nevertheless kept the knife steady. "So you're going to break that mirror, release that familiar spirit without a proper body nearby, and kill my little brother, is that it?"

"Maybe. Or maybe you could do me a little . . . favor."

Despite her tension, Dagmar had to suppress an urge to roll her eyes. "And what favor would that be?"

Ramdane continued to retch. Dagmar was sure he must be empty down to his toes by now.

"There's a little town called Daralis north of here," the greasy man said, "and they have a little problem. A gorgon."

"Ugly woman? Snakes for hair? Turns people who look at her to stone?"

"You're smart for a sword-swinger. At least one person

has already disappeared, and a huntsman saw a statue in the woods. Gorgon." The man held up the mirror. "I'll trade this bit of glass for its head. The talismans I could make from the hair snakes alone will set me up for life."

"How," Dagmar asked levelly, "are we supposed to cut the head off something we can't even look at?"

"I recommend shield polish," the greasy man said. "Just come back to this charming little grove with the head. I'll find you." And with that, he backed into the bushes and disappeared.

Dagmar flung the knife down and hauled Ramdane to his feet. "Dammit! Dammit dammit dammit!"

"Thanks for the sympathy," Ramdane said, staggering. "We're just talking about a piece of my soul, here."

Overhead, a bluebird twittered cheerfully. Dagmar would have cheerfully strangled it. Instead, she picked up Ramdane's hammer and started pounding the tent stake again. She swore in time with the rhythm.

"What are you doing?" Ramdane asked incredulously.

"Setting up camp. Are you up to hauling water? I need to wash like you wouldn't believe."

"What I don't believe is that we aren't packing up and heading out."

Dagmar sat back on her haunches. The cool breeze blew up stronger for a moment, making the canvas ripple. "You go on ahead. Me, I don't much care for stumbling through brambles after dark and turning my foot in gopher holes I can't see. Daralis isn't going anywhere."

"But my soul is!"

A little girl inside Dagmar jumped up and down and chanted *Told you so! Told you so!* But Ramdane's face was haggard, and his whipcord build looked even leaner than usual. Tiny lines of fear had already etched themselves around his blue eyes. Dagmar bit the inside of her cheek. There are times when even older sisters aren't allowed to say certain things aloud.

"Water," was all she said, and went back to pounding the stake.

"We're looking into the disappearances," Dagmar said, "and the innkeeper told us you could—"

"Well, it's about time," the woman snapped. A baby

squalled in the house behind her. The sound mixed with shouts and screams from voices of varying ages, and Dagmar caught a heavy whiff of unwashed bodies. "Ever since that lazy, ungrateful little slut ran off, I haven't had a moment's rest. Who's supposed to scrub my floor and clean my fireplace? And do the mending? And wash the dishes? And—"

"How dreadful for you," Ramdane interrupted. "Can you tell us how she disappeared?"

The woman snorted. "I sent her into the woods to look for flax."

"Where in the woods?" Dagmar asked intently.

"North of here. Told her not to come back until she had enough to start my new dress." She turned and shouted a threat into the screaming morass. "Brats."

"Horrible," Dagmar said.

The woman bristled. "My children?"

"Your dress."

"Oh." The woman looked confused, and Dagmar wondered if she were related to the greasy talismonger. "Anyway, that was the last I saw of her. A week after she disappeared, that idiot Dillon Hunter rushes into town blithering about seeing her statue in the woods. Serve her right if she got turned to stone."

"Can't think of a better punishment," Dagmar said.

The woman looked at Dagmar sharply, but Dagmar kept her face blank.

"Well," she growled, "if you find her, tell her not to expect any back pay." With that, she marched into the house and slammed the door.

Ramdane gave Dagmar a long look. "So you still want kids one day?"

Two hours later, brother and sister were resting beneath a huge maple tree. Occasional red leaves drifted down around them like tattered feathers.

"I hate this," Ramdane muttered. He was holding a small stone in his hands. "We must've talked to the entire village and haven't found anyone to guide us north. Not even Dillon. They're all too scared. Chickens."

"Too bad you weren't chicken about giving Crystamel a new body," Dagmar said, and instantly regretted it when

she saw the look on Ramdane's face. She sighed and gestured at Ramdane's rock. "That talisman will reverse what
the gorgon's done?"

"In theory. I've never dealt with anything like this before,
though." Ramdane's fingers gleamed, and the stone in his
hand went soft as clay as he carved one final rune with
the nail. When it was finished, he threaded it onto a leather
thong and hung it from his belt.

"How's Crystamel? You can still feel her, can't you?"

"She's scared," Ramdane replied shortly. "What's our next
step?"

Dagmar got to her feet with a clinking of mail. "I think
we should wander around the woods for a while. North of
here."

"Dagmar," Ramdane blurted, "how are we going to get
the gorgon's head?"

"With a shiny shield and a pure heart."

Ramdane grimaced. "I don't trust that greasy guy."

"You think I do?"

"If she dies, I die, so what's to prevent him from sending us off on another monster hunt after this one?" Ramdane
hooked the finished talisman onto his belt. "Threats and
blackmail for the rest of my life. Gods, Dagmar, there's a
twenty-ton rock hanging over me on a thread."

The little girl inside Dagmar jumped up and down. *Told
you so! Told you so!* Dagmar told her to shut up.

"Let's take it one step at a time," she advised. "And our
first step should be toward the woods. There must be a trail
the girl was following. Let's find it."

There was a trail, actually. It even led north. Brother and
sister followed it under crisp, colorful leaves and over
browning grass. Twice they lost their way and had to scour
the forest floor to pick up the trail again. The air was crisp
and fresh as a new-picked apple, and Dagmar's internal little
girl was filled with a desire to roll in leaf piles and stuff
dead twigs down Ramdane's shirt like she had done when
they were small, in the days before magic and swords had
taken over their lives. Those days were over now, though
Dagmar couldn't resist scuffling through crunchy leaves when
Ramdane wasn't looking. And then, in mid-scuffle, she
stopped and stared.

"Flax," Ramdane said, pointing to a ground-hugging patch.

"Statue," Dagmar said, pointing to the trees. A motion-less, white figure stood visible among them.

Ramdane caught his breath and went into a crouch. Dagmar whipped her shield off her back and followed suit. They crept closer, trying to be quiet but constantly betrayed by crunching leaves. Dagmar kept her highly-polished, sil-very shield in front of her as she crouch-walked forward. Her mail shirt jingled at every move.

"You look like an armored duck," Ramdane complained in a whisper. "And you're twice as loud. Here." He took a dog's ear from his amulet belt and hung it around Dagmar's neck.

"Hush," Ramdane said. The amulet glowed red and faded. Then the pair continued creeping toward the house, but silently.

After a certain amount of nerve-wracking shuffling ahead, Dagmar could see the statue more clearly. It was a teen-age girl carrying a basket and wearing the ragged clothes of a poor servant. She looked thin and tired, and it seemed as if she would gladly collapse to the grass if her muscles hadn't been carved from solid white marble. Behind the statue, the roof of a small cottage peeked above a tall, well-kept hedge. Dagmar blinked.

"I think," Ramdane whispered, "we've found our gorgon."

Dagmar eyed the cottage suspiciously. "It lives in a house?"

"Let's get the head and worry about details later."

"Easy for you to say. You aren't carrying the sword. No, don't say it. I'll scout. You take care of . . . her."

Without waiting for a reply, Dagmar slipped up to a gap in the hedge. She positioned her shield so it would reflect the view inside. The shield showed a well-kept little yard and a red front door with a fair amount of gingerbread molding.

Weirder and weirder, she thought nervously.

Ramdane, meanwhile, sidled up to the statue. With trem-bling fingers, he slipped the new talisman over its head and whispered, "Change."

A moment passed. Then the stone amulet shattered with a light popping sound that made Dagmar jump. A spot of fleshy pink formed on the statue's chest and spread with a wet, peeling noise. The young woman's cheeks acquired a rosy blush which crawled down her neck and swiftly suffused the rest of her body. Then the statue's arms plopped to the ground, followed by the head, torso, and legs. Ramdane leaped backward. Within seconds, the entire figure had collapsed into a mushy red pile at his feet. Dagmar stared.

"What," asked a querulous female voice, "have you done to my statue?"

Dagmar, who had been watching the statue instead of the yard's reflection, yelped and accidentally dropped her shield. It showed a perfect reflection of overhead green leaves.

"Watch out, Ramdane," Dagmar barked, fumbling madly for her sword and trying to recover her shield without raising her eyes. "Don't look at her."

"Too late," came the sour reply.

Startled, Dagmar snuck a glance in her brother's direction. Ramdane was leaning back on his elbows and looking directly past Dagmar. She could see reflected in the shield an elderly woman with a dark, raisin-like face. Obsidian eyes flashed in anger. She was standing in the gap in the hedge. Belatedly Dagmar realized she was staring at what must be the forest gorgon.

"I repeat," the woman said. "What have you done to my statue?"

"Are you the gorgon?" Ramdane asked cautiously.

It was the woman's turn to look surprised. "Gorgon?"

A rather pretty teenage girl stepped around the hedge, and Dagmar inhaled sharply. It was the young woman whose image lay squashed on the ground, only she wasn't nearly as thin and tired-looking.

"Granny, who are you talking to?" the girl asked.

"A pair of statue wreckers."

"Uh, we came from Daralis," Dagmar explained uncertainly, eyeing the girl. "Someone is missing from the village and—"

"What Dagmar is trying to say," Ramdane put in, "is that there's supposed to be a gorgon living in the forest and she's been turning people to stone." He peered intently at the old woman a moment longer, then got to his feet, brushing bits of . . . flesh? . . . from his clothing. "But if you're the gorgon, why haven't you turned *us* into stone? And did I or didn't I free her from your spell?"

"You didn't free anyone," the woman snapped. "I'm a sculptor, not a gorgon."

Dagmar blinked. "Say that again?"

"You deaf, girl? I said I'm a sculptor, not—"

"I'm dead," Ramdane whispered. "Oh gods, I'm really going to die."

"What's wrong with him?" the girl asked. She had a low, sweet voice.

"May we go inside?" Dagmar asked levelly, though her heart was sinking. "This would be a lot easier to explain sitting down."

"And so I retired from the guild," Granny Carver finished. "But I kept getting people who wanted advice about this piece of work or that bit of chipping. So I moved out here. The house used to be the summer home of a talismonger who liked his privacy and I figured I could finally get some peace and quiet. The talismans he used to cloak this place must be wearing off, though, which is how Kate found it." She nodded at the girl. "I offered to give her a place to live if she would help around the house and pose for some pieces, one of which you destroyed, young man."

They were seated in a rough but comfortable parlor sipping tea from paper-thin stone cups. Several small stone figurines had been arranged tastefully on wooden shelves and stands about the room while a round, bas relief carving of some species of demon glared moodily from its perch over the mantle. Dagmar was staring at the latter, fascinated, but she looked away when Granny addressed Ramdane.

"Sorry," Ramdane apologized. "The talisman was supposed to turn stone back into flesh. It worked. Sort of. If the statue had been human in the first place, things would have worked differently. As it is . . ." He trailed off with a shrug.

"You could always have barbecue for dinner," Dagmar couldn't help saying.

Granny Carver looked thoughtful, and for a dreadful moment Dagmar thought she had taken the remark seriously. Ramdane blanched.

"Um, you're an awfully fast worker," he said quickly. "I mean, carving that statue—and making all these in here— should have taken years, shouldn't it?"

The woman held up her wrinkled old hands and showed Ramdane the fingernails. They were glowing faintly.

"I've got the talent for molding," she said, "but not for enchanting. For me it's like working clay."

"Look," Dagmar broke in, "why don't you two come down to Daralis and tell the people what's going on? After that, you could come with us and explain to that greaseball of a talismonger that there's no gorgon."

Kate vehemently shook her head. "I signed a serving contract," she said. "That woman could make me work for her if I went back. And her husband tried to . . ." Her hands twisted uneasily in her lap as her voice dropped to a whisper. "I'm not going back to Daralis, not ever."

"And if *I* went back to explain," Granny put in, "everyone would know where Kate went."

Dagmar puffed out her cheeks in vexation. "I don't think you realize what's going on here. Ramdane needs to give that damned talismonger a gorgon's head or he'll break the mirror. If the mirror breaks without the proper spell and a proper new housing, Crystamel will disperse—and Ramdane will die."

"What do you expect me to do?" Granny growled. "Conjure up a gorgon's head out of nothing?"

Ramdane screamed and fell across the coffee table. Cups and teapot crashed to the floor. Startled, Granny and Kate shrank back in their chairs while Dagmar rushed to her brother's side.

"What is it?" Dagmar said helplessly. "What can I do?"

"Nothing," Ramdane panted through clenched teeth. Dagmar helped him sit up, and he opened his tunic. "Look."

Everyone looked. Three ugly welts on Ramdane's chest formed the numeral one.

"The greaseball is scratching that mirror. He's telling me we've only got one day left to meet him—with the gorgon's head," Ramdane gasped.

Dagmar assisted Ramdane to a chair. For once her internal little girl was quiet. "There's nothing to worry about," she soothed without believing it for a minute.

"Right," Ramdane replied dully. "We've been in worse spots. Maybe we could set up an ambush."

And then a thought struck Dagmar. She looked at Granny Carver's fireplace, then at Ramdane. Her internal girl clapped her hands with wicked glee.

"No," Dagmar said. "I have a better idea."

✧   ✧   ✧

"Did you bring me the head?" the greasy talismonger demanded from his vantage point across the clearing.

"Right here," Dagmar said, holding up a small strongbox. She held her still-polished shield in the other hand. "We'll bring it out as soon as you show us the mirror."

Grinning crookedly, the greasy talismonger dipped into a pouch and pulled out the bit of glass. "Do you feel your familiar, talismonger?" he taunted. "Can you sense her fear? One little accident is all it would take."

He dropped the mirror.

Dagmar and Ramdane let out a single cry. Time slowed, and Dagmar watched the mirror turn end over end as it headed for the rocky ground. The talismonger negligently flipped his foot, allowing the mirror to bounce off one toe into a patch of grass.

"Clumsy," he clucked, squatting to retrieve the object. He straightened and looked mockingly at Ramdane. "I'm sorry. Did I frighten you both?"

Dagmar opened her mouth but her heart was beating at the back of her throat and she couldn't formulate a reply. Apprehension warred with red-tinged anger.

Kill him! urged the internal little girl, and Dagmar *really* wanted to listen.

"I'll just put the box in the middle of the clearing," she called quickly. "After I've backed away, you come and exchange it for the mirror. And we'll all be home in time for supper."

The talismonger nodded jerkily. "Hurry up," he ordered. "The sun's going down."

Dagmar stumped past the boundary of trees and set Granny's heavy, metal-bound box on a flat stone in the exact center of the tiny meadow. Then she backed away, careful to keep her shield pointing in the talismonger's direction. Sunlight glinted off the shiny surface, creating a wobbly circle of light on the grass. The talismonger's eyes flicked toward it, then back to Dagmar.

"Don't try to blind me with that," he warned.

"Wouldn't dream of it," Dagmar said, still backing away. "I can see you're way too smart to fall for that trick."

The talismonger looked suspicious, but didn't reply. Dagmar waggled her shield one more time, sending the bit of light dancing across the ground. Behind her, she heard Ramdane chanting softly, though the greasy talismonger didn't seem to notice. His attention wandered between Dagmar, the box, and the light.

That's right, you bastard. Pretty light. Look at the pretty light. Never mind what Ramdane is doing. Pretty, pretty light.

Once Dagmar was safely back on the other side of the clearing, the talismonger sidled cautiously out to the box. Exultant avarice gleamed in his eyes as he opened it and reached inside without looking, examining the contents by touch alone.

Three . . . , Dagmar counted, *two . . . one.*

The greed dropped from the talismonger's face, replaced by a thunderous fury. With a screech, he snatched a handful of stone chips from the box—refuse from Granny's workroom—and flung them furiously to the ground.

"You *lied* to me?" he screamed. "Your life is forfeit!" And he hurled the mirror to the stone at his feet just as Ramdane finished his chant.

The mirror struck the rock and exploded into a hundred cloudy shards. A fine gray mist fogged upward, then sucked itself down into the stone at the talismonger's feet. Laughing, the talismonger ground the fragments into dust beneath his heel.

"Now we'll see," he crowed, "how a talismonger dies."

And a wild scream of pain and terror cut through the laughter.

"I don't want a new body," Crystamel said, hunched at Ramdane's feet. "I like viff one."

"Don't you think it's awfully heavy?" Ramdane commented.

"The voice is really grating," Dagmar put in. "And the extra fangs make you sound like a leaky teakettle."

"Vere iff vat," Crystamel acknowledged. She scratched her ear with one claw and ran a long tongue over improbably pointy teeth. "Fwitching bodief would alfo take the tafte of vat talifmonger out of my mouf. He waf awfully dirty."

"He should have looked where he was standing," Dagmar observed as she plucked the strongbox from a bloody mess of ragged clothes and ruined talismans.

"I'm rather glad he didn't," Ramdane replied. "He'd have

known something was up if he'd noticed the stone on the grass was Granny's demon carving." He sighed heavily. "The woman bargains like a moneylender. It'll take me weeks to make enough talismans to cloak her house again."

"It's the only fair way to pay her back," Dagmar remarked. "Between the demon carving and the meat statue, you've ruined two of her better pieces."

"Fo when do I get my new body?" Crystamel asked. "You ftill have the cat ftatue, don't you? You could fange me right now."

"No!" Dagmar and Ramdane said together. Then they laughed.

The Truth About the Gotterdammerung

Eric Flint

Since Loki's alibi was airtight, suspicion fell on God.

"That Bum's always had in it for us," grumbled Frey. Thor roared and bellowed, splintering tables with his hammer.

"Justice! Justice!" Valhalla rang with his thunderous basso profundo. As always, the gigantic hall was packed with heroes, who immediately took up the cry.

"JUSTICE! JUSTICE!"

Then:

"Death to the Christian God!"

At these words, the hall fell silent. Men and gods craned to see who had spoken. A huge and extraordinarily inebriated warrior clambered onto a feasting table. Several times, actually, before he finally managed the feat.

Swaying back and forth, spilling great quantities of mead from a tankard, this worthy spoke again.

"Hear me, gods and heroes! I am Hunkred Thorvaldsen, called the Cropped-Head, and I am accounted the fiercest berserk in my district! It was I who slew Gunnar Hairybreeks with one thrust of my spear through his liver after he took his sword and wounded my third cousin Ingmar, called the

Reckless, after Ingmar cut off Gunnar's brother Harald's arm at the fjord with his ax after Harald killed my brother's wife's uncle's grandson's dog after the dog pissed on his leg after Harald stole a bone from the dog at the midwinter festival after the dog had seized it fairly from the feasting table after Harald's nephew Bjorn, called the Ungenerous, refused the dog his fair portion."

Great applause resounded throughout Valhalla. Many toasts were drunk to the downfall of miserliness. After falling off the table three more times, Hunkred Thorvaldsen resumed his wobbly stance and continued his speech.

"Therefore do I, Hunkred Thorvaldsen, called the Cropped-Head, call upon the gods and heroes of Valhalla to avenge the murder of our beloved deity"—here the berserk, sobbing tears, pointed to the pallid corpse of the god Loki which was lying face down upon the floor of Valhalla, a knife sticking out of its back—"and seek satisfaction upon the mangy body of God, called the Almighty."

As one man, the heroes of Valhalla leapt to their feet, tankards held high.

"DEATH TO GOD!"

The excitement of the moment was irresistible. Heroes seized their weapons and charged out of the hall, led by the gods Heimdall and Thor. The former blew his great horn, the latter swung his hammer gaily. Taking his place at the head of the entire parade was Odin, riding his eight-legged horse Sleipner. His two great wolves, Freke and Gere, paced by his side.

As the gods and heroes poured out of the great feasting hall, the goddesses and Valkyries hastily donned their breast-plates and rushed out to bid them farewell.

Wincing, most of them.

"Breastplates and fond farewells are a lousy match," grumbled Odin's wife Frigga, after the gods and heroes were gone.

"You're telling me?" groused Thor's wife Sif, trying—gingerly—to pry her breastplate loose. "Breastplates are a lousy match with anything civilized. At least your husband isn't a damned weight-lifter."

As he led the procession across the heavens, Odin's expression was grim and stern, as befitted the Allfather of gods and men. It grew grimmer and sterner at the words of the ravens perched on his shoulder. Hugin and Munin, they were called.

"This is a bad idea," observed Hugin.

"A *really* bad idea," added Munin.

"Shuddup," growled Odin. "What do you know, anyway? You're just a couple of stupid birds."

"They don't call God the Almighty for nothing," pointed out Hugin.

"Omniscient, omnipotent, omnipresent," added Munin.

"Not like you, Odin, who's just a—"

Odin's divine temper boiled over. His spear missed the ravens, although a few tail feathers went flying. The birds cawed derisively and flew back toward Valhalla.

"Don't say we didn't warn you!"

"And they call us bird-brains!"

But Odin had no more time for impudent avians. Even now was the mighty host drawing up before the Pearly Gates of Heaven, so rapid is travel through the outer planes of creation.

High atop the Pearly Gates stood the resplendent figures of two angels. The one on the left held a great trumpet. Gabriel, his name. No doubt in the hopes of abashing the lout, Heimdall blew a mighty blast with his horn. But even before the sound of Heimdall's horn faded, Gabriel was improvising upon the tune, developing themes and varia-tions which were not only dazzling in their divinity and awesome in their cunning, but which also—especially the little riff which he added as a coda—exuded musical derision.

"O Heavens!" cried the other angel, Azrael. "We are besieged by a mighty host of flea-bitten barbarians!"

"O, what shall we do?" sobbed Gabriel.

The two angels convulsed with laughter. The assembled heroes of Valhalla bayed with fury. But at a gesture from Odin, they fell silent.

"Stand aside, lackeys!" cried the Allfather. "Open the Pearly Gates! We've business with your Boss!"

Azrael sneered. "God's busy."

"Deciding the fate of the universe," added Gabriel.

"Not that it's really necessary," mused Azrael, "seeing as how He figured it out right from the start when He made the whole thing. But He likes to check His work."

"A real precisionist." Gabriel.

"Not like some deities I could name." Azrael.

"And isn't that a good thing!" cried Gabriel. "Can you imagine the lopsided universe created by a god with only one eye?"

The insult was too much to bear. With a great curse, Odin hurled his spear at Gabriel. Alas, he missed. By quite a large margin, actually.

"Just like you said, Gabriel," giggled Azrael. "No stereoscopic vision."

Odin's curse was now joined by a multitude of others. A hailstorm of spears and axes was hurled at the Pearly Gates. With no noticeable effect, alas, although Thor's hammer did produce an impressive booming sound.

The ensuing comments by Azrael and Gabriel did little to improve the temper of the assembled gods and heroes of Valhalla. They were especially affronted by the angels' offer to find Thor a job ringing the bell in a cathedral, provided he agree to abstain from sin and grow a hunchback.

But their fury was suddenly stilled by the manifestation of an infinite Presence.

"Now you've done it," complained Azrael.

"God's here," added Gabriel. Quite unnecessarily, for the Presence of the Almighty is a unique and unmistakable phenomenon.

WHAT'S UP?

(Quotation marks cannot properly be used to indicate God's Voice. He is, after all, Unlimitable.)

The charges against Him were babbled forth in an unruly and not entirely sober manner.

YOU THINK *I* STABBED THIS—WHAT'S HIS NAME?— LOKI CHARACTER IN THE BACK?

An overwhelming sense of infinite amusement.

WHAT A BUNCH OF CLOWNS.

The assembled gods and heroes of Valhalla suddenly found themselves attired in the ridiculous costumes of circus clowns. Odin's mount was now an eight-legged elephant wearing a fez. His wolves were poodles, yipping with rage at the absurd cut of their pelts. Thor's hammer was a rubber mallet, with which, seized by an overpowering compulsion, he began hitting himself on the head. Heimdall's great horn was a carnival noisemaker.

Other indignities followed, but there is no need to dwell upon them. Suffice it to say that the assault of the gods and heroes of Valhalla upon Heaven turned out very badly in the end, even as foretold by the ravens.

On their way back, slouched and miserable, Frey complained to Odin: "When you made yourself the father of the gods, why didn't *you* assume omnipotence?"

"Do I look like an egomaniac?" snarled Odin.

"He's not the only Almighty, you know," came a voice. Turning, Odin and Frey beheld a slender but well-muscled stripling striding alongside.

"Who're you?" demanded Frey.

The stripling swelled his chest. "I am Lothar Halversen, called the Skinny, and I am recognized as the fiercest berserk in my district. It was I who slew Knut Ohtheresen, called the Heavy-Sleeper, after—"

"Forget all that!" roared Odin. "What did you mean—when you said God wasn't the only Almighty?"

The youth grinned gaily. "Oh, there's at least one other. Goes by the name of Allah. I heard about Him when I was raiding in Spain. The Moors are some fighters, you know? Of course, that didn't stop me from slaying twenty-eight of them at—"

"Shut up! I never heard of him. Allah, you say? And He's another omnipotent god?"

"According to the Moors, even more than God. And they say this Allah hates God with a passion."

Odin's grim face grew stern with thought.

"It's worth a try," he muttered.

And so it was that the host of heroes and gods of Valhalla came to Paradise, and sought an audience with Allah. This they were immediately granted, without obstruction by insolent servants, for Allah runs a strictly One-God show.

Alas, it went badly. No sooner had Allah heard Odin's proposal that He lead a charge on the Pearly Gates than the universe was filled with an overwhelming sense of fury. Allah's voice filled the infinite void.

GOD'S A HERETIC AND AN INFIDEL, BUT AT LEAST HE'S NOT A PAGAN.

And so saying, Allah visited a rain of toads and brimstone upon the heroes and gods of Valhalla, followed by locusts and seven lean years.

On their way back from Paradise, the gods and heroes of Valhalla regained some of their strength by eating the stripling Lothar Halversen, called—unfortunately—the Skinny. Such is the lot of those who give bad advice to ill-tempered gods and heroes.

"Still and all," mused Frey, picking his teeth with one of Lothar's fingerbones, "the kid's general idea wasn't bad. Just picked the wrong Almighty, that's all. But there must be one omniscient, omnipotent and omnipresent Deity around who'd be willing to take a crack at the Pearly Gates."

And so it came to pass that the gods and heroes of Valhalla sought out the various Almighties for aid and assistance in their quest to seek justice for the foul murder of Loki. Finding these Almighties proved simple. True, the Void is infinite and eternal. But, on the other hand, it is in the nature of Almighties to be omnipresent.

Finding them, therefore, proved easy. Obtaining their help, on the other hand, proved otherwise.

The interview with Yahweh went sour right from the start. The gods and heroes of Valhalla offered Yahweh a feast of pork baked in goat's milk, with steamed shellfish on the side, and it was all downhill from there.

"What does that Guy manage to eat, anyway?" grumbled Thor, as they crawled their boil-infested way across the limitless desert into which Yahweh's wrath had cast them.

But it is well said of the northern gods that they are a stubborn lot, and so they persisted in their search. All to no avail.

The Hindu Trinity couldn't seem to agree on anything, and Shiva wouldn't go it alone even though he was all for the idea. The Buddha just babbled nonsense, and Confucius wouldn't stop droning on and on about filial piety.

The time came when the gods and heroes gave up the hopeless quest and made their way back to Valhalla. Imagine their outrage when they finally came home—much the worse for wear—and saw that their great feasting hall had been turned into a Victorian mansion.

Odin stormed through the door, calling for his wife Frigga in a tone which boded ill for domestic tranquility. But he didn't get far before he was confronted by a huge wolf, fangs bared.

"You're ruining the carpet!" snarled the wolf, who was—as all the gods and heroes immediately recognized—none other than the great monster Garm.

"You're supposed to be guarding the Hel-Gate!" roared Thor.

A look of satisfaction came upon Garm's horrid visage. "Got a better gig," he said smugly. Then, eyeing Odin's wolves, who were yipping at him fiercely, Garm announced that he was in the mood for raw poodle. Freke and Gere immediately shrank back, wagging their pom-poms furiously.

"Out of my way!" bellowed Odin, who made to push past the great wolf. But Garm seized his leg in his maw and brought the Allfather down.

"I said," growled the wolf around Odin's leg, "you're ruining the carpet."

"What carpet?" demanded Odin, vainly trying to pry the great jaws loose. "There's no carpet in Valhalla!"

"There is now!" came a shrill voice. Looking up, Odin beheld his wife Frigga. Her appearance made him goggle. She was wearing an elaborate gown, with high heeled shoes and—and—her hair—

"What'd you do to your *hair?* What happened to the braids? Why are you wearing shoes?" With a particular air of complaint: "*And where are your breastplates?*"

Frigga ignored the questions, gazing down at her husband with a look of immense disfavor.

"I suppose we'll have to go through this unpleasantness," she snapped. Then, making an imperious gesture:

"Oh, let him go, Garm!"

The wolf obeyed. But no sooner had Odin scrambled to his feet, swearing sulphurously and promising great mayhem upon the person of his spouse, than Frigga drew forth a tiny bell and tinkled it vigorously. A moment later, a giant stepped into the foyer. (And that was another thing the gods and heroes were outraged about—who ever heard of a foyer in Valhalla?)

"Thrym!" cried Frey.

"King of the Frost Giants!" exclaimed Heimdall.

"Why are you wearing that ridiculous outfit?" demanded
Thor.

Thrym gazed down at his formal suit. "I'm the butler,"
he replied complacently. "And if you don't mind, I prefer
to be called James."

Frigga clapped her hands briskly. "James, see these—
gentlemen—into the parlor, if you will. But I insist that they
remove those muddy boots before they ruin the entire
carpet."

The scene which ensued was most undignified, for the
gods and heroes of Valhalla objected strenuously to the
removal of their boots. After Thor began hammering Thrym
(James, rather) with his rubber mallet, the butler felt it
necessary to call for assistance. Moments later the foyer was
flooded with fire and frost giants who proceeded to forcibly remove the boots of the gods and heroes of Valhalla.
Not too gently, either, for the giants were much aggrieved
at the damage inflicted upon their nice new footmen's
uniforms.

And so it was that the gods and heroes of Valhalla were
ushered into the parlor which was located where the feasting
hall used to be. "What's a 'parlor,' anyway?" groused Tyr.

"And will you look at that?" demanded Heimdall. "It's
a—what *is* it, anyway?"

"It's called a piano, sir," sniffed James.

Even at that moment the fire giant sitting at the piano
brought a dazzling mazurka to a close. The audience, which
consisted of goddesses, dwarves and giants dressed in evening
wear, burst into applause. An enormous serpent which
encircled the entire room hissed its mighty approval.

"Watch it, Odin!" murmured Heimdall. "That's the Midgard
Serpent."

But Odin's concern over the presence of the great rep-
tile was immediately overridden by Thor's bellow.

"Surtur, get your filthy paws off my wife!"

The thunder god's fury was understandable, for the
pianist—who was actually Surtur, the King of the Fire Giants,
although the gods and heroes hadn't immediately recognized
him because he was wearing a tuxedo and the flames which
formed his hair were shaped into long flowing locks—was
stroking the back of the goddess who was leaning over him.

She, for her part, was cooing admiration of his musical artistry.

"*And why aren't you wearing your breastplates?*" roared Thor at his wife.

Sif looked up and glared at him.

"I'm not your wife, you loudmouth! I got a divorce three weeks ago!"

Thor's eyes bugged out. He gabbled incoherently. Sif giggled.

"Look at him!" she exclaimed, She gazed around the room. "Can any *civilized person* blame me?" The murmurs of the assembled giants, dwarves and goddesses indicated their profound agreement with her sentiments. Sif ran her fingers through Surtur's flaming hair, which is the kind of thing goddesses can get away with, but is not recommended for mortals.

"Surtur is so much more genteel," she said. Then, laughing gaily: "And much more passionate! You won't ever find *him* complaining that I'm not wearing those stinking breastplates."

"It's my artist's soul," murmured Surtur.

Thor lost his temper completely at that point and set upon the King of the Fire Giants. But the affair went badly, for Surtur insisted upon a proper duel and before you knew it the two opponents were facing each other across the room, Thor hurling his rubber mallet and Surtur firing one unerring shot after another right between Thor's eyes with his dueling pistol.

No harm came to the thunder god, of course. It's one of the advantages of being immortal. But it certainly made him look foolish.

Then all the gods and heroes felt even more foolish when it occurred to one of them (Rolf Gunuldsen, called the Bigfoot, who was accounted the fiercest berserk of his district because he slew—well, never mind) that since the bullets weren't actually hurting Thor, even though he looked like a jackass, that it was a mystery how a knife in the back had done in Loki who was, after all, also immortal.

No sooner did Rolf utter these words than the gods and heroes of Valhalla heard a snicker behind them. Turning, they beheld Loki himself, entering the parlor with a beautiful giantess on his arm.

"I was wondering when you saps would finally figure it

out," sneered the god of discord and strife. He advanced to the center of the room, scratching his back.

"Still itches," he grumbled.

"Try wearing breastplates!" laughed Frigga. "You want to talk about *itching*?"

Loki smiled sympathetically. Then, with a laugh:

"And will you look at these idiots? They find me with a knife in my back, which isn't the kind of thing which would do any real harm at all to an immortal deity, and the cretins not only jump to the conclusion that I've been murdered but that the culprit was none other than God Almighty Himself."

Loki bestowed a great sneer upon the assembled gods and heroes of Valhalla. "Let me explain something to you, dimwits. When God Almighty decides to do somebody in, He does not—repeat, *not*—stab them in the back with a knife."

I CERTAINLY DON'T, came a voice which filled the universe.

The gods and heroes of Valhalla jumped with surprise.

"Where'd He come from?" demanded Frey.

I'M OMNIPRESENT. ALSO OMNIPOTENT, WHICH IS WHY I DON'T STAB PEOPLE IN THE BACK WITH A KNIFE. MUCH PREFER HEAVENLY CATASTROPHES— COMETS, ASTEROIDS, THE OCCASIONAL SUPERNOVA. BIT INDISCRIMINATE, I ADMIT, BUT I HAVE A REPUTATION TO MAINTAIN.

"Then who stabbed Loki in the back?"

"I did," said Thrym (James, rather). "It was Loki's idea, of course, but we all thought it would be appropriate for me to do the actual deed. After all," he concluded proudly, "I'm the butler."

"But why?" cried Odin.

"To get you out of here!" snapped Loki. "So we'd have some time to set everything right."

"Not to mention some peace and quiet!" exclaimed Frigga. "It's been so heavenly since you left—no more sleepless nights caused by your carousing and brawling."

A furious chorus from the assembled giants, dwarves and goddesses indicated their complete agreement with these sentiments. The goddesses and Valkyries seemed especially aggrieved on the subject of breastplates.

Needless to say, the assembled gods and heroes of Valhalla

were not slow to indicate (even more loudly) their own sentiments, which were quite the opposite. Indeed, the whole thing turned into quite a scandal, but when all was said and done the gods and heroes found themselves pitched out of Valhalla with firm instructions not to come back.

The goddesses were adamant on this last point, each of them whipping out a bill of divorce on the spot. They weren't printed on mere paper, either. Each bill of divorce was engraved on a brass placard made from melted-down breastplates.

"You can't divorce me, Frigga!" cried Odin. "No power in the Universe can divorce the Allfather of the Gods from his wife!"

OH, YES I CAN, came the voice of the Almighty.

"That's not what the Pope says," complained one of the heroes. "I know, because when I was raiding in France I tried to force this priest to marry over this hot wench to me but he said he couldn't because she was already married and the Church had forbidden divorce."

A slight tinge of pink embarrassment colored the entire universe, for just a split second.

WELL, THE POPE TENDS TO BE A LITTLE RIGID. AND IT'S A FACT THAT I DON'T GENERALLY APPROVE OF DIVORCE. BUT I MAKE EXCEPTIONS IN EXTREME CIRCUMSTANCES, OF WHICH YOU CERTAINLY FIT THE BILL. I WOULDN'T FORCE A PIG TO STAY MARRIED TO OAFS LIKE YOU. MAKING YOUR WOMEN WEAR BREASTPLATES WAS THE FINAL STRAW! HOW WOULD *YOU* LIKE TO HAUL AROUND TEN POUNDS OF BRASS ON YOUR TITS? A FLAGRANT CASE OF DOMESTIC VIOLENCE, WHAT IT IS. THESE ARE MODERN TIMES, YOU KNOW.

And that was that. The gods and heroes of Valhalla eventually got it into their thick skulls that things had changed, and they slouched off into the wilderness.

But they made a comeback, of sorts. Once they calmed down enough to think about it, they realized that the worst thing was the damage to their reputations. It wasn't as if any of them were actually going to miss their wives, after all. Making love and breastplates were a lousy match.

"The old story of Ragnarok was so much more dignified,"

wailed one of the heroes. "Now we're gonna look like chumps!"

It was Bragi, the god of poetry and song, who came up with the idea that saved the day.

"There's no point in fighting progress," he explained.

So Bragi went down to Middle-earth and brought back an opera composer named Richard Wagner. After Wagner heard what the gods had to say, he assured them that he could take care of the whole problem.

"For money, of course."

After the gods agreed to his terms, the detailed negotiations began. Wagner was particularly adamant about protecting his artistic reputation.

"It's great for people to think I have divine inspiration, but it can't look crass. So we'll have to figure out a way to launder the money."

And that's why Odin the Allfather caused King Ludwig of Bavaria to go mad and shower Wagner with patronage and largesse.

Wagner also insisted that the opera had to be in German, which would involve some changes in names.

"Wotan," mused Odin. "Wotan," he said again. "It kind of rolls off the tongue, doesn't it? Okay, I can live with that."

For their part, the gods were deeply concerned that the opera put forth the proper moral lessons.

"The giants and the dwarves have got to be the bad guys," insisted Tyr.

"Piece of cake," said Wagner.

"The women have to come to a bad end," demanded Thor.

"How's being burned alive grab you?" snickered Wagner.

"I get to sing a lot," specified Odin sternly. "After all, I'm the Father of the Gods."

"No sweat," assured Wagner. "I'll call it 'Wotan's Narration.' It'll go on and on and on and on and on and on and on and on and on. Then we'll repeat it. Over and over and over and over and over again."

Finally, after the gods were satisfied that Wagner was their kind of composer, Odin turned to the assembled heroes.

"How about you mortals?" he asked. "Got any requests?"

The heroes of Valhalla talked it over and, after they came to agreement, they appointed one of their number to act as their artistic spokesman. This fellow was muscled like Hercules and had no discernable forehead.

"I am Siegfried Siegmundsen, called the Brainless," he said, "and I am accounted the fiercest berserk in my district. It was I who slew Fafnir the Hutmaker after that lousy snake in the grass demanded payment for—"

"Shut up!" roared Odin. "Get to—"

"No, no, let him talk!" cried Wagner. "I'm getting an idea."

So Siegfried Siegmundsen was allowed to finish his very, very, very long but monosyllabic recitation of his accomplishments. Wagner took copious notes. At the end, Siegfried explained the central concern of the heroes regarding the opera.

"We just want to be sure the hero won't be some kind of pansy," he growled. "No eggheads, fretting over all kind of silly stuff. A stout, simple hero type. That's what we want."

"Absolutely!" exclaimed Wagner. "In fact, I'm going to model the hero after you personally. Uh, how well did your mother know her brother?"

The hero's face turned beet red.

"I knew it!" shrieked Wagner, clapping his hands with glee. "Oh, it's going to be the greatest opera ever written! Very profound. Very uplifting. Worthy of my genius!"

And that's how the gods and heroes of Valhalla managed to salvage their reputation. They all agreed that Wagner did a magnificent job. In fact, attending the season at Bayreuth has become their favorite pastime. You can always spot them in the audience, if you're in the know. Look for a crowd of beefy middle-aged men obviously uncomfortable in their suits, tugging at their ties. Their breath will smell like a brewery, and they'll be complaining loudly about the avant-garde set design.

That's them. The Aesir.

Defender of the Small

Jody Lynn Nye

Dawna Keen-Eyed upended her water skin and drank the few last drops. Walking the rough horse track between villages was thirsty work, but she was happy. It was better to be breathing country air full of the smells of new-cut hay, wood smoke and pig poop than blood, rot, burning oil and the smell of corpses beginning to decay. The way the land sloped, the river shouldn't be far ahead, and by it the town where perhaps a decent meal and a clean bed waited. Her longsword, carefully cleaned from the last battle and wrapped in its oiled cloth, and her shield with its red stripe down the center bumped against the tall woman's back with every step she took. The red pennant that indicated her status as a mercenary fluttered from the hilt and tickled the back of her neck under her long, brown braid. King Drealin III himself had handed the pennant back to her with a brief statement of gratitude, at the same time that the paymaster gave her her fee. The money wasn't much, but it ought to last long enough for her to reach home. For the moment she longed to sit down. Her legs were tired, and she had finally worn through the thin place in the sole of her left boot.

CABBAGE TOWN, the gold-lettered plaque read, as the track changed from mud to gravel at the edge of the village. Dawna glanced around with pleasure. Life was here, not death. It was market day. Hearty merchants wrangled with their customers, apple-cheeked women in kirtles and wimples, or tall men with colorful liripipe hoods. Farmers argued about the relative merits of this or that cow. Dogs slept in the sun.

A plump gray puss slept tucked up on a window sill beside a scarlet flower in a pot. An orange-striped mother cat, her teats heavy with milk, wound about the legs of the tables on which the merchants' goods were displayed.

A group of shouting and laughing children ranging in age from five to ten or eleven years old raced up the hill along a lane that led up from the river that Dawna could now see from the village's main street. They stopped to stare at the mercenary in armor with her pack and sword slung upon her back. She smiled at them.

"Good day to you," she said, shifting the heavy load to the other shoulder.

Immediately the children went wide-eyed with distrust and curiosity.

"Are you here to conquer us?" asked a little girl with long plaits tied with blue ribbon.

Dawna laughed. "No, I'm just back from the wars."

"You were fighting?" asked the biggest boy, hair the color of fresh wood and eyes of leaf green.

"Indeed I was. I killed eight men in the last battle at Songhelm. I and my fellow sell-swords were in the front line when we laid siege to the pirates' stronghold at Valorin on the coast. We broke the walls down in only three days, and saved the town."

"Ooohhh!" the children gasped, awed.

"Did you burn their boats? Did you meet the king? Did you find bags of gold?" Now that she had proved friendly, questions bubbled up out of the children like steam in a stewpot.

"Perhaps I'll tell you a tale or two later. I just want a rest now," Dawna said, with a smile. She turned back to the butcher, who was hacking a slab of meat into collops. "Where's a good place to get a meal and a bed for the night?"

The man stuck the tip of his carving knife into the chopping block and consulted the sky. "Oh, well, there's Brenner's tavern, or Mistress Peck's . . ."

The biggest of the boys, bored by such ordinary talk, picked up a stone and heaved it at the orange cat. It struck her in the side. She let out a cry and skittered underneath the weaver's table, next to the butcher.

"Stop that," Dawna ordered. The boys paid no attention. They picked up more stones and continued to pelt the cat, who mewed piteously, trying to find a place to hide. "For Gods' love, what's the matter with you? Whose children are those?" she asked the tradesfolk.

"Just children," the butcher replied, with a shrug. "Just a cat. What do you care?"

"It's wrong," Dawna exclaimed angrily. "Cats are the Gods' creatures, the same as we are."

The man blew a derisive raspberry. Dawna felt her temper flaring. Those brats were hurting an innocent animal, and he didn't intend to do a thing about it. After all the killing she had seen, senseless cruelty fired her blood.

"Mind that for me," she said, thrusting her pack into the butcher's arms. She drew her sword and stuck it, point quivering, into the nearest tree. No need for it in what she intended to do.

As she turned the children instantly divined her intention. They dropped the rest of their stones and fled down the street towards the river. A coracle lay on the churned-up mud bank. No doubt they intended to make their escape in it, leaving the woman unable to follow them in her heavy leather-and-bronze armor. They had the advantage of lightness, but her temper lent speed to her feet. With a surge of strength she hurtled down the hill, angling to come up in front of the largest boy, the initial stone-thrower.

"Now we'll see how much *you* enjoy a thrashing," she said, grabbing him by the arm. She sat down on the coracle's edge and swung him over her knee. "*That's* for assaulting a poor innocent beast. And *that's* for harming a mother. And *that's* for not listening to your elders." Her open hand smacked down hard on his upturned backside again and again.

The other children fled as soon as their leader had been captured. By the time Dawna marched her captive up the hill, a crowd had gathered.

"What the hell do you think you're doing to our children?" demanded the weaver.

"They needed a lesson," Dawna stated, thrusting the boy

toward the crowd. He immediately ran to a prosperous-
looking man whose sandy-blond locks suggested to her that
he was the boy's father. "Cruelty to animals is a sin." The
gray cat had been awakened from his nap by the shouting. He wound around the legs of the crowd. The weaver
distractedly aimed a kick at it when it brushed against him.

"Get away with you," he growled.

Dawna turned on him. "You're no better! Children learn
from their elders. You should teach them kindness. These
animals are your friends and protectors."

"Oh, please," the weaver groaned, rolling his eyes. "Don't
spout your animist noises at me. The Father put all creatures under the command of humans. If He wishes us saved
from plague, He will be the one to save us, not some dumb
animal." From the sound of the grumbling, the rest of the
crowd agreed with him.

"Dumb! Can *you* catch a rat with your hands?"

"You're a fine one to talk about holding life sacred," a
gaunt, gray-haired woman declared, shaking a finger at her.
"That red flag of yours gives you away. You work for a price,
killing for pay."

Dawna walked over to the tree beside the butcher's stall
and pulled her sword free. The crowd watched with worried eyes as she sheathed it. "I accept a fee to defend what
I think is right, goodwife. I only use my weapon in worthy service. I never harm anyone who cries me mercy and
lays down his weapons. Thank you." She tugged her pack
out of the butcher's limp arms.

"Fine words," the prosperous man said, "but you were
quick enough to paddle a harmless boy."

"It's a lesson he had coming, if not from you, then from
me," Dawna said frankly. "If the king's marshalls saw him
he'd have gotten more than a swat, I can tell you that. His
punishment was with my empty hand. I will never draw my
sword against an unarmed man, woman or child." She sighed.
"I am only passing through your town. I'm not looking for
a fight. But don't doubt that I can defend myself well without it. I don't want a fight with you. All I want is to sup here
and sleep, and I'll be on my way in the morning."

"Not in my establishment, you won't. You stay out of my
inn," the wrinkled old woman ordered her.

"And mine," added a stout man.

"Leave our town," the boy's father declared, shaking his fist. "We don't want you here, sell-sword. No one here wants your services, or your presence."

Dawna growled to herself. If she hadn't been so tired she'd have given them *all* the flat of her hand. If anyone she'd ever met needed spankings, it was these people. "I'm on the common property, and I claim the king's peace." She raised an eyebrow, defying anyone to disagree with her.

No one did. The king's peace meant they couldn't drive her off the green or within a body-length of any public highway. Paying her no more mind the townsfolk closed up their market stalls and went in to dinner. Dawna watched longingly as a cluster of merrymakers followed Mistress Peck through the cheerfully-painted wooden door at the corner of the square. *Beer*, she thought, wistfully, *roast beef*. Tempting smells floated out to her on the evening breeze.

No chance getting a hot meal from Mistress Peck or the other innkeeper, nor of paying a villager for a share of their supper. Dawna sat down against a tree and began to rummage in her pack for dry, tasteless journey biscuit. It'd gripe her belly more than usual knowing that good food was so close by.

She jumped back in alarm as something cold and slimy fell on her hand. The tabby cat she had rescued sat at her feet with tail wound around its paws, looking up at her with big, green, saucerlike eyes. The thing that had now fallen off Dawna's hand was a freshly caught trout.

"Taking pity on the hungry traveler, eh?" she said, reaching down to scratch the cat behind the ears. "Thank you. It'll be most welcome."

With flint and tinder from her pack she struck a small fire, gutted and staked the fish over it to cook. It was delicious. The cat watched her eat, accepted a morsel and no more, rubbed against Dawna's knee, then disappeared into the darkness. Dawna banked the fire and settled herself uncomfortably against the tree. With the townsfolk unkindly inclined toward her she didn't dare strip off her armor. After a few drinks they might be bolder. She hated fighting with drunks; they always threw up on her, and bronze took so much polishing.

The blanket of twilight began to draw across the sky. Now that the sun was down the chill river mist was rising. She pulled her gray wool cloak out of her pack and wrapped it around herself, tugging the hood down over her forehead. Not warm enough, but it would have to do. She'd have to sleep with one eye open and her sword at her side. It'd be a cold night and a wakeful one.

Birdsong woke her at false dawn. Dawna's free hand clenched on something unfamiliar, which squirmed. She struggled to sit up. A heavy weight on her chest and legs shifted. Her hand fumbled for her sword. Instead of metal her fingers touched fur. Her eyes flew open. Green eyes in a wedge-shaped gray head regarded her from an inch away.

"Wha'?" Dawna sputtered, thrashing. "Gah?"

The gray cat was curled up just underneath her collar bone. More of the weight on her moved. She raised her head to look. Behind the gray cat a blanket of felines rolled or stalked off Dawna's body, leaving behind cold morning air. Dawna gaped in amazement. They had spent the night on her, providing her with a living blanket. But that was not all. From the protected hollow in the crook of her arm four kittens, two gray, one orange and one calico, looked up at her with trusting eyes. The mother cat unwound herself from a ball next to Dawna's head and came over to rub against Dawna's jaw, then began to lick the kittens vigorously.

"Well, so much for my reputation for vigilance," Dawna said, touching the little ones' delicate heads. The kits were so young their ears were still rounded. The mother cat's rough tongue pushed her fingers away from the calico's ear. "I'm glad my sisters-in-arms weren't here to see me sleep through that. Thank you for keeping me warm. I was comfortable. A kindness for a kindness."

The mother cat arched her back upward, stretched forward and back, then stalked away, leaving her kittens in the curve of Dawna's arm.

"Wait, I'm not a nursemaid!" Dawna called, then chided herself. How could she expect a cat to understand what she was saying?

It wouldn't be long before the townsfolk emerged to take up their chores for the day. If Dawna hung about too long they'd begin to gather in small groups, eventually working up enough mob courage to drive her out of the village. She intended to be on her way long before *that* psychological moment arose, but in the meanwhile, her damaged boot needed attention.

Gingerly, she peeled off the battered black shoe. It would have been nice to have the local shoemaker fix it for her, but under the circumstances he'd most likely be afraid to do business with her. Never mind: she had pieces of leather, waxed cord and a needle in her pack, same as she used for patching her armor.

The kittens crawled in her lap and batted at the end of the string. Dawna gently pushed them away as she took another stitch.

"You still here, sell-sword?" a voice demanded. Two very nice, honey-colored boots stopped just over a body's length from her knee. She'd have liked to have a pair like that. Dawna looked up, in no hurry. In them was the weaver, wearing a defiant expression, though his eyes were scared.

"I'll be gone soon enough," she said.

"Sooner's better than later," he replied. It *almost* sounded like a threat. Dawna went back to her work. The weaver hesitated for a moment, the beautiful boots rocking back and forth with indecision, then strode away. Dawna dismissed him. He wouldn't be the one to attack her, but he'd stand at the back and shout encouragement to the stupid ones at the front. Dawna knew his kind.

A soft but insistent mew interrupted her thoughts. The orange cat had returned, laying another fish at her feet. Her right paw was wet up to the shoulder, but the rest of her was dry. A good hunter.

"You've decided to feed me, eh?" Dawna said, picking up the fish. It was a mature brook trout, twice the length of her hand. Plenty of good meat on it. The cat chirruped, expectantly. "Is it out of gratitude?" Dawna asked. "Because you already thanked me last night."

The cat chirruped again, and settled down with her paws tucked under her breast. Dawna had had few dealings with cats except on her father's farm. They seemed curious, independent, brave and cowardly at the same time, taking their business and pleasure equally seriously, just like people. But she'd never taken the time to talk to one, assuming their comprehension was limited to their own language. This one listened carefully, her orange-striped head cocked to one side, almost as if she understood. Then, to Dawna's surprise, the

cat walked from the fish to the pennant hanging from
Dawna's shield and back again, rubbing up against the
mercenary's knee with each pass. Dawna let the corners of
her mouth perk up in amusement.

"You couldn't be . . . hiring me?"

The cat chirruped again.

"How can you understand what I said yesterday? How
could you possibly know what I do?" The cat gave her a
wise look. "What is it you want me to do, then? Protect
you? Or you *and* your babies?"

It was a test. The cat passed it. She climbed into Dawna's
lap, briefly licked the top of each kitten's head, then stared
up at the warrior again as the kittens burrowed in toward the
tabby's nipples. "By the Gods, I believe you *are* hiring me.
Why not? Very well. It's a bargain." She put out a hand to
seal the deal, as she did with her human clients, and laughed
at herself as the cat sniffed her fingers. "Here, then," she said
formally, unhooking the pennant. "My gage is the symbol of
my service. Carry it until my duty to you is discharged."

She wound the streamer twice around the cat's neck, tying
the loose ends in a bow. "A bit gaudy with your coloring,
my lady, but not too bad."

The cat seemed pleased, and began to wash her wet paw.
The kittens were well into their morning meal.

But how to discharge her commission? Dawna thought,
pushing the needle through the hard leather. She could hardly
follow the cat on her morning rounds, nor shadow her as
she stalked vermin. The cat solved the dilemma by departing
abruptly from the mercenary's lap, leaving the now sleeping kittens behind. The mercenary shrugged and went on
with her repair.

As morning began, the smaller children emerged carrying slates and headed toward a house at the opposite corner of the square, where a goodwife was waiting with her
hands on her hips: the village schoolteacher. The older
children who were apprenticed were already on their way
to and fro, discharging commissions for their masters. They
all gave her a wary look as they passed her, sitting under
the tree in the middle of the green, especially the blond boy
whom she had spanked.

Once in a while the cat returned to feed her kittens. She
had decided Dawna's lap was by far the best place for the

job. The butcher passed by with a cart full of meat, saw the red streamer around the cat's neck, and snorted.

"How much is it paying you?" he asked.

"Two fish a day," Dawna replied. "I've had better wages, but I've had worse, too."

"You're mad," the butcher informed her. "That's the silversmith's cat. He'll do as he pleases with her, scarf or no scarf."

"If she has the wits to ask for my help, then she's master of her own fate," Dawna said.

Word spread quickly through the small town about her contract with the cat. From her vantage point on the green she could see all the comings and goings. Even the boy, who appeared to be apprenticed to the brewer, gave the orange cat a wide berth as he wheeled kegs of beer up and back from the brewery. The cat strutted, proudly displaying the red scarf around her neck as she went about her business.

One dark-haired lad did work up the courage to shy a stone at the orange cat. It just missed her, striking dust up from the pathway directly under her belly. The cat levitated in surprise, spun around to glare at her attacker, then she turned and stared directly at Dawna. No doubt remained in the warrior's mind that the cat understood what she had commissioned. Dawna, grinning, began to rise from her seat under the tree. The boy's face paled in fear, and he fled into an alleyway, his loose shoes pattering on the cobblestones. Dawna settled back again. She doubted he'd ever try again.

As long as she was there, that was. Dawna could not stay in Cabbage Town for long. By her reckoning she had perhaps a day, maybe two, before the townsfolk decided they were tired of the looming presence of an armed mercenary, one they thought was at least a little mad because she considered herself employed by a cat!

Shouting voices drew her attention to the river path. She saw nothing at first, but a small black-and-white cat came tearing up the hill, running full out. Its eyes were round with terror. It spotted Dawna and made directly for her. As it neared, Dawna saw blood, bright red on its fur. A cluster of children pelted up the hill ten steps behind it, throwing stones and clods of earth. By the time they reached the green, the black-and-white was crouched underneath Dawna's shield, trembling. Its eyes lifted to hers, beseeching. The blood dripped from a cut in its side.

"I won't give you away, little one," she said, laying a gentle hand on its neck.

The children cast about, looking for their prey. "It got away!" one of them shouted. "Let's go find another!"

They shot Dawna defiant glances. So that was the way of it, she thought. As long as the orange cat was off limits, they were going to have their fun with other animals. She loathed this town and everyone in it.

She opened her pack. "Stay there, little one," she said, as the black-and-white began to edge away from the strange sounds. "I've got salve that will ease the pain and stop the bleeding." The little cat held still for its physicking, then lay purring weakly as Dawna tied a makeshift bandage around its middle. When the orange cat returned she touched noses with the newcomer, then gave it a good washing before lying down to feed her kits. Dawna had a new client.

"Nay, I'll not sell you red cloth, nor anything else," the weaver said severely, spreading his hands protectively over the stock on his counter. "I'd suggest you go visit the priests and see if they'll pray for your sanity. Now, leave."

Dawna gave up the argument and departed from the white-painted shop. She had not gone five paces out of the door when something bumped her leg. She looked down to see the gray cat, a long, red ribbon trailing from its mouth. It draped the end over her boot and blinked moonlike eyes at her. She groaned.

"Not you, too! Does no one treat their beasts with respect in this town?" Dawna glanced about to see if anyone was watching her. She took a small coin and wrapped it in a scrap of cloth. "Give this to your master for pay," she said. "I won't have either of us in trouble for theft. I accept your commission."

The gray cat dipped his head as if nodding, and trotted back into the store with the little bundle in its mouth. Dawna strode hastily up the hill, not wanting the weaver to come bursting out and accuse her publicly of sorcery.

Word had spread among the four-legged denizens of Cabbage Town, too. When she returned, her small camp was occupied by a dozen cats. Some of them bore the marks of recent ill-treatment; still others had old scars and limbs misshapen from being broken and left untreated. None of them had come empty-handed, or, rather, empty-mouthed. A little pile of offerings guarded by the orange-striped mother cat included sausage links, a raw chicken leg, a silk handkerchief, a child's purse containing one copper coin and a thumbprint-sized religious medallion depicting the Forest God. The length of red ribbon from the weaver's was barely long enough to make collars for all the worried-looking felines huddled near her. More clients. That night, they once again provided her with warmth, fresh fish, and not a few fleas. If she was going to be the protector of the local cats, she was going to have to pick them some fleabane.

"Rats!" the silversmith declared, confronting the warrior nose to nose as she stumped back up the hill after making a rough toilet at the river's edge. The orange cat followed her, her latest catch clasped proudly in her jaws. "There are rats in my shop, and *my cat*," he pointed accusingly, "has spent all the last day up here with you. Release the witchery you've placed on her so she can do what I keep her to do!"

"There's no witchery," Dawna replied, glancing at the cat, who'd taken her favorite spot among the knobby roots of the tree. Her kittens, looked after by her other charges, played with their mother's tail, a leaf and a strand of hair from Dawna's comb. "She'll go, but your son must promise not to abuse her."

"Er . . ." the silversmith began. If he thought it was sorcery how could he argue? "Er. Done, then."

He rushed away. Dawna glanced at the orange cat. "In your own good time, then. We'll see if his word's his bond."

She was beginning to enjoy the company of cats. In many ways her little enclave on the hilltop reminded her of the war camp she had just left. Each warrior had her job to do, but was glad of the society of fellow warriors at the end of the day. She wished they could talk as well as understand. Dawna missed human conversation. Her keen hearing allowed her to eavesdrop on the innkeeper's guests at the edge of the green.

" . . . Say the war's over, so I guess that female up there was telling the truth . . ."

" . . . Raspberry season down south. It'll start here soon . . ."

" . . . Sixty dead in one town. Can't tell *me* that's not sorcery from the enemy!"

" . . . Never happen here. Come on, let's have another drink."

By the next morning Dawna could feel that the town's tolerance limit had been reached. Though they couldn't tell she knew what they were doing, the adults went about furtively, peeking at her from behind trees, ducking into one another's shops and homes, coordinating what they planned to do, to drive away the invader. She had plenty of time to divine their intention. By the time they'd formed up into a mob, three hours after they had begun, she had had time to bathe, enjoy a hearty breakfast of grilled fish and pur-loined sausage, pet and doctor all the cats, and don her full armor, including her buckler and newly-polished sword. The gleaming hilts of dirks poked out of both boot tops, and a war hammer, her least favorite weapon but a good one of last recourse, hung ready at her belt. She had fifteen cats with her now. Most of the adult felines of the town had come to her during the last day, bringing an offering, hoping for protection. They clustered behind her heels.

Led by the silversmith, nearly the entire human popula-tion of Cabbage Town stalked into the common and surged partway up the hill where she held her vigil. They were carrying tools of their trades, such as shears and hammers, or garden implements like hoes and spades. Only two bore themselves like former soldiers: the schoolteacher and the dyer, who both carried short-swords of uncertain age. The rest held their makeshift weapons with no conviction. Dawna felt certain she could defend herself if it came to a fight, but she intended that no fight should begin. A few of them stopped dead when they saw how she was attired. She smiled. Half the battle was already won.

Pushed by the others, the silversmith finally stepped forward out of the mob. He cleared his throat.

"Sell-sword, we've concluded . . . all of us," he turned to gesture at the crowd, "that, er, it is disruptive to the, er, well-being of our town, of which you are not a citizen, that . . . that . . ."

"That I should leave?" Dawna finished for him.

"Um . . . er . . . yes," the silversmith squeaked out, surprised at her capitulation. He seemed to take heart. "I mean, that is, forthwith. You must be on your way at once. Carrying only what you came with. Er. Yes. You must leave our cats behind."

"Very well," Dawna said, crossing her arms. "I won't touch a single one." Muttering erupted amongst the townsfolk. She had agreed so easily. What were they missing? They would be missing quite a lot, soon, if she was not wrong. She raised her voice. "I've got a few words to say that I want everyone to hear. I wish to thank the citizens of Cabbage Town for the use of green for the last two nights. It would have been a cold and uncomfortable place to stay, if not for the hospitality of your cats. They've shown me the common courtesy that I thought humans owed to one another, certainly that which one might expect to be extended to fellow subjects of this kingdom.

"To my hosts and clients, then," and she turned to look into the round eyes of the cats huddled at the foot of the tree, "I depart now for my home town of Marigold Down. If you are afraid to remain here, you may come with me. I'll find you somewhere better to live where you need never again fear a boot or a stone. I know my father would be grateful for good hunting cats. His barley harvest is much troubled by rats."

"Now, sell-sword!" the silversmith protested. "Didn't you just agree not to take our cats with you?"

"Now, silversmith," she countered, turning to face him. "They're dumb creatures, aren't they? You've all said as much for the last two days. You don't honestly believe that they can *understand* me, do you?"

"Uh. Er. No. I suppose not." The muttering in the crowd got louder. Dawna pitched her voice so it could be heard clear down to the bottom of the hill.

"I swear to you by my soul that I will not take a single animal out of this town. If any follow me, it will be by their own volition. Will that satisfy you?"

"Not me," the butcher growled, stepping forward with a cleaver in his hand. "I'll see you to the edge of town, mercenary, just to make sure you don't steal anything of ours."

"And I!" exclaimed the weaver.

"And I will, too," said the barber-surgeon, a dark-complected man with beefy arms. In all, six of the boldest elected to act as her escort. Dawna glanced back as she marched down the hill with her honor guard trailing behind. All of the cats who had been there had melted away into the undergrowth.

"Go on about your business," the butcher ordered the rest of the crowd. "We'll see she doesn't turn back."

Dawna led the six townsfolk toward the northern edge of town. Six days' march would bring her within sight of Marigold Down, and another half day to her father's home to the northwest.

"Goodbye," she said, nodding to her escort.

"Good riddance," the butcher said. As one, the men turned and stumped back toward town.

"Same to you," Dawna said under her breath. The sooner she shook the dust of Cabbage Town off her feet, the happier she would be. And now to see if her speech had had any results.

It had. As soon as she left the clean, gravel track for the muddy forest path, cats began to appear like magic out of the surrounding undergrowth. The orange cat popped out from beneath a flowering gorse bush with her kittens marching in a file behind her, and claimed the warrior with a cheek swipe along her boot top. Dawna stopped only long enough to scoop up the little ones and put them in a makeshift sling made of a fold of her cloak. The gray cat and the injured black-and-white came running from another hiding place. In all, eighteen cats and a couple dozen half-grown kits would be making the long journey northward with her. As soon as she felt safe stopping, she would tie red ribbons around the necks of each to show the people they met that these cats were under her protection. She hoped she wouldn't run into anyone as thick as the denizens of Cabbage Town.

"Come along," she said to the cats, setting a light pace once she was out of sight of the town. "We've got a long way to go, and I've always found a story helps to pass the time. Now, let me tell you about the siege of Valorin . . ."

The kittens against her chest purred their approval.

Of Mice and Chicks

Harry Turtledove

It is a wide country, and a steep one, and how it can be
both those things at once no one is quite certain, but
nonetheless no one doubts that it is. There are rivers in the
valleys and castles atop the hills; here, everybody would be
surprised if this were reversed, but it is not, and so nobody
is. Some of the rivers have fish in them and brush growing along their banks. None of the castles has fish in it,
save only when the fish is smoked or salted. Nor do the
castles have brush around them, because otherwise the serfs
might have time on their hands, and it just doesn't wash
off.

At this point, the narrative goes, uh, went from present
to past tense. Gods knew, uh, know why.

"Tell me about the rabbits again, Georgia," Lani said.
"Aw, for cryin' out loud." Georgia was a short, compact
woman with a scar on her cheek who wore her mail shirt
as if she'd been born with it for skin. Her face was tanned
and weathered, her eyes narrow and shrewd. She looked
over at Lani with affectionate annoyance. "I done told you
about 'em a million times already."

"Tell me again. You know how I forget things." Lani paused. "Tell me again. You know how I forget things." She was twice Georgia's size, four times Georgia's strength, and had not a brain concealed anywhere about her person. Other things, yes, but brains? Afraid not; they must have been plumb out that day. "Tell me again. You know how I—"

"For gods' sake, how can you forget about gods-damned rabbits?" Georgia broke in. "You're riding one, you miserable dummy!"

"Well, yeah." Lani reached out a large, callused hand to pat Thumper between his fine, upstanding ears. Thumper was about the size of a horse, but since they didn't have horses in that world the comparison makes more sense to you than it would have to Lani and Georgia. Nobody, but nobody—not even Lani—would have thought about carrying a rabbit's foot around there. Trust me on that one. Lani went on, "Tell me how we're gonna raise 'em, Georgia."

"Oh, all right. Maybe it'll shut you up." Georgia lolloped along on Clumper, a war bunny much like Thumper except for an ear with a bend in it. Once upon a time, Thumper had been called Floppy, but then everything went to CD-ROMs and DVDs. "We're gonna get us a stake—I reckon six hundred pieces o' silver'll do it. We're gonna get us a stake, and we're gonna buy us a farm, and we're gonna raise rabbits to sell to other knights instead of goin' off to war ourselves. We're gonna raise 'em, and they're gonna breed—"

"They're gonna breed like bunnies! Like bunnies, Georgia!" Lani clapped her hands with excitement.

"Yeah. Like bunnies." When Georgia promised Lani's old Uncle Hugo she'd help take care of her after he kicked off, she hadn't known just how much fun it would be. Every day brought a new lesson. If Uncle Hugo hadn't dropped dead, she would've killed him. As things were, she pointed toward the castle on the hill. "Come on. That's where we're going."

"Where we're going to raise the rabbits?"

"No. Gods, but you're an idiot. We've got to fight for Baron Howard. That's the guy the castle belongs to. With what we get paid and whatever loot we grab on the field, we ought to have enough to buy us a bunny ranch. Have you got that through your thick head?"

"I sure have, Georgia," Lani said. Georgia doubted it, but Lani went on, "First we fight, then we get the rabbits. Did I say it right?"

"You said it right," Georgia admitted wearily. "But when we get up there, you keep your big mouth shut, you hear? I'll do the talking for both of us. Have you got *that*?"

"Yeah," Lani said, and then, "Tell me about the rabbits, Georgia." Georgia clanged the visor down on her helmet.

Baron Howard's castle was like most of the ones in that part of the country: gray stone, foursquare, towered at each corner of the outwall, with a moat full of waterweeds around it that stank to high heaven. Given the castle's sanitary arrangements, such as they were, the stench was hardly surprising.

After the portcullis went up and the drawbridge came down, Georgia and Lani's rabbits hopped into the courtyard. Baron Howard's son, a handsome—almost pretty—young man in fancy parade armor, came out of the keep and met the mercenaries there. "I'm Curls," he declared. "What can you girls do?"

Georgia gave her name. Then she said, "Lance, sword, bow—you want it dead, I'll make it dead for you."

Curls rounded on Lani. "How about you, sister?"

Lani didn't say anything. Quickly, Georgia did: "She's good with the same weapons I am."

"Well, how come she doesn't talk for herself?" the baron's son demanded.

"She ain't real bright," Georgia said, which would do for an understatement till a bigger one came hopping out of the old briar patch. "She ain't bright, but she'll kill anybody you reckon needs killing. Point her at 'em, turn her loose, and get the devils out of the way."

"Well, she'll have her chance." Curls strode off, clattering.

"Ooh, Georgia, he's cute," Lani breathed. "Can we keep him instead of the bunnies?" Her taste in men was as bad as it was in everything else: it would have had to improve to make it catastrophic, in other words. Georgia knew a coldhearted serpent when she saw one. That he was a baron's son only made things worse; it turned him into a spoiled, cold-hearted serpent.

"Let's get the rabbits into the hutch," she said. "After that, I'd like to dump you in the bunny trough to get the heat out of your britches." Lani laughed, for all the world as if Georgia had been joking. She wished to the gods she were.

Once Georgia saw the rostler knew what she was doing and the hutch hands were reliable, she left Thumper and Clumper with them without too many regrets. Then, carrying their weapons and their few personal belongings, she and Lani went to get settled. The top sergeant was a weathered veteran people seemed to call Slim Jim. He was more to Georgia's taste than the baron's son; she had no interest in handsome beef if it was jerky, too.

Slim Jim led her and Lani to the women's dorm and pointed out a couple of empty straw pallets on the slate floor. Some of the other women warriors greeted them as they set down their gear. Slim Jim was just leaving when another woman came to the doorway and said, "Anybody seen Curls? I've been looking for him."

She was no warrior. She didn't fight. People fought over her. She knew it, too, knew it and reveled in it. Her dress, such as it was, clung to every curve. She wore enough perfume for a portside joyhouse the day the war galleys came in. Not even Slim Jim was immune to her. That disappointed Georgia without much surprising her. The sergeant said, "You weren't lookin' real hard, were you? He just went back to the tower after he sized up our two new gals here."

She sized up Georgia and Lani, too. Georgia she dismissed after one quick glance. Lani, on account of her size, was briefly interesting. Nobody but herself was more than briefly interesting to her. "Well, I reckon I'll just find him there, then," she said, and sashayed away with hip action she must have practiced for years. Slim Jim followed her, smiling. He would.

"Ooh, Georgia, she's mighty cute, too." Lani sounded as if she were surrounded by cuddly brown-and-white puppies.

Georgia sat down on her pallet and buried her face in her hand. "For gods' sake," she said. Lani liked girls every now and then, the only problem being that her taste in them was even more appalling than it was with men. Georgia glared up at her. "Don't mess with that one," she snarled. "Don't, you hear me? Don't! She's poison, nothin' else but."

"I didn't mean anything by it," Lani protested.

"You never mean anything by it," Georgia said. "But you can't keep your damn hands to yourself. That's how come they ran us out of Crabgrass. Remember that? *Do* you?" Unhappily, Lani nodded. Scowling still, Georgia went on, "So just don't. Not that one. She's a chippy, nothin' else but—teases for the fun of it. People like that are no stinking good. Just pretend she's not around, all right?"

"She smelled awful pretty, though, didn't she?" Lani said. Georgia buried her face in her hands again. But before she did, she aimed a glare at Lani that should have buried *her.*

The other women mercenaries listened with interest not far from fascination. Some tried to pretend they were doing no such thing. Others didn't bother. New faces meant new gossip. New gossip was always welcome. By the look of things, there'd be plenty of new gossip to go around. Georgia hated gossip. No, that wasn't quite true. Most of the time, she liked it as well as anybody else. What she hated was gossip about her. With Lani in tow, that was a forlorn hate.

Baron Howard went to war with his southern neighbor, Baron Ritz, for the most common reason any two barons tangled: over grazing rights. Baron Ritz's rabbits had taken to hopping the fence between the two domains and stuffing themselves on Baron Howard's meadows. Baron Howard squawked. When squawking did about as much good as squawking usually does, he undertook more direct action. His archers started shooting the trespassing bunnies. That increased the hasenpfeffer ration at Castle Howard. It also made Baron Ritz squawk. Baron Ritz's squawks to Baron Howard did as much good as Baron Howard's squawks to Baron Ritz had done. This being the case, Baron Ritz undertook direct action of his own. His archers started shooting Baron Howard's archers.

And so. A war. Adding a few strands of barbed wire to the damn fence would have saved both barons silver and casualties, to say nothing of rabbits. It never entered either of their heads. Not a whole lot of things did.

Georgia got all this in bits and pieces from Slim Jim and the other mercenaries as they bounced across the meadows toward battle. Curls led the Howard war party. Lani didn't care about what was going on one way or the other. She knew which side she was on, and the side she wasn't on was the enemy. Georgia wished the world were as simple as Lani made it out to be.

"Who's going to be in charge of Baron Ritz's men?" Georgia asked.

"Probably his son, Al," Slim Jim answered. "He's the oldest Ritz brother."

"Is he any good?"

"He ain't bad. His pa's a lot ritzier, though, if you know what I mean." The sergeant dropped his voice. "Of course, same thing's so about old man Howard and Curls. What worries me is, folks say Baron Ritz has hired a bunch of crackers up from the south. Some o' them are rough customers."

"They'll all be in gray, right? And their captain'll wear one of those fancy plumed hats?"

Slim Jim nodded. "Sure sounds like crackers to me. You *have* been around the block once or twice, haven't you?" Georgia warmed at the admiration in his voice. But he went on, "What about it?"

"I'll tell you what," Georgia said, and she did.

"You reckon that'll work?" Slim Jim asked, and then, "You want we should do it, or should we leave it to Curls?"

"We oughta take care of it," Georgia said at once. "Either that Curls won't do it at all or else he'll do it the wrong kind of way."

The sergeant glanced over toward Baron Howard's son, who was lolloping along on his war bunny without a visible care in the world. "I reckon you sized him up right the first time. All right—we'll handle it." Georgia nodded, pleased with herself and him both. Maybe friendship was blossoming there, maybe even something more. Whatever it was, she'd worry about it after the battle.

When they got to the fence between Baron Howard's land and Baron Ritz's, Ritz's archers shot at them till Howard's bowmen made the enemy soldiers keep their heads down. The rest of Baron Howard's men used cutters to open a way through the wire. What that meant, of course, was that till the fence got fixed the rabbits on both sides could go wherever they pleased. Rabbits going where they pleased was most of what the war was all about. Nobody seemed to worry about that, not even a little bit. They could have been fighting about rock oil coming up out of the ground or something else equally stupid. Every so often, they just wanted to fight.

As soon as they'd hopped a little ways into Baron Ritz's lands, Georgia saw why his bunnies were leaping the fence. Baron Howard had much better grazing country, full of clover and alfalfa and buckwheat and other tasty things for the little rascals to eat. Baron Ritz's border country was bloody boring, and would have been boring to a bunny, too.

Horns blared. Ritz's riders bounded toward Baron Howard's. The border country was about to get bloody in the literal sense of the word.

There was the cracker chief—sure enough, plumed hat over gray surcoat. Before setting spurs to her own bunny, Georgia and Slim Jim both smacked Lani on the back. "That one! Go get that one, Lani!" they yelled. "The one with the feather!"

"The one with the feather," Lani agreed. "I'll do it. You betcha I will." She couched her lance, let out a war cry that didn't have any words but that made every hair on Georgia's head stand bolt upright anyway, and thundered down on the foe.

And the rest, as they say, is history, or possibly fantasy.

A battlefield after a battle is not a pretty place. The only thing worse than fighting a battle, though, is fighting it and losing it. If you've fought a battle and lost it and you're still on the field afterwards, the most likely explanations are that you're a prisoner or you're dead. Neither of those is anything to write home about. Of course, if you're dead you probably won't start writing *War and Pieces* any time real soon, no matter how much you might know about war or be in pieces.

Bits of Ritz's army bucketed off in all directions—anything to get away from the ferocious warriors and fierce bad war rabbits who fought for Baron Howard. Curls was beside himself with glee—and if one of him was annoying, two would have been downright obnoxious, to say nothing of excessive. "We whupped 'em!" he shouted to anybody who would listen. "We beat the bastards, and we bounced their buggering bunnies!"

He wasn't wrong. That didn't make him any less irritating. Georgia stayed as far away from him as she could. Slim Jim made much better company. Surveying the chili con carnage, the sergeant nodded to Georgia and said, "Well, you was right, no two ways about it."

"About what?" Georgia wasn't beside herself with glee. The looting hadn't been as good as she'd hoped. Baron Ritz's troopers must have been as broke as she was. Now a lot of them were not just broke but broken.

"That Lani, she fights like a son of a bitch," Slim Jim said. "Them crackers just weren't the same after what she done to their captain."

"Oh. That." Lani had unrabbited him. She'd bent over and plucked the lance out of his hand and broken it across her knee. And then she'd leaned down in the saddle and given him a big kiss. There he was, standing with a bunch of other captives and looking as if he wished she'd only killed him. How was he supposed to live this down? Who'd hire him now? What would people call him? The Cute Mercenary? He'd have to go to night school and study accounting or something.

"Be damned if I don't think Baron Howard'll pay her a bonus for what she done," the sergeant said.

"Yeah?" That made Georgia perk up.

Slim Jim looked as if he was afraid he'd said too much. Quickly, he added, "I can't promise, mind you. It's up to the baron. But if it was up to me, I sure would."

Georgia knew what that meant. It had almost as much tease in it as Curls' wife. "Well, we'll find out," she said, which was a lot politer than hauling off and kicking something—preferably Slim Jim.

Curls had the brains to post scouts to make sure Baron Ritz's men didn't regather and counterattack during his march back to his own lands. That surprised Georgia, who wouldn't have bet he could add eleven and ten without dropping his pants. But Ritz and the crackers had truly crumbled. They stayed away. Georgia was willing to bet it would be a long, long time before the beaten baron's bunnies bounded over the barrier between the baronies.

When they got back to Castle Howard, sentries on the wall shouted questions, asking how the fight had gone. "We made stooges of 'em," Curls shouted, and they burst into cheers.

Up rumbled the portcullis. Down creaked the drawbridge. In bounded the rabbit riders. In plodded the prisoners. Out rolled the beer barrels. Backwards ran the sentences.

The sun set. A wizard set a small fireball floating above the courtyard, just to work a little bit of magic into the story. Georgia took care of Clumper while Lani saw to Thumper. Lani might mangle mere men, but she was always kind to bunnies. Once every whisker had been washed and Thumper's cottontail curried, Lani said, "See how they're all happy out there, Georgia?"

"Yeah, I see." Georgia longed for a mug or three of beer herself. Sometimes keeping an eye on Lani was singularly unrewarding. Other times, by contrast, it was plurally unrewarding.

"I won't do nothin' bad, Georgia," Lani said. "Honest I won't."

She always said that. She always meant it, too. Except on the battlefield, she didn't have a mean bone in her body. Even then, she just smashed people. She didn't dislike them—not that the difference did them any good. Off the battlefield . . . Off the battlefield, things had a way of going wrong. "Remember what happened in Crabgrass?" Georgia asked.

A few days earlier, Lani had. Georgia could tell she didn't now. She wondered why she'd bothered to ask. Lani wouldn't have remembered her head for long if it wasn't stapled on. Georgia muttered a curse. The only way she could have kept Lani out of the celebration was by sitting on that empty head. Georgia was damned if she would. She'd earned some celebrating of her own.

"Just keep your hands to yourself," she said. "You got that?"

"Sure thing, Georgia." Lani was obliging. She was always obliging. That was part of the problem.

People cheered when the two of them came out into the courtyard. Hard-bitten, beer-swilling mercenaries shouted out Lani's name. Some of them shouted Georgia's name, too, but Lani was the one who'd made sure the cracker captain could never admit his real name in a hiring hall again. The cheers and the shouts made her blossom like a sunflower.

"They like me. They really like me!" she said.

"Yeah." Georgia eyed the soldiers. Some of them—quite a few of them—were liable to like Lani altogether too well. What had happened in Crabgrass hadn't been unfriendly. Oh, no. A lot of other things, sure, but not unfriendly. That was Georgia's last thought before somebody thrust a foaming mug into her right hand and somebody else thrust another one into her left. She had to get rid of them—she had a reputation of her own to uphold, after all. But by the time she came up for air, she didn't see Lani any more. Then a different somebody else gave her some more beer. Once she'd downed that, her own head started to swim.

Curls' wife whirled through the crowd in a dress that couldn't have been any tighter if it were painted on. By the way the mercenaries, male and female, rubbed up against her, they wanted to find out if it *was* painted on. By the way she giggled and swayed, she didn't mind in the least.

Curls whirled through the crowd, too, but somehow never in the same part of it as his wife. The happier she looked, the more sour he got. Georgia had noticed she was drinking hard. If anything, Curls was drinking harder. That might turn out to be . . . interesting.

Georgia really would have wanted to see Slim Jim, but he seemed to have disappeared. A little muzzily and more than a little resentfully, she looked around for Lani. She didn't see her, either. And, for one of the rare times in her life, she had enough beer in her that she didn't much care.

Curls went by, his face red and angry as the sunset before storms. He scowled at Georgia and breathed hoppy fumes into her face. "Have you seen my wife?" he asked.

"Just a little while ago," she answered. "She came right by here."

"Well, I don't see her now. Do you?" Curls went on scowling. By the way he asked the question, he might have suspected Georgia of owning a system of eyesight different from and superior to his own.

For her part, she wished she were in a different barony, one where things like this didn't happen. She shook her head. "No, I don't see her now." As if to prove the point, she looked around again. She still didn't see Curls' wife. She still didn't see Slim Jim, either. Yes, that could add up to trouble.

She looked around some more. And she still didn't see Lani. Not seeing Lani added up to trouble almost by definition. Lani got in trouble even when you did keep an eye on her. When you didn't . . .

"I'd better go," she said to Curls.

"How come?" He grabbed her left arm in a way that made her want to reach for her knife. "Are you looking for her, too?"

"By the gods, no!" Georgia said. If Curls' wife was with Lani, then Georgia *was* looking for her, but not the way the baron's son meant. She would sooner have cozied up to a barrel of Greek fire with the wick lit than had anything to do with Curls' wife *that* way. Some things were more trouble than they were worth. That was how Georgia saw it, anyway. Thinking ahead of time about how much trouble she might land in never once occurred to Lani. Lani leaped before she looked.

More than what Georgia said, the way she said it convinced Curls she might mean it. "I'm going to find her," he ground out, "and when I do find her—" He stopped. His hands closed into fists.

He stomped off. Georgia followed him. She didn't need to be subtle about it; Baron Howard's son had forgotten she existed. She wondered why he'd married a woman like that. It had probably seemed a good idea at the time. A lot of things did, even—or maybe especially—if they weren't.

Had Curls been sober, he would have prowled. Had pigs had wings . . . But pigs didn't, and neither did Curls. He wandered and weaved and wobbled like a sailboat in heavy seas and contrary winds. That wasn't because of the crowd he was navigating through, either. Even when he was by himself, he still stumbled sottishly.

He meandered through the keep, Georgia in his wake. He kept yanking doors open. Georgia wouldn't have done that if she were him. There were a lot of things Georgia wouldn't have done if she were him, but she thought that one likely to prove hazardous to his life expectancy. The squeals and gasps that rose when he did open doors did nothing to disabuse her of her opinion.

Luckily for Curls—probably more luckily than he deserved— none of the squealers or gaspers turned out to be in a homicidal mood. None of them turned out to be his wife, either. To Georgia, that was a good thing for all concerned. Finding her squealing or gasping probably would have turned Curls homicidal.

He didn't find her anywhere in the keep. "Why don't you just have yourself some more beer?" Georgia said when he went out to the courtyard again. "I'm sure everything's all right."

"I'm not," Curls snarled. Neither was Georgia, though they could have put her on the rack before she admitted it.

Curls grabbed another mug. Georgia hoped he would grab the serving girl, too—that would have been good for what ailed him. But he didn't. And the beer didn't prove good for what aled him, either. It just made his glower grimmer than ever.

Georgia found herself with a fresh mug in her hand, too. She couldn't have said how it got there, but there it was. Plot contrivances are like that sometimes. Stay tuned. Curls' wife wasn't in the courtyard. Neither was Slim Jim. And, more importantly to Georgia, neither was Lani. Georgia started worrying in earnest.

With Curls, it wasn't worry. It was swelling rage. He growled, "When I find her, I'm going to . . ." He still didn't say exactly what he'd do. That left Georgia unsurprised. Curls didn't strike her as long on imagination. But, if the time came, she suspected he'd think of something.

He went into the rabbit hutch. Georgia wouldn't have wanted to fool around in there. It stank of war bunnies. Of course, the returning soldiers stank of war bunnies, too. Maybe, if you weren't too fussy, that evened things out. Georgia's worrying advanced from earnest to downright sincere. Lani had never, ever, been fussy.

Georgia right behind him, Curls peered into a stall that should have been empty. He gasped. He squealed. So did all three people in there.

And so did Georgia. All the participants in what looked very complicated were violating at least one commandment in somebody's religion. Curls' wife was violating at least two, but she was more limber than her . . . associates? No, they were pretty definitively friends by then.

Curls made a noise like red-hot tearing metal. He started to draw his sword. Georgia broke her mug of beer over his head. (See? Told ya it would come in handy.) He groaned and crumpled.

"I'm sorry, Georgia," Lani said.

"Yeah, tell me another one," Georgia said. "Come on. Put your clothes on, for gods' sake. We got to get out of here before laughing boy wakes up." She prodded Curls with her toe.

"Take me with you," Curls' wife said urgently.

"Not on your life, sister." Georgia shook her head. "If you're anybody's worry, you're his." She jerked a thumb at Slim Jim. She sighed. She'd hoped for better from the sergeant. She'd actually liked him, and thought he'd liked her, too. But men had a way of going for what looked nice first. If wasn't as if she hadn't seen that before. She'd hoped for better, yeah, but she couldn't really say she'd expected it. She rounded on Lani, who, despite her size, was pretty well rounded herself. "Get dressed, I told you!"

Two war bunnies rode out of Castle Howard. (A little later, two more rode out, but they aren't part of this story any more, so you can forget about them.) "You gals already get your pay?" one of the gate crew asked as they let down the drawbridge.

"We got what we needed," Georgia answered. Lani didn't say anything. By the silly grin that still spread over her face, though, she'd damn well got a good part of what she needed.

They hopped along for a while in silence. Georgia chose forks in the road almost at random. She didn't want those other two bunnies following them. She didn't think Slim Jim would, but she wasn't nearly so sure about Curls' wife—or, more likely, ex-wife. (Oh, wait. You were supposed to forget about those other two. Never mind.)

After a bit, Lani started to fidget. After a bit more, she said, "Georgia? Tell me about the rabbits, Georgia."

"Oh, shut up," Georgia explained.

About the Authors

John G. Hemry is the author of *A Just Determination*, the first SF military legal series, as well as the Stark's War series. His short fiction has appeared in *Analog*, *Amazing* and *Marion Zimmer Bradley's Fantasy Magazine*. He lives in Maryland with his wife (the enigmatic and incomparable "S") and three challenging but great kids.

Laura Frankos has published a mystery novel and short fiction, as well as science fiction and fantasy short fiction in venues as diverse as *Analog* and, well, this one. She also indulges her love of Broadway trivia by serving as quiz-mistress at *fynsworthalley.com*.

Mike Turner is a university dropout who served in the Air Force and has worked as a receiving clerk, warehouse manager, convenience store night clerk, store Santa, door-to-door vacuum salesman, school lab attendant, machinist, and security guard. He spent half a decade living in Japan, has lived all over the United States from Hawaii to Alaska to Rhode Island, and currently resides in Colorado Springs with his wife, three obnoxious teenage sons, and a dozen or so cats.

Jan Stirling hails from Massachusetts originally and misses it something fierce. But she happily left there in '88 to marry

SF author S.M. Stirling and move to Toronto. Thinking this would be the biggest change ever to occur in her life, she little suspected they'd end up in New Mexico, a much more foreign country than the middle of Canada. She also never suspected she'd end up writing but she caught the writing bug from Steve (she swears it's contagious) and computers, bless 'em, make it possible for her to write comprehensible prose. And the rest, as they say, is history.

Cassandra Claire is a twenty-something writer living in New York City, where she has painted her apartment green. She has loved fantasy since her father introduced it to her when she was a child. This is her first published story.

Yvonne Coats says, "I'm originally from Dubois, Wyoming, a town where the wintering bighorn sheep outnumber the humans about ten to one. I now live in Albuquerque, New Mexico, a city with more people than the entire state of Wyoming . . . but a lot less snow. I share space with my handsome mathematician husband Mike Collins and our bad-but-beloved cat Magpie. My first story was published in *Marion Zimmer Bradley's Fantasy Magazine*. I have also been published in the Penguin/Roc anthology *Treachery & Treason*, and I was shortlisted for the first James White Award in 2000."

Catherine Shaffer is a writer, a mother, and a molecular biologist living in the Detroit area. She has now tickled funny bones on both sides of the Atlantic, since her first story was published in Great Britain, and a small collection of silly ferret stories first published on the web have been translated into Swedish. Her science articles have appeared in various newsletters, newspapers, and magazines, including *Analog*. In her free time, she plays the violin, runs, swims, and tries not to acquire ferrets, which is a more difficult thing to avoid than it would seem.

A wise writer once told **Jim C. Hines** that, to be a writer, you should avoid stressful day jobs that keep you hard at work and sap your brainpower. Otherwise you end up too tired and drained to write. Following this advice, Jim quickly landed a job as a state employee. So far, so good—he has been published in numerous magazines and anthologies, and his humorous fantasy novel *GoblinQuest* should be hitting the shelves this month. He lives in Michigan, along with his wife and daughter, and 2.75 cats.

D. S. Moen has finally achieved one of her lifehood ambitions by combining shopping, surfing, Herb Alpert tunes, and swords into a single story. She lives in the San Francisco area with her husband, their cat, and a glow-in-the-dark jellyfish.

Nebula Award winner **Esther Friesner** is the author of twenty-nine novels and over one hundred short stories, in addition to being the editor of six popular anthologies. Her works have been published in the United States, the United Kingdom, Japan, Germany, Russia, France, and Italy. She is also a published poet, a playwright, and once wrote an advice column, "Ask Auntie Esther." Her articles on fiction writing have appeared in *Writer's Market* and Writer's Digest Books. Besides winning two Nebula Awards in succession for Best Short Story (1995 and 1996), she was a Nebula finalist three times and a Hugo finalist once. She received the Skylark Award from NESFA and the award for Most Promising New Fantasy Writer of 1986 from *Romantic Times*. Her latest publications include the novelization of the movie *Men In Black 2* and a short story collection, *Death And the Librarian And Other Stories* from Thorndike Press.

Raised on the Southwestern Pennsylvanian farm where her father, grandmother, and great-grandfather were born, **Wen Spencer** is slightly bewildered as to how she ended up living outside of Boston, Massachusetts. It had something to do with owning four houses in two states, an eighteen-month pause in the Berkshire Mountains to finish construction on one of said houses, and stock options. Currently her family is down to one house and resisting all offers to move them out of the country. Wen is a two-time finalist for the John Campbell Award for Best New Writer. Her books include the recently released *Tinker*, whose heroine is a chick that kicks butt. Excerpts from all her novels can be found at her web site at *www.wenspencer.com*.

✧   ✧   ✧

Selina Rosen's short fiction has appeared in the new *Thieves' World* anthology, *Turning Points, Sword and Sorceress 16, Such a Pretty Face, Best of MZB's Fantasy Magazine, Volume 2*, and *Distant Journeys*, to name a few. Meisha Merlin Publishing, Inc. has released several of Ms. Rosen's novels. Among them are *Queen of Denial* and the sequel *Recycled*, and the *Chains* trilogy, the first two of which (*Chains of Freedom* and *Chains of Deliverance*) are out, and the third (*Chains of Redemption*) is due out in April of 2004. *Strange Robbie*, another of Ms. Rosen's novels scheduled for release by MM in September of 2004 will be her first hardcover release. She and a few other masochists own Yard Dog Press, a micro press that specializes in truly odd work and is presently producing four perfect bound trade paperbacks per year in addition to a variety of chapbooks and smaller anthologies. Their motto being: "If anyone else wants it, we probably don't." She edited the children's book *Stories That Won't Make Your Parents Hurl*, and the sequel *More Stories . . . Hurl*, and the shared-world anthology *Bubbas of the Apocalypse*. *The Host Books, The Bubba Chronicles, The Boat Man, Fire & Ice*, and *Hammer Town* have been published by Yard Dog Press—about which Ms. Rosen says: "It's so hard to get published by your own publishing house. There's all the writing and then the telling yourself 'yes' over and over again. It can be quite tiring." You can write to Ms. Rosen from her website *www.yarddogpress.com*.

Lee Martindale's short fiction has appeared in numerous magazines and anthologies, including three collections and both *Bubbas of the Apocalypse* anthologies from Yard Dog Press. She edited Meisha Merlin's first original anthology, *Such A Pretty Face: Tales of Power & Abundance*, and has a story in its second, Lee & Miller's *Low Port*. When not slinging fiction, Lee is a Lifetime Active member of SFWA, a member of the SCA, a member of the SFWA Musketeers, and a Named Bard. She and her husband George live in Plano, Texas, where she keeps friends and fans in the loop at *http://www.HarpHaven.net*.

J. Ardian Lee is the author of historical fantasy novels *Son of the Sword, Outlaw Sword* and *Sword of King James*, all featuring hot, sweaty men wielding long, hard weapons.

She is a former actor, a former journalist, and a former award-winning short story writer, and began writing fiction for publication at a late age when she finally realized it was the only way to make the voices in her head earn their keep.

Lesley McBain *could* tell all sorts of tales about herself—following her familial predilection of never letting the truth stand in the way of a good story—but That Would Be Wrong. (Worse, that might provoke the Wrath of Esther Friesner, which would be Very Bad Indeed.) She *will* tell two truths here, though: this is her first fiction sale, and she wishes the *real* Father Doonan were still alive to read it.

K.D. Wentworth has been channeling biographical information from Hallah Iron-Thighs for some time now, and is under strict orders to GET IT RIGHT. Hallah is an exacting subject and tolerates no mistakes in her chronicles. Wentworth has seven novels in print now, including *This Fair Land,* an alternate history Cherokee fantasy, and *The Course of Empire,* written with Eric Flint. In her spare time, she writes short stories and serves as Coordinating Judge of the Writers of the Future Contest. She is owned by a hundred-pound Akita named Bear, and lives in Tulsa with her husband.

Robin Wayne Bailey is the author of numerous novels, including *Dragonkin, Night's Angel,* and *Shadowdance.* His short fiction has appeared most recently in *2001: The Best Science Fiction of the Year, Future Wars, Thieves' World: Turning Points,* and *Revisions.* He's also edited *Architects of Dreams: The SFWA Author Emeritus Anthology* and *Through My Glasses Darkly: Five Stories by Frank M. Robinson.* He's the current chairman of the Science Fiction and Fantasy Hall of Fame, an avid book collector, and student of Ryobu-kai Karate. He lives in North Kansas City, Missouri.

Laura J. Underwood is the author of over 150 short stories, articles and books reviews, as well as several novels and short story collections. Her latest publications include, "The Gingerbread Man" in *Femmes De La Brume,* and a collection titled *Magic's Song: Tales of the Harper Mage* from Wildside Press. Future publications include her novels *The*

Black Hunter, Dragon's Tongue, and *Wandering Lark.* When not writing, she is a librarian, a SFWA Musketeer and an occasional harpist. She lives in Tennessee with her family and a feline of few grey cells that she fondly calls Gato Bobo.

Steven Piziks teaches English in Walled Lake, Michigan, and he is appalled that the school requires him to teach *Romeo and Juliet,* which contains horrifying violence and shocking dirty jokes. His students think he's hysterical, which isn't the same as thinking he's hilarious. When not writing, he plays harp, dabbles in oral storytelling, and spends more time on-line than is probably good for him. Writing as Steven Harper, he has produced the critically-acclaimed Silent Empire series, which so far includes *Dreamer, Nightmare,* and *Trickster.* Visit his web page at *http://www.sff.net/ people/spiziks.*

Eric Flint was born in southern California in 1947, and since lived in France (as a child) and in various states around the country before settling in Indiana. Although he began dabbling in writing in 1970, he didn't turn his hand to it full time until more than twenty years later, and in between was a political activist, longshoreman, machinist, and glassblower. He has collaborated with such authors as David Drake and Mercedes Lackey, and his own series, which began with the novel *1632,* has spawned a sequel, with more books set in that universe to come. He has also tried his hand at editing, with reissues of James Schmitz's and Keith Laumer's works in progress.

Jody Lynn Nye lists her main career activity as "spoiling cats." She lives northwest of Chicago with three of the above and her husband, author and packager Bill Fawcett. She has published twenty-five books, including six contemporary fantasies, three SF novels, four novels in collaboration with Anne McCaffrey, including *The Ship Who Won*; edited a humorous anthology about mothers, *Don't Forget Your Spacesuit, Dear!*; and written over seventy short stories. Her latest books are *Myth-Told Tales* and *Myth Alliances* (Meisha Merlin Publishing), co-written with Robert Asprin.

❖   ❖   ❖

Harry Turtledove is known for his alternate history, but does other things as well. His recent books include *Ruled Britannia*, *In the Presence of Mine Enemies*, *Conan of Venarium*, and, writing as H.N. Turteltaub, *The Sacred Land*. He also enjoys getting silly every now and again.